TRANSLAT[ED]
PRONUNCIATIONS

- Eriu – "Air-ooh"
- Iseult – "Ee-salt"
- Tynan – "Tie-nan"
- Cillian – "KILL-ee-in."
- Fionn – "Fee-yun"
- Bratva – Russian organized crime or Russian Mafia
- Pakhan – Head of the Russian Mafia
- Mo stoirin- my little darling – "Mu store -ee"
- Daragaya – Dear
- A Thiarna dean tròcaire – Lord have mercy on me
- Eta suka okhu el – This bitch has lost his mind
- Mogu ya yego ubit? – May I kill him?
- Na zdorovie – To health (Russian version of "cheers")
- Pozdravleyu – Congrats

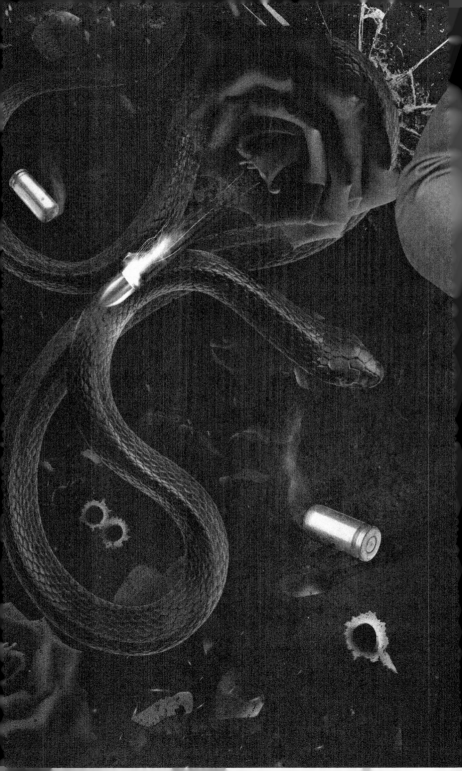

ONE

DEVLIN

"**L**etter for you, McHale." A prison officer tosses an envelope into the slot of the six-by-eight box that's been my home for about a year.

That is, of course, when I wasn't stuck in solitary for killing a man. I had no choice, though. It was a hit. He was out for my blood, so I took his. Choked the life out of him.

He didn't stand a chance against me. No one ever has.

I don't know who sent him, but whoever it was must've been connected to the guy I'm accused of killing and the reason I'm in here.

I've got a feeling it was Gio Marino of the Messina crime family who organized the hit. Would be fitting. I did murder his friend, after all. Or so he thinks. But the bastard deserved it. Was connected to a trafficking ring.

Gio came to see me some months back, asking questions about

that night. Wanting to know what happened. I'll never tell him the truth, though. I'll be taking that to my grave.

Don't know why he'd wanna associate with the likes of that fella. The Messinas never were the type to dabble in people.

But let him think it was me who killed his friend. That was the point. I'd take the fall for it every single time just so I could keep Eriu safe.

She's not just anyone. She's the youngest daughter of Patrick Quinn, the man I work for and the head of the Irish Mob in Boston.

After I got out of solitary, Patrick forced the warden to erase the incident from my record. Pinned it on someone else who's serving a life term for killing some kids. The Quinn family is powerful, and their connections run deep.

I get to my feet, already knowing who the letter is from before I even open it. She's the only one who cares enough about a bastard like me to write them. I've got no one else who gives a damn. Family's all dead. Hers is the only family I've got left.

As I trace her name on the envelope, my body strains, knowing it's wrong to think of her the way I am right now. She's only eighteen and, most importantly, Patrick's daughter. She's not meant for me.

But in the last few months, my feelings for her have become more than I can endure. I never dared to think about her that way, not until a few months ago when she confessed in a letter that she has real feelings for me.

And for a moment, I wondered what that would feel like. To have someone who actually loves me.

Of course, I told her nothing could ever happen. That she was being foolish. She was merely a child. Yet she isn't much of a child now, is she?

But she's still far too young and impressionable. Innocent

beyond measure. She's got the kindest heart and purest soul. Too good for me. I have nothing to offer her.

So why do those bright green eyes haunt me when I close mine? It's then that I see all of her: those lean, sun-kissed legs, those curves men would spill blood over just to sin at her altar.

She's never realized the effect she has on men, though. She was always shy, and her cheeks would turn pink every time I looked at her. I realize it's because she had feelings for me.

Now I'm the one hiding my feelings for her.

My Eriu.

A temptation far too enticing.

One taste, and I'd forever be hers.

So I have to keep my distance. Make her think that nothing can come of our mutual attraction. We are of different worlds. We always will be.

I'd never simply fool around with her, either. She's far too special for that. And I'd also never disrespect her father by suggesting I take his daughter's hand. Someone like me would never be good enough.

I have too much respect for the Quinns. Patrick has done a lot for me. Helped me start over after my brother, Keegan, was killed. Recruited me to become an enforcer for the family.

It's the only thing I've lived and breathed until she came along. Until her father asked me to be her bodyguard when she was only thirteen.

After that, I swore to give up my life for hers. I vowed to protect that girl with everything I had, and I always will.

I'd die behind these prison bars if it meant she could be safe. If she could shine her light on the world like I never will.

I knew I needed to protect her. It's one thing I couldn't do for my brother. It's why he died. Even while I thought I was doing what I had to do to protect him, it still wasn't enough.

Francis Palmer was the leader of the gang I worked for before I joined the Quinns. The one I betrayed. And the one who killed my brother.

Keegan had nothing to do with the Palmers. He was just a way to get to me. To punish me for what I did.

My brother haunts me when I sleep. Accuses me of killing him. And he'd be right. I might as well have held the knife to his throat.

His last few moments of life constantly play in my mind. No matter how much I try, I can't ever escape that day.

And I never will.

"Come on, Francis, just let him go."

Two of his men hold me back, while another points a gun at my head.

His people are everywhere, surrounding me across the acres of land he owns. I could fight off the ones holding me, but I know Francis would instantly kill Keegan if I tried.

Francis tilts up his mouth, his eyes narrowing, a sharp blade against my brother's Adam's apple.

Keegan trembles, tears rolling down his cheeks.

Feck! How will I get him out of this?

I don't know what the hell to do!

Think, you arsehole, think!

"You thought you could double-cross me and live to tell about it?" Francis laughs coldly. "After I kill you and your addict of a brother, I'm gonna fly to Ireland and personally cut out your parents' hearts. It's too bad you won't see me do it."

"Don't do this! I swear, I won't say any more shite to them. I'll say I lied. Please, just let him go!" I hate begging this feck, but for

my brother—my blood—I'll do anything.

My mother was right. She said I'd kill him one day. If he dies and she finds out…

Pain shoots through my chest. This will kill my parents. I can't allow it to happen.

"Do you think I'd ever trust you again?" He drills me with a sharp look. "If you don't kill a rat and teach the other rats where not to shit, they'll never learn their lesson."

Keegan's eyes connect with mine, slicing with fear, his body continuing to tremble.

I'm sorry, *I mouth, heaviness weaving through my chest.*

I can't lose my baby brother.

This is all on me. I got sloppy. I let them find Keegan.

I was always careful. Never met up with him unless it was at our secret spot in the park at night. He knew I worked for unsavory people, and I knew he was selling crack. I tried to stop him, but then he got hooked on it. I attempted to get him help, even though I knew he had fallen beyond anything I could do.

But still I had to try. He was family. You don't give up on family.

So when he called me one day, saying someone was trying to kill him, I came running. But Francis's people were following me. I knew there was a chance they were. But I took the risk anyway. I couldn't let Keegan die.

I did get him out of trouble, but we landed in a whole new one.

"P-please, I don't w-wanna d-die!" Keegan cries.

"Hush, hush." Francis gently slaps his cheek. "There's no point in wasting your voice. You will die today either way."

A sob shakes through Keegan's body.

"It's all your brother's fault. If he'd been loyal, we wouldn't be here. Isn't that right?" He glares squarely at me.

"I didn't have a choice." *I know I won't convince him of that, yet still I try.*

"We all have a choice, and you made yours. Now you get to live with it."

"Please, Palmer. Just kill me. This isn't his fault!"

"I know." He holds the edge of the knife to the side of my brother's throat. "It's yours."

It's over in a second. One slice to Keegan's carotid, and I'm watching my brother die.

I let out a guttural scream while his life slowly and painfully slips away.

"No!" I headbutt one of the men and kick the other, then rush to my brother's limp body, his blood seeping like a slow-moving river. "You feckin' son of a bitch!"

Keegan drops to the ground, grabbing his throat, fingers covered in crimson, his eyes wide and filled with equal parts shock, fear, and goodbye.

That part hurts the worst. I'll never see him again.

"I'm so feckin' sorry." I grip the back of my head.

He struggles to say something back, but all that comes out is a grumbling strangle as the blood chokes him.

"It's okay," I whisper, trying to keep it together.

He's dying right in front of me and there's nothing I can do about it. Nothing to stop this except hold him in his last few moments.

"I've got you. I'm not letting go." My voice breaks. "It's okay. Don't fight it."

I blink back my own anguish. And then his body sags, and in seconds, he's dead.

Gone.

Forever.

"Feck!" Heaving, my gaze filled with rage, I stare up at a grinning Francis, who points his weapon at my head.

"Before I kill you, there's one other thing I want you to do for me." He wipes the blade over his shirt, my brother's blood penetrating the white cotton.

"Go to hell! I'm done doing anything for you," I spit through clenched teeth, my pulse slamming in my ears.

"Fine. The men will cut your brother's body into a thousand tiny pieces for the fish. Or…we can bury him."

"You son of a bitch!"

He chuckles. *"The only condition is we bury him here, on my land."*

"No way!" I clutch my brother tighter. *"I'm taking his body with me."*

Francis laughs, the crinkling around his dark eyes deepening before his face grows enraged. *"This is where he will be buried, so you'll know that I have him forever."*

More men surround us, cocking their weapons at me. A good ten of them.

"Get up." He hands the knife to one of his men. *"Better start digging before it gets dark. Maybe if you're lucky, I'll even bury you together."*

With a roar, I slam a fist against the wall, but I barely feel the pain. I hate remembering that day, hate seeing him die right before my eyes.

My association with the Palmers destroyed my brother, and if I'm not careful, it'll destroy Eriu too.

After I dug his grave, they threw his body inside like cattle. They were gonna kill me too, but help finally arrived. The rival gang owed me a favor. If they'd only shown up on time, maybe my brother would be alive today.

We killed some in the Palmer crew and they killed some on our side before Francis and his sons ran off. I wanted to find them. I tried. But I couldn't, so I left that life.

Until Patrick came calling. He knew exactly who I was.

Back in Ireland, when I was fourteen, I fell in with a bad crowd who did work for some gangs. That's how it started. Can't tell you why. Maybe I liked the attention, the respect. Maybe I was just a savage.

I had my hands in everything. Roughed up the boys who couldn't pay their debts. Killed my first man at fifteen. I had a reputation. The neck-breaker. When they saw me coming, they'd run the other way. That hasn't changed much.

When I decided to come to the States, my parents refused to come with me, but my brother followed me. I wish he hadn't.

We landed in California, and it didn't take long for me to be recruited by the Palmer gang, a bunch of thieves who would go after museums carrying high-priced items. They were skilled, and I liked my time with them.

Until my allegiances changed. Until my brother paid the ultimate price. And that was when my parents turned away from me completely.

My parents knew I had to be involved in what happened to him, and they hated me for it. My baby brother had his problems with drugs, but he was a good man. Nothing like me.

When I had a chance to save him, I did in the only way I knew how. But it cost us both everything. My brother was dead at twenty-one, only two years younger than me. I wanted more for him. More than I had. But that didn't quite work out.

It's been twelve years, and the Palmer gang hasn't found me. Maybe they've given up. Too much time has passed for them to still look for me. Then again, revenge has no expiration date.

They may still want blood for what I did to protect my brother. For everything I took from them.

They never knew my real name, though. They never knew Devlin. They knew me as Scott.

But they could still find me. I can't ever let my guard down. If it was me, I wouldn't stop until every last one of them was dead.

When they come, I will be ready. I will end this once and for all.

I've looked for them over the years, but they've been quiet. Too quiet. Part of me hopes they're all dead, but I'm sure they're still alive somewhere, hating the very thought of me.

I can't let this touch Eriu. I can't let her die like my brother did. She has too much life inside her to let someone like me take it away.

I must do right by her. I must keep her away from me. I must not entertain her wild fantasies of us. They're nothing but fairy tales.

Yet she comes to visit every month like clockwork, and I refuse her every time. How she still comes, how she still wants to be near me after I had failed her so gravely, is something I'll never understand.

It was my job to protect her, even from herself. I should never have drunk the glass of water she gave me. I should've been smarter than that. But I did. And she drugged me, then snuck out with her friend to go to that club.

That changed everything. That landed me in prison. That has prevented me from keeping an eye on her.

I have all the letters she's been writing, but I only ever wrote her back twice. Once after the first letter, then to tell her to stop writing when she confessed her feelings for me. Told her that her fascination with me was one-sided.

But that's nothing but a lie.

My hunger for her grows the longer I'm in here, the longer I'm away from her.

I remove the folded piece of paper from the envelope and clutch it in my hands. These letters are enough to kill me, to make me want to hold her in my arms or spank the holy hell out of her for doing what she did.

If I hadn't been tempted by her, none of this would've happened. But we got to talking, and I missed it when she slipped something into my water that knocked me out cold. If I ever get out of here, it'll never happen again.

I brought shame to my name and my job. Patrick is never going to want me back. I should be used to disappointing people by now. I did a lot of that with my own family.

It was a true honor to be assigned to the boss's daughter. Many wanted the position. But I failed to carry out my duty, and I can't do anything to take it back.

If I get out and Patrick doesn't reinstate me as her bodyguard, I'll still watch her. She'll always be mine to protect. That'll never change.

I'm lucky Patrick pays my attorney bills. He didn't have to. I could afford twenty with what he's paid me, but the gesture means there's a part of him that can forgive me like my parents never could.

I settle on the lower bunk. It's nice being alone. My cellmate was stabbed and is still in the hospital.

As soon as I glance down at the letter and see her handwriting, my breaths grow shallower.

Her emerald-green eyes appear as though before me, and I start to read her prose, unable to stop my pulse from drumming.

Dear Devlin,

I keep writing, yet you never write back. I know you're getting my letters. I won't stop writing them. Not until the moment you're free.

I know you said you forgive me, but I don't forgive myself. And every day you're gone, I play that night in my head, wishing I'd done things differently.

I regret it. What I did to you was wrong. I'm not making excuses, but you know how strict my father has always been with me. I was always treated differently than all my siblings. And I hated that. Still do. I'm eighteen, and still nothing changes. I'm forever a child in his eyes.

It's like he's waiting to marry me off. And the day he announces that I've been arranged to marry someone is the day I die.

I know it's coming soon. I don't want to marry someone my father chooses. but I can't tell him that. He sees me as a girl who obeys him. who does what's best for the family. But I don't want to. Devlin. I want to be free. Want to do what I want. And what I want. what I've always wanted. is you.

Why can't you be the one to marry me? My father adores you. He still does. I know he does. He would accept you as my husband. even with the age difference. He knows you'd lay down your life for me. That's what he wants in the end. Someone to protect me. And you've always protected me.

I know you feel something for me too. I'm not imagining it. How long will you spend denying that there's something between us?

Please. Devlin. I need you. I don't want to be anyone else's wife but yours.

Love,
Eriu

My heart bloody well stops beating. With a fingertip, I trace the trinity knot she has drawn with utter perfection. She signs her name next to it in every letter, like she's tellin' me that we're bound for eternity.

She's right about one thing. She *was* always treated differently.

But that's because she's innocent in every sense of the word.

There's more to her, though. Eriu is a woman of many talents, and I long to know everything I can about her. Yet I can't. She's not meant to be mine, no matter how badly I want her to be.

With a roar, I crumple the letter in my palm.

The thought of her marrying someone else sends me over the edge.

If I was a good man, worthy of her, maybe I would ask her father for her hand.

But I'm not that man, and the sooner she comes to terms with that, the better it'll be for the both of us.

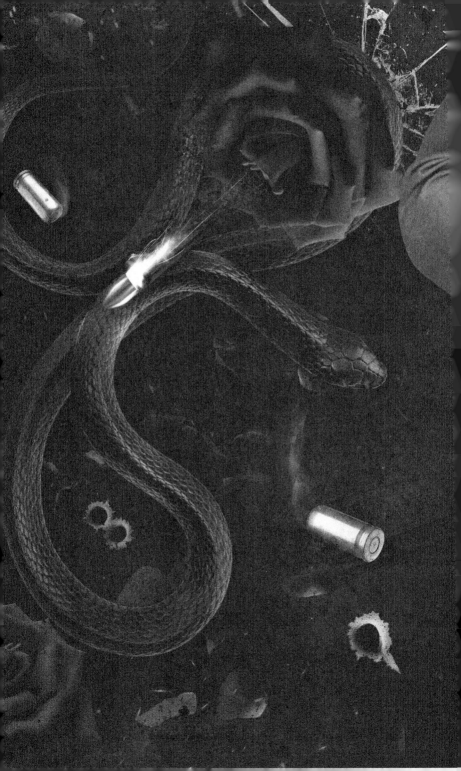

TWO

DEVLIN

D ays later, inside my cell, I stare up at the poorly painted white ceiling, drips frozen in time as though long forgotten.

The air is thick with the smell of sweat and disinfectant, fluxed into something putrid.

It's not the first time I've smelled it. Been to jail back in Ireland. I was stuck alone in a tiny cell for a few days for a fight. Nothing stayed on my record, though. Being part of a gang and having connections helped.

My brother was the only one who cared I was even there. He was all I had.

I was eighteen, and my parents had lost hope of me becoming someone by that point. To them, I was nothing but a lost cause, always feckin' off, embarrassing them. Mother used to tell me a fella like me would never find anyone but a floozie to love him.

Maybe she was right.

I often remember the night she kicked me out of the house once I got out of jail.

I had come home after having just killed someone, blood on my knuckles, my shirt. As soon as I walked in, she was there sitting in the kitchen, the lights off until she turned them on.

I didn't notice the luggage beside her, not at first. But then she told me how she knew I was never going to change and how I was going to destroy my brother's life in the process.

I don't want to lose the only son I have left, she said.

Hearing that had hurt, but she wasn't wrong. I was a feck-up. I'd always be a feck-up.

After I left, I had stayed with one friend, then another, until I had some money saved up from the shite I was doing. By twenty-one, I decided I needed to get out of Ireland and out of my family's life. Where they could be safe from me.

I landed in California, but I wasn't alone. It broke my parents' heart when my brother decided to follow me, but he didn't see me the way they did. I should have told him to stay, but instead, I was happy he was coming with me. Happy that someone in my family actually gave a shite about me.

Now they're all gone.

And I'm alone.

Mom wasn't unkind growing up. I had good parents, but I had become a disappointment, and I don't blame them for hating me in the end.

Because I hated myself too. If I'd been different, Keegan would still be alive.

The door opens, and I look to find Officer Doyle stopping at the threshold.

"She's back, McHale." He lifts a gray brow. "Either go see that poor girl or tell her to stop showin' up."

Worry gnaws at me. Why is she here today? She doesn't usually come for another week. What if something happened after she wrote that letter?

I can't just abandon her. I need to see her.

But the very thought of being around her after all this time…

Hell, I have to stay strong. I can't show her what she does to me: completely unravels every messed-up inch of my heart.

With a groan, I rise. "Fine."

"Man of many words." He laughs.

He's the only one who tolerates me. Not sure why. I barely talk to him. Barely talk to anyone. I prefer to use fists. That's the only language I've ever known.

He slips the cuffs on me, and together we step into the hall, walls of prison cells lining both sides. Taking the stairs, we make it around the bend. He scans his card, opening the double doors before leading me into a room filled with people sitting around white tables.

I don't see her at first, inspecting the vast space like a hungry man starving for air. And when our eyes connect, my heart rips right out of my chest. It's been so long since I've seen her, I'm not even sure if she's real.

My fingers tighten into a fist. All the air completely evaporates from around me.

She's here. This beautiful goddess only has eyes for me, and this immediate possessiveness nabs me whole. I'd do anything for her. Kill anyone who hurts her. It's that simple.

Her chestnut hair spreads across both shoulders, slight waves at the ends, glistening and soft. She's in a light pink blouse, a button popped above her small breasts. I shouldn't even be thinking about them, but here I am, dreaming of us in bed together, her eyes on mine as I wrap my mouth around a nipple and suck.

"Keep it moving." Doyle pushes me from the back.

I hadn't even realized I had stopped walking.

"Mm-hmm." With a grumble for a response, I continue forward.

Her radiant gaze is a blend of peridot and the wild green ocean. A rarity in all her glory. Yet I can't touch or taste her. This is all we'll have: stolen glances and torn hearts.

I should gouge out my own eyes for the things I'm doing to her in my mind, but I've never been a righteous man. Never even wanted to be, not until her.

Her eyes pop as I approach, and there's real mirth caught within them.

I don't want there to be. I don't want her here. She needs to be far away from me.

I grab a chair and settle into it, keeping my expression tight even when every molecule in my treacherous body fights to make her mine.

"Got ten minutes, McHale," Doyle blurts out before he buggers off.

"What are you doin' here?" My voice carries indifference or even a bit of anger.

She shouldn't be in this awful place, making time for me like I'm important.

She clears her throat and fumbles with her fingers on the table. "I'm surprised you showed up. I kinda got used to sitting here alone before someone tells me you're not coming."

Her face grows sad, and I hate myself for it.

"Better go home, love. This is no place for you." My tone softens, and this is how I want to be with her. A man who's never been soft with a damn thing in his life.

Her gaze widens as a result.

It's then I realize what I called her.

It was a slip. A moment of failure.

Because it is something I dare to only call her in my dreams, where she is mine and I am hers.

It's the only place we make sense. Because here, in our world, we never will. I'm darkness where she is light. We don't mix. We don't even exist in the same orbit. Too outside the realm of possibility.

"My place is wherever you are, Devlin." She reaches her hand and grabs mine, but I quickly pull away.

Her nostrils enflame with her anguish and she blinks rapidly, stopping her tears from forming. But I see them, and I know I'm the one to blame.

"You need to stop coming here, Eriu. I mean it. I only came to make sure you were okay."

"Why wouldn't I be?"

"You come around the fifteenth. You're a week early." I run a hand through my hair, brushing it away from my eyes.

"So you *do* notice when I come." Her lips twitch.

I grind my jaw in return.

"It's fine. Don't say anything. Glad to know you pay attention, even though you like to pretend you don't." She huffs. "Is that easier?"

"Is what easier?"

"Pretending I don't exist."

I ball a hand on the table.

Couldn't pretend you didn't exist if I tried.

But I don't tell her that. It'd be leading her on.

"Why'd you come?"

Her features deflate, real hurt caught in the tendrils of her gaze. "Because I was hoping that if I showed up earlier than normal, you'd wonder if something was wrong and actually show up. Guess I was right."

She looks bloody proud.

I am too. She knows me too well.

"And is there? Something wrong?"

She nods, her brows tugging. "My father, he's been talking to someone." She swallows harshly. "He's gonna marry me off, I think."

God damn it!

"You have to do whatever your father tells you to do."

Her eyes slant with curtained fury. "Is that what you really think? Or is that you running?" She slants her body closer. "What are you afraid of? That we would actually make sense?"

Her fingers feather across the top of my hand, and this time I don't push her off. My skin burns, tingling like it's been dead until this very moment.

"I'm thirty-five. You're eighteen. You even comprehending what you're saying?"

"So you've thought about it?" Her gaze fills with some semblance of hope that I'm about to shatter into pieces.

"No. I haven't. I think it's laughable, really." I chuckle coldly, pushing myself back into the chair. "You're a child. I'm a man. I'd never marry you, Eriu, let alone feck you."

Her mouth parts, and tears paint her lower lashes. I remember my mother's words then, that I'm not good enough for a woman. Never gonna be good enough for her.

"How—how can you say that?" She sniffles under her breath. "Right before you went to prison, we really connected. You told me about your family. Your brother. How much you loved him. Did you forget?"

She swipes under her lashes, and I want to be the one to touch her silky skin, to replace her tears with her beautiful laughter.

But I'm nothing but a damaged, rotten corpse, breathing just to exist. I can't ruin her, and that's exactly what I'd do if we were together. She milks goats, for feck's sake. We're different in so many ways.

I shouldn't even want to be her bodyguard again. Nothing good would come of it.

How long will I be able to fight this attraction? How will I be able to remain unaffected when I'm around her all the time?

Maybe it would be a good thing if Patrick didn't want me back. I could disappear somewhere and forget all about her.

A pang hits my chest at the thought of not seeing her every day.

I used to see her all the time—holidays, birthdays, watched her grow up. Her family is close, and I was a part of it.

I can't be that way anymore. I must let that part of my life go. But what do I have without them? Nothing. That family is all I know.

Patrick owns acres of land in Boston, beautiful farmland with homes he's built for his children and the soldiers who have no place of their own. So he gave them one. Built an underground school for the future enforcers of the generation too, everything connected through intricate tunnels, dorms for the students and more space for anything they need.

It's where I started, and where I taught on occasion before I ended up here. I didn't just teach, I led by example. I've killed more men for the Quinns than I can count, and I'd do it again if they'd let me. At least that would keep me away from her.

"I haven't forgotten the things we discussed," I finally tell her. "But it didn't mean what you thought it did."

It meant everything.

I had never opened up like that before. Not even to my brother when he was alive. No one knew how much I missed him. Not even me. Not until I sat on her sofa and told her stories about him.

And she listened. My God, did she listen. She took every word like it was gold, and after that, she fed me. She can cook like the best of them. The flavor of that curry chicken was like tasting heaven.

She shakes her head, her wounded gaze sinking into my soul. I want to walk out and act like I never saw her. Like I didn't just break her beautiful heart. Like I didn't just hurt someone who doesn't even realize how much she means to me.

"You should go, Eriu. And this time don't come back because you won't see me again."

Defeat flits through her features. "Is your lawyer working on your appeal?"

"Aye. Trying to get me out on some technicality I don't understand."

She breathes a sigh. "How soon will we know if you're out?"

"Don't know." I start to get to my feet.

"Wait!" With one look, she begs me to stay, to take her in my arms and confess every sordid detail of my past.

Would she accept me for who I am? Would she even want me if she actually knew the kind of things I've done?

"Call me. Just call me when you get out. Please, Devlin."

"Aye." I have to agree. It'd be too cruel not to.

Goodbye, mo stoirín.

As soon as I turn around, I hear a small sniffle.

From over my shoulder, I glance back at her. "Whoever he is, he'd be a lucky man to have you."

Then I walk away before I flip every table in this goddamn place and get myself stuck here for eternity.

Well, maybe that actually wouldn't be such a bad idea.

THREE

ERIU
FIVE MONTHS LATER

I toss my shoulder bag onto the desk in my dorm room, breathing a sigh as I climb into my bed and press my head into the pillow.

I still can't believe my father allowed me to change schools my freshman year. I was attending a university in Boston, not too far from home, but after I was taken a few months back by someone who hated my family, everything changed. As a result, my father agreed to let me attend school in New York City shortly after.

It wasn't until the moment of my kidnapping that I truly realized what my family was capable of. Of course, I know who we are. I'm not as naïve as they all think I am. But it's one thing to know it and a whole other thing to see it.

After I was freed, my sister, Iseult, told me she wasn't just a Quinn, but an assassin for us—the Mob.

The word seems so strange to me. I don't think of us that way. We're just a normal family.

My mother died when I was five. I was always made to believe it was an accident, but it recently hit me that she probably died because of my father and what our family does.

I miss her terribly. How do you miss someone you never truly had?

An ache builds behind my eyes. All I have are her photos. Her deep brown hair was exactly like mine, and it's the only connection I have to her. My eyes are as green as my father's. Mom's were hazel gold.

After she died, my sister was always there for me. She was fourteen at the time, and she grew up taking care of me. She still does. My three older brothers—Tynan, Cillian, and Fionn—were protective, just like my dad was, but Iseult was my person. She'll always be the one I go to when I'm lost and need guidance, when I need a shoulder to cry on.

It doesn't hurt that she now lives with Gio Marino on Long Island, right outside of the city. It's one of the reasons my father agreed to let me go to school here.

But there was another reason, and I'm sure it was the biggest one.

Devlin came with me. 'Cause he's once again my bodyguard.

Yay…ish.

I groan to myself.

I mean, don't get me wrong. I want him here. But not as my bodyguard. I want more than that. I always will. Time hasn't changed much about my feelings for him.

I'm doomed.

After I visited him in prison and he told me never to return, I didn't. I was too hurt to face him. Then, soon after, his lawyer was able to get him out on a technicality.

He kept his word and texted when he was released, but told me not to visit him. He was blocking me from his life completely, so I was done.

I didn't go see him.

I didn't write.

I pretended he didn't exist.

Of course, that was impossible, but I was bitter over the constant rejection. I think it finally hit me that he's never going to want me.

He was my first crush, the first man I dreamed about kissing. But he never looked at me as more than a child.

As I grew up, that never changed.

Of course I know how ridiculous I was back then. I was young. I had no business having a crush on a grown man, but I couldn't help myself. I still can't seem to get him off my mind.

Except now I'm not a child, though he still seems to treat me that way. When will everyone stop treating me like I'm a little girl?

Our age difference is a huge issue for Devlin, but not for me. My father would most likely not approve either, but I would've fought for us.

But I'm done fighting. I can only try for so long.

When I was kidnapped, Devlin was already out of prison. He went looking for me. And once he realized I was already rescued, he stormed into my father's home like a man straight out of hell. When those sapphire-blue eyes met mine, I felt something, and I know he did too. I could just see it. And I thought he'd finally admit his feelings for me.

But after the dust settled, he went back to keeping his distance.

It was a big deal for Devlin to show up at my father's. No one except Iseult knew he was even out of prison. He didn't want them to know. Wasn't ready to face my father for failing to keep me safe, for allowing me to slip something in his water.

My father, of course, forgave Devlin for my drugging him and all that. He'd have been ridiculous not to. The man went to prison for me. That means something to someone like my father. It was honorable, and there's nothing more that my father respects.

Thankfully, Dad hasn't brought up marriage. Not since Gio. Yes, my sister's husband was originally supposed to go to me. So glad I dodged that bullet.

Luckily, he was already in love with my sister. I wish Iseult would have told me right away that she met him first, way before my father arranged my marriage to him. It would've been easier. But she was afraid of feeling something for anyone, and of course she didn't want to disappoint our father. He would've thought she was having an affair with Gio. To him, loyalty is key in a marriage, and he doesn't take infidelity well.

But he would've believed her. He loves Iseult. And after what happened to her when she was seventeen, when the Russians tortured her, he would do anything for her.

It all worked out how it should have, though. My sister and Gio were meant to be. Both insane and head over heels. She was always unwilling to give herself to someone else, but it took the right person. I don't even remember her having a boyfriend. But with Gio, she found love. And nothing makes me happier.

As for me, I'm bound to be stuck with a man who will probably be someone in the Mob or Mafia, a man who thinks of me more as a steppingstone than a wife he's supposed to cherish. That's how many of these men in my circle are. I've seen enough of them in my home when Dad didn't think I was watching. I'd hear how they talked about their own wives, and it would make me sick.

I don't want someone who will be unfaithful, who will treat me poorly. I'd rather die alone with a bunch of cats, maybe a puppy or two. Sounds much better than what my father plans for me. Marriages in our circle are not about love. They're about alliances, money, or power. Usually all three. It's sad when you think about it.

I consider running away often. Starting a new life somewhere. But, of course, that's a fantasy I can't afford. You can't live on your own with no money. And I don't have any of my own.

Hopefully I have some time before my father finds another man I don't love to marry me.

My mind instantly zips to Devlin. Things are so much more awkward now than they were when he was previously my bodyguard. Because now he actually knows how I feel about him.

Way to go, you. You just made things a lot worse for yourself.

In the past three months since he's been in New York with me, he's barely said a word, and when he does, it's to tell me what to do.

When he accidentally touches my hand or my arm, I swear I catch on fire.

Does he feel it?

If he does, he never shows it. And my heart breaks every time.

I hear someone at my door, entering the code, and I know it's Karen, my best friend. She's the only one who has it besides Devlin.

She walks in, huffing as she drags her feet toward the love seat and lies on it. I swear she spends more time in my room than her own.

My father arranged for me to get the whole room to myself, and for Devlin to be allowed anywhere on school grounds. Probably donated a crap-ton of money to the university for that.

"I'm shot." She yawns. "Wanna grab some lunch?"

"Not really hungry." I twist my lips, and that has her sitting up, brushing her long, sunny blonde hair off her face.

Her dark eyes squeeze as she gives me a once-over. "What's wrong? Is that hot guard giving you hell again?"

"Don't call him hot." I swear I get jealous every time she ogles him like she's imagining him doing things to her he should be doing to me.

"Well, he is." She wags her brows. "That damn simmering gaze and that long hair." She blows an exaggerated breath. "How the hell haven't you jumped his bones already?"

My eyes roll. "You can't jump the bones of a man who doesn't want you."

She waves off my remark. "You just haven't tried hard enough."

"What do you mean?"

"Well, remember how he tossed you over his shoulder earlier this month when you went out with Kayla to that lounge?"

"Yeah…" I shrug. "And nothing happened afterward. He brought me back to the dorm and left."

Kayla is my other friend. She's close with Elsie Marino, the wife of Michael Marino, the head of the Messina family. They're one of the Italian crime families of New York, I'm told.

Iseult told me that when Kayla, Elsie, and their other friend, Jade, were nineteen, they were trafficked by one of the five families. An evil syndicate that no longer exists. A group of brothers who hated them, the Cavaleris, killed them all off.

After Kayla was rescued, nine years after she was taken, she wanted to go to college. Something she never got to do. So Michael arranged for her to attend the same school I'm attending now.

Karen giggles. "The fact that he threw you over his shoulder because you were dancing with another man obviously means he was really jealous. So you step up your game. Go out more. Dress in skimpier outfits. Make him crazy. Until he blows." Her lips thin

3

into a calculating grin. "You have to challenge him. See how much he can take. It's the only way he'll fuck that virginity out of you."

I grumble and throw the extra pillow over my face.

"I knew I shouldn't have told you," I mumble.

"It's not a big deal." She scoffs. "I mean, I don't know that many eighteen-year-old virgins... Actually, I don't know any." Her laughter echoes. "But that's okay. You want him to be your first. I bet he'd fuck you so hard the bed would break."

"Jesus!" I toss the pillow away. "Can you not?"

"Aww, are you blushing?"

She loves to tease me about my lack of experience. I know it is all in good fun. I do wish I was more like her, though. She has boys lining up to date her, and she knows all the tricks to make them want her. I know nothing. I once read a magazine article talking about what a man wants in the bedroom, and there's no way I could do any of that. I've never even seen a live penis before.

My face heats up just thinking about Devlin naked or getting naked in front of him, touching him everywhere. Oh geez, I can't even think about that stuff without my body tightening. He'd get so turned off by my lack of experience that he'd never want to touch me again.

"We're going to a party tonight," Karen announces, jumping to her feet, her face beaming with excitement. "The boys of Psi Zeta are throwing a huge bash at their house, and you will *not* say no."

Devlin at a frat should be interesting...

I bite onto my lower lip. Maybe I *can* get him jealous enough to try something.

"I'll do your makeup and you can borrow one of my dresses." Karen grins.

"What's wrong with how I do my makeup?"

"Nothing! You're gorgeous. But I'm gonna make you all sultry

33

and sexy. He won't be able to resist you."

My skin prickles with excitement. "Okay. I guess we're going to a party."

Can't wait to see the look on his face after Karen is done with me.

FOUR

DEVLIN

I didn't expect to get released from prison as fast as I did, but the lawyers figured out some loophole. Sometimes the law works in your favor.

When I first got out, I was too ashamed to face Patrick. He had to know I was out since he was paying my attorney bills, but he didn't try to contact me either. So I stayed in my house—the other one I own, not the one I lived in on his estate. I didn't think he'd want me there.

But after Iseult told me that Eriu was taken, I went out on my own to look for her. I was in a deep state of torture knowing someone could be hurting her.

I was worried that it was the gang I was a part of, but I quickly learned it wasn't them.

It was someone else: Sergey Marinov, father of the current Pakhan of the Bratva.

The war between the Irish and Russians all began with that prick. After a disagreement between Patrick and Sergey over land, he took Eriu's mother and killed her. Patrick, of course, took revenge and killed one of Marinov's sons. An eye for an eye. That started an all-out war, and in the end, Konstantin, the oldest, and his three brothers called a truce.

Their father disappeared soon after that, but waited three years before he came after Iseult when she was seventeen. She fought like hell and escaped, but not before she took one of his eyes, and the bastard waited a long time before he took Eriu as payback.

Now he's rotting in the ground. Thank feck nothing happened to her. I would've raised hell on that entire family.

After Eriu was rescued and I saw for myself that she was safe, I returned back to my home. Until one day, weeks later, I got a call from Patrick, asking if I wanted my job back.

I didn't hesitate. I said yes. Of course I'd say yes. Why did I think I'd refuse if I ever got the chance to be close to her? To protect her? I'd never turn that down. I didn't want some other man where I belonged.

I didn't even care that I had to move to New York. I'll be there for Eriu, and I won't fail her this time. She is under my constant care and protection.

Patrick did forgive me for what transpired with Eriu the night she drugged me, but he also knew me well enough to appreciate that I was ashamed for failing at my job. But he told me he trusts me, and that meant more to me than he realized.

So I won't fail him again. I watch her every move.

Before Eriu moved into her dorm, I had it bugged. Didn't want to add cameras so I don't invade her privacy that way. I also added a tracker to her car. Even her cellphone is tapped. I ran background checks on her friends too, who all came out clean.

I know every move Eriu makes before she makes it. Just like I know she'll be going to a party tonight, where I'll be watching everything she does.

She needs to be protected. Too many could use her as a pawn in the dangerous world she's a part of. She doesn't truly realize the danger she's in just by existing. Her father has many enemies, and to add mine to the mix is even worse.

I continue to listen to her and Karen talking about the party, about how Eriu should seduce me. It's too bad I'm a lot stronger than either of them gives me credit for.

The things I want, she'll never know.

When I'm alone, when it's safe to think about her, that's when I let my true intentions roam free. Her as mine, the object of my every desire, my wife, the mother of my children. It's what I want.

But we don't all get things we want in life. I should know. I lost everything when I lost my brother.

I'm relieved I wasn't married. They would've killed my wife. They would've killed our children too. They have no limits.

They could be anywhere. They could bloody well be in New York, waiting for the perfect time to take me out, and everyone I care about.

I won't let that happen.

I won't let Eriu die.

It's why we can't be together.

It's too bad I can't tell her that.

ERIU

I pull down the fiery-red minidress, hoping my behind doesn't pop out of this thing as we stride up toward the frat house.

37

I don't dress like a nun, but this is way too short. But Karen insisted, and I didn't want to disappoint her or ruin my chances of Devlin eating his heart out.

Maybe that's what he likes, women who dress like this. I guess we'll see.

She wasn't lying about my makeup either. I look like one of those pinup models: smokey eyes, pink lips, blush and shimmer on my cheeks. My hair is down, the large curled ends hitting the small of my back.

"You look hot," Karen whispers. "Stop fidgeting."

We stroll up the steps toward two guys who are checking people in by the entrance. They appear visibly high or drunk, I can't be sure which. And they seem to only be letting the girls in and refusing many of the guys.

Peeking behind me, I find Devlin moving closer, his eyes concentrating on mine. For a moment, I find them drifting from my head to my legs, and I immediately shiver.

When I do, he catches himself and his jaw flexes.

I gulp down the nerves riding up my throat and fight to shake off the goose bumps threading my skin.

But that'd be hard to do.

He noticed me.

He was staring at me like a man would look at a woman he wanted, and it thrilled me.

I definitely noticed him too, but then again, I always do.

He looks incredible in a suit jacket, a baby-blue button-down beneath, with navy dress pants. Every sinew, every muscle is on full display. I start to wonder how he looks without his shirt on. I bet he has abs for days, and I crave to have my hands on him, to feel those ripples.

Oh my God… I can't believe I'm picturing him like that.

My face goes hot, and I peer back at him, wondering if he knows what I was just thinking about. His eyes are hard and unrelenting.

Of course he doesn't know what I was thinking. That would require him to read minds. Then again, this is Devlin we're talking about.

I glance at the girls standing behind him, and they sure notice him too, whispering with each other as they peep at him with flirtatious smiles. Some of them are aware of my connection to him, but not all of them.

I don't even know how he'll get into the party. Those guys are going to wonder why he's here. He doesn't pass for a twenty-year-old. They'll think he's someone's father, and Devlin won't take no for an answer. Then we'll have trouble.

Maybe I can convince them he's with me.

As soon as we're one person behind to get inside, Devlin strolls up to the back of me, his warm, howling breaths skating down my nape, making it hard to breathe.

"That dress is far too short," that husky timbre drawls out with a deep whisper. "You shouldn't be wearing it."

I gasp when his palm cups my elbow, jolting every molecule. I'm not sure if he doesn't like me in this dress because he's jealous or because it doesn't look good on me.

"Too bad I don't care what you think," I breathe with a quick glance behind my shoulder, swallowing down the jittering nerves.

His eyes turn arctic and dangerous, and a growl deepens in his chest. But he doesn't say anything else, though his hand remains on me as we climb a final step until we reach the top.

"Hey, Karen!" One of the guys hugs her. "You two can go right in."

When Devlin tries to follow us, the guy stops him.

"Whoa, dude." He chuckles dryly. "I don't know where you

think you're going, but you can't go in."

Crap.

Devlin curls an arm around my lower back and brings me flush against his side. My entire body shivers. This is the closest I've been to him.

His eyes take on a demonic turn as they zero in on the college guy.

But it's hard to concentrate on how bad this situation could get when he's touching me this way, the woodsy, masculine scent of his cologne invading my nostrils.

Thoughts of his mouth on mine, thick fingers stripping off my clothes, pummel into my mind and I almost let out a moan.

"He's with me, boys." Karen gives them one of her sultry smiles. "I promise he won't cause trouble, right?"

She tries to loop her arm through his, but he gently flings it away, holding on to me tighter.

She passes me a knowing smirk.

Devlin eyes the kid like he's about to remove his head from his shoulders. And he just might if we don't get him inside.

"Okay, cool," the guy retorts. "Just keep the beast on a leash, will ya?"

He laughs, and Devlin's body jolts.

"Okay, come on, you two." Karen struts inside while I try to yank Devlin, who's rooted, staring at the guy.

"Devlin," I whisper. "Come on before they kick us all out!"

"That wouldn't be so bad," he spits through clenched teeth, zeroing his concentration on my lips.

His gaze turns hooded, cheeks hollowing, and I almost forget how to breathe.

Quickly facing forward, we start for the door. I'm grateful he hasn't thrown me over his shoulder and taken me back to my dorm yet.

As soon as we're all in the house, Karen grabs my other arm and gives him a once-over when he refuses to leave my side, holding on to me, his fingers digging into my hip.

"You can let go now. She's safe with me."

"Right," he mutters gruffly, but his hold on me disappears, and I feel a chill that wasn't there before.

"Stay back and behave," Karen tells him. "Eriu deserves a fun night with how hard she studies. Nod if you promise to behave."

She pops out her large breasts; her dress is blue and just as tiny. I know she hopes to get his attention, but his eyes don't budge from mine, and he doesn't nod or say a word as he crosses his arms.

"Okay, well…" she adds. "I will take your silence as a yes. We'll be going now."

But as we head for the table filled with alcohol bottles and plastic red cups, he follows me, keeping just enough distance that I don't feel his body pressed up against mine like it was before.

He stands there, surveying the place, the bustling of college kids and loud music not fazing him at all. I'm sure he's been at his share of college campuses and parties, though I don't really know much about his past, other than his brother's death. He never actually told me how he died. Once he got arrested, I never brought any of that up again.

I often wonder about his past and who he was before he began to work for my father. He's always been secretive. I just wish he wouldn't be with me.

"He's intense." Karen bumps my shoulder, already drinking some concoction she created. "This is for you."

She passes me a cup, and I take it, inhaling the smell of something sweet.

"What is it?"

She scoffs. "Alcohol. Drink it and have a good time, for fuck's sake!"

I gander a look at Devlin, whose eyes narrow as he sees the cup in my hand.

He doesn't want me to drink…

The corner of my mouth tips up, and as it does, I toss the alcohol down my throat and gulp it down. My insides burn, but the sweetness nicely masks the liquor.

His nostrils flare, and the intensity written on his features sends my pulse thumping. He's always so stoic. I like getting a rise out of him, even when it's miniscule. It shows I can make him react. And the more I try, the harder he will have to work to fight it.

I drop the cup on the table.

"More," I tell Karen while my eyes remain fixated on his, and the small shake of his head, telling me to stop, has me popping a brow and smirking.

"That's my girl!" Karen gets all giddy as she makes me another drink.

When she's done, I drink that too and…well…that one, I'm definitely feeling.

"Did you add more alcohol to this one?" I cough out into her ear, hoping he doesn't notice.

"Hell yeah, I did! Maybe if you're a little drunk and wobbly, he'll have a reason to touch you. Then who knows what'll happen?" She winks.

"You're worse than Kayla."

She also thinks it's a good idea for me to make Devlin jealous.

"That I am." She tilts up her chin and grins. "I just want you happy, and you haven't stopped talking about that man since the moment you transferred. So, Mission: Fuck Your Bodyguard is in full swing."

I laugh, shaking my head. She's always been supportive of my infatuation with a man I have no business crushing on.

Karen doesn't know who my family is. All I told her was that my father is a businessman in Boston and he has always been overprotective, so of course he wouldn't allow me to attend college in New York without eyes. She easily bought it.

"Ladies!" Adam and Camden, two guys I know from some classes, pass by, giving us both a hug.

I've grown suspicious of everyone. It's hard to trust people with everything my family and I have gone through. But I have to be a normal person too.

The guys make their own drinks while Adam gives me sheepish glances. His tall, rugged athletic vibe would potentially interest me, especially with his pretty-boy looks, but there's only one man I want. The one who's currently staring a hole into the back of my head. I don't have to look behind me to know he is.

"Wanna dance?" Adam asks.

Of course I don't. He's not Devlin.

As though hearing the question, I find Devlin moving up a few steps from the corner of my eye, only a few feet between us now.

I want to say no. I should. I don't want to lead a guy on. But it's just a dance, not a marriage proposal.

"You better say yes," Karen whispers into my ear. "Devlin is going to lose his shit with some guy being all up on your ass looking the way you do."

"You think?"

"Hell yeah, I do!"

Adam comes to stand next to me, his body a bit taller than my five-four. Not like Devlin, who is a good foot taller.

I let out a wistful sigh. Will I always compare every man against him? What is it about Devlin that makes me like him?

He's barely said much to me in the years he's been my bodyguard, but when he does… Those moments are what I wait for.

I know behind that rough exterior is a man who wants someone to love him. Why can't that be me? Why won't he allow it?

Because you're eighteen and he's thirty-five, and your father would probably hang him for it, especially if he takes your virginity.

My virginity is like a gift for my future husband. This patriarchal nonsense has me wanting to sleep with just about anyone so that maybe whoever my father finds for me will no longer want me. I don't want a man who values my purity more than me.

Would Devlin care? I doubt it. He doesn't seem like the type. But I've saved myself for him anyway.

Guess that will be for nothing since he has yet to ask my father for my hand, and once my father finds someone for me, he won't have the chance anymore.

"So, how about that dance?" Adam's hazel eyes glimmer with interest, and not the creepy kind.

He genuinely seems like a nice kid. I've never heard anything bad about him around campus.

"Sure." I smile politely. "I'd love to."

Maybe this is, in fact, what Devlin needs.

Adam grabs my hand and leads me to where a bunch of people are already dancing. At first, he keeps a distance, but as the song progresses, he curls his hands around my hips and brings me close, staring down at me, a smirk on his face. He seems shy, not like your typical jock.

As he spins me around, I find Devlin's clenched jaw and a fist tight at his side. He looks ready to rip the poor guy's head off.

Instead of being afraid of what he might do, I grin and throw my arms around Adam's shoulders, gyrating provocatively. Devlin has never seen this side of me, and frankly, neither have I.

When I continue, I feel the heat of a body behind me, and I instantly know it's him. Adam's brows knit as he stares past me.

"Stop dancing with him. Now," Devlin warns into the crook of my neck.

That seductive tone, the warmth of his breath, makes my heart race. But I ignore him, letting him think he's in control.

His growling is hot and heavy against my nape. "Eriu…I'm not playing." His palm lands across my hip and my pulse quickens. "You're barely dressed, and you're dancing all over him."

"Excuse me?" I turn around abruptly, before blurting a quick apology to Adam, asking him for a minute.

He nods, giving us a curious look before he leaves.

"I'm having fun," I snap at my broody jerk of a bodyguard. "I don't know who you think you are, telling me how to dress or how to dance, but you have no say in my life."

His expression narrows. "We're leaving. You're drinking too much. Anyone here could spike your liquor."

"Well, you'll be here, won't you? Knight in shining armor." I pop a sassy brow. "Last time I checked, you don't own my body. You're here to watch me, and there's nothing I'm doing wrong. Daddy never cared if I drank. So go ahead. Call him and tell him what a bad girl I'm being."

I fold my arms over my chest, and his eyes turn to slits as his vision follows my movement, seeing the way my breasts pop.

"Like what you see?" A grin spreads on my mouth. "I won't tell."

"Eriu…" In an instant, he slants his face close to mine, his hot breath caressing my lips. "You're playing a real dangerous fecking game."

"Maybe it's time I dabbled in a little danger. Would fit right into my family, wouldn't I?"

FIVE

ERIU

H is eyes flash with something warm and inviting, our gazes battling. My racing heart doesn't stand a chance against what he does to me.

His lips near, almost against mine. "You're gonna get yourself into lots of trouble with that feisty mouth."

My body stills.

Waiting.

Hoping.

Praying for this very moment.

But then he grabs my wrist. "Let's go."

His demeanor shifts and he starts to pull me away.

"Hey! Stop!" I tell him, trying to keep my temperament at bay so no one calls the cops.

My dad would be furious with me, and I hate disappointing him. I've never done that except that one night I drugged Devlin.

I've always done what my father wanted. I was willing to go through my marriage with Gio because I knew I had no other choice. But faith intervened and I was saved. That won't happen again. A girl can only get lucky so many times.

Devlin stops mid-stride and turns to me. "You're either coming with me or I will throw you over my shoulder and take you out of this place. You know my word is good."

"Would like to see you try." I slant up my chin and keep a brave face, and when he cuts the distance between us and grasps my jaw possessively, I almost collapse.

The way my skin tingles, the hungered way his eyes cut into mine, it's all too much. My nerves hit my stomach, and my knees buckle.

His thumb reaches for my mouth, and slowly, he brushes it across my lips.

Every breath is trapped within me, the ability to utter a sound impossible, not with the way he touches me, holds my stare like we're one.

He moves nearer until I place my soft hands on his hard chest, those eyes never leaving mine. "You need to stop fighting me, love. I always get what I want."

Before I can say anything more, he grabs my hips and throws me over his shoulder as promised.

"Put me down!" I'm afraid my behind will be on full display, but he keeps his arm secured there.

"Next time, maybe wear a dress that covers your arse, because this one sure as hell doesn't."

"Right…" I scoff. "I forgot you hated my dress."

"Never said that," he grumbles.

Did he just admit he likes it?

"Why does it even matter who sees my ass? It's not like you

care."

"In fact, I very much do care about your arse." He cinches his hold on it with a dry laugh. "It's why I'm taking it out of this place, full of boys who'd do wretched things to it."

I scoff, rolling my eyes. "Protecting my virtue, are we?"

I hate him right now. Absolutely despise him. I'm only half-kidding…

As we pass Karen, she gives me a thumbs-up. My gaze narrows at her, but she grins wider. Only she'd be excited for me to get dragged out of a college party by my bodyguard.

Not like anything exciting will happen. Not with Devlin. He's a hardheaded brute of a man.

"You need to be careful around everyone. You understand? Your family's got too many enemies." He places me on my feet as soon as we hit outside, peering at me intensely, his irises deepening.

My stomach rolls.

"I don't want anything to happen to you."

And the way he says that, I know he cares. It's there, caught between his words, the true meaning, his true heart.

Or maybe I'm just dreaming it all up because I want him to care. I'm desperate for anything he gives.

His hand reaches for my face, fingertips stilling in the air between us like he's fighting the need to touch me. The anticipation causes me to shiver.

My God, I wish he would touch me. Just once, I want to feel this man's hands on me. What will it take for him to do that?

Heat builds between my thighs—this familiar, yet foreign feeling that I've never done anything about. I've been too shy to touch myself. But I bet he knows just what to do.

I wish I was more like the other girls, like Karen. She's had sex with plenty of guys. She knows what she likes and she's not shy about it. But I know nothing about my own body, and that's a little pathetic.

"I'm aware of how much danger I could be in." I clear my throat. "I'm not stupid."

"Don't go and put words in my mouth. Never said you were." His eyes scan my body. "You're cold."

It's when I glance down at my arms that I find them covered in goose bumps.

But it isn't the cold that caused it. It's him.

"I'm not." I bend my arms around my body.

His mouth flattens. "Put this on."

He shrugs off his suit jacket and holds it out for me to wear.

"Fine." I pretend he's doing me a favor.

Of course I don't want him to know how much I'm still obsessed with his grouchy, insufferable ass.

But really, my chest warms at the thought of wearing something that belongs to him. And as soon as I slip my arms into it, all I smell is Devlin. I practically sigh, feeling like I'm surrounded by heaven.

"Come on, let's get you home," he says while I fight not to smile.

I follow him down the stairs, but just as I do, I yelp when my stupid heel gets caught in the concrete, and I almost drop to my knees.

But his arm snaps around my back and he steadies me, tugging my body right up against his, chest to chest.

Always keeping me safe…

"You okay?" Warm exhales bathe my lips. "Almost took a real bad tumble."

His mouth lifts into a half-smile, and I forget I'm supposed to breathe.

His fingers sink deeper across my hip, keeping my body right up against his, close enough for the swell of his erection to push into me.

"Oh, God," I whisper, unsure if he heard it.

"You drunk?" He searches my gaze with concern.

Drunk on you, maybe.

My heart flips, and I swear I could cry with the way I love this man. And I know that's what I feel. Pure love. Yet loving someone who doesn't love you in return is unending torture.

"No, not drunk," I tell him. "Maybe a little?" My mouth winds up a fraction. "I'm a lightweight."

"Well, you're not twenty-one yet. I shouldn't even be letting you drink." His eyes dip to my mouth and his jaw strains before he looks back at me.

"Let me?" I laugh. "I don't belong to you, nor are you my father."

He releases an exasperated sigh. For a split second, he closes his eyes, and once he stares back at me, his arms scoop me up bridal-style.

I fist his shirt, and for a moment, I feel his skin and my body zaps with pleasure. "What are you doing?"

But I don't really care, because he's cradling me. My arms wind around his neck, and I could truly die happy right now.

"Carrying you. If you get hurt, I'll have to hear it from your father, and the last thing I want is to piss him off more than I did before."

My face falls. "I'm sorry. I'll spend my life apologizing for what I did. It's not your fault."

"Of course it is. You were seventeen, and I was your protector. I failed you, and I won't hear you blaming yourself anymore. Understand?"

His fingers roll up and down my shoulder, and with my sharp intake of breath, he instantly stops, like I'm made of acid or fire. Or both.

But his touch remains there long after it's gone, like a ghost I ache to hold on to.

SIX

DEVLIN

What the hell am I thinking, touching her, holding her this close? But it was like I couldn't help myself, needing my fix.

I rationalized it in my head. Told myself I was only making sure she didn't end up hurting herself. That's what I'm here for, aren't I?

But that's not what this is. I wanted her. I wanted to feel her skin on mine, no matter how we got there.

Her arms stay wrapped around my neck, and I'm *this* close to kissing her. What would she do if I did? Would she tell me to stop, or would she let me taste her?

Too bad I'll never know.

We make it back to her dorm room and I realize she's more inebriated than she even thought.

Gently, I drop her to her feet as we enter her room, and I lock up behind us. She plays with the hem of her dress, appearing uncomfortable to be this close to me. And if I'm honest, I'm damn uncomfortable too.

She's dressed in such a way that should have me lookin' the other way, but I can't help but rake her body while she doesn't see me. Makes me feel like a dirty feckin' man. But nothing about my true feelings for her is dirty.

I saw the way those guys at the party were staring at her body, and I hated it. Wanted to take off my shirt and wrap it around her.

She flings her shoes off and tosses them to the side while shrugging off my jacket and handing it back to me. I lay it over the back of her chair.

"My God, these are the worst things I've ever worn." She sighs.

"Why did you, then?" I glance at the long, thin heels. God knows why women do that to themselves.

"Because…" She clears her throat. "Never mind. Ugh, I have a headache."

"Shouldn't have been drinking, then." My brows bow.

"Okay, Daddy. Promise to be good next time."

A low, savage growl emanates from deep in my chest. Why did that spunk just make my dick hard?

Her lips thin, head slanting all innocently, and I swear there is a deviant little devil inside that girl dying to come out. Sure as hell won't be comin' out when I'm around. Lots of trouble could happen if she pushed me hard enough.

I may be strong enough to resist her for now, but day by day, it gets harder not to pin her to the wall and rip her clothes off until I'm balls-deep inside her.

I bet she's submissive. I bet she'd like it rough.

My God, what the hell am I doin', thinking these thoughts?

I back off a bit at a time. "Let me get you some meds and put you to bed before I go."

My feet are moving to her bathroom to grab some pills and a bottle of water from the mini fridge. I open it for her as I return, handing her both.

She swallows the meds before placing the water down on the desk.

I stalk to her dresser and retrieve a pair of leggings and a t-shirt that can cover that breathtaking body of hers.

Staying at that party, seeing those guys looking at her… It was hard not to lose it. Too much I wanted to do to those boys. None of which would be a good thing for the Quinns or me. Can't be headin' back to prison. She needs me.

When I hand her the clothes, she eyes me curiously and her gaze thins.

"How did you know which drawer those clothes were in?"

"Lucky guess."

She scoffs. "Right. I bet you've been in this room, looking through all my things when I've been in class. Is that it?"

"No."

Yes. Know where everything is, love. Would've preferred cameras, but didn't think that'd be the right thing to do.

"You and my father—my whole family, for God's sake—you all hover and manage my life like I'm a child. I can't wait to move somewhere far away from everyone so I can live without the constant eyes on me!" Her voice simmers, and I can't help but laugh. "What's so funny?"

"I think it's cute that you think you can get away from your family—or me, for that matter. I thought you were a smart girl."

"Screw you."

Now don't go putting those thoughts in my head.

"When do you talk like that?" I remark instead.

"You underestimate me." She prowls closer, her eyes gleaming with her irritation. "I say a lot of things when I'm not around my family. It's why I was glad to be away, but of course you…" She digs a finger into my chest. "…had to follow me and report everything to *your* daddy."

She sneers in a mocking demeanor, and my jaw pulses with the desire to flip her against the wall and erase that smugness with my mouth.

"If I was reporting everything to your father, I would've already been callin' and telling him what a brat you're being."

"Brat, huh?" she snickers. "Not your type, I'm guessing?"

She runs her fingers up and down the top of my abdomen, and every muscle in my body contracts from her mere touch. Wonder what it'd feel like to have that hand wrapped around my cock instead. This wee little thing would probably get all shy and not know what to do.

A smirk teases my lips.

"Do you even have a type, Devlin?" she mocks, and I'm close to pinning this woman to her bed and showing her just who my type truly is. "Or are you cold as stone? Unaffected by the female population?"

"Eriu…you need to stop." My tone is an icy threat.

She giggles. Even her being drunk is adorable.

"You're always so serious."

Her pout is damn right sexy and irritating as hell. She shouldn't be sexy, not to me. She's Eriu. Once an innocent teenager…who has blossomed into a gorgeous woman.

Feck! My mind is corrupted.

'Bout to kiss the hell out of you just to show you how serious I really am.

"Go into the bathroom and change so I can put you to bed and leave."

"Why not join me and keep me warm all night? Promise I don't snore."

"Lord…" I grip the back of my neck.

Her laughter rings in my head, making me want to hear her moaning my name instead.

She starts to back off, and I release a silent prayer to the gods for her finally listening. But instead of heading to the restroom, she drops the clothes I gave her. I have no idea what she's doing until her hands reach behind her and that dress starts to come undone.

"Bloody hell! What are you tryin' to do?" I turn away in a snap, unable to comprehend that she's removing her dress in my presence.

"Making you see me…"

I see you, love. I see you so damn much, it hurts to be near you.

When I don't say anything back, she laughs.

"You told me to change, so I am." She sounds all throaty and sensual as hell.

A rumbling groan emerges from my lungs. "Go in the bathroom, Eriu, I swear. This is inappropriate."

I continue to face the other way.

"Why? Afraid you'll get hard? Maybe if you don't, I'll finally realize I'm not your type."

Not my type…

I chuckle to myself. If she only knew.

"Anyone with eyes would be attracted to you."

She inhales sharply, and I realize maybe I shouldn't have said that, but I didn't want her thinkin' low of herself. She's stunning.

"But I'm not the one you're gonna be with." I throw that in so she realizes I have not changed my mind.

"Why?" Her voice goes small and sad, and I want to reach for her and hold her close.

"Because I'm way older, and my life will only lead you to further danger. I've no plans to marry anyone either way, and when your father finds you a husband, it'll be because it will create a strong alliance for the family. Marrying me wouldn't do that for ya."

She snickers. "The family. Right. What happened to people falling in love and marrying for those reasons? My sister did."

"She may have, but she got lucky. Doesn't happen that way for many of the people in your position, and you know this."

"I wish I wasn't a Quinn…" She sniffles. "I wish…ouch!"

"Eriu?" I flip around immediately and find her on the floor, her foot twisted.

And she's still very much naked.

Lord have mercy on my soul.

"Tripped on the chair."

She winces as she tries to cover her breasts with her arms, but my God, I've seen the whole lot of her. I can't ever forget it.

"Can you stand?" I reach a hand to help her up, looping my arm through hers.

"I don't know," she mutters, rising to her feet while trying to cover herself, and I do my best to close my eyes while assisting her.

I look back just to find the clothes she dropped on the floor.

She continues to cover her breasts, keeping her knees locked.

"Think we're past bein' shy now, love. Seen everything there was to see." My lips jerk, and her cheeks grow in color. "You did take off your clothes for me." I grasp her jaw and near my lips to hers, so close I can taste her scattered breaths. "Didn't think things through, did ya?"

Her inhales grow shallower as my thumb inadvertently runs

across her full mouth. I should teach her a lesson so she never does this again.

There I go, rationalizing it again…

My blood's laced with desire as I take in her doe-eyed expression. Her father would kill me for this, but he won't know.

"Raise your arms in the air. I'll help you get dressed."

She shakes her head.

"Wasn't asking."

I drop my hand from her, wishing it could stay there. When she still doesn't do what I said, I tilt a brow.

"I'm waiting. You wanted me to see you, so here I am, looking. Arms up."

My cock throbs at the shy way she peers at me, no longer the courageous woman who stripped, hoping to get me to give in to those wild curves.

But I'm doing this for her. She needs to learn that she can't be doing things like that. And knowing she no longer wants me to see her this way is exactly why it needs to happen.

Her chest rattles, a nervous glint in her eyes, and slowly, she backs off, her arms trembling down her body until I find a rosy nipple peeking through, hard and small.

Wanna tug it into my mouth and watch her face grow with pleasure.

I fight those feelings as she lifts her arms all the way, making me grow and ache in my slacks.

Her eyes lower there, and her mouth parts when she catches the thick outline of my hard-on. Bet she's wondering if it'd fit inside her.

With a finger, I beckon her closer, and she comes standing a few inches away.

"Good girl."

Her lips tremble as her eyes lock with mine

It's a shame I have to cover her up. The shirt slips over her, and when I pull it past her chest, my finger accidentally rubs over her nipple.

She gasps.

"Sorry," I mutter, almost coming in my pants. This is damn inappropriate. "Sit on the bed, and I'll help you with your pants."

Her breathing grows raspier and so damn hot. I wanna bury myself deep between her warm thighs.

"I can do that myself," she whispers.

"I told you what's gonna happen, didn't I? Now sit down and do what I said."

"But…but you're gonna see me. There…" Her face just about turns red.

"Where?" I tug her jaw to me. "Say it."

She pinches her eyes closed and grimaces.

"Say it, Eriu. Tell me where I'm gonna see you."

Her pretty mouth parts, yet she still doesn't look at me.

"Look at me and say it." I stroke her lips with my thumb.

"Jesus," she breathes, but those eyes lock with mine for a moment before she glances at her lap. "My pussy. You're gonna see it."

I knowingly smirk and incline her chin with the back of my hand. "That's right, I will. But you only have yourself to blame. I warned you not to start trouble. This is your punishment. After tonight, you'll never attempt anything like that again. You'll never try to seduce me. Nod if you agree."

Tears brim in her lower lashes, and I hate that I made her cry, but I need her to stop with this fantasy of us. It's never going to happen.

"I hate you," she pants softly as she lowers onto the bed.

"That's exactly what I've been waiting for."

I kneel before her and take her right foot, gently massaging her toes, not wanting to stop touching her. As I slip her foot into her leggings, it's hard to avoid her bare core, warm and wet. My body turns rigid with desire, my blood pumping, needing a taste of her.

This is too much to bear.

One kiss and I'd be done for. That's all it'd take. And I've never been a man who cared much for kissing. But Eriu? I'd kiss her until my soul gave out. She owns me.

She closes her eyes and practically trembles as I put her left foot in.

"You're beautiful," I whisper, my heart racing so quickly, I didn't know it was capable of such things.

Her lashes flutter, and she peers at me with a quivering jaw.

My hands still, fingertips warm against her silky skin.

My heart beats out of my throat as her eyes no longer hold tears, but passion and sin. She's going to bring me to hell for what I wanna do to her.

"You think I'm beautiful?" Her question rings incredulously.

How could she ever doubt herself?

I nod once. "Too beautiful. So please, Eriu…please stop this." There's pleading in my voice that's never been there before, not like this.

"You're never gonna want to try, will you?"

That pain in her eyes returns, and I wish I had a different answer.

"Go." She sniffles. "Get out of here!"

Her hollerin' rises until she's hopping on one foot, yanking her pants all the way up, then pushing me with two palms on my chest.

But it does nothing but keep me rooted in place. A small thing like her doesn't stand a chance against me.

"Sit down before you hurt yourself." My hand snaps around

her wrist.

"I don't want to look at you right now. Please..." Her voice drops. "Just go."

My pulse gallops in my ears. I hate seeing her upset. It wasn't my intention, but I can't make her think there is a chance for us when that's impossible.

She has to learn that her life doesn't include me.

"I'll go. But I'll be here tomorrow, as always."

"Wonderful." She puts pressure on her foot that she may have twisted.

"You wanna go see a doctor for that?" I glance down at it.

"No." She sits on the edge of the bed. "I'll be fine."

I don't like this. She's probably just saying that to get rid of me.

I start for the door.

"I'm sorry." The words echo as my back faces her, unable to look into her eyes any longer.

She doesn't say a word even as I walk out. But I remain on the other side long after, hearing her soft sobs undoing me one tear at a time.

SEVEN

ERIU

Groaning, I stretch my limbs across my twin bed, recalling the events of last night. What I did. What he did.

Maybe it was all just a terrible dream. Or more of a nightmare.

But once I rotate my foot and a bit of pain radiates across my ankle, I realize there's no such luck. It all happened as I remember it.

Forcing myself up, I place both feet down while seated, testing it out some more.

Nothing too crazy. I'll live.

I run a hand down my face. I can't believe I stripped for him. How stupid could I be? What did I think would happen? He'd take one look at me and decide, *yep, this is the girl for me. Just look at those nipples.*

I laugh dryly at my own childishness. Instead, what I gave him was a full view of everything. Then he decided to enact his version of revenge and really humiliate me. What a jerk!

I seriously can't believe he did that. Punishment? I scoff. Well, hope he got to enjoy the view, because that's never gonna happen again. Devlin will never see me naked unless he puts a ring on it. Or at least buys me dinner first.

I really hate him right now, really dreading seeing that sexy, rugged face of his. My God, I love his thin stubble across that firm, sculpted jaw. Want to run my fingertips across it as he kisses me.

I grumble and reluctantly get to my feet, knowing that in reality, there's nothing about that man I can hate.

I take a couple of steps, and though I can walk on my injured foot, I decide I'm skipping class today. It still hurts, and I'm afraid I'll do more harm when walking from class to class. Plus, it would help *not* to see Devlin all day if I don't have to.

My face flushes just remembering what happened between us. *Stupid, stupid, stupid!*

Getting back to bed, I get my cellphone from the nightstand and shoot Devlin a text, knowing he'll be showing up here to follow me to class.

ERIU

Not going to class today. Headache.

DEVLIN

Does your foot still hurt? I'm bringing you to the doctor.

ERIU

What? No. It's fine. It only hurts a little. Nothing to get crazy about.

DEVLIN
Fifteen minutes. Be ready.

I shake my head in frustration, knowing there's no way to make this man reconsider. I force myself to the shower and slowly strip my clothes off before getting in. The water is hot, and I'm careful so I don't fall.

The last thing I need is to call Devlin for help while I'm naked. Again. No, thank you. Once was plenty.

Karen, of course, is still not back at her dorm. She would've texted if she was. Unless she's still sleeping, which is possible. I'm thinking she's probably with some guy she met last night. She does that a lot. Wish I was more like her.

She's free, untethered by family obligations. Or, you know, her virginity?

If I was more experienced, maybe I'd know how to properly seduce a man like Devlin instead of falling on my behind and embarrassing myself.

Once I'm done, I step out and dry off, brushing my hair as I let the blow-dryer whisp through each strand. With a quick touch of makeup and ChapStick, I'm out the door.

And as soon as I am, there he is, waiting for me. Those strong, muscular arms crossed over his defined chest.

My pulse gallops in my throat, and my heart practically weeps. But I tuck those emotions in, that inexplicable longing, and I hide behind it.

His harsh expression softens just a fragment before it returns to its previous state.

I hate it. I hate everything about this.

I want to scream. Cry. I want to hate the world. Not even because he will never choose me, but because my father will eventually choose my husband, and there's nothing I can do about it. Devlin was my only shot at happiness, and he's never going to change his mind about us.

His eyes narrow while I try to stop looking at how handsome he is. A dark navy suit jacket is fitted over his white dress shirt with a button popped open. So insanely attractive, it hurts to look at him.

He assesses me with deep concentration, a furrow between his brows, not a hint of the seductive man who made me show him my body yesterday. He's back to his broody self.

He glances down at my foot. "How is it?"

"Fine." I exhale dramatically and speed past him. "Let's go. I have things to do."

"Like what?" He appears before me in an instant, his palms rounding my hips as he takes me into his arms like I weigh nothing.

"What the hell are you doing?!"

"Carrying you. If you're still in pain and can't go to class, it must still be bad. Wouldn't want you to make it worse."

I roll my eyes.

"Don't roll your eyes at me." His mouth tremors.

"What are you gonna do about it? Dress me again?"

He grunts. "Don't bring that up."

I arch a brow. "Why? Regretting it?"

"I regret nothing." The thick vein in his neck throbs. "But we're done with that. I'm here to keep you safe. That's all this will ever be."

"Yeah, I got the message." My teeth grind as he carries me out the entrance and down a flight of stairs before we make it to the parking lot.

He opens the passenger side door and settles me in like I weigh nothing. As he clips my seat belt, his eyes hold mine for a moment, and I almost forget where we are.

He blinks away the flaming connection between us, rounding the SUV before entering and putting the car into drive.

My body deflates like a balloon.

Is it always going to be this way?

We're on the road in no time, and I hate being this close to him, smelling the woodsy cologne in the air, remembering the way he looked between my thighs when he put my leggings on. Placing one leg over the other, I attempt to quench the desire coursing through me. I take in each silent breath to relax myself, but it's no use, not when he's this near.

My cell rings in my bag, and I'm relieved at the disruption. I find Karen's name on the screen.

"Hey! How did it go last night?" I glance at Devlin from my periphery.

"Well…after you ditched Adam, he needed a shoulder to cry on, and I had one he liked." She giggles.

"Oh my God," I whisper. "No, you didn't."

"Sure did, and man, was he good. You really missed out on a great fuck."

My cheeks bloom with heat as she continues.

"He would've popped your cherry, and you would've loved it."

"No, thank you…"

"Yes, because Plan: Fuck Devlin's Brains Out went so well…"

Of course she knows I didn't get any. Devlin is a force too hard to break.

"It's okay," she says. "I'm just teasing, but you really should move on from him. If he didn't fuck you after last night, it's never gonna happen."

My sigh is doused with exhaustion. She's right, I know she is. But every time I want to give up, I'm right back to wanting him and wanting to fight for him.

"Anyway, I need to tell you the best part," she goes on, and I'm immediately curious. "After Adam and I were done with the best sex of my life, he told me all about his father and how connected he is. He's some congressman, yada, yada." She skips over that, as though that isn't a huge deal. "So he said because of his connections, he knows the best places to party. Exclusive places."

"Okay…" Not sure where she's going with this.

She laughs. "He invited me to some pop-up club."

"What's that?"

"It's when the party is at different locations every time. No one knows the address until the invitation is sent."

"Sounds interesting…"

That kind of thing isn't my jam. I know Karen would love it. I'm happy for her.

"It's exclusive. I mean *really* exclusive, Eriu." Her voice grows with excitement. "Like you need ten K just to be let in. And after you're accepted through some application process, they send an anonymous text with the address, then the text disappears after sixty seconds of opening it. Isn't that cool?"

"Umm…sounds like a good way to die."

"Orrr…and stay with me…" she teases. "A good way to have fun! Never know, maybe it's the perfect place for you to finally lose your virginity."

"Wait…" My eyes widen. "Is it a…you know?"

I sheepishly peek at Devlin, who glances at me suspiciously.

"Yes, it's that kind of club." Her short, mocking laugh slips through the line. "And Adam said I can invite you! He said he would sponsor us both, so we don't even need to pay! We'd be full members!"

No way can I go. And did she say I'd be a member? Of a sex club?! What? Did she forget who I am? Miss Virgin of the Century?

68

"You don't have to do anything there. You can just watch. Maybe learn a little something. Come on! You have to go with me! I need a wingwoman."

Watch people have sex? Okay, that's insane. Of course I can't do that. And here's the biggest issue: I wouldn't be able to step foot inside without Devlin. Unless I figure out a way to lose him. I've done it once before…

If he can't find me, he can't stop me. I can deal with his wrath after I'm back.

What am I even thinking? I can't do that to him again.

"When is it?"

Am I seriously considering this? But I did say I wished I could be more like Karen. I have to start somewhere. Just didn't think sex club was on my bingo card.

"In three nights." She tries not to sound excited just in case I tell her no. "What do you say?"

"Let me think about it, okay? I can't talk now. I am being driven to a doc appointment. May have sprained my foot last night."

"Oh shit, Devlin is there. Got it. Okay, let me know what the doc says. Love you. Debauchery, here we come. Also, what the hell happened to your foot?"

"Ugh, don't ask…"

"Ooh! Something did happen with sexy bodyguard man." She giggles before I end the call.

I can feel Devlin's eyes on me.

"What was that about?" he tosses out coarsely.

"Nothing." I throw on an innocent smile. "Just Karen being Karen. You know how she is."

"Mm-hmm. That's what I'm afraid of."

The appointment lasted all of twenty minutes, then we were out. Was told to take some painkillers, ice it, and elevate, but that I should be fine to go to school tomorrow as long as there is no major pain. Everything I already knew, but Mister Overprotective had to drag me out for no reason.

"I can walk, you know," I huff as he carries me into my dorm building like a child. Students whisper as they see us. "This is embarrassing. Seriously, the doctor said I won't die. You can put me down."

His bicep muscles tense around me, and the veins on the top of his hand ripple. "Not until you're in your room. Then I can go."

"Fine…"

I know there's no use in talking to him. Once he has his mind made up, a fight is hopeless. He always wins.

Entering my code, he opens the door and carries me to my bed.

When he gets ready to go, I have every intention of making him stay. But I know there'd be no point. He'd just sit here staring at me. The days when he could open up to me are long gone.

"Can you pass me my backpack?" I ask him, eyeing the black canvas bag on the desk, hoping to get some reading done for my literature class.

He reaches for it, and as he does, a book on creative writing slips out.

Shit. He can't see that.

He might realize I'm taking writing classes and report it to my dad.

My father believes I plan on becoming a vet. He has no idea I decided to follow my true passion and become a writer. I want to write for online magazines, or maybe even novels one day. But my father doesn't believe there is a career for writers, not one that is worthy of our name, so I have resorted to lying, but I know he'll find out eventually. I'm just not ready for that day yet.

I've been accepted into a small writing class for advanced students by Professor Montgomery. She's brilliant and has become a mentor of sorts. I've told her how my father has never been supportive of my passion. That he doesn't believe an English literature degree is going to take me anywhere. But this is what I want.

Once I get a job doing what I love, maybe he'll finally believe in me. Until then, this must remain my secret. Even Iseult doesn't know. I can't risk her slipping it to someone.

"What's this?" he asks.

"Um. Nothing. Just a book."

"On writing? Are you taking writing courses? I thought your father told you not to."

I grind my molars, my pulse racing in my ears.

Think. Think!

"Eriu…"

"You can't tell him!" I advance on my feet, dragging myself toward him, grabbing the collar of his shirt in my trembling grasp. "Please, Devlin, don't take this away from me."

His blue eyes soften, and for a moment, I wonder if it's sympathy.

"Why don't you tell him? Secrets are always bound to come out."

I snicker. "You know how stubborn my dad is! He'd never allow it. He'd take me out of school and move me back home. Then I'd have no life. I'll be married to some man who will probably beat me and I'll—"

In an instant, he cups my chin and his eyes bore into mine. My breaths still.

"Lass, I'd never let that happen." His gaze turns intense, blazing with promise. "If you think that my vow to protect you will end when you're married, then you don't know me. Your husband will have to deal with me for the rest of your life."

My eyes lower to my feet. "You swear?"

Instead, I want to ask him how he can allow me to marry anyone but him. Is it that easy? Do I truly mean nothing at all?

"I swear it, love."

That word. I instantly melt. I could listen to him say it over and over again.

Our eyes lock, and through it, he brushes a thumb over the corner of my mouth.

My breath catches, and my pulse spikes.

He holds my gaze, his throat straining, and I don't so much as move, afraid of risking this moment, whatever it means.

My God, he smells good. And his chiseled jaw, the sharp edges of his face, that domineering appearance... It all does things to me.

I have no business feeling what I currently am. Yet here I am, feeling everything, wishing he was mine and I was his.

His cellphone rings, and it instantly has him dropping his hand off me and retrieving it.

"It's your father," he says before he answers. "Sir?"

I can't hear what my father says, but Devlin focuses on me as he continues to listen.

"I'll bring her right over."

"What?" I whisper.

"We will see you in a few hours."

When he drops the call, he stares at me, and there's something there I can't yet name. But it sends a jolt of anxiety through my limbs.

"What is it?" My heartbeats skip in my chest.

"Your father requested the family for a meeting. It's important."

"Why? I'm never included in those meetings. Why now?"

They're for the rest of them, the killers.

"He said you must be there, so come on, we've gotta leave ASAP. We have a long ride ahead of us."

With nerves jittering in my stomach, I run into the bathroom and grip the faucet, staring at myself in the mirror.

Something unsettling prances across my flesh, like a warning that whatever I'm about to walk into won't be good at all.

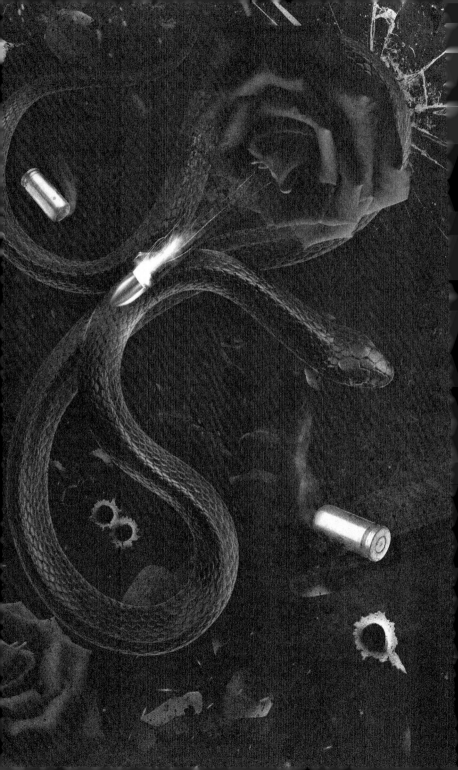

EIGHT

ERIU

We've been on the road for hours, and in a short while, we'll be at my father's. I texted my sister to find out if she's heard about this meeting and if she'll be there too, but she hasn't called me back yet.

I glance over at a tense Devlin, his knuckles going almost white with how hard he grips the steering wheel.

He knows something. He has to. But he hasn't said a word, even when I asked. I'm almost afraid to know why I've been invited. Maybe that's why he hasn't told me.

My body sags as I lay my head against the window.

"You alright?" he asks, the timbre of his voice low and deep.

I shake my head in response. "I know you're hiding something from me."

He doesn't even deny it. His jaw visibly clenches, and that's all the confirmation I need. Devlin has never been a liar. Even when he doesn't want to tell me the truth, he just won't say anything instead.

My phone vibrates, and I discover a text from my sister. Finally.

ISEULT

No one told me about any meeting. But don't worry, I'm heading to Boston. Just told Gio I'm gonna surprise Daddy. Bet he forgot my invitation.

I laugh aloud before I reply.

ERIU

I'm scared it means he found someone for me. I can't marry a man I don't even know. Please, Iseult. Find out what's going on before I get there.

ISEULT

Look, if our darling father found you a husband, I'll make sure the guy becomes permanently tied up. You get me?

ERIU

Um. I think so? But I don't actually wanna write that in a text.

ISEULT

Smart girl. Now, listen. You don't have to worry. You won't marry anyone you don't like. You make the rules. Fuck our father and fuck whoever he may have found for you. Got it?

ERIU

I love you. I don't say that enough.

ISEULT

I love you too. Always. Now let me drive,
because I'm going too fast, and if I die,
Gio is gonna kill me.

ERIU

Yeah, don't die. I need my sister. See you
in a few hours.

I slip the phone back in my handbag. Iseult won't be here for the meeting. No way she'll make it on time, no matter how fast she drives. Not that I want her in danger. I just need her. She's the only one on my side.

All the men I'm surrounded by—my brothers, Devlin, my dad—all they care about is honor and doing the right thing. I don't care about that.

All I want is to fall in love like in the books I read. I want my pulse to flutter, my body to grow weak. I want to be nervous my first time, I want to feel my heart soaring. I don't want my marriage to be a contractual negotiation between my father and some man he's chosen.

But do girls like me really have options? Even with Iseult's reassurances, will my father bend?

She can't possibly murder my future husband.

Can she?

My heart sinks as soon as we step out of the car and head up the cobblestone steps to my father's home.

One of the guards welcomes us into the large foyer of the mansion, a sparkling chandelier hanging above the cathedral ceiling, filled with paintings of angels floating in a vivid blue sky.

My father is grandiose in his décor. There are various Renaissance paintings throughout his house. He has an unhealthy obsession with that era. The furniture is similarly styled, gold and old-fashioned, but still beautiful.

The home is surprisingly silent. There are usually staff cleaning one of the many rooms. But I do smell my father's chowder, and I know for certain he's entertaining guests somewhere inside. He always cooks his chowder when he's welcoming company.

I still in my tracks, and my hands visibly tremble. But Devlin's fingers slip into mine, his body so close I register his rigidness against my shoulder, the slow rise and fall of his chest consuming me with panic.

"What's waiting for me there?" I whisper, my tears throbbing behind my eyes.

He sighs, and his brows snap almost painfully. He turns all the way to me, a hand cupping my cheek, holding it as our eyes connect.

My heartbeats quake louder, beating tumultuously in my chest.

"I won't let anyone hurt you."

It's an oath he means, but it's not enough. If he really didn't want to hurt me, then he'd have asked my father for my hand, and he hasn't.

His touch vanishes, and I grow colder without it.

"Come on now. We don't want your father waiting."

But I need to stall. I need Iseult here. I can't face whatever is there without her.

Sudden footfalls start closer, light and tapping nearer, until Fernanda, my father's new wife and Gio's mother, appears.

"Hey, sweetheart!" She embraces me tightly. "I heard you were coming in. Hello, Devlin."

"Ma'am." He nods.

"Hey, nice to see you," I say. "Do you know why Dad had me over?"

"I do not. Your father tends to be secretive about certain things." Her forehead scrunches in frustration.

Because he probably knows she'll hate this as much as I do. With her past being as it was, she isn't a fan of arranged marriages.

She was once married to Giancarlo Marino, the former head of the Messina crime family, until he died. But my father and Fernanda were apparently high school sweethearts, and though they were in love, they weren't allowed to get married. She comes from an old-school Italian family who arranged a marriage for her to Giancarlo, a cruel man from everything I've learned. But my father and Fernanda never stopped loving each other.

Iseult was angry with him because she always suspected he didn't love our mother like she deserved, but in his way, he did. He just loved two women, and I can't fault him for that like she does. I almost feel sorry for my dad and Fernanda. To love someone and not be allowed to marry them… I know how that feels.

I glance at Devlin, and my heart breaks, wanting him more than I can say.

More footsteps come, this set heavy and foreboding. And I know instantly it's my father.

"Darling, there you are!" He appears, his green eyes full of joy, a large grin on his face with no hint of anything amiss.

He kisses Fernanda. "Hello, my beautiful bride."

She shakes her head playfully, and her cheeks turn all red.

And Devlin? He's staring at me with unspoken emotion, and I wonder if he wants that to be us one day as much as I do. But that's ridiculous because the man is made of stone. Nothing could make him love me.

I force a smile, throwing my arms around my father in a tight hug, one that he returns.

He kisses my forehead and places his hands around my face. "I'm so glad you're here. We've been waiting for you."

"We?" I gulp.

"Aye. You have to meet someone very special. It's why you're here today. Now, come. They're in the study."

"Who, Daddy?"

"What are you doing, Pat?" Fernanda tsks.

"I'll tell you more in a bit, my love. Why don't you go relax, and I will join you shortly?"

Her eyes follow me with melancholy until we grow distant.

I just wanna run far away from here. Every cell in my body is screaming to get away, but I can't. No one would help me.

My father loops an arm through mine and leads me down a narrow corridor, with Devlin close behind.

One turn leads to another, my father's men all around us, and when we enter the den, I find my brothers standing around. Tynan, the oldest, appears serious as always, but somehow more so than normal. My other brothers, Fionn and Cillian, don't appear happy either.

What's going on?

As my eyes scan the rest of the room, I find two strangers here too, seated on a sofa. I didn't see at first, not when my brothers were blocking my view.

One is around my brothers' ages, and one is older, like my dad.

That's when I know what I feared is finally happening.

That's my fiancé.

It has to be.

Nausea curls in my gut.

I'm gonna throw up.

I glance behind at Devlin, but he avoids me, and my heart sinks into despair. He comes to stand across from me behind an empty sofa, and I can't stand to look at him right now. He knew and he didn't tell me! He's letting this happen!

"Darling, this is Mason Reynolds and his father, William." My dad winds an arm around my back, and I try not to tremble from my overwrought emotions.

The elder one nods curtly while the younger man assesses me through hazel eyes, like I'm a car he's buying. He's handsome with short brown hair and high cheekbones, but there's something about him, something deeper, that makes him unattractive.

The sharpness of his gaze has me growing uncomfortable, and the air around him makes it clear he comes from money. Lots of it, and he wants the world to know it too.

"It's nice to meet you both." I feign a smile like the good Quinn girl that I am, but sorrow fills my veins.

"Please sit," Mason tells me with a hand slicing through the air.

As though I need his permission to sit in my own damn home! Asshole!

Devlin's gaze hardens, and a muscle in his jaw pops as he glares at the man I'm supposed to spend my life with.

My lips thin as I lower onto the leather, crossing my legs while my heart pounds in my ears. I try to shut down the tears from forming, but it's getting harder to breathe.

"So, I'm sorry to make you two drive here on such short notice, but this was important," Dad says. "Mason and his father are busy with business, so this had to get done today."

I swallow the nausea down.

"What had to get done, Daddy?" My voice quivers, hoping I'm

wrong about this, but of course, I'm not.

Mason's mouth twitches on one side, like he enjoys the meekness in my tone.

"Well, my darling daughter…" My father faces me. "After your marriage to Gio fell through, we needed to find you a new husband. And I found you one."

He takes my hands in his, blocking my view from the man I already hate.

"It will be okay," he says quietly. "You will be okay."

Please, I mouth silently. *No.*

I shake my head, tears starting to fill my eyes. But my dad's face hardens, and with a kiss to the top of my temple, he lets both of my hands go.

"Mason is thirty," he goes on. "And already an established businessman. He and his father own architectural firms all over the world, and this marriage will unite our worlds together."

"That's right," William adds. "Mason has heard so many good things about you. Your plans to become a vet, and your work prior with the animals on your dad's farm."

I nod, my whole body shaking, and I try not to cry, yet I'm sure they can all tell I'm about to burst into tears.

"Though you'll never have to work when we're married," Mason adds, leaning over his knees, and something catches in his eyes. Something cold and calculating. "My wife will not need to earn her own money."

My eyes enlarge. He wants to control me. Keep me in line by making sure I only rely on him. I can't go through with this!

"That's right. Marriage is a bond," my father adds.

But I don't think that's what Mason meant. Not from the leery appearance in his eyes. No. He would prefer I depend on him for everything, but that's never gonna happen.

"I want to work." I tilt my chin, needing to establish some semblance of authority over my own path.

"Well, we will discuss it when we're married, but your ethics are commendable."

"Thank you." I don't know what else to say anymore.

"The wedding will take place in two months."

As soon as those words leave my father's mouth, my head spins and tears sting the back of my eyes.

Two months? That's it? I stare at Devlin with a quivering jaw. How can it all end like this?

Devlin is instantly there, grabbing my hands in his as he kneels before me.

"Are you okay?" he whispers, searching my gaze, emotions threaded within his eyes. "Do you need water?"

I nod.

"I'm her fiancé now. I'll get her the water." Mason slaps Devlin on the shoulder, and they lock in a stare.

The look Devlin gives him would scare anyone. But Mason only chuckles dryly, as though taunting him, before he heads to the table filled with food and drinks.

"I can't do this," I tell Devlin. "Please…"

He shuts his eyes, and when his mouth moves, Mason appears again like a cockroach. He hands me a glass of water and attempts to cut in between us.

But Devlin remains there as he rises to full height, and the look shared between them could start a war.

Maybe it should. Devlin would win…

"Let's let the young people get to know one another." My father throws an arm around Devlin, practically pushing him out.

The room slowly empties until it's just my future husband and me.

My throat closes as he walks over to make himself a drink, pouring whiskey into a crystal cut glass.

"You're prettier than they said." He settles back down on the sofa. "Please…" He pats the seat beside him. "Come here."

My insides gnaw, and I fight my legs and slowly head toward him. Clearing my throat, I lower to the spot, feeling the weight of my anxiety as he places a hand over my knee and squeezes. When I shiver, he laughs.

"So, you're a virgin, like your father said?"

He what?! They were discussing it?

"I…"

"That's a good thing." His thumb massages me right above my kneecap, and disgust fills my gut. "It's what I want in a wife. I have no use for a whore."

My heart drums louder until my body and my head all feel like they're going to explode.

That would be a relief.

"You will remain a virgin until we're married. Do you understand me?" He pops my chin with a finger, forcing me to look into his eyes that have no kindness within them. "I know you're in college and around guys all the time."

"I don't have a boyfriend." I swallow thickly.

"Not even that bodyguard?" He hikes a brow.

"Devlin? No!"

I wish…

"Good." His leery grin sends my pulse into a chaotic rhythm. "Will you be faithful to me?"

I don't think he will. He doesn't appear like the type of man who would be.

"Of course. It was one of your father's requirements, and I always stick to my end of the bargain."

"What will this marriage get you?"

"Is having you not enough?" He laughs sarcastically.

"I know I'm not the reason. I'm not naïve."

He scoffs. "That's a good thing too. Don't want a stupid wife either."

My body shivers. There's cruelty right behind those eyes. He doesn't even need to hide it.

He leans back and outstretches his arms around the top of the sofa. "With your family's connections, we can expand even more and get permits we need much easier. And with our connections, your family can get property for more underground casinos they want to open across the world. We can get them access to land they couldn't get without us. It's a win-win for both sides."

Yeah, everyone except me.

DEVLIN

My rage has me reeling, unable to utter a fecking word. Afraid what will come out of it.

I can't believe this is who Patrick found for her. That bastard was about to get himself killed for staring at me like he owned her.

Eriu is mine. She'll always be mine. He'll never have her the way I do.

Mason is a rat. Nothing more than skin and bones with money. His father is the one who worked his entire life, coming from nothing. His son is poison. He's heavy into gambling and whores. Patrick has to know that.

This makes no sense. Why would he choose someone like that for his daughter?

"May we talk?" I ask him while Eriu is stuck in a room with

that arsehole.

"Sure. Come on in."

He leads me into his office, and I shut the door behind me.

"Sit, please." He settles on the chair behind his desk.

"I'd rather stand."

"Alright. What can I do for you, son?"

"She can't marry that bastard." My palms clasp the edge of his desk.

He chuckles. "Right to the point. One of the things I always liked about you." He releases a sigh, looking too intently at me. "You're so protective of her. Always have been. It's why I knew you'd be perfect to keep her safe from the time she was a little girl, but she needs more than a bodyguard, Devlin. She needs a husband." He looks me dead in the eyes. "Someone who can continue our bloodline. Someone who will love her and respect her and be there for her. Mason can do those things."

Sure, he feckin' can.

I should be the man to do all those things. No one else.

But I squash those thoughts and focus on the problem at hand: getting rid of Mason.

"Oh, come on!" My voice rises, and he snaps a glare. "I mean, with all due respect, he doesn't have a good reputation. Never has."

"Well, neither did Gio, and look how well that union turned out. He's a good husband to my Iseult. So you should trust my judgment."

I don't at the bloody moment.

"I spoke to Mason about the women, and he assured me all that will stop."

"And the gamblin'?"

"I can't tell a man what to do with his money. That's his business. I care about him sleeping around, and that will end once they're married, or he will pay the price."

A fist clenches at my side. I can't let this marriage happen.

Because you wanna be the one to marry her, you bastard.

Feck!

She deserves more than Mason. More than me. Someone like Eriu deserves the world, and I'm gonna make sure she gets it.

"Eriu received a threat today. It was a note left in my mailbox." Patrick takes a deep breath, a furrow between his brows.

"She *what*?"

He nods. "It was a personal threat, and whoever wrote it said they're gonna come for her. I want eyes on her twenty-four seven. You understand?"

I nod.

"I need her married, Devlin. I need her as protected as possible, and you know the Reynoldses are connected to the highest people in government. Senators, even the fecking president. I need her to marry someone like that. It's the only thing I care about, her protection. When I'm gone, I want to know my baby girl is safe. She's never been like the rest of us. She can't protect herself like we can."

I can keep her safe...

Couldn't even keep your brother safe. What makes you think you're capable of keeping a wife safe?

My own thoughts sabotage every chance I could have with her.

"Can I see the note?"

Fear settles deep in my gut. Maybe it's the gang I was associated with, but why would they send a letter to Patrick and not me? If they found me and found my connection to the Quinns, they would threaten her by sending me the note.

This makes no sense. It has to be someone else. But who?

He reaches into a drawer and hands me the paper, the words

typed out.

> She'll pay for what you've done. I'm coming for her. And
> there's nothing you can do about it.

My pulse rings in my ears as I read the words over and over. It could be them. They'd know I work for the Quinns and that I'd see this letter. They'd find an indirect way to taunt me.

"Do we know who it's from?" I ask him.

"We don't. Not yet. We're all looking into it, but don't tell Eriu. I don't want her worried."

"Aye."

When I start to leave, the door swings open, and in walks Iseult, bright red fiery hair swinging as she marches in with more rage than I've seen in a while.

"Devlin," she grits before her eyes zero in on her father and her palms slap across his desk. "Really, Father? Mason fucking Reynolds? Are you insane?!"

"Hello to you too, darling. Please do come in." He gives me a look that says *help me*.

Yet I do no such thing. I turn the hell around and leave him with a pissed-off Iseult.

Nothing will change. He always gets his bloody way. But two months is a long time and a lot can happen.

To Mason, that is.

NINE

ERIU
TWO DAYS LATER

"**Y**ou can't marry that sleazebag." Karen recoils as I tell her what transpired when I met my horrible future husband.

I can't believe my family just stood there, letting this sham of an engagement happen. Doesn't anyone care about what I want?

"I know I can't. But what choice do I have?"

"Kill him?" She laughs before turning to face her laptop, clicking a few buttons and checking out photos of Mason on various tabloids.

He's not only rich, but famous, apparently, and he isn't shy about it. Picture after picture is of a different woman on his arm.

With a silent huff, I stare back at myself in the full-length mirror in Karen's dorm room. The tight emerald-green dress hits right below my ankles, with a slit going up way past my knee. It's sexier than any evening dress I've ever worn.

But the dress code for this sex party we're going to said black tie or lingerie for women, and I sure as hell won't be wearing lingerie.

I have no idea what I'm getting myself into. It's probably worse than I'm imagining. People screwing around everywhere...

I didn't need to buy anything for the occasion, thankfully. Karen always has more than enough dresses. Her mom is a buyer for a high-end clothing store and gets her beautiful things that she, of course, shares with me.

I'm beyond nervous to get caught by Devlin, though. We did set this up well, so I hope he doesn't suspect anything.

He's parked in front of Karen's building, not knowing I plan to head to the party. He thinks we'll be studying all night and that I'm sleeping over here.

Little does he know we'll be making an exit through the basement and out the other side of the building, then slip into her car. He won't be looking for it. It's one of many in the large parking lot.

It'd be a lot more fun if he was going. If he was in a mask. If we forgot who we were for a single night and let things happen...

A girl can dream.

Meanwhile, I'm stuck with the likes of Mason, a man whore by all accounts. I'll be married to a guy who cheats on me.

Was that always my fate? To live in a loveless marriage?

Mason already texted me twice today, asking about what I'm doing and who I'm hanging out with, warning me against being around college guys so he doesn't get a bad reputation for being engaged to a slut. I angrily deleted the texts and told him not to worry. I wasn't going to give him details of my life.

I've only known him for a couple of days, and he already has me seething.

I pick up the mask Adam sent over, the one I'm supposed to wear tonight. Mine is gold and hits the bridge of my nose, with an intricate loopy black design that glistens with tiny clear stones.

Karen's is red with the same black design. Both are beautifully crafted and clearly expensive. We're not allowed to put them on until right before we reach the penthouse where the event is being held. I don't know who the place belongs to, but I'll be finding out shortly.

Nerves skitter in my stomach. I can't believe I'm doing this. I don't know exactly what to expect, but part of me is…dare I say, excited?

I run my hands down my hips, the material silky soft. And I imagine Devlin's palms running down my dress, his body pressed to mine from behind, fingers discovering places laid dormant.

My nipples grow taut, scraping against the material. I probably should've worn a bra, but with this dress, it's impossible. The back is completely open, exposing my entire spine.

If Devlin saw me in this, I don't know what he'd do.

"If this idiot cares about your virginity so much…" Karen interrupts my thoughts. "…maybe you should tell Devlin to fuck you so Mason doesn't marry you." She grins, completely serious.

"Yeah 'cause he'd be so willing to deflower me." I roll my eyes.

"Well…" She quirks a brow. "Maybe you can find someone else to deflower you. Then you can tell Mason, 'Hey, jerkoff, I fucked a random dude just so I didn't have to marry your loser ass. How does that make you feel?'"

"Ew. No." My face twists. "I'm not sleeping with some random dude just to avoid marriage."

Or maybe I should, because what other option is there?

"Fine." She shrugs a single shoulder. "Marry Mason. Have his babies and let him treat you like shit."

I narrow a glare. She makes it sound like this is so easy to avoid.

Iseult could kill him… All I have to do is ask, and she'll do it, no problem. And if I tell her what he's said to me, she'd kill him without my having to ask.

Ugh, what am I thinking? I can't be responsible for someone's death.

I settle back on the bed and shake my head. "This is hopeless. I guess you'll be my bridesmaid in two months."

"Of course. I'd be honored. As long as you don't put me in some ugly-ass dress." She makes a gagging expression and laughs.

When I drop my face into my palms, I hear her moving closer.

"Look…" She places a hand on my shoulder. "We'll figure this out, okay? Let's just have fun tonight. Don't think about anything else."

I nod and peer back up.

"I want you to pretend you're someone else when you're there. Do things Eriu wouldn't do. Pretend you're me." A big grin spreads across her face.

"You just want me to screw someone." I squint knowingly.

"Would that be so bad? Then we could swap stories. The first time sucks anyway. Might as well get it over with and save the good time for Devlin." Her lips thin with a smirk.

"I thought we already established that Devlin doesn't want me."

"Not yet." She rubs her palms together like she's a master planner of fate. "We just haven't motivated him hard enough."

I shake my head at her resilience. "If me marrying someone doesn't wake him up, nothing will."

Karen and I arrive at a four-story contemporary glass building with masked people in expensive cars driving us, so many of them I lose count.

The valet drivers all have masks on too, taking keys and parking the vehicles in the multi-story adjacent garage. We park here, though, up the gravelly road, the building yards away before us.

Hordes of bodies strut toward the front double doors where a tall, scary-looking security guard with a red devil's mask greets them.

There's something dangerous about not seeing faces. Yet the anonymity is exciting in its own way. I can appreciate the appeal of doing things with strangers that you'll never see again.

Of course, I wouldn't do anything here. It's not why I came. It was curiosity more than anything.

Once we get out of the car, the masks already on, a man in a tux and a simple black masquerade disguise heads our way.

"That's Adam," she whispers to me, practically bouncing.

She really likes him. I've never seen her this way before.

"Ladies." He nods, giving us each a quick kiss on the cheek. "You both look incredible. I hope you're ready to have fun."

"Ugh…" is all I can manage.

"Don't mind her." Karen waves me off. "She's just nervous. You'll be fine!" she says to me.

"You don't have to do anything you're not into," he offers as we start for the entrance. "You can just watch. There's a lot to see here."

"When is the next party?" Karen asks, her tone full of excitement.

He chuckles. "I think the next one is the following week. They usually pop up every weekend."

"That's so cool!" Karen grabs my hand and gives it a little squeeze.

I don't think any of this is cool. Insane and wild come to mind, and I haven't even been inside.

When we arrive at the entrance, the guard scans our masks, which apparently have devices in them that contain our membership numbers. This is terrifying. What if someone connects me to the number somehow? My father would have my head.

"Phone." The man in the red devil's mask outstretches his palm, a plastic bag in his other hand.

"We have to give them our phones?!" I whisper to Karen.

Adam answers instead. "Yes. It's required so no one takes pictures or videos. They can't let anything get leaked. The bags are attached to our membership numbers, and they are placed in a secure area."

"My God… Who runs this place?" My eyes wander to the large crystal chandelier beyond the closed entry doors centered in the lobby, the marble beneath sparkling white.

"A very rich and powerful family," he murmurs into my ear. "You don't want to know them. Trust me."

A shiver runs up my back. Whatever waits for us inside is going to have me running back toward the exit. I guarantee it.

Once we're done checking in, we're ushered inside by a woman in a red strappy gown, who takes us into an elevator.

She enters after us, and with the press of a button, we rise in seconds to the top floor.

My stomach dips with adrenaline and I start to regret this. I'm Eriu Quinn. A good girl. I don't go to sex clubs!

Ding.

As soon as we arrive, Karen's pulling me out, rushing toward the sultry music beating from all around. It's not as loud as you'd find in a dance club, yet still enough to mask the noises I'm sure we'll hear the further we go.

Two masked men in tuxes nod at us as they each open a door and welcome us inside.

I expect to see sex immediately, but instead, there are people dancing, dressed to the nines. Blingy jewelry, sweeping gowns. Men in tuxedos. The room lit up by dark purple and blue LED lights.

If it wasn't for the knowledge of where I am, I'd think I was at a fancy wedding or something like that, but no, this is just an illusion.

Once we continue onward, the doors shut behind us, and my heart skips a beat.

We move past into a large area, where more people dance and kiss one another. Adam leads us down a corridor, and as I glance into the rooms we pass, I know exactly where we are.

People are doing things to each other.

I gulp. When I get the sense to run, Karen grips my hand even tighter.

"Don't be a baby about it." She shoves me playfully with her shoulder. "Have you never watched porn before?"

"No…"

Adam laughs. "Leave her alone."

We continue into another large room, but this time, most of the people are not fully dressed.

A woman in a black corset dress and black mask leads a naked woman by a leather leash, a gold collar chained to her neck and a white feathery face covering on her.

In a separate corner, three men are all over a single woman. Her body is bare, lying across one man who's inside her, while another pleasures her between her thighs. The third strokes himself before he shoves his dick into her mouth. This is insane. How are they doing this in front of people, and why am I getting aroused as I watch them?

"Isn't that hot?" Karen whispers. "Wouldn't it be amazing to have three men at once?"

"Uh…no…"

I've never even had one.

I immediately think about Devlin and me. Him naked, touching me, not knowing who I am. Maybe that's better…if he doesn't know it's me. Maybe that's the only way he'd ever have me.

But that's ridiculous. Of course he'd know who I am. He'd hear my voice and realize it immediately.

I keep walking like I'm hypnotized, strutting down past another corridor, finding another room with many beds, all filled by people who are partaking with one another. Multiple people stand on the side and watch.

This isn't me… I shouldn't be here.

But maybe that's the problem. This sort of thinking is why I'm still a virgin at almost nineteen.

Further I go, spotting more private rooms, all with different things happening. In one, a man is nude, his erection hard as a woman is chained from the ceiling. Her wrists cuffed, ankles too, while he uses some kind of flogging thing. I think that's what it's called. Her mask is beautiful, black with gold peacock feather designs drawn into it. But it's the sounds she makes that have me rooted.

In his hand is a device of some kind, one that hums. It's got a circular end, and when he places it around her core, she cries out and her body convulses as she moans, over and over until she screams. But he doesn't stop. He continues until she does it again. He tortures her with orgasms, and I'm immediately jealous.

Is that how good it feels? I want to have just one, to know what it would be like.

She has another one, and my throat goes dry, my body warm all over. I shouldn't be watching this.

"Karen, I should—"

But when I turn my head, I realize neither she nor Adam are here anymore. I hadn't even noticed that she was no longer beside me. I didn't even look to see if she was following me. Where is she? I can't even call her because they took our damn phones!

I force myself to calm down even as my pulse pumps in my throat. I'll find them. They have to be around here somewhere.

I continue to walk further, past another room where a woman lies on a wooden contraption. Her wrists are tied above her head with thick rope, a black-and-red polka-dot mask on her.

Her nipples are concealed by crystal teardrops that have a large diamond in the middle, like an eye, and the collar she wears is all black. The man standing next to her is wearing a black devil mask.

I remain still, watching him use a leather whip on her, tracing her breasts, her thighs, before he snaps it across her hip. She yelps, her legs twisting while he now traces his fingers down her arms.

I grow insanely uncomfortable—not from watching, which I hate to admit I'm liking. It's the tightness in my body, the throbbing at my center that has my throat dry. The need to touch myself overtakes me, but I've never done that before. And I definitely can't do it here.

"You're new," a deep Russian accent husks behind me.

I gasp, spinning around to find an exceptionally tall man in a suit, an ornate gold mask on his entire face. Two buttons are neatly undone on the gray dress shirt beneath his black suit jacket. I have to look up just to meet his face. Maybe he plays for a basketball team.

"Uh, yes. Sorry, I—I should go."

He laughs huskily. "No, stay. Please. Everything is private here. Every thought. Every act. Feel free to do what you want, and with whoever you want. No one has to know, daragaya."

Daragaya... I've heard that word before.

"You're Russian."

Well, that was stupid since his accent basically gave him away.

"I am. Do you know the language?"

"Not at all." I shuffle, every nerve ending in my body warning me away.

"Mm-hmm," he replies thoughtfully.

Though I can't truly see his eyes, I know he's staring at me, dissecting me. My body shivers, and I get the sensation that a man like him enjoys my skittishness.

"Does your father know you're here?"

I gasp, and something both hot and cold swallows me. Panic like I've never known takes hold.

He can't know who I am! How would he? He's just trying to scare me.

"My—my father?"

"Yes." He chuckles. "You're Eriu Quinn, are you not?"

My knees grow weak, and behind my mask, my eyes practically explode.

His tone though, is full of amusement. "See, I know everyone who joins my club. I personally oversee the applications and mask assignments."

His club! Oh my God! My heart beats faster.

And that's when Adam's words come to haunt me. Rich and powerful... Of course he knows my family. My father knows many people, and this man, whoever he is, may not even like us.

He could hurt me for revenge. Or he could tell the world that I was here! He could even lie and say I did things! Oh my God, I'm so screwed.

Please, universe, forgive me for being reckless. I promise to be a good girl from now on and never come here again.

"I—I need to go. I'm not…uh…" My words stay trapped as he grabs my wrist, thick fingers curling just hard enough to make me know who is in charge.

"I'm not here to hurt you. Your secret stays between us. I promise."

"Why don't I believe you? Who are you, exactly?"

He chuckles but it's got danger written all over it. "Adam's father and I go way back, and when Adam told me he was planning on inviting two young girls, I decided to allow it. But when I found out you were one of them…well, that was a welcome surprise. I know your family well, but I won't break your trust to your father. A woman should own her sexuality, and this place may be just what you need."

My head grows dizzy. I don't believe him at all. This man could ruin everything. But it's too late now. He already knows exactly who I am. Denying it seems pointless.

"Please, promise me you won't tell anyone!" I clasp my hands together to steady my nerves. "If my father doesn't kill me, my fiancé will."

"Fiancé? Well, congratulations are in order." He nods once. "But I can see how that may be a problem."

His laughter sends hot coals to the pit of my stomach.

"It's not that kind of marriage. I just met him a few days ago, and he's…never mind." Imagine he knows Mason and tells him what I said.

"Ah…" He nods knowingly. "You don't like him."

"Not even a little."

Why did I just say that?! When will I learn to keep some things to myself?

"My sincerest apologies. But I assure you, sometimes these things work themselves out."

"Not this time." Tears burn my eyes, and I'm thankful this stranger can't see them.

"Well, I won't tell him either. You have my word, and my word means a lot. Now, I must go. Business calls. If you need anything, just ask any of the people wearing the red collars. They work for me."

I glance around and find a good few of them. "Thank you."

But when I look back, he's gone. Just like a phantom, disappearing as quickly as he came. Whoever this man is, I don't want to know him. He scares the crap out of me.

I start in the opposite direction, needing to find Karen so we can go home. As I pass more rooms on each side of me, sounds of pleasure spill into the hallway. How big is this damn place? Before I can head back the other way, something catches my attention.

The room is set up like a theater. A stage is at one end, and a man with a full-faced black mask stares out at a seated crowd. There are definitely over a hundred people here.

What the hell is this?

Discreetly, I slip into an empty seat at the end of one row, curiosity keeping me here as the emcee continues to address the crowd.

"Welcome to the auction." He throws both arms in the air, but no one claps or cheers.

They stay silent, their eyes on him.

Leaning into the woman beside me, I get her attention until she faces me through a black lace mask, bright red lips slightly lifting up.

"What sort of auction is this?" I whisper.

"A virginity auction, dear." She says it so plainly, like this is completely normal.

"A wha—"

But I don't get to finish the words as the emcee continues. "The first young woman is nineteen, beautiful, educated, and willing."

A woman with a black gown and red collar brings out the girl out by the hand.

The young woman wears a see-through white gown, her entire body on display, a mask on her like the others. Hers is white, made of lace and feathers.

"You've never been here before, I gather," the woman beside me says.

"No." I shake my head.

"That's okay." She scoots closer, a finger running up my arm. "You have a gorgeous figure."

"Thank you?"

"Don't sound so offended. I appreciate beauty in all forms. Have you ever been with a woman before?"

I shake my head again, my throat going parched.

She laughs seductively. "Have you ever been with a man?"

"No." My entire face ignites with heat.

"Oh." Her interest is piqued even more. "Well, you have a lot in common with the girls on stage, then."

"And…and what happens to them?"

"Well…" She peers at the young woman as people begin to bid on her, lifting up one of those auction number signs. "The lucky winner gets to fuck her and take her virginity tonight, and we get to watch if we want to."

"What?!" I holler, and all eyes go to me.

The woman beside me laughs. "Don't mind her. Do go on."

The emcee continues as she focuses on me again.

"The women sign up willingly. They get a lot of money for this. But yes, they will all lose their virginity tonight. That's how it works. They're taken to rooms, and the winner or winners get to play with them as long as they want."

I press my thighs together at the thought.

Her lips curve a fraction as she observes my movement. "Have you ever thought about that?"

"Thought about w-what?"

"Losing your virginity in a room full of strangers."

I clear my throat. "No. I definitely haven't."

"Well, that is something to ponder, now, isn't it? You might enjoy it."

She turns her body forward and continues to watch as the emcee places his hands on the woman and slowly slips off her gown, until she's in nothing but a white thong, her nipples covered with white round sparkly coverings.

As the bidding reaches five hundred thousand dollars, a winner is announced, and an older couple comes and claims their prize.

This is insane. I could never do this.

I mean, if I did, Devlin would find out and kill me.

But…what if this is the only way I can avoid marrying Mason? Can I handle one night of misery instead of a lifetime of it?

I doubt Mason would come after the Russian man I met. He'd be an idiot. Something tells me he's a lot more powerful than Mason's entire family.

And if Mason drags my name through dirt, let him. I can handle it. My father will be mad, but he'll forgive me. Eventually.

Maybe this way, I can ensure no one from our circle marries

me. Most of them want an untouched little virgin. It'd be a win-win.

I'm totally fine being a cat lady forever. They're nicer than most people out there anyway. But the thought of doing something like this... Being naked on stage. Having someone touch me, someone who isn't Devlin.

No. I—I can't.

Clearly this place is making me someone I am not.

If you don't stop your marriage to Mason, you'll be miserable and wish you had done it.

I can't think straight. I don't know what to do right now, but I have less than two months to decide.

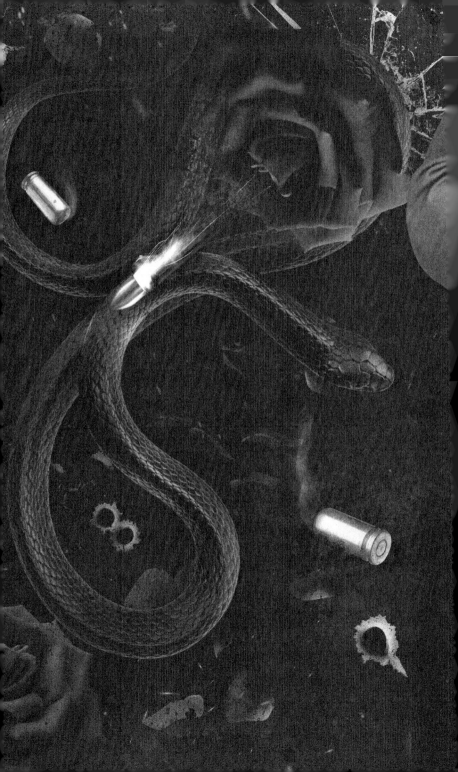

TEN

DEVLIN

Eriu has no idea that, after what she pulled on me the day she drugged me, I'm even more prepared for the bullshite she's capable of. Like tonight, when she told me she'd be at Karen's studying.

My hands tighten around the wheel of my car as I follow them, unsure of where they're going. But I had Karen's sedan tagged with a tracker, so wherever they go, I'll be one step behind.

When I saw Eriu walk out of Karen's dorm dressed in strappy heels and a dress with a high slit she has no business wearing, I wanted to throw her over my shoulder and cover her up.

I don't want anyone looking at her like that. Like I was. She's so damn beautiful, I can't stand it. It's like she's punishing me every time she's near.

But I didn't do any of that. Instead, I wanted to see what she was up to. Because I very much wanted to know where she was going dressed like *that*.

My mind travels to Mason feckin' Reynolds. Thoughts of him undressing her, touching her, fecking her. Never gonna happen. Never gonna happen with anyone, if I can help it.

My teeth grind together at the thought. She has no idea how badly I want her. I want everything with her, even when it makes no bloody sense for us to be together. But I want her still. Yet I know that can't happen.

One whiff of her, and my enemies will come runnin', and they will destroy her and leave me with pieces of my broken heart.

I like to pretend I don't have one. It's easier that way. But with her, all my heart does is beat, and I often wonder how it'd feel to love her. To feel her love in return. Until then, all I have is her from a distance.

I continue following Karen's car, which is driving too damn fast. My hand curls around the wheel, tighter the quicker she goes. If anything happens to Eriu, she's gonna have me to answer to.

Where the hell could they be going? A club, I'm assuming. Didn't she learn her lesson the last time? My God, what is she thinking? Too much alcohol and danger at those places.

I know she wants to experience things she never has in her sheltered life. I get that. But she has to be careful, more than any other girl her age. And sure, that's not fair, but we don't get to choose the life we're born into.

They get off at an exit, and I'm right behind. I doubt they're even paying attention to anyone around them. Hell, there could be a bloody assassin after her, and she wouldn't feckin' know.

I should charge in front of that car so I can drag her back to her dorm room. But that will only get her pouting and angry, probably causing me more of a headache.

Better to stay back and keep her safe. And if anyone tries

anything, I'll be there to stop them. Permanently, if I have to.

They take a few more turns until they arrive at a contemporary building in the middle of nowhere, surrounded by commercial properties, many of which aren't in operation.

What the hell is this place? She gets out, and both girls are now wearing masks. So are all the people around them.

What the feck?

A guy approaches them wearing one too. He seems to know them both. I hate not knowing who that is.

Looking around, I realize I'm the only idiot without a mask. How the hell am I getting inside this place without one? I exit my car, trying to be as hidden as possible, but I stick out like a sore thumb.

I don't like this. She's getting the hell out of here.

Karen loops her arm through Eriu's, and together, they head for the entrance. A guard scans them before they hand in their cellphones. They then rush into an elevator and they're gone.

"Shite…" I mutter.

I'm bound to lose her here.

My eyes scan the perimeter, spotting men securing the doors inside, looking strapped. I inspect the roof for more guards. I'm sure they're up there. That's what I'd do. Have snipers on the ready. Keep the muscle hidden to keep up whatever appearance the owner of this place is trying to achieve.

But who's running it? I've gotta find out what the hell Eriu has gotten herself into. Again.

With hands in my pockets, I strut closer to the entrance. I'm really screwed. Can't bloody well shoot my way inside.

"Excuse me," a feminine voice says from behind me while two women pass by.

Both of them are in high heels and skintight white dresses that reach the ground. They glance back at me and laugh.

"They won't let you in without a mask, handsome. You should go get yours, then come find us."

What the hell did she just say?

"No, thank you. Where do I get one?"

She scoffs, but doesn't say a word, rushing into the place instead.

When it's my turn, the security guard stares through dark eyes, his face covered with one of those bloody masks too.

"No mask, no entry. Get lost."

"How do I get one?"

He straightens himself, taking a few steps into my space. "How the hell did you find this place?"

That must be his weak attempt at scaring me off.

"A friend told me about it."

His fingers lower to his waist, and I know he's going for his weapon. Matching his intensity, I reach for mine in my holster.

"Then you and your friend are both dead." He snaps a fist to my shirt, and before he knows it, my nine is pointing at his balls.

That's when his grip loosens.

"If you don't want to lose your tiny dick, you'll give me a feckin' mask and let me inside."

He laughs wryly. "If I let you in without being on my list, I'll lose more than just my balls because the boss would hang me."

"And who's your boss?"

Before I can get an answer, I register cold metal against my nape.

"Drop your weapon. Now."

He's Russian, whoever he is. Could this place be tied to the Marinovs?

He's clearly ready to pull the trigger. But so am I.

"I'm gonna turn around," I warn him. "I'm not here to cause trouble."

His chuckle is more like a threat, and when I pivot, I find he's not wearing a mask. Don't think I've seen him. Dark eyes, dark hair. About six-three, the same height as me.

"How the hell did you find this place?" Indignation fits his gaze.

"I followed a girl."

His sinister grin widens.

"Kill him and make it quiet," he tells the guard, and starts to walk away.

A pair of women gasp and rush inside.

When the guard tries to grab me, I flip his arm, and he can't hide his groan.

"Don't feckin' move, or I kill you right here, then shoot your friend."

That causes the Russian to return his attention to me, a sneer lining his face.

"Now, can we have a talk?" Heated rage shapes my words. "Or should we start a war and see who comes out on top? Either is fine by me. I like it bloody. But I'm betting your guests don't."

My hold on the guard tightens.

"Kto eta dalbayop?" he asks the guard in Russian.

And with a quick jerk of his hand, he returns to pointing his gun at me, so I return the favor.

"Wanna see who shoots first?" My mouth twitches.

Before I can pull the trigger, a taller man comes out of the front door, towering over everyone else. When he slips off his mask, I immediately recognize him.

Konstantin Marinov. The damn Pakhan of the Russian Mob. Now it's a party.

I knew he had something to do with this place. It has his

family's name written all over it.

Eriu sure knows how to land her pretty arse into trouble. First, she lands me in prison; now she's gonna have me fighting the Bratva. For her, though, I'd do anything.

"Now, now, Aleksei," Konstantin says to the man pointing his gun at me. "Is that a way to treat our friends?"

He chuckles, but it's the kind that would scare a sane person. But I've never been sane.

"What the hell are you talking about? Who is this?" Aleksei doesn't lower his weapon, and neither do I.

Konstantin walks up to him and pushes his arm to his side.

"My brother can be trigger-happy sometimes." He forces my weapon down next. "Devlin. Nice to see you, old friend. What can I do for you?"

"You know this idiot?" Aleksei snaps his glare at me.

"Da. Devlin is a friend of the Quinns." He turns to me. "Can't say I expected to see you here, though. But you're here now, so how about you tell me why you came here looking to die?"

Konstantin is the craziest motherfecker I've ever met, and that says a lot. He wouldn't hesitate to kill me while his guests watched.

"I need inside. Patrick's daughter is here, and I'm on her detail."

He lifts a thick brow. "Iseult is here?"

"No. The other one."

"Ahh…" He nods. "The little one. Yes, I don't think this is a place for a young, innocent thing like her. One wrong turn, and she may end up tossing both her green attire and inhibitions to the ground." He smirks.

I instantly know he already saw her here. Only way he'd know what color her dress was. In fact, I'm sure he knew she was coming before I did.

What the hell was she thinking?

"I need to get inside to get her out. If Patrick gets a whiff of this, it won't be good for either of us."

He snickers. "This has nothing to do with me. She came here on her own. And I'm a businessman first, so unfortunately for you, I can't just let you inside. Friend or not. Normally, you need to be vetted properly and pay a large fee."

"Who paid hers?"

"A friend. Don't worry. She doesn't owe me a dime." His grin expands, and my worry only grows.

"I've got five on me. Will that do?"

Of course, he knows I mean five grand.

"It's ten, but for you? Sure."

His smile is sinister. He's gonna want something in return.

"Come on..." He throws an arm around my shoulders. "Let's go find your girl."

"She's not my girl."

He leads me inside. "After tonight, she can be, old friend."

"We're not friends."

He chuckles. "I only have friends or enemies. You choose."

I get his meaning perfectly. But I would barely call us friends. Acquaintances, maybe, and that's only because of the Quinns.

"Let's get you a mask so you can see what awaits you inside. Never know what could happen when the masks are on."

That's what I'm bloody afraid of.

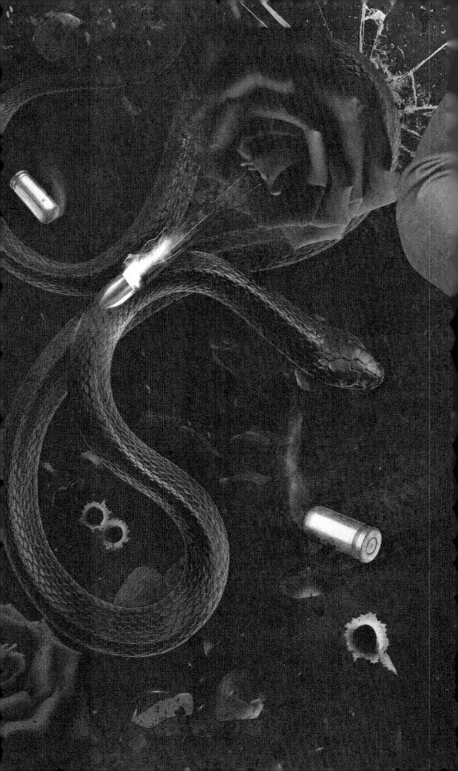

ELEVEN

DEVLIN

Minutes later, and I've got myself a black mask that covers half of my face. I doubt she'd recognize me just from my mouth. But that's all Konstantin would offer.

I look around the place, ignoring the Russian beside me.

There are so many people here, I don't know how I'll find her.

"Want to know where she is?" Konstantin leans over. "All you have to do is ask."

Hell, I hate asking him for anything. Every favor seems altruistic until you uncover his true motives. He never does anything for no reason.

The Marinov family are known psychopaths. All four brothers, even their cousins, are insane. No one compares. None that I've met. I've watched Konstantin rip a guy's neck…with his bloody teeth. All because the man stole a few hundred from him. You can't cross the Russians. They will come after everyone you love.

No one is spared. Not women. Not children. Not a soul can escape them.

So for Eriu to be at one of his clubs... It's not good.

I've heard about them, these clubs. He has a few of them around the world, all under the same umbrella.

The worst part is, Eriu has no idea that the man who killed her mother is none other than Konstantin's father.

Iseult and the rest of the family have shielded her from the gruesome details of her mother's sudden death. No child should bear that sort of pain, especially someone so young. She thinks her mother died in a car accident.

The Quinns have done what they can to protect her from what they do. I know she's aware of who the family is now, yet she's only touching the surface.

I march ahead, still ignoring Konstantin, but he appears beside me, reaching into his pocket for his cell.

"One click, and I can tell you where she is right now. You'll be here all night looking for her."

He's gloating. The bastard wants me to need him.

I keep moving past him, determined to do this without his damn help. But he's up my arse, like a bloody roach.

I should just fecking ask where she is and be done with it. But I keep searching through the rooms, hoping she isn't on some bed or tied to the damn ceiling. The very thought makes me see red.

Eriu wouldn't do that. She's a good girl, a virgin, and losing it this way isn't like her.

But what if she's desperate? What if she thinks this is how she can avoid marrying Mason? He wants her to be a virgin, that much I know. If he told her that, she might see this as her only way out.

Jesus Christ, I can't let that happen. The thought of her with anyone else, anyone but me, makes me straight-up homicidal. If I were to see it, the man attached to her would be dead. I don't care what Konstantin does to me as retribution.

I keep searching in every crevice, but she's not here! Feck!

"Fine! Just bloody tell me where she is!"

"Ahh…finally." He clicks a few keys on his phone. "Go straight ahead and turn left. She's standing there. You can appear behind her. Touch her. Kiss her. No one will know. No one but me, of course." His laugh slinks with malice.

Would feel so good to put a bullet between his eyes.

He knows I like her. He somehow knows everything. Got eyes everywhere. I should be careful.

"I'd never touch her."

"Then let her experience it from someone else. Seems to me she's about to marry someone she can't stand, and she's looking for something he can't give her. And if you're too much of a coward to give it to her, then maybe someone else should."

In an instant, I have his shirt in my fist. "Don't you touch her, you filthy feckin' animal."

His laughter mocks, like I wouldn't kill him if he dared to touch what's mine.

Sure, he's probably got snipers around the place, and with one sign from him, I'd be lying bloody on the ground, but I won't let anyone talk about Eriu like that. Not even him.

He leans in. "I'd take it easy before one of my men gets trigger-happy. I do often remind them it's not safe to play with guns, but they just can't help themselves, I'm afraid."

I loosen my grip and eventually drop my arms to the side.

"I get it. The youngest Quinn belongs to you, though you've done nothing about it."

"It's complicated." I curl a fist at my side.

"Life is complicated, brother. But when you want something, you grab it and you drag it to hell with you."

"Maybe that's your way, but it isn't mine. I don't want her paying for my mistakes."

"Well, she'll be paying for someone else's. Why not yours?"

Before I can come up with a sensible comeback, he walks away, leaving me there to ponder whether Eriu and I could really have a future. But even if nothing from my past stood in the way, her father would never accept us, and without his approval, I'd never marry her.

Heading the way he told me, I rush past people, ignoring everything else but the thought of seeing her.

As soon as I happen on the back of that bright green dress and long, wavy brown hair, I know it's her. My heart beats faster, the air around me tightening in my chest.

I move closer until I'm right behind her, so close I can smell the rose scent in her hair from the shampoo she always uses.

Her eyes are on a man and a woman, him flogging her while she's tied up on a wooden bench, her ankles and wrists cuffed to it, her eyes blindfolded.

Is that what Eriu wants? Does she think about me doing it to her?

Better be me and me alone. She's the only woman on this planet who'd have a chance to ruin me, and I'd let her every time.

My fingers inadvertently reach for her soft hair, and I gently brush them down her locks. When I accidentally touch her shoulder, she turns around and jerks her head.

"Uh, hi?" she chokes out with a nervous, innocent laugh, her full lips parting—so damn kissable, I almost beg.

I can't apologize or say anything, because she'd know my voice.

I can pretend to be a mute. Anything to disguise myself.

"Did you mean to touch me?"

I nod once, and she clears her throat.

"Okay…umm, I'm not really into all of this. I just came here to see what it's about, ya know?"

I nod again. She's awfully nervous, and it's sexy as hell. I've never been the kind of man to want to be a woman's first, to want to take it and own it the way I do right now.

"Do you come here a lot?" she asks.

I shake my head.

"Do you talk at all?"

I shake my head again.

"Oh! Well, that's okay. My friend Karen tells me I tend to talk too much, especially when I'm nervous." She laughs just under her breath. "Like now…'cause this place is crazy, right? I mean, oh my God. Can you even do things like this in public?"

I'd never allow anyone else to see you bare.

When I don't respond, she just goes on.

"Right. Me neither. Though it would probably get me out of an engagement since he cares more about my virginity than me."

I knew it.

Don't do it, love. You'd see me in a very bad light if I have to kill a man in front of you.

"My God, I have no filter." She giggles, fumbling a hand through her strands. "Must be the champagne I had a bit ago. I'm too much of a lightweight."

She continues talking about how her friend drinks, but she barely ever does.

My mind, though? It's still on her wanting to lose her virginity and how I want to be the one to take it.

Mason better have not said anything insulting to her. If he did,

I'll gut him and send his carcass to his father.

She toys with a lock of her hair, and my heart aches to touch her again. Maybe she'd let me. But I'm nothin' but a stranger.

Still, I reach my fingertips and draw them down her arm.

Her chest rises and falls, and she watches me as I do it again. The back of my other hand glides down in between the V of her dress, wanting to slip it off and have her submit to me.

A woman's virginity has never been a factor for me, but with her, being her first is somehow something I now covet.

Her head lolls to the side, her pretty lips quivering, her nipples growing harder the more my hands remain on her silky skin. I draw nearer as my hands slip behind and down her bare back. A growl escapes me, an unending need and desire coiling in my gut, my cock so hard it could cut glass.

"Fuck," I mutter under my breath, trying to mask my damn accent.

"Wh-what?" she groans as my fingers slip into her hair, massaging her scalp as a little moan escapes her mouth.

She definitely heard me, but I hope she didn't recognize me, especially with the loud music.

My palms fall to her shoulders, and I slowly turn her around, back to the people she was watching.

I remain behind her, my fingertips brushing up and down her arms before I run a palm between her breasts and down her abdomen.

She gasps, but remains against me as I gently caress a thumb over a single beaded nipple.

Her feminine whimpers drive me insane, my hard-on heavy and throbbing. Before I can stop myself, I pinch the hard tip between two fingers, and she pants, grabbing hold of my thigh, so close to where I want her hands.

I hate that she's letting a stranger touch her this way, even when that stranger is me.

I want to touch her everywhere, want to rip off this dress and find the nearest wall to feck her up against, to tear her virginity from her until it's mine.

My thoughts are making me insane. This place is poison, yet I want it all with her.

My lips fall to her neck and I kiss her there, groaning as I do, teeth raking up her soft skin while her pulse beats life into my cold, dead heart.

When she moves a little closer, I palm her abdomen and pull her flush against my body so she can feel the effect she has on me.

My teeth grind when I remember that she has no idea it's me who's touching her this way. It's me she's moaning for. She thinks it's someone else, and she's letting him do this to her?

Feckin' hell.

I should rip off this mask and flip that dress right over and punish her for it. Would serve her right.

But that wouldn't be good. I wouldn't be able to stop myself from doing more when those beautiful eyes stared back at me.

I snap a hand around her throat and squeeze just a little until she gasps and pants like a deer in headlights. Her nails sink deeper into the muscle of my thigh, my breaths scattering wildly across her neck.

The fingers of my other hand ride down her stomach, lower, until they feather between her thighs.

She jolts, her cries morphing into gasps.

I growl and squeeze harder, roughly lifting up her dress until…

"Feck," I grunt under my breath once I feel her bare core.

She's not wearing panties. Jesus Christ! What is she thinking?

I'm not doing much thinkin' either, but right now I need this, and so does she. I slide my fingers through her wet cunt and she fights not to scream, gasping for air when I roll a thumb over her clit. Her ass arches into my cock, making me want to bend her over right here and take what belongs to me.

"Yes! Oh my God!" she cries as I continue to rub her.

That's all I'll have. I can't finger-feck her. Not like this, not her first time.

"I—I shouldn't," she groans, but I increase my pace until she whimpers, her head falling backward against my chest.

I bite down hard to stifle my own thirst, to stop myself from saying anything, or she'll discover it's me.

My thumb swirls faster, then slows a fraction before I rub her again, teasing her entrance with a tip.

She shudders and writhes against me, her release so close I can taste it—and holy hell, I wish I could right now.

I take her clit between my fingers and stroke until she trembles.

"Yes, yes. Oh, God, what's happening?"

I chuckle deep in my chest. *Making you come, love.*

Quivering and shaking against me, she screams as her pussy contracts with her orgasm. "Yes! Oh, God!"

Fisting her hair, I yank her head back, my teeth gritted as our eyes connect.

The way I want you right now would get me killed. Yet here I am.

Konstantin wasn't wrong. The mask…it adds a sense of courage I wouldn't have without it.

When she's finally finished, I tighten my grip on her soft strands and slowly draw her dress down. Pulling my fingers into my mouth, I moan as I taste her for the first time, her eyes hooded as she watches. Her chest heaves as she struggles to catch her breath.

"Why do you feel so familiar?" she whispers.

Mason doesn't deserve her. No one ever will. Not even me.

"There you are!" Karen suddenly appears, and I immediately drop my hands off her.

Eriu instantly tenses and straightens herself, clearing her throat, but her friend eyes us both.

"I've been looking all over for you…" Karen's attention jumps between us.

"Sorry, I've been here. Once I lost you, I just started to wander around."

"And who is *that*?" Karen loops her arm through Eriu's and stares at me.

"He's…uh…no one. He doesn't talk."

She jerks her head back. "Like he can't or won't?"

Eriu shrugs.

"Well…this is interesting!" Karen tilts up her chin.

"Oh God, we should go before you say something inappropriate!" Eriu tries to pull Karen away, but she remains there, continuing to ogle me.

"Inappropriate? Me? Never. I mean…I was gonna suggest you take Mister Hottie into a room and let him show you how good it can be." Her mouth curls. "You can do that, can't you, sir?"

"Karen!" Eriu huffs.

"What?" She laughs, a look passing between them. "Don't mind her. This poor girl's been holding out for someone else. This…uh, young and very handsome gentleman." She giggles. "And he's not interested. She's eighteen, almost nineteen, and still a virgin, and at this point, it'd be better if she weren't."

But my ears are ringing. She's interested in someone? Someone young? She wants *him* to take her virginity? Over my dead body.

"Shut up!" Eriu smacks her lightly on the chest. "I'm sorry about her. She likes to butt into my business quite a lot. It was, uh,

121

nice to meet you. Have a great night."

I watch her go, and as she does, she glances at me from behind her shoulder one last time.

Is she thinking about what just happened? How she let some stranger bloody touch her and make her come like that? My exhale howls out of me.

Now I find out she likes someone else?

I'll find out who she's doting on, and I'll make sure he no longer exists. I know I'm not being fair, but fairness has nothin' to do with it.

If I can't have her, no one can.

TWELVE

ERIU

"Are you alright?" Professor Montgomery asks the next day as the other students start to leave the room, our advanced writing class now coming to an end.

She slides a little closer on the sofa in one of the study rooms in the library, her auburn brows tugging in concern. I'm generally not this spaced out in class—especially in hers—but today, my mind is elsewhere.

It's back at the club from last night. I can't seem to get that stranger out of my head, or what we did together. The way he smelled, the way he sounded when he did utter a word, it was…I don't know…

He could've been anyone.

But I felt like I knew him somehow, or maybe I'm just hoping I did. Would be easier to stomach that than the fact that I let a complete stranger touch me like that. Give me my first orgasm.

Shame fills my gut.

Why does it feel like I cheated on Devlin? He isn't mine, yet I feel bad anyway. Like I just betrayed him.

"Whatever it is, you're always free to talk to me," she says. "I know it's hard for you to talk to your father. It's hard growing up with a strong male figure in your life who still views you like a child. I understand. My father was the same."

Her golden eyes glisten with kindness as she forms a tight-lipped smile.

"How did you get past that?"

"Well, time, I guess." She laughs solemnly. "But everything was a fight with him. He always viewed my brothers as the strong ones, always underestimating me." She sighs. "But it took proving to him that I'm a capable person before he gave me the same respect that he gave them."

She throws one long leg over the other, her red stilettos as beautiful as she is. She has this refined sophistication about her. But it's not her beauty I admire. It's her mind and her talent. She's an author of many psychological thrillers that have hit bestseller lists, but she's said that teaching has always been a passion of hers.

The professor has been such a support to me through this—hiding what I want to do from my father. She's given me books on improving my writing, given me extra work to better my character development. I don't know what I'd do without her. She really wants her students to succeed.

"I want you to know that you're not alone." A line forms between her eyes. "It's hard being a young woman in today's world. But you're a strong, capable woman who can accomplish whatever you want. The path you set for yourself is yours to take. You're the driver. No one else." She grabs my hand and squeezes.

"Don't let anyone steal your shine, Eriu Quinn."

I nod, knowing that Mason will suck all the joy from my life. He will suck every drop of my willpower and talent until I have nothing left to give.

"Are you married?" I ask her.

We've never discussed her personal life, so I have no idea if she even has kids.

"No." She shakes her head and scrunches her nose. "I never had any desire to settle down with just one person."

"I get it." I bow my head.

"Is your father making you get married?"

I raise my eyes to hers and nod.

"Oh, God." She rolls her eyes. "You're just a child! That is outrageous. Is this an arranged marriage situation?"

I nod again. I shouldn't be saying anything to her, but who would she tell? She knows nothing of my family, and it's not like I'm a minor. Even if she Googled me, she'd find nothing. My family looks clean on paper.

"It'll be okay." I shake it off and bear a grin. "My father means well, and the guy he chose for me isn't too bad."

I almost sound believable.

"You can't lie to me." She runs a hand through her shoulder-length brown hair, giving me a comforting look. "You should tell him it's not what you want. Stand firm."

"Yeah, I'll try that." I almost laugh, because that wouldn't matter to my father. "I should go. I need to grab some food before my next class."

"Of course." She reaches into her briefcase. "Before you go, I have a few more craft books for you on different writing techniques that you may find interesting."

She hands me a set of three, and I grow giddy with excitement.

"I can't wait to read them. Thank you so much!"

"You're my best student. I want to watch you succeed. Just don't tell the others I said that." She laughs. "Now go, get out of here. I have papers to grade."

I rise to my feet with the biggest grin. "Okay. See you next week."

"Yes. Bye now."

With my bag slung over my shoulder, I head out of the building and toward my car, hoping to grab some off-campus food. But when I reach my vehicle, I find an unwelcome surprise.

Mason stands there, leaning against the driver's side, his eyes flashing with visible rage. "Where you been? Your class has been over for a while."

Does he have my schedule?

Nausea churns in my gut, and my insides curl from fear.

How can I marry this man?

Maybe the professor was right. Maybe I can make my father see reason.

"Uh…hi? What are you doing here?"

My pulse hammers from his icy glare. How quickly can I make him leave?

"I'm your husband. I don't need permission to see you."

Breathe.

Just breathe and calm down.

"You're my fiancé, not my husband." I force a smile.

He chuckles humorlessly and his jaw tightens before he returns that ugly stare that has me bathed in fright.

"I asked you where you were."

My body shivers.

Where's Devlin? He has to be close. He always is.

Mason backs off the car and marches directly toward me. I

jump a step back, my breath hitching.

"I—I was talking to a professor, and now I'm heading to lunch."

He stares down at me bitterly, as though unsure whether he finds my answer acceptable.

"Great, let's go get lunch. I have my car, so we can stop by that retro diner not far from here." He grabs my hand, but I tug it away.

"Eriu? Everything okay?" Devlin's voice is a welcome relief.

Tears threaten behind my eyes when I whirl around toward him, suddenly feeling safer now that he's here. I rush over to him, and though he doesn't reach for my hand, his finger brushes mine, and I almost burst into tears. With just that touch, every cell within me blossoms to life. My chin trembles and more tears gather.

Mason comes to stand between us.

"Devlin," he says coolly by way of greeting. "You don't need to follow her around when I'm here. That's my job now."

Devlin eyes him intensely and stalks closer until his chest meets Mason's. "Until her father tells me otherwise, Eriu is under *my* protection. Wherever she goes, so do I. I don't take orders from you. We understand each other?"

Mason's nostrils flare, his mouth set in a wry smile. "Clearly." He backs off just enough to give me space. "Assuming you're going to be joining us for lunch?" He cocks a brow.

"Aye." Devlin holds his stare while my throat throbs and anguish fills my chest.

He sees it. Devlin sees my pain, and instead of telling my father he wants me, instead of saving me from it all, he watches me walk away with a man who isn't him.

When will I ever learn? I'm alone. I always will be.

We arrive at the diner and immediately take a seat at a table, with Devlin taking his at the one beside us. His attention never leaves me, and the severe look on his face should terrify Mason, but he acts like he's untouchable, grinning at Devlin as though saying *what the hell will you do?*

I can sense the anger in my future husband, feel it as though he's hurting me already. Like I know he will once we're married.

I won't do it. I'll find a way out of this on my own.

A waitress approaches us. Her sunny disposition does nothing to quell the fear breathing life within me.

"Can I get you two something to drink?"

"Just water for me." I force my features to look anything but terrified. I don't know if I've succeeded.

"And for you, sir?"

Mason grabs my hand and drags it into his own. His thumb roughly brushes my skin as he looks up at her with a smile. It's one of those smiles that would melt a woman, but I know who he truly is.

"I would love some iced tea." He gives a momentary look to her name tag. "Thank you, Macy."

"Not a problem. Coming right up."

A minute later, she's setting the drinks before us, and we place our orders.

He still has my hand in a tight grip as she struts away, and I'm afraid he'll cause a scene if I yank it away. I pass a glance at Devlin, who's staring at us with a predatory glare, his gaze bouncing to our hands.

"Stop looking at him," Mason barks.

I dash my attention to him immediately, finding his face twisted with rage.

My own anger shoots through me, and I bite down hard to stop myself from having an anxiety attack. "Why are you really here?

Are you spying on me?"

My heart races almost out of my chest from my bravery. He doesn't seem like the kind of man who appreciates being questioned.

"Now, is that how a fiancée talks to her future husband?" He jerks my hand closer to his until I feel my shoulder pull.

When I groan, there's a satisfied look on his face.

"I'm gonna make a few changes once we're married," he goes on. "For starters, you're no longer gonna have that bodyguard watching you. I will have one of my family guards on your detail. At *all* times. I'm also going to tell your father that I want to move the wedding up. Why wait?"

Nausea hits my gut.

Nonono. This can't be happening.

My pulse drums faster until I grow lightheaded. He keeps talking, but I just can't be here anymore. I'm gonna pass out.

He leans in as he says, "A few days before the wedding, I will take you to my family doctor and have you checked to make sure your virginity is still intact. And if it's not, we're done, do you understand me? If someone else has touched you before I do, I will destroy you. I will paint you as a whore, and no one will want you."

My chest rises with quickened inhales as I peek at him breathlessly.

His eyes narrow, irises turning darker as he takes me in with revulsion.

I will not allow him to demean me this way. I yank my hand out of his grasp.

"That's insane," I snap with a whisper-shout. "I will do no such thing."

With a mocking smirk, he roughly grabs my wrist until his

fingers pinch around it. But before I can ask him to stop hurting me, Mason's screaming in agony as Devlin bends his hand backward until his fingers look like they're about to break.

With my hand released, I rub at where he's hurt me as eyes from other patrons land on us.

"Um, is everything okay here?" our waitress asks.

"Oh, yeah. We're fine." Devlin grins. "Just teaching the fella how to be a gentleman. Isn't that right?"

He stares at Mason, and when he doesn't nod, he bends his hand some more. With a groan, Mason starts cooperating and nodding.

"Doing just fine here," he spits through gritted teeth.

"Okay…" The waitress appears terrified. "But please end this before my manager calls the cops."

"Not a problem. Almost done here."

Her mouth trembles right before she stalks off in a hurry.

As soon as she's gone, Devlin looks at me. "Did he hurt you?"

I nod.

Devlin's entire face transforms, and I shudder. He leans in toward Mason's face.

"Touch her like that again, and you're gonna bloody well see what I'm gonna do to the rest of your hand." Then, without another word, he bends one of his fingers hard until a popping sound is heard.

Mason starts to scream.

"Shut up now, or I break another finger."

He grunts, his exhales heavy, chest rattling.

"Now you listen, because I won't give you another warning. If you hurt her in any way again, I'll cut off your entire hand. Stay away from her, and don't you dare come around her again. Understand me, arsehole?"

He drops Mason's hand, and he immediately jumps to his feet, a wide-eyed glare bouncing between us.

"I'm gonna have your head for this, you fucking Irish bastard!" He holds on to his finger like it's made of glass. "You're gonna find out how powerful the Reynolds name is when I'm through with you."

"That's all very exciting," Devlin taunts with a low, dry chuckle. "Let me know how I can get tickets to that pretend show of yours."

The more he laughs, the redder Mason's face gets.

With a frustrated growl, he rushes out of the restaurant, still grasping his hand.

Devlin immediately turns to me, concern fitted in the furrow of his brows. "Are you okay, love?"

He cups my cheek in his large, masculine hand, his eyes full of affection and worry.

Would he care if he were to find out that I let another man touch me? Do things I've wanted him to do to me?

He slides in next to me, still holding my face, his other hand now grasping my fingers, like he doesn't wanna let me go.

Moisture builds behind my eyes as I shake my head. "I'm never going to be okay married to him. I have to talk to my father. I have to make him see reason. Mason told me he wants to move up the wedding!"

"Feckin' bloody bastard." A thunderous expression washes over his face. "I tried to speak to your father."

"What?" His thumb draws circles to the corner of my mouth and I shiver.

"I tried to tell your father Mason wasn't the right fit for you the night you met him, but he wouldn't listen."

"Of course he wouldn't." For my father to see reason, I need something bigger on Mason.

But losing my virginity is the easier solution. If Mason backs out of the wedding himself, that will alleviate all of my worries.

The waitress brings the food over and sheepishly places two plates down before disappearing. I can't even look at food right now. The thought of eating the chicken panini I ordered makes me sick.

Devlin picks up a knife and fork and starts to cut into it. Good. I'm glad he'll get to enjoy the food I won't eat.

The back of my hand glides down my cheek where his touch was, and my heart clenches.

"Open up for me." He nears the fork to my mouth.

"What are you doing?"

The instant our gazes meet and the blue within his eyes shimmers with that affection, I almost forget why I'm upset in the first place.

"I'm feedin' you, you brat." His slight smirk makes my heart flutter. "Now open up. You've gotta eat."

He places the small bite of food past my lips. As he does, his attention falls to my mouth and he watches me through hooded eyes.

My body instantly prickles. It's like his hands are there, brushing over my skin, tempting me with his body and his heart.

Does he feel it between us? This indescribable connection?

He continues to feed me until all the food's gone, but all I've been focused on is him.

"How was it?" His deep, sultry voice settles in my gut, coiling down my body until I'm warm and wanton.

"Delicious," I whisper, my heartbeats quickening the more his eyes bore into mine.

He grunts as he peers at my lips like he wants to kiss me, and I wish he would. I lean in closer, our knees touching, butterflies erupting from within me.

"You've got a little something." He points to the corner of my mouth, and I fumble as I wipe. "No, not there." His lips spread into a half-smile. "Let me."

I hold my breath as his thumb feathers over my mouth, and it stays there for long moments while his gaze remains locked with mine.

"Eriu…" he breathes.

"Yeah?"

My heart beats faster. Every feeling is amplified, wanting so badly to kiss him.

Please tell me you want me as much as I want you. That you'll marry me and end this hell.

"The check whenever you're ready." The waitress zaps us out of this moment, and he immediately turns to her.

"Yep, gonna pay now."

He hands her a credit card, and she walks away with it.

"I'll drive you back to school," he tells me.

"Yeah, thanks." I play with the hem of my shirt, unable to look at him with what I'm feeling.

Will it ever stop? Will I always be in love with Devlin McHale?

I can't imagine anything worse than that. Not even my marriage to Mason Reynolds.

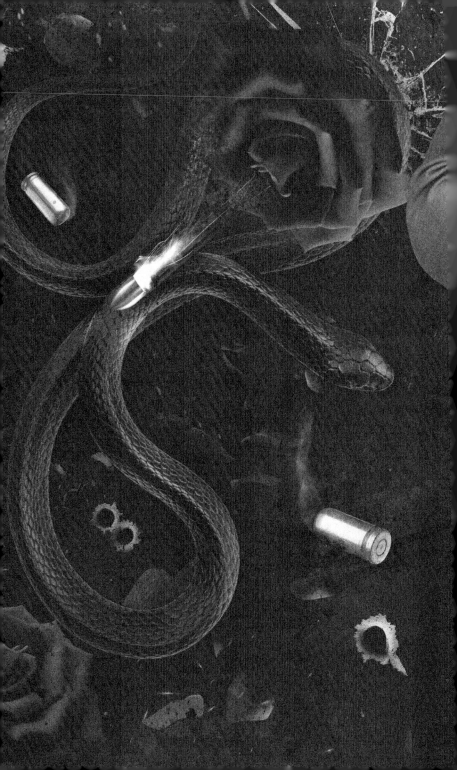

THIRTEEN

DEVLIN

A s soon as I drop her back off at school, I remain in my
car and ring Tynan as she enters her dorm.
"Yeah?"

"How the hell do I get your sister out of this feckin' marriage?"

He laughs briskly. "Find someone more suitable before the
wedding."

"I'm serious."

"Me too. My father cares about her protection. If you can find
someone better suited, he may change his mind about Reynolds."

"I can protect her." The words come out instantly, and I close
my eyes, realizing what I said and how it sounds.

Silence greets me. "What are you saying? Are you asking for
her hand?"

Yes. I'm in love with her, and I have no idea how to stop it.

How the hell can I let her be with someone else? It makes me wanna rip out my own bloody heart. But how can I claim to be capable of keeping her safe? My past could be comin' for her at any moment. She would be safer away from me.

But no matter how many times I tell myself that, I can't seem to let her go.

"No. Of course not," I reply instead.

"Shit, for a second there I thought you were about to tell me you're in love with my baby sister." He chuckles like it's something unfathomable. I guess it would be, since I've known her since she was young.

Makes me an arsehole, doesn't it? But I can't help what I feel. What I'll always feel. She's written into my DNA. Like a code imprinted into my marrow. It's impossible to exist without her.

"Look," he goes on. "I don't like him either, but my father... You know how stubborn he is. He doesn't listen to me or Iseult. But if you can give him another option, someone powerful enough to keep her safe, then he might agree."

A deep guttural grunt rolls out of me. "I can't let this happen."

"What did he do?"

"He manhandled her, grabbed her wrist too hard on purpose. So I broke the bastard's finger."

"Good. Maybe it'll teach him a lesson to keep his hands to himself."

"Doubt it."

"We could kill him," Tynan says matter-of-factly. "But if Reynolds Senior finds out, it will get us into a war."

"You're serious."

"It's an option if you think she's not safe with him."

"She won't be. But give me a little time. I'm hopeful I can find something on him that will make your father decide to break this arrangement in case him being aggressive isn't enough."

"Okay. I'll talk to Iseult. I mean, you know her. She'd be ready to throw a dagger into his eye at a moment's notice."

I let out a laugh. She's one skilled assassin on a bad day. On a good day… Well, any son of a bitch who crosses her or those she loves should watch their back.

"You know…" he says. "It's too bad you never had those kinds of feelings for my sister."

"What?" My voice fills with shock. "What the hell are you bloody insinuating?"

"I'm just saying. My father loves you like a son. He'd be open to it."

Is he really saying this? He wouldn't be if he knew my past. The gang that could get his sister killed.

I can't be the one to ruin her life. I won't do it.

"I'm way too old for her, and I've got no connections like the Reynoldses and their kind do. I'm nothing."

"You underestimate yourself." He exhales a short breath. "Don't matter, anyway. It's a pointless conversation since you don't feel like that about her, and what the hell do I know about relationships anyway? Never had one to begin with."

"Why is that?" I keep my vision on her dorm, making sure Mason doesn't decide to return.

"What are you, my fucking shrink?"

"No." I snicker. "Just asking a question. Isn't your father all about continuing the bloodline? He's gotta be demanding it."

"Fuck you, McHale," he mutters.

"I knew it. He's on your case to tie the knot and make a family, isn't he? We all know he's retiring soon and putting you in charge. You knew it was coming. We all did."

Patrick is getting older, and he wants everything in place before he retires. As the oldest, it would be Tynan's rightful place to lead the Quinn family.

"Yeah, yeah. How about you shut up and worry about your own fucking bloodline?"

"My bloodline would be best to die off with me." I let out a sigh. "No reason to bring a woman into my shite and ruin her damn life."

"Yeah… It's a lot to ask of a woman to marry into the kind of family we belong to. Unless she's getting something out of it, there's no way in hell someone would willingly sign up for this."

"Maybe if you're lucky, one would actually love your crazy arse."

"Yeah, right. Love. What the hell do you know about it?"

More than you realize.

My heart beats faster because it's her face that I see. Those green eyes glistening, that radiant smile. The ones that are all mine.

It's then my mind runs to dirtier corners, the night at the club. How nervous she was. The way she tasted on my tongue. How badly I wanted to rip that dress off her body and claim every untouched inch of her.

"Never getting married," he mutters, dragging me out of my illicit thoughts. "And love is nothing but a weakness."

A chuckle rolls out of me. "Your father's gonna want heirs. You've got no choice."

He groans. "I'm hoping once he retires and puts me in charge, he forgets all about it."

"Have you met your father? He won't forget shite, and you bloody well know it. So I suggest you start making a list of potential wives, or he may arrange a marriage for you."

"Don't joke like that." I swear that's the first time I've heard fear in this man's voice.

"I'm serious."

"Fuck off," he snaps. "Last thing I wanna do is mess things up even more for Brody. Bringing some random woman into the house when he barely even looks at me won't help. And I won't do anything that hurts him."

I immediately feel for the boy, and Tynan too. Brody is his cousin's kid, the one who was killed by Raph Marino when he thought the Quinns killed his wife. Tynan stepped up and adopted the eight-year-old child. Tynan and his cousin, Aiden, were close, and it broke everyone's heart when he died—including his wife's, who committed suicide, leaving poor Brody without parents.

The trauma caused Brody to stop talking. And no matter what Tynan and the family have tried, nothing has helped.

"Let me know if you find anything on Reynolds we can use." Tynan changes the subject. "I don't know what else you can get on him that we don't already know."

"There's always something a man like that is hiding, and I'm gonna be the one to find it."

As soon as I hang up with him, I dial a number I've never had a reason to dial. But Grant Westfield is a friend of Gio and Iseult, the best hacker around, so if there's anything to find on Mason, he'll be the one to do it.

Grant's a filthy billionaire. His company developed the best cellphone currently on the market, and he does some crazy stuff with AI too. I think he's developing robots or some shite.

His cell rings a few times before I hear his voice.

"Yes?"

"Grant, hey. You don't know me, but I'm Devlin M—"

"I know who you are. How can I help you?"

"Need a favor. Not just for the Quinns, but for me personally."

"Any friend of Iseult's is a friend of mine. Now, how about you tell me what that favor might be?"

"I need everything you can get on a Mason Reynolds. I'll send you a photo."

"Come on, man. I don't need a photo." He chuckles. "How much dirt are you looking for?"

"Everything you can find on him. Every text. Every e-mail that he deleted. Every meeting he's had, every girl he's screwed. I want it all. Anything. And I mean *anything*. I don't care how small."

He blows a breath. "Wanna tell me what he did?"

"He's supposed to marry Eriu. And he's a feckin' arsehole, so I wanna stop it, but I need to find something on him first. Think you can have it to me in a week or two, tops?"

"Yeah, that's more than enough time."

"Alright. Thanks. I owe ya."

"No, you don't. I'll be in touch."

He ends the call, and I slip the phone back into my pocket, leaning my head against the headrest.

This has to work. If her father doesn't see what a big mistake he's making, then I'll do everything I can to protect her myself.

Except marry her.

FOURTEEN

ERIU

Karen stuffs a tortilla chip in her mouth while Kayla takes a bite of her burrito. I sip on my strawberry smoothie, happy to be out to dinner with both of my friends.

I haven't done anything since the incident with Mason a few days ago. I haven't been able to stop thinking about him and what he plans to do to me.

The things he could say about me to everyone would humiliate not only me, but my father and our family. But I just don't know what else to do. If I don't lose my virginity, I'll have to lose it to him, and I won't allow that man to touch me.

Shivers erupt across my skin, like tiny spiders scurrying up my flesh.

Luckily, I haven't heard from Mason since that day. I also haven't spoken to Devlin at all since then. Of course, he still follows me, but he refuses to have a conversation of any kind. It's as though he's ignoring me.

But what else is new? I should be used to it by now. It's like whenever we get just a little closer, he pulls even further away. Those moments at the diner, the way he fed me… I can't seem to forget them. Those memories keep me warm at night when I'm at my loneliest.

"I seriously cannot believe Mason told you he's gonna take you to the doctor to check your virginity. Eww." Karen's face twists, her features warping with disgust.

I've filled both Kayla and Karen in about what happened that day. I wasn't going to. I knew Kayla would worry and Karen would tell me how I needed to lose my virginity, and I didn't want to hear it. Not then.

But now that I've had time to process it all, I think she'd be right. I just wish there was someone I could lose it to. Someone I actually had feelings for. Like Devlin…

"I swear, he's so lucky he didn't say that in front of me," she continues, dipping another chip in some guacamole. "I would have punched him in the face."

"Would've paid to see that happen." Kayla laughs before her eyes grow tense. "He hasn't hurt you, right? Because if he has, you have to tell me."

Something in her gaze turns darker, and I almost feel a chill in the air.

"No." I shake my head. "He hasn't."

Not yet… Not in the way I know he plans to.

"At least Devlin broke his finger." Karen grins at Kayla. "There is a God, after all."

We all laugh, though none of this is funny. After what Devlin did, Mason's going to be even angrier, and he's going to take it out on me.

Mason is not the right one for me. In fact, he's not the right one for anybody. The sight of him makes me want to vomit.

"I can't do this." I throw my face into my hands.

"It's why I've told you losing your virginity is the best way to get out of this engagement."

I look up at her, my heart beating so fast at the thought of spending my life with a man who will never love me. It hurts so much I can barely breathe.

I can just see it now. Unhappy. Crying. Afraid.

Why is this happening to me? I'm not a bad person.

I close my eyes, and all I see is Devlin. The way he protected me from Mason, the way he always protects me. I'm always safe with him. That's what I want in a husband. Why can't my father see that?

"You don't need to lose your virginity if you don't want to," Kayla adds. "You're in control of your body and your future."

I nod, while Karen's face falls.

"Look, I know I don't always give the best advice and you probably think I'm ridiculous and super slutty—"

"I don't think that." I take her hand in mine. "I think you're brave and amazing and I wish I was more like you all the time."

"Aww, that's so sweet." She pouts. "But let me finish, okay?" Her expression grows sincere. "You're one of the best people I know, and I want you to be happy because you deserve that. It's why I think you have to lose your virginity, because that is how you'll be rid of that horrible guy. I know losing your virginity at the club probably sounds like an insane idea, but I don't know what other option you have."

That's because it *is* insane. I can't do that. How can I?

But how can you marry Mason?

Her eyes fill with the same sadness that's currently ripping through my chest.

"Devlin seriously won't help you?" Kayla asks. "Have you tried begging?" Her brows pinch with a melancholy smile.

"I've tried everything I can think of."

"Damn hardheaded idiot."

"That's why I think you have to do this at the club." Karen's attention zaps between us. "It's like the perfect place. If you don't do it there, then you have to do it with someone else, and that would be way harder. But at least there, you'll have a mask on and no one will know it's you."

Except the owner…

"Do you know who runs the club?" I ask, and her eyes immediately pop.

"Why…"

"I—I think I met him that night." I shift uncomfortably. "And I think he knew me."

"Wait, what?!"

I don't wanna tell her that he definitely knew who I was. I don't think I'm ready to fully admit it to myself either.

"Wait, he talked to you?" Her mouth pops, and she looks horrified.

"Yes, why?" I quirk a brow.

"Oh, God!" she whispers, resting her forearms on the table as she leans closer. "Okay, don't freak out, but I heard from Adam that the owners of the club are Russian Mafia."

"What?!" I shriek, practically jumping out of my seat.

A few curious eyes go to me and I give them an apologetic smile, trying to temper the strain of my quickened heartbeats.

"Why the hell didn't you tell me?! I would have never gone!"

"Okay, guys, that's dangerous." Kayla leans back, concern

fitting her features.

But I know she would never break my confidence and tell anyone about any of this. I trust her with my whole heart.

"That's exactly why I didn't tell you," Karen adds. "Who cares who owns the club? Not like we're doing anything that could get us killed."

"Oh my God…"

I can't believe this. The Russian Mafia…

Then again, I am the daughter of an Irish mobster. And now it makes sense why the owner knew who I was.

There's no way I can go back there now. And the fact that I was even thinking about it is insane.

I shouldn't want to go back there. But a part of me was kind of excited to go again. Maybe see that man in the mask one more time, the one who didn't talk back. It's strange, but I felt so drawn to him. Maybe I was just in a trance from the illusion of being in that environment. It's like when you step inside that place, you leave a little of yourself behind.

Maybe if I keep going back, I'll get used to it and will be brave enough to actually lose my virginity there. I've already done more than I ever thought I would.

Okay, maybe that was stupid. I think Karen is rubbing off on me too much. I'm obviously not thinking with a straight head.

But my thoughts instantly rewind back to that man. The way he felt. That tall, strong build. The way he lifted up my dress and took what he wanted. But he was gentle too.

I thought of Devlin the entire time, wanting to scream out his name, but I was afraid someone would hear. I squeeze my thighs together, imagining it was actually Devlin doing that to me.

"Oh, no." Karen narrows her eyes. "I can see the wheels turning in your head already. You're gonna say you don't wanna go back to the club, aren't you?"

"She shouldn't. Neither should you." Kayla gives her a stern look that she briskly ignores.

"We'll be fine!" She waves a hand in the air.

"I can't go back there."

"Oh, come on, Eriu. If you really admit it, you want to go back."

I do. I want to see that man again. The one who touched me, but never spoke a word—except once when I thought I heard him.

That voice…

It sounded so familiar, which of course is nuts.

But is some stranger really worth putting myself in danger? The Russians could use me against my family.

"There's danger everywhere," Karen adds as though taking a ride in my mind. "This is about having fun! And it looks like your days of fun may be numbered."

"Are you planning on going back to the club soon?"

"I am. This weekend."

Oh, God. That's soon.

Kayla shakes her head and folds her arms across her chest.

"Adam told me about the text that's going to be sent out the day before the event," Karen adds. "Please tell me you're gonna come with me. I hate going alone."

"I don't know…"

"Just one more time. If you really hate it or if you feel unsafe, we don't have to go back."

"Promise?"

Am I really doing this?

Of course, the right decision would be not to go. But here I am thinking about it anyway.

Kayla grabs my hand, and our eyes lock. Worry weaves through her features.

"Please be careful. I don't want you to ever get hurt the way I—" But her words die in her throat and her jaw sets tight.

She's scared I'll fall prey to the same evil she once experienced.

I grab her forearm. "I know you're worried about me, and I appreciate that."

"There are too many evil men in the world, girls. Don't be reckless."

She forces her back straighter and picks up her drink, swallowing a few big sips.

My eyes bounce to the corner of the restaurant, where Devlin sits watching me, and every hair on my body stands up.

It only takes a single look to feel this pull between us. This energy we create drowns the air from my lungs, penetrating my pores until all I feel and know is this man I crave more than I've ever craved anything in my life.

"Would you stop looking at him?" Karen tsks. "I don't think that's going to help you get out of your upcoming marriage."

My gaze jumps to her. Blowing an exacerbated exhale, I think about the club and everything else and my head spins from these overwhelming thoughts.

I need to get out of here. I need to think.

"I'll consider it." I raise a finger to call over our waitress, who arrives immediately.

"Anything else I can do for you girls?"

"Just the check, please." I reach into my handbag to retrieve my wallet.

"Oh, that's already been taken care of," she informs us.

My brow furrows. "What? By whom?"

"That gentleman."

She points to Devlin, who nods once, and she scurries off, leaving me dumbfounded.

Why would he pay? He doesn't typically. Why now? What does it mean? Is he just being nice?

I can't stop these thoughts from flying.

Karen laughs as I rise to my feet, unable to stop looking at him.

She leans into my ear as she gets out of her chair. "Well, well, maybe someone is finally starting to show his feelings."

Is that what this is? Devlin is a puzzle that isn't easy to solve.

He throws some money on the table and gets off his chair. His face is tight as he stalks over. I swallow the bundle of nerves climbing up my throat, my body heating up the nearer he gets.

"Are you ready to go?" He reaches a hand for my elbow.

That simple touch has me gasping for air.

"Mm-hmm, all done."

He allows us to go first, and I register his body heat behind me. The closer he gets, the harder it becomes to breathe.

His hand is suddenly across my right hip. I try not to collapse to the ground from the weight of his touch, from the way my nipples bead and my thighs quiver. I love it when he touches me, even while everything in me wishes that nothing about this was innocent.

But Devlin has always been a hard shell to crack, and I'm not sure anything I do will be enough to break him.

FIFTEEN

ERIU
FOUR DAYS LATER

I'm seriously doing this.

I told myself I wouldn't go back to the club, but here I am, staring at myself in the mirror in Karen's dorm room, pretending I'm studying again.

Her roommate is usually sleeping over at her boyfriend's apartment, so she's barely even here, which is nice for Karen.

I'm nervous Devlin will find out I've been lying. He isn't stupid. Then what? How will I explain myself?

Then again, I don't owe him an explanation. I'm a grown adult. If I want to go to a sex club and watch a bunch of people fuck each other's brains out, then I will.

My mind soon travels to the auction. I've thought about it. Would be the best option to lose my virginity and get money for it. If Mason still decides to marry me, I'll have cash to run away with.

"That dress looks so hot on you." Karen curls her hair in the bathroom while giving me a once-over from the doorway.

I do love this gown she picked out. A royal-blue halter dress with a collared neck and a full open back. The slit, though... It hits way too high on my thigh, like the green one did. But Karen insisted, and she's usually not one you want to argue with.

Her dress is equally beautiful, an ivory beaded gown with an even higher slit and a plunging V-neck and V-back.

"Are you sure it isn't too much? This dress costs over a grand." I'm fully aware of the brand and how much it is.

"My mom gets them free! Don't worry. We have to look the part to fit in. We may be the youngest people there!" Her full red lips spread into a grin.

"I envy your excitement. I wish I was less nervous."

She drops her curling iron and unplugs it before walking over to me. I can easily see her from where I stand.

"You've been too sheltered in that family of yours," she says. "It's why the universe sent you to me."

I roll my eyes and push her away playfully. "We ready to go or what?"

"Yep!"

She gathers her mask and her handbag, while I get my stuff from my bed.

"Okay, let's go get you laid."

"I'm not—"

But she fully ignores me, dragging me out of the room.

With the same masks as we used last time, we're ushered up to the penthouse, with Adam beside us.

My heart pumps faster as the elevator dings, and before I know it, the familiar sound of music floats through the open doors.

Karen grabs my hand, probably to make sure I don't run away as we're let into the main room. People are dancing like before, bodies pressed together seductively as the LED lights skirt around them.

We make it further, past the familiar rooms, sounds of pleasure coming in waves. Karen stops at one, forcing me to do the same.

"This is so hot!" she whispers into my ear.

I press my thighs together, unable to stop staring at a woman who's being taken on all fours. She's got a gag in her mouth and an expandable metal bar with cuffs attached holding both ankles, spreading her legs apart.

Adam throws an arm around Karen and whispers something in her ear, causing her to laugh. I don't bother asking what he said. I'm sure it wasn't meant for my ears. Not wanting to be the third wheel in this relationship, I start for the room next to this one.

Glancing over at Karen, I see her still watching that couple, while I find myself before a room with two people.

The man's in a black skull mask with ram horns and the woman is in a full-faced red mask, lying on her stomach on a table of some kind. Her legs dangle in the air, held apart by a spreader and cuffs, which are attached to the ceiling. Her arms are facing down, bound to the legs of the table.

But the wildest thing about this is the machine that's currently inserting a large fake penis into her pussy.

She screams in pleasure while the man runs a whip down her spine.

This is insane. How is she enjoying being tied up and screwed by a machine? I turn around, intending to return to Karen and Adam, but of course, they're gone.

Lovely.

Here we go again.

When I rush to look for them, I bump into an insanely tall man made of steel. But once I see that ornate gold mask, I know immediately—it's him.

The owner of the club.

The Russian mobster who will probably kill me.

"Well, it looks like you've returned, Eriu Quinn."

I don't dare deny that it's me. He already made it clear he knows everyone who steps foot inside here.

I can just see the smirk beneath his mask. I wonder what he looks like.

"Yes, uh…but I should go. This was a mistake."

He slants his head. "Why is that? Is my club not up to your liking?"

"No, it's great!" I giggle nervously. "It's just not for me. And if my father or Devlin find out, then I'm basically dead."

"What would you do if Devlin were here?"

"What?" My pulse jumps out of my throat.

"Is…is he here? Have you seen him?" My eyes widen and my heart races.

He can't be here.

"I simply asked you a question. What would you do? Would you seduce him? Make him think you're someone else?"

"Um, no. Why would I seduce him?"

"You've known him a long time. You must have some feelings for him, especially when engaged to the likes of Mason Reynolds."

Oh my God. Does this man know everything about my life?

"How…"

"Don't worry yourself, daragaya. I promise I will not tell Devlin how much you enjoy my club. You know…" he says, leaning into my ear, his voice low, yet dark. "We're always looking for new virgins. And we pay well. You could take that money and run."

He chuckles, and the sound sends shivers down my spine.

How does he know I'm a virgin? Is it written on my forehead?

I jerk back a step, my heart beating so fast I almost faint. "I could never. My father would find me. I'm not like my family. I don't know how to hide."

"Hmm." He nods. "You're certainly a lot different than your sister."

"You know my sister?"

"Oh, yes. I'm particularly fond of her. She's got quite a temper. I admire that in a woman." His scoff is ominous and full of danger. "Now, that Mason Reynolds? He's more like a bug. Wouldn't you say?"

I can't disagree…

He reaches into his pocket and takes out his cell. "I've sent you an email. It's a discreet link to the application."

"Application for what?" My voice trembles.

"The auction. I hear Mason wants a virgin bride. Seems to me you have yourself a dilemma. And I'm in the business of solving them."

"I—"

I don't know what to say. Can I really do this?

"What if someone finds out?" I ask. "What if the person who wins hurts me?"

"We have a strict policy on that. As part of your application, you write down your likes and dislikes. If someone does anything you don't approve of, I will personally oversee their permanent removal."

"By removal, do you mean…"

He chuckles, and there's something callous hiding in plain sight.

My God. I've stepped into the lion's den.

"I do hope you join one of the scenes here at the very least. I promise it'll change you. Now, I must go. But you have yourself a wonderful evening, Ms. Quinn." He picks up my hand and kisses the top of it. "Always a pleasure."

Then he stalks away like the devil in a suit he is.

DEVLIN

I can't believe I let her return to the club. And yes, she's only here because I allowed it. That's because I'm a bastard who wants more of what happened the last time.

She thinks she's clever, running off in Karen's car once again, but I'll let her have her fun, thinking she got the better of me.

As soon as she walks into the club with her friends, I'm at the door with the mask on my face. Same one Konstantin gave me last time.

The doorman scans it, then his attention bounces between me and the tablet screen in front of him.

"Wait here." He removes a walkie-talkie and says some shite in Russian.

Great. Gonna have myself some trouble, aren't I?

He slips the device back in his pocket, then scans the others gathering behind me.

From the back of the building, a man walks out. He doesn't wear a mask, like he's unafraid to be seen. His mouth twitches as he marches up to me, tats running from his neck up to the side of his head.

"You're not welcome here," he informs me. "Go. Before I change my mind."

"Not sure who you think you're talking to, but I'm not going anywhere. I'm a member now."

He whips out a nine-mil and points it at my head, and some of the women gasp and run inside.

"Not a great way to do business. What would your boss think?" A smirk eases onto my mouth as I enjoy the irritation growing on his smug face.

He's a little younger than Konstantin, and I see some resemblance: dark eyes, dark buzzed hair. This must be another Marinov.

I reach my hand into my waistband.

"If you try to get that gun, my men on the roof will have your brain splattered on the floor before you can even remove it."

"Maybe, if I'm lucky, I'll have blown your balls off before you get your shot."

"Eta suka okhu`el." He laughs with the doorman.

"Not polite to speak in another language while you've got company."

"I called you a little bitch." He grins, pressing his thumb on the trigger.

I wanna kill this smug son of a—

"Ah, look who's back." Konstantin marches out the front doors while the guests all rush out of his way. He isn't wearing his mask either. "Now, what is this ruckus, Kirill? Is that any way to treat our fine guest?"

Kirill Marinov. Of course. Another brother, as I thought. At this point, I'll meet the entire family. My God, they're like roaches, appearin' from all over.

"Mogu ya yego ubit'?" Kirill continues to point the gun at me while my palm grabs a hold of the butt of my own weapon.

"Now, now, I don't want to have to ruin this fine evening with bloodshed, so how about we let our friend Devlin in now that he's a member?"

"You made this asshole a member for half the cost. He owes us. And he will pay every fucking dime." Kirill's brown eyes narrow while my hand curls tightly around my weapon.

I don't care who he is. If he wants to fight, we will fight.

"It seems you have had a rough start at meeting my family. I promise Anton is the nicer one. More or less." A miniscule smile twists one side of Konstantin's mouth, and with a finger, he motions for his brother to lower his weapon.

With a grunt and a snarl, he does.

"Good dog." I chuckle.

"You son of—" Kirill rushes for me, throwing a punch to my face while I return the favor, getting him in the nose.

"Enough!" Konstantin hollers, and his brother stops, swiping the blood trickling from his mouth.

All I want to do is get inside and keep my eyes on Eriu; meanwhile, I'm stuck here with this idiot.

"Now, Devlin, you will have my money by tomorrow, yes?" A muscle in Konstantin's jaw twitches. "I don't like it when I'm owed. You know that well."

He throws an arm around my shoulders like we're best friends. I swear, this family is full of psychopaths.

"Aye. I'll have the rest of it tomorrow."

"See?" He glances back at his angry brother. "All good. Now, we shall go inside and find your woman." His words are meant for me this time.

"She's not my woman, and you bloody well know it."

His laughter grows as we make it inside and into an elevator.

"The night is young, my friend. You never know where it will lead. Now, come on. The first drink's on me."

The music grows as we enter the room, people all over each other. I hate it here. I only stomach it for her.

The more I follow him, the more my mind takes me places where I long to sin…with her. Where I take her up against the wall, with my palm wrapped around her pretty throat. Rip that dress right off and see how much of me she can fit before she cries.

Konstantin shoves a shot of God-knows-what into my chest.

"Na zdorovie." He tips up his own drink and drowns it in a single gulp.

I do the same, the liquid burning nicely down my throat. "Now tell me where she is."

"First, I'd like to show you something."

He removes his cellphone and clicks a few buttons, playing a video. At first, I don't understand why I'm looking at two people fecking, but then I realize…

"Mason?" I cock a brow. "Here?"

"Not here, no. But he likes to frequent my L.A. club. That one is unmasked. He comes with a woman." He smirks.

"Why are you showing me this?"

"Because you should know what the girl is getting herself into."

"I'm aware that he's a feckin' prick. I'm trying to do something about it. Not sure how much this will help, but I can use the video to attempt to convince her father."

He nods, and within seconds, my phone vibrates. I check it to find an email with a link to a drive to download the video.

"I don't even know how the hell you got my email, but thanks. Not sure why you're helping me."

"Not you. Her." He slips his cell back into his pocket. "Consider it an olive branch for what my father did to her and her family."

"You lost a brother too."

His jaw clamps. "I did. And it's not something I've forgotten.

But I would've done the same as Patrick did. Probably worse." He smirks, then his eyes turn hard. "Marry her."

"What?" I let out a wry snicker. "You playin' matchmaker now, Konstantin?"

"You just don't see what's right before your eyes." His palm lands on my shoulder. "You, my friend, have yourself a good evening."

He starts walking away.

"Wait, where is she?"

His mouth tips up. "If you want her, going to have to find her yourself this time."

Then he disappears.

"Feckin' Russians."

SIXTEEN

ERIU

The music pounds as I rush past bodies, needing to find Karen. I can't believe the owner found me again.

Why is he fascinated with me?

My skin crawls. This was a mistake.

I have to leave, and I definitely have to delete that application he sent. I'll find another way.

As soon as I step into another corridor, I run into a hard body.

As I glance up, I realize it's *him*. The man who touched me. The one who gave me my very first orgasm. The one I can't seem to forget.

I instantly want to run, feeling dirty at the thought of what I let him do. What I wanted him to do.

As he looks at me, that familiar feeling returns, and I can't seem to shake it. I want to step closer toward him to look at his eyes, but it's dark here and I can't make out the eye color.

His lips jerk and he nods, as though in apology for banging into me.

"I'm sorry about that. It was my fault." I laugh nervously. "I lost my friend again, the one who wouldn't shut up last time, and I wasn't watching where I was going."

He doesn't say anything, simply remains there staring at me.

Why are you still standing there? Leave! Before whatever happened last time happens again.

He holds out a hand, and I don't know why, but I take it.

Why am I lying to myself? I do know why. I like how he makes me feel: like a woman who's desired.

Devlin…

Thoughts of him scatter in my mind as the stranger pulls me in, my back to his front, like he doesn't want me to know who he is as much as I don't want him to know who I am. His arm circles around my front, his hard bulge pressing into the small of my back, while a hand sinks into my hair, his nose running down my neck as he pulls my head back.

My eyes close and my skin flushes.

His low, rumbling grunt has a moan slipping from my lips. His rough hands on me feel too good, while his mouth brushes down my throat, leaving my pulse thumping loudly as he does wicked things.

My body aches to be kissed, to be touched. I want to feel what he did to me the last time. A whimper escapes me, and his fingers drive lower, brushing between my thighs as I hum with need.

When my eyes open, I stare into the room we're currently in front of. A woman hangs from the ceiling while a man uses a toy between her legs.

The man behind me presses his palm into me there and my arousal grows until it burns to be put out. The more he touches me, the more I watch what's happening to the woman, the more I hunger for something deeper, something to take this ache away.

His fingertips stroke back up my body, from my stomach to my breasts. And I gasp when his thumb brushes over my erect nipple.

"Shh," he whispers into my ear, his teeth sinking around my earlobe as a heady moan makes its way out of my lips.

He pinches one after the other before a hand slips under my dress to feel them bare. He easily fits his hand through the side of the exposed material. His hands on me feel good, too good, and my shame morphs with pleasure until I don't know which part is winning.

He palms my breast and kneads it in his expert hands, and the way I want this right now, it's unexplainable.

I want to fight it, this insanity that is happening, but I'm too far gone, rubbing my behind on his very hard erection. He cups my other breast and tugs on my nipple.

"Oh, God," I cry out, realizing I enjoy this.

And the more I groan in pleasure, the more he touches my breasts. How would his mouth feel on them? His teeth…

Devlin…

That's who I'm picturing right now. It's him behind me. His hands on me. Him as those fingers drop to my thigh and start lifting the dress up.

Oh God, I want him so badly.

My eyes fall to a close, and I drop my head on his chest. His grunting only makes me widen my thighs for him.

I didn't wear any underwear like the last time. These dresses are too thin.

He growls when he finds me without any, fisting my hair as a single finger dips and strokes between my soaked lips.

"Yes, please," I beg this stranger to make me come.

If Karen or Adam see me like this, I may die.

"Mm-hmm," he growls, and when his finger rubs my clit, I'm done for.

It wouldn't take long, just a little and I'd be flying.

"Don't stop," I groan. "I need this."

His breaths storm out of him, wafting across the curve of my ear. His touch is rough, yet somehow softer too.

And the scent drifting from his neck…it reminds me of Devlin. Can it be?

No. Of course not. He wouldn't do that. He wouldn't touch me like this. He'd be furious that I was even here and he'd march me right out.

The man is careful not to sink a finger inside me, keeping his rhythm fast, then slow, around my clit as he coaxes the orgasm free from my body.

"Oh my God, so good!" I gasp as he starts upping his pace.

My eyes roll, my knees buckle, and when he gives it a little pinch, I scream out in pleasure, not caring who hears or sees. The feeling is all-encompassing, like I'm being thrown off a cliff, the air hitting my face fast as my body rushes for descent.

But as I hit the ground, I wake up. My eyes widen, and my breaths come in gasps.

I just did that. Again. In a club. In front of everyone.

There are people all around us, but they're not really paying attention. The owner probably watched me, though, ready to tell my father what a whore I am.

"I—I…" I pry myself out of his grasp and get ready to run.

He holds out the fingers he just used on me and runs them over my lips, forcing them into my mouth.

I suck on instinct, tasting myself as our eyes lock. My heart races, but something about this is exciting and hot.

His mouth tips up in approval as he slips his fingers out.

"I have to go. I…uh…" I tremble out and rush out of here like my ass is on fire.

Karen. I need Karen. I need to go home.

DEVLIN

I told myself that wouldn't happen again, but I've simply been lying to myself.

I wanted more. More of her. Her body, her taste on my tongue. I wanted to be the one to give her that again, something I know she's never felt before me.

But what's worse is that she thinks it was someone else who made her come.

I did that. Me!

Feck! She's gonna go on thinking some random arsehole made her pussy do that? Everything in me wants to tell her the truth. But I can't feckin' do that.

A growl rumbles out of me, hands fisting at my sides. Want to spank the holy hell out of that woman for letting me touch her like that again.

I watch as she returns to her dorm room, in regular clothes now—leggings and a hoodie—pretending to be a good girl, like she wasn't just at a club coming all over my hand.

As soon as she enters her building, I'm following her. Not sure what I plan to do, but I need to see her. Need to make sure she's okay after she rushed out so quickly.

She enters the elevator and rides up while I wait for the next one.

I get out on her floor, but she's already inside her room.

Knocking once, I wait until she appears a few seconds later, like a vision straight from every dirty movie I've ever watched.

"Devlin?" she whispers. "What are you doing here?"

"May I come in?"

"Sure."

She moves out of the way, and I step inside.

"I just came to check on you." I decide on the truth. "You looked upset after coming back from Karen's."

She shrugs, but her chin wobbles in this adorable way that has me wanting to hold her close and make everything better.

Before I can stop myself, I wrap her in my arms. "I've got you, love."

She sniffles against my chest, and all I do is grip her closer until my heart just about gives out.

On my fingers, I can still smell her arousal, the way she gave me that. Or gave *him* that. This is hell, her thinking it was someone else.

I weave back and cup her face in both hands, searching her eyes for more. More of anything. I love her too damn much. Life isn't fair sometimes.

"I've just had a bad day." Her mouth thins, and her eyes fill with moisture. "Will you…"

"Ask me," I tell her.

Because in this moment, I'd give her anything.

"Will you stay with me? I just don't want to be alone right now." Her voice breaks, and I want to be the one to put it back together.

"Aye." I can't stop looking at her, and the more our gazes twine, the more our hearts do too.

My hand lowers until my fingers slip through hers, and she's pulling me onto her bed.

She climbs in first, and I remove my shoes and slip off my jacket before sliding in beside her. It's soft as I land on her pillow and smells just like her. My Eriu.

She faces me, and the back of my hand brushes down her cheek. Her lashes flutter and her lips part.

"Tell me what has you upset."

"Everything?" She laughs, but it's more like a cry. "I'm scared, Devlin. I'm really scared I'm gonna have to marry him, and I'm running out of time."

"I promise I'll figure it out."

The more she stares at me, the more I want to kiss her as I glance down at her soft, tempting lips.

"There's no time left," she whispers. "Before I know it, I'm gonna be walking down the aisle toward that man, and I can't do it." She swipes under her eye. "I'll do anything to avoid it."

"Mm-hmm." I lose all sense being this close to her body, remembering how good she felt when I touched her sweet pussy.

Gently, I push away a loose strand of hair from her eyes. "It's gonna be okay. I won't let anything happen to you."

"Devlin…" she whispers, her fingers reaching for my face, feathering over the stubble of my jaw.

I release a low groan, unable to contain it, not when she's touching me this way. She holds her breath; her awestruck look has my cock throbbing. Like a little deer stuck in headlights. Wanna feck it right out of her.

Before I can stop her, she lowers her mouth to my jaw and gives it a little kiss.

"Christ. What are you doing?" I grunt.

My hand clutches the back of her head, but I make no attempt to push her away. Instead, the devil in me fights to keep her. Her lips on me is like tasting the poisoned apple from a tree. Now I just want to sin and take everything she offers.

"This is wrong." My fingers sink into her hair. "We can't be doing this."

But I don't even sound like I mean it.

Her eyes search mine, brows hunched in frustration. "None of this feels wrong."

She swipes a thumb across my lips, and I give it a little nip, unable to control what's happening. She tries to lean into my mouth, but I take a fistful of her hair and jerk her back.

With a whimper, she palms my chest. "Stop fighting me, Devlin. Don't you wonder what it would be like? For us to be together?"

"All the bloody time." The confession slips out easily.

Her eyes burst.

"Then why? Why won't you be with me?" she asks so vulnerably.

I ache to tell her none of it is her fault. It's all mine.

"Because you're far too good for someone like me, Eriu. You have no idea the kind of past I've had. The kind of things that could hurt you."

"Being a Quinn is already dangerous. What's a little more?" Her eyes grow sad.

My palm falls to her nape, and I bring her to me until her forehead meets mine, until her breaths become my own, until her mouth is all I crave to consume.

"You don't know how badly I want to kiss you right now."

"Then kiss me," she says. "Just this once. Because for as long as I live…" Her lips brush mine. "I will never love anyone the way I love you, so don't you dare refuse me right now."

Feck. I can't kiss her. If I do, it won't stop at that.

"Eriu…"

She registers the battle in my voice, and when she peers

back, her face grows with anger. "Maybe I should ask my father for a different guard. Maybe this isn't something that we can do anymore."

She fights back tears, and as soon as she tries to get out of the bed, my hand snaps around her wrist and I yank her soft body right on top of me.

"Mine," I growl, an unexplainable possession taking hold. "You're all mine, you hear me?"

She gasps, not understanding what the hell I'm doing. I've not got a clue either.

My fingers slide into her hair and my gaze bores into hers, devoured by her beauty, too consumed by it.

"Devlin…" She takes a shaky, shallow breath.

"Right here, love." I grab her jaw, my eyes lingering on her full mouth before I smash my lips to hers, kissing away the shock on her face, needing this like I need air.

I hold her face in both hands, kissing her with beating passion and fiery longing. I kiss her like the world is about to end and all we have is the two of us.

My tongue sinks inside and rolls with hers, taking everything.

Tasting her, I get so bloody lost, I don't know how to climb back out. My teeth bite and nibble her bottom lip, and the sounds she makes, so feminine and innocent, are tempting me to lose all my control.

My God, she makes me weak. I'm not used to that. But I wanna be.

I jerk my hips up, my cock stirring to life, growing hard and ready, but that can't happen. I can't just take her virginity.

I let myself taste her, make love to her mouth, and that's all I'll allow myself. She makes small little erotic sounds, and I flip her beneath me, rocking between her warm and willing thighs.

Before I can stop myself, I reach and yank her leggings down, lowering them around her upper thighs. This time, she's gonna know who's making her come.

She moans against my mouth, the sounds vibrating deliciously around my tongue. I pull back a drop to look at her and my soul comes undone.

"Please." Her begging has my cock jerking. "I need this with you. You don't know how badly after—"

My eyes darken; I know what she wants to say. "After what?"

My hand edges up and fastens around her neck, the span of my large palm covering her delicate throat.

"After everything with…you know…everything?" She swallows nervously, her pulse slamming wildly against me.

"Hmm." I palm her pussy with my free hand. "Forgot your panties, baby girl?"

As I massage it, she groans. "Oh my God."

"You like walking around bare like that?" I nudge the column of her throat with my thumb.

"Yes…" she pants, her teeth snapping around her full bottom lip.

"You want my fingers right here? Want me to rub this clit and make this sweet pussy come?"

"Oh my God, is this really happening?" she pants with a tantalizing groan.

I chuckle, rubbing my thumb over that spot, and her back jerks completely off the bed.

"That's right, it is. You've been driving me mad. And I've been waiting too long for this to stop now."

My lips drop to her jaw and I kiss and suck along its path, leading to her throat, lowering my elbow onto the bed.

Her pulse hammers beneath my touch as I stroke her clit,

making her sound so bloody good, I almost come too.

"That's it, scream for me. Let me hear what I do to you, mo stoirín."

She doesn't speak my tongue, doesn't know I just called her my little darling. But that's what she is to me.

The urge to sink my fingers inside her overtakes me, and instead of fighting it, I do. I push past her entrance until my first knuckle, not enough to take her virginity, but enough to feel her stretch for me.

"Oh God, Devlin! More! Please." Her fingernails dig into the muscle of my bicep, her eyes lost with mine.

My thumb circles around her clit while my fingers sink a little deeper, curling inside her.

"Shite, you're so tight. Can't even take my cock, now, can you?"

She nods. "I can. I'll learn to."

I chuckle.

"Can't believe I'm doing this," I hiss as her walls suck me in.

"Yes! Oh, God!" Her back arches. "I knew it would be this good. Just you. That's all I've ever wanted."

My hand returns to her throat, squeezing as her eyes fill with even more desire.

She's close. And I want her just like this when she comes. Palm wrapped around her throat, at my mercy. When I swipe my finger this time, she screams.

"Devlin! Yes! I'm…I'm—"

The way she moans…I want to consume it.

"That's it. Good girl. Come for me."

I continue to work her, wanting every drop that belongs to me.

Her jerky movements and the ripples of her walls send me over the edge.

My cock throbs to be free, to feel her mouth and pussy around it. But this was about her. I don't want nothin' in return.

She's slick, soaking wet, and when I feel the sheets below her, I know she just made a mess.

"Think I just made you squirt, love." My mouth curls.

"Wh-what? Is that what I felt? Like a balloon that was about to pop?"

I let out a rumbling laugh as her chest climbs higher with every inhale, trying to catch up with her breaths. I slide over to her side and take her to my chest, kissing her forehead.

"That's right. How did it feel?"

She drops her chin to the top of her hand. "Amazing."

There goes that lip bite again, which is not helping the massive hard-on I'm carrying in these damn pants. I reach down there and, as politely as I can, I re-adjust myself.

She immediately notices and rises on her elbow.

"Do you want me to…" Her words are caught in her doe-eyed expression.

A smirk appears on my face. I want to see how far she will take this.

"Do I want your soft hands wrapped around me? Your pretty mouth sucking my cock?" I hum with a growl.

The tip of her tongue licks her lips like her throat has gone dry.

My little siren. She may not know the kind of power she has over me—not yet—but she's starting to suspect. I can see the glint in her irises.

Slowly, she reaches down, her hand hesitating to touch me there.

"Wanna feel how hard it is for you? How much I want to feck you rotten?" I grasp her jaw in a rough palm and stare deep into her eyes. "Wanna know how many nights I've lain awake just wondering what your pussy would feel like when I claimed it?"

Her face flushes, but she nods, those eyes widening with every word. And that pretty hand lies against my hard-on.

She squeezes a little, and I let out a deep-chested moan, putting my hand over hers, showing her how I want it. I grip and stroke with her hand beneath mine and let her take over.

"Too many nights, Eriu. I've wanted you since that first letter you wrote me. When you told me how much you saw me. I was afraid that I was seeing you too, and I was ashamed of it." My knuckles brush her cheek. "You were a Quinn and I was a McHale. Our worlds weren't the same. I was never anything special. But you always were. And even now, just to be with you this way, it's not right, but I couldn't refuse you anymore. I didn't have the strength."

"You *are* special, Devlin. Don't say that." Her dark brows pinch. "Does that mean…does that mean you'll marry me?"

"Eriu…"

She snaps her hand back. "No! Don't tell me you can't. God! Why? Just give me *one* reason why!"

I pinch my temple. "Even if our ages weren't enough, I've got people after me who wouldn't hesitate to kill you or our children just to get to me."

Her face goes white.

"That's right. I'm not a good man. I've done things, and there's no coming back from that. Not for me." I kiss her with a groan, my pulse racing. "So I'm doing what I can to protect you. But I swear I will get you out of that engagement. You won't marry him."

She falls backward on the bed beside me and stares at the ceiling, sighing with exasperation.

"Can you spend the night?" Her body turns to me and her eyes are sad again, causing my heart to break. "Just to sleep?"

I curl my arm around her back and pull her to my chest. Her cheek rests against my ravaging heartbeat. "I'm not going anywhere. I'll be right here when you wake up, I promise."

With that, she settles, her body sagging against me. I lift her thigh and let it rest on top of me, ignoring my still-pulsating hard-on.

But I want every inch of her body on me. I want this moment to last as long as possible. Because tomorrow, we'll wake up, all of this will be forgotten, and we'll go back to how things used to be.

SEVENTEEN

ERIU

"**S**o, are you finally going to tell me what happened at the club last night and why you wanted to go home so badly?" Karen gives me a knowing look as her eyes bounce between the rack of clothes at the mall and me.

"Nothing happened." I run my fingers through the selection of tops hanging on a metal bar, hoping she completely forgets about this line of questioning.

She's going to think I've lost my mind if I tell her I had not one, but two orgasms last night, and by two different men. Or she may throw a party. One never truly knows with Karen.

She shimmies toward me, holding a blue crop top over my chest. "So hot. We're getting this for you. We need to spruce up your wardrobe."

I roll my eyes. "Whatever. Just give it to me."

I grab it from her, not hating it, though I'm not one for crop tops.

"Did Devlin stay the night?" Her gaze zeroes in on me intently, a curious sparkle in her eye.

Does she know? How can she? Was she spying on me?

"Why would you ask that?" I raise a brow, my pulse doing a frantic dance in my throat.

"Well…" She inclines her chin inquisitively. "I saw him come into your building after I dropped you off at your dorm, and I have a sneaking suspicion he never left until the next day. Am I wrong?" Her mouth curls.

"Ugh! You're so annoying."

She gasps, her eyes enlarging. "Oh my God! I'm right, aren't I?" Tugging me to the corner of the store, she grabs my shoulder. "Tell me everything."

I shake my head and pinch my eyes to a close for a moment. "Fine. But we have to make it quick, and please don't overreact."

She gets all giddy. "Oh my God, did you fuck? Please tell me he fucked you!"

"Shut up!" My gaze grows as I peek at Devlin behind her, standing by the entrance watching us.

She zips up her lips, but can barely contain her excitement.

I drag her behind an array of evening gowns and take a harsh breath. "Okay, so remember the guy from the club you met the first time who didn't talk?"

"Yeah…?"

"Well…he kinda gave me an orgasm." I grimace and pinch my eyes closed. "Twice."

"What? Oh my God!" she shrieks.

"Shh!" I smack a hand over her mouth. "Quiet!"

"Okay, okay, sorry! Shit, so twice the same night. Damn!"

"Uh, no…just once last night and once that first time."

She stares, open-mouthed. "And you never told me?"

"I was kinda in denial that it even happened. Then I felt super guilty because it wasn't Devlin and it was like I was cheating on him."

She gives me a sympathetic look. "You weren't cheating on him. Because you're not with him. So, good for you! But what does this have to do with Devlin?"

"Oh, right. That…" I scratch my temple. "So, he did come over last night and I asked him to stay because I was sad about the thing that happened at the club, and one thing led to another and…"

"He fucked you?" She grins.

"No."

"Ugh!"

"But…"

Her face grows with excitement.

"He gave me an orgasm too." I slap a hand over my eyes.

"Oh my God!" she whispers. "Two men in one night! I'm so proud! Did he use his fingers or his mouth?"

"Fingers! They both did. Shut up before he hears us!"

"Did he say anything?" She's practically jumping around.

"He told me he's thought about being with me, but that we can't be together because of our age."

She rolls her eyes. "Men. But this is a start! It means he wants you. We can use that."

"Let's not get too excited."

"Too late." She grabs my hand and pulls me toward a row of jeans, grabbing a few for each of us. "You never even thought this would happen. Now look at you, getting fingered by two men in one night. There should be some sort of award for this."

I scoff with a laugh. "Are you done yet? We have a test to study for."

"Ew. Studying. Fine. Let's go pay for our things, then grab some coffee."

"Okay."

We head toward the register, where the cashier is keeping the clothes for us so we didn't have to carry them.

After paying for it all, we start the four blocks toward our vehicles, hers a few streets away from mine. We could've taken the train like almost every college student in Manhattan, but that would mean we have normal parents.

My father doesn't want me taking public transportation. Too dangerous, he says. That was one thing he wouldn't budge on. Wanted Devlin to drive me around, but I wanted to have my own car so I didn't have to depend on anyone. I won that battle. Sure, Devlin still takes me places, but I take myself places too.

Karen's mother is just as overprotective and refused to allow her to step foot in a subway. It's why we walk to most places when we can. So much easier than finding parking. That's what hell feels like. It took us forty-five minutes just to find these spots.

Devlin drove my car in just so he didn't have to take his. His SUV would've been way worse to park than my sedan. On campus, at least there's a parking lot. Nothing big, and you need a special pass that my father was able to get us.

"Alright, I'll see you back at school." I give Karen a quick hug before she gets inside and drives off.

With Devlin beside me, we start toward the rest of the way.

"How are you feeling today?" he asks.

My cheeks heat up when I glance at him. I get all shy whenever I think about what happened between us.

"Good, yeah, fine."

He doesn't say anything in response, remaining silent the entire way while I grow insanely uncomfortable at this awkwardness between us.

When we're finally in front of my car, I rush toward the passenger side, clicking the doors open, more than happy to let Devlin drive in the city.

When I open the door, though, I find a note on my seat.

"That's weird…" A creepy sensation crawls up my spine.

"What is it?" he asks, coming around just as I open it.

"What the…" My breath hitches as I read the mysterious words.

Do you really know who Devlin is? He's a liar. Has he told you what he did to his brother? Maybe you should ask him.

My hand jitters, fear settling deep in my gut. Who left this for us?

"Eriu?" He snaps the note from my grasp.

When he reads it, his nostrils flare, and he crumples the piece of paper in his palm.

"Who sent that?" I whisper, not sure what any of this means.

His brother died. He couldn't have done anything to him. Could he?

"Get in. We need to get out of here. Now."

"What? Why?"

His anxiety level causes mine to soar.

"Stop asking questions and get in, Eriu."

He grabs the keys from me, but when he starts the car remotely, there is a beep that wasn't there before.

The rest happens in the blink of an eye.

One second, I'm standing on the sidewalk beside him. The next, he's pushing me out of the way as my car explodes in a wild blaze.

I fall hard, my back throbbing with stinging pain.

"Devlin!" I shout, not seeing anything besides the fire.

Tires screech, vehicles beeping.

My body quivers, panting, as I stare wide-eyed in horror and shock.

"Devlin!" I scream, jumping to my feet, needing to know that he's okay.

I run toward the car, whizzing past a crowd of people gathering in the middle of the street, traffic completely halted on both sides.

"Devlin!"

I can't see anything from the fire.

When I brush past more bodies, I find him unresponsive, lying on the concrete with a large gash on his forehead and blood pooling around his head.

"Devlin! Can you hear me?" I place a palm on his cheek, registering the loud ring of sirens coming closer. "Please, please wake up!" I cry, calling his name over and over.

But he doesn't even move. And his pulse? It's faint, as though slowly dying.

This can't be happening. He can't leave me. My tears fall down my cheeks.

This can't be over before it's even begun.

DEVLIN

"Help me!" His eyes plead, but I'm unable to do a goddamn thing.

My brother is gonna die. I know it's comin.' And there's nothing I can do, because I did this to him.

"He can't help you. He's the one that got you into this mess."

Francis Palmer holds the knife to Keegan's throat while I fight the men holding me down, another with a gun to my head.

"Just let him go! I'll do anything you want!"

Francis's malicious grin cuts into me, and I know this is the end. My brother and I are both going to die. I should've done things differently. I thought I was helping him, but instead I'll be killing him.

"Please, Palmer. Just kill me. This isn't his fault!"

"I know. It's yours."

"No!"

My eyes pop open as I jump up to a seated position, reliving my brother dying all over again.

"Eriu?" I instantly remember the explosion, and my heart beats so loud I swear it's gonna rip right out of my chest.

She can't be dead!

I glance around, not sure where I am or where she is.

"Eriu!"

My pulse thrums in my neck, nausea hitting me as my head spins. I'm on a bed, wires sticking out of me, the damn lights above my head bright as hell.

"Where the feck am I?" I mumble, attempting to get this shite out of my arm.

"Relax, sir," a woman says as she walks in. Think she's a nurse, from the blue scrubs she's wearing. "You're in a hospital. You've been—"

"Where's Eriu? I need to see her. Now!" There's a buzzing in my ears, and I try to ignore it so I can focus.

I rip the IV from my arm.

I knew having her close would put her in danger! Why did I

think I ever stood a chance with her?

"Sir! You can't do that! Please relax so I can put that back in your arm," the nurse huffs. "I will get someone to find the young woman you're looking for. Just please relax. You'll do more harm than good."

"So she's alive?" Hope springs in my chest, and I pray she is, 'cause I can't live without her.

"Yes, she was unharmed. You can relax now, sir. I swear she's fine."

I breathe in deeply and lie back on the bed, thanking my brother in heaven.

"What hospital is this?"

She sticks the damn needle back in my vein.

"This is a private hospital. I'll get the doctor. Please just don't go anywhere." She gives me a sympathetic look before she rushes out of the room.

I start looking for my cell, but don't see it. "Feck!"

It must've gotten messed up. My mind rushes back to the incident. The note. It had to be Palmer. There's no one else who would bring up my brother like that.

Now that they've made it clear they're coming after her, all bets are off. I'm gonna find them first, and I will kill every last breathing Palmer.

Footsteps pummel in the distance, growing closer until my door opens and Tynan enters.

"Where's your sister? Where's Eriu?" I sit up again, my heart racing. "Is she really okay?"

"She's fine. Worried as hell about you."

"How long have I been out?"

"You hit your head. You've been out for hours. Doc said you may have a concussion. And they checked you out for internal damage, but you must have someone watching out for you because you're lucky as hell."

My chest tightens. I know it's my brother. It has to be. No one else up there gives a feck if I'm dead or alive.

"Where am I?"

"The Messinas run their own hospital on Long Island. Underground and private, just the way we like it. We checked you out from a local hospital against medical advice and brought you here."

"Look, I need to leave. I need to find them before they try hurting her again."

"Find who?" He crosses his arms and narrows his eyes. "Do you know who did this?"

Shite, I don't know how much I should tell him. They may never trust me again. Once a rat, always a rat, and rats are killed. But I can't carry this any longer either. If they want to kill me, then maybe I deserve it.

"The Palmers. I used to run with their crew before your father recruited me."

I press the heel of my palm between my brows and start at the beginning. When I'm through, he blows a breath and settles down.

"Jesus. Now I know why you never said anything before. But you have to talk to my father. We need to all be on the same page."

"I will." I nod, knowing that Patrick may not look at me the same way again, but it's the price I have to pay. I've kept this in for long enough. "But before I do, I need to see Eriu and make sure she's okay. Can you ask her to come in?"

"Yeah, sure." He slaps his palm over my shoulder. "Glad you didn't die. You're one of the few I don't hate."

"That's a compliment coming from you." I chuckle, then groan from the pain in my ribs.

He walks out of the room, and a few minutes later, I see her, and all the air stills in my lungs. She stands in the doorway, shutting it behind her, eyes shimmering with anguish.

"Devlin," she cries, bottom lip quivering.

"Come here, love." I reach out a hand, and with a sniffle, she rushes onto the bed and into my arms.

As soon as I have her, I breathe a sigh. My eyes pinch shut and my palm clasps the back of her head, holding her to my beating heart, because she is my heart. I breathe in that familiar scent of roses in her hair, feeling at peace knowing she's alright.

I tug tighter, ignoring the pain shooting down my torso.

"I thought you were dead." Tears fill her eyes as she pitches back. "I thought I'd lost you."

I clasp both sides of her face and stare into her eyes, feeling like my soul is slowly coming undone.

"I'm right here, baby. Even the devil couldn't take me."

Away from you, is what I want to say. But how fair would that be when I refuse to make her mine?

I press my mouth to the top of her head. "Don't cry. I hate knowing you were worried. I'm sorry."

She looks at me through those wet eyes that just about break me. "Who wrote that note, Devlin? Who's trying to hurt us?"

Us....

But it's her I'm worried about. I don't care what happens to me.

I should tell her everything too. What happened to my brother. What I did. Maybe if I tell her, she'll truly understand why I've kept her away, kept refusing her.

"When I was younger, I was part of a gang of thieves and killers."

She sits up straighter, staring intently for me to continue while I wait for some kind of judgment. But it never comes.

Is it that easy? Could this woman's love be unconditional?

But love isn't that way. It's never given freely. When we mess up, those we love stop loving us back.

Sometimes it takes a few feck-ups to get there, and other times, it takes one monumental act to change someone's feelings—to make them see you like they never have before—and that's when their love simply vanishes. I saw it happen with my parents. Their love wasn't free. Hers won't be either.

"We did a lot of shite. We stole expensive artwork and jewelry. Hurt people to do it, too many people, and we got away with it thanks to me."

Her brows furrow, and my fear grows that this will be the end of us.

"They trusted me. Most of them did, anyway. Francis Palmer, the head of the gang, had two sons, and one of them, Roy, never liked me. He tried to get me kicked out, but Palmer treated me more like a son than his own kids, and I think that's why his son wanted me gone."

She takes my hand in hers, squeezing reassuringly. I don't know why she'd want to touch me knowing what I've done.

"I didn't think of them as family. My brother was my only family, and I'd always look out for him. So, when he fell into drugs and started dealing, I was approached by the feds."

Her expression slides into a frown.

"They had two options for me. Rat on the gang or let my brother get taken to maximum security federal prison, where they told me they'd have him killed."

"My God…" She shudders.

"I tried to find another way out, but I failed. I chose my brother over the gang, and Palmer found out."

"Oh, no!" Her hand cups her mouth.

"Yeah… He killed him right in front of me, then made me bury my own brother on his property."

"That's… I'm so sorry, Devlin," she cries, throwing her arms around my neck, holding me like a child before she perches back. "How did you get away from them?"

"I had some help from some associates. Then I disappeared to the East Coast. This is going back twelve years, but I guess they know how to hold a grudge."

"So now they want to kill me to get back at you some more?"

"Aye. They know I don't give a shite about myself, but you?" I clasp her face and stroke the corner of her mouth with my thumb. "I'd do anything for you, and it seems like they've bloody well figured it out."

Her hand comes over my wrist, her eyes misting over with fresh tears. "I'm sorry you had to make such a difficult choice. I don't know what I would've done."

"I'm sorry you're getting caught up in my mess. It's what I wanted to avoid, but it seems like they won't let that happen."

"What are we gonna do now?"

"You're gonna lie low, and I'm gonna find them and kill them."

Her inhale stills in her lungs. "You say that so easily."

"That's because it *is* easy for me." I lay a palm over my heart. "But feeling what I feel for you? Now that's scary as hell, Eriu." My forehead meets hers as I take a deep breath. "It's why I can't let myself have you. There's too much that could hurt you, and I'd die before I let that happen."

Her bottom lip trembles, too close to mine, too close to where I can taste it again. My body pumps with blood, needing her in my veins.

She pulls away a fraction, and I ache to feel her body against mine again.

"You'll always have my heart, Devlin McHale. Nothing will change that. Not even a little car bomb." Her sad smile rips at my soul. "But I can't be the only one wanting this. So I guess this is it."

Those words, they cut deep. More painful than any bullet.

I want this.

But I just can't, God damn it! Why can't you see that?!

I hate hurting her, but being selfish and keeping her for myself isn't right either. If it's not the gang, it'll be someone else. And I can't be responsible for her death too. I won't bear it.

Eriu Quinn was never meant to be mine, even though every molecule in my body fights to keep her.

But my focus needs to remain on finding Palmer and his team now that they've come out of hiding. I will get payback for my brother and for what they tried to do to Eriu.

She sidles closer, and I tug her to me, both of us silent as my fingers stroke up and down her back. Being this near her and knowing she's never gonna be mine is feckin' hell.

There's a sudden knock on the door, and she jumps to her feet and my heart misses her already.

Her face goes red and she backs up another step just as Patrick marches in, looking sternly between us.

His attention settles on me. "I'm glad you're awake, son." He smiles softly at his daughter. "Darling, would you excuse us? It seems like we have a lot to catch up on."

"Sure, Daddy." She glances at me shyly. "Bye, Devlin."

Patrick settles on the chair across from the bed as soon as she's gone.

"Tell me what's going on. Tynan says it's important that we speak."

With a brisk sigh, I look into the eyes of the one man who's been like a father to me, and I tell him everything, no matter how much I could jeopardize between me and this family.

He stares with a tight glare, a tautness in his jaw. Wish I knew what the bloody hell he's thinking. It feels like an eternity before he finally speaks again.

"How am I supposed to trust that you won't do the same to us?"

I stare at him and straighten my back. "Because you all are my family, and I would die for each one of you."

His mouth thins.

"I had to save my brother. I had to do what I thought was right. I understand if you no longer trust me to work for you." I curl my fingers at my side. "You don't ever have to see me again if that's what you want. I don't deserve your forgiveness."

"Well, let's not get all dramatic." He waves a hand in the air. "I know I can trust you with my family. If I didn't, I would've pulled out my gun and shot you right here. I just wanted to hear you say it." He starts to rise. "Now, you've gotta rest. We'll look into these bastards while you get the proper care. I've assigned another guard for Eriu in the meantime."

No way in hell!

"That's not necessary. I'm fine." I force myself to ignore the dizziness as I sit up, then get to my feet.

Don't want anyone else around her. She's my responsibility.

Stars erupt before my eyes, and I clench my teeth together just to remain standing.

"I say it is necessary. You're gonna rest up, and once you're cleared, you can return. Until then, you listen to whatever that doctor says. You hear?"

"Yes, sir," I grumble.

Nothing is gonna keep me away from her, though.

Nothing.

He strides for the door. "I'll see you soon."

That went a lot better than I anticipated. Though the real trouble is imminent.

When I face Palmer again, he's going to regret coming after my woman.

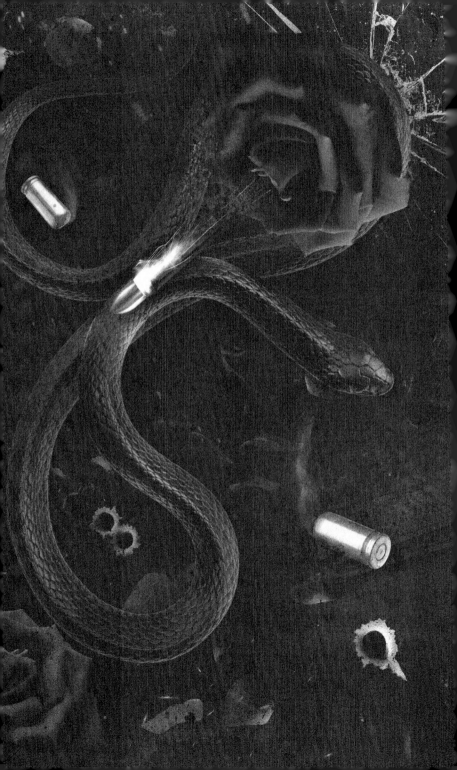

EIGHTEEN

ERIU

"I can't believe your car caught on fire!" Karen shakes her head while we finish breakfast at a café on the Upper East Side.

The accident was two days ago, and it feels like it was all a dream. Like it happened to someone else.

But it didn't. It happened to me. To us. My God, Devlin could've died. I could've lost him forever.

A pang hits my chest.

"Yeah...me neither." I feign shock. "My father said the fire department ruled it as bad wiring."

Now, that's not true, obviously. My father paid them off. That's what Iseult said. It seems like my family's connections are deeper than I've realized. Who else have they paid off, and for what sorts of things?

It makes me wonder back to my mom's death, and I plan to ask

Iseult about it when this all dies down. I'm not a child anymore. I should know what happened to my own mother.

I finish off my bagel with cream cheese and crumple the wrapper in my palm, starting to get up and head out.

"Where are you off to today?" She tosses her breakfast burrito wrapper and empty coffee cup into the nearby trash can.

"I'm gonna go see Devlin. He came home from the hospital today, and I don't want him to be alone." I grab the bagel I got him just in case he didn't eat this morning.

"Aww, look at you, taking care of your man."

"Shut up." My lips flicker, and I playfully shove her. "If it hadn't been for him, I could've died."

Her face grows somber. "I'm glad you didn't." She twists her mouth. "You're my favorite bitch."

"Thanks for the sweet compliment. You always have a way with words." I give her a big hug. "Please be careful getting back to the dorm."

"Why?" Her brows furrow. "Think my car is gonna blow up too?"

She laughs, but I don't find it funny. Whoever is after me could come after her. When it comes to evil people, there are no innocents. Everyone can fall prey. I'm starting to learn that about my life.

"Of course not." I let a reassuring smile slip even as my pulse kicks up. "It's the city. You always have to be careful."

She shrugs off my concern. "Please. The city is as scary as the rats in the subways. Harmless. Now go see that sexy bodyguard of yours." She eyes Rogue, my current replacement until Devlin gets better. "Now, the new one? He's mine."

She grins at him flirtatiously and gives him a little wave. His dark eyes narrow at her, and his bulging arms remain crossed as he sits at a table near ours.

She leans in toward my ear. "I think he likes me."

"Uh…if you say so."

When we start heading for the door, Rogue gets up, his large frame easily six-five. He's someone I'd see around my dad's academy, a school for elite soldiers in his little army. Yes, he has an army. And I assume they do more than just defend his massive estate or protect us.

Rogue follows us out, and Karen gets in her car after a long walk to where we parked. But before he allows me into his Rolls-Royce, he checks it for bugs and bombs, using a small circular device someone on my father's team created.

This is my life now. Danger everywhere. And now my dad won't even let me drive.

"Okay, Rogue, I think we're safe."

"Can never be too careful, ma'am." His face is stoic.

I swear these men who work for my dad are paid to look pissed off.

Once he's satisfied, he allows me to get in and follows to the driver's side.

"Just going to Devlin's."

"Yes, ma'am." He starts the engine and takes us to the Upper West Side, where Devlin has his apartment.

Thirty minutes later, we've found a spot a few blocks away and arrive at his building.

Rogue is right behind me as I head into the complex and ring Devlin's doorbell from the lobby.

"Who is it?" His voice is a rough, yet soothing concoction.

A smile spreads on my face. "It's me. I just wanted to see—"

The door buzzes instantly, and I rush inside and into the elevator with Rogue. He remains silent, staring at the door while I ache to see Devlin. To hold him. To make sure he's okay.

Ding.

When the elevator arrives, I dash out of it and straight for his apartment, knocking on his door just as it opens.

I inhale and hold my breath.

Unable to do much else.

Because…uh… He's shirtless. Kind of sweaty too, like he's just finished a workout, which would be insane considering he just got out of the hospital. But this is Devlin, of course.

His palm lands on the doorjamb, the veins in his hand and forearm throbbing, practically ripping through his skin.

My tongue slips past my lips, my body growing taut and warm.

Gray sweats hang low on his hips, exposing a deep V. And his abs… I'm counting eight, and they look like they're cut from glass.

Am I supposed to talk? Don't think I can manage that right now.

I've never seen him shirtless before, and a shirtless Devlin with those thick veins running up his arms is a sight I wasn't ready for this early in the morning.

I don't miss the bandage wrapped around his upper arm. I didn't realize he had an injury there. And there's a smaller gauze pad on his forehead too.

My heart tugs, wanting to take care of him.

"Come in." His smirk drops right into my stomach, heavy and overwhelming, and I know he's caught me staring.

More like gawking. My cheeks heat up instantly.

Suddenly, his demeanor shifts, and his glare sends a cold shudder down my spine as his attention zaps to the man behind me. He looks like he wants to take his head off.

"This is Rogue." I quickly glance back at the man.

They both stare at one another, and something passes between them. Nothing good.

Rogue's mouth twitches, if one can even call it that. "We've met."

I clear my throat, needing to defuse this unfriendly interaction. I start inside, hoping Devlin follows.

"I'll let you know when I'm done here. Thanks, Rogue."

Devlin grabs my hand, sending a tingle running up my arm, and pulls me all the way inside, kicking the door closed with his foot.

"What was that about?" I whisper, not wanting Rogue to hear.

Devlin keeps our hands locked as he takes me further into the lavish penthouse apartment he's rented. It's a one-bedroom, but the living space and size of the rooms is huge, and I know it costs a pretty penny.

Devlin isn't the kind of man who acts like he has money, but he's got a lot of it doing what he does for my father. I'm sure he's saved most of it too.

"We trained together at your father's academy. He was always too cocky. Thought he was too good until I beat him." He huffs a chuckle. "Don't like him, and I sure as hell don't like him being assigned to you."

Nervous butterflies soar in my gut. "Got it. Well, if it makes you feel any better, he's been nothing but nice, and definitely not cocky. Maybe he's changed since you knew him."

He snickers. "Doubt it."

He winces as he pulls me into the kitchen, and I almost forgot about the bag in my hand.

"What do you have in there?" He eyes the contents, and he gives me one of those Devlin smiles, those tiny flickers into the real man. The one he shows just me.

I've missed those smiles.

"I got you breakfast." I lift the bag and shake it a little. "Did you eat yet?"

"No…" His voice drops and turns deep as he prowls closer, tugging my jaw in his calloused hand. "But now I'm suddenly famished."

My eyes widen, and I gulp down. His stare is intense and full of unrelenting prowess. And something in it makes my heart beat faster, because it almost feels like he's hungry for *me*…

His eyes sear into mine, leaving a trail of heat and awakened desire behind.

"Thank you for thinking of me, love," he husks, and my throat goes dry.

That seductive baritone makes every inch of me come alive.

"Welcome." My voice comes out tinier than I intended, but I'm insanely nervous, and having him looking at me this way, touching me this way… It makes me recall what happened between us that night.

"Did *you* eat?" he asks, cupping my cheek, his lips dropping lower, his arm curling around my back and molding my body to his.

My lungs still as I wait, hoping for his mouth to meet mine.

I nod, a shiver rushing up my spine.

"That's too bad." He brushes his thumb over my lips. "I was hoping to feed you."

Am I allowed to change my answer? Because I'm suddenly starving.

My God, what is happening? And how can I have more of this every single day?

His responding chuckle makes every inch of me tingle.

"Come on, I'll make you a cup of coffee. I know how much you like coffee." He drags me into the kitchen, his hand in mine, and this feeling drops into my stomach where your heart's actually smiling. Really smiling.

He pulls out a stool for me in front of the white marble island and clutches my hips to help me up. But instead of moving away, he remains there, between my open thighs, his palms remaining right above my knees, massaging my skin. His breathing grows raspier, a muscle in his neck popping.

My chest rises and falls with every exhale.

"I'm glad you're here, mo stoirín."

Me too…

I go breathless, wishing I knew what he just called me. Before I can ask, he drops his hands away, heads toward the coffee machine, and proceeds to make me a cup.

His back flexes, every sinew rippling, and I've immediately come to realize I have a thing for backs. Or maybe just his back. His body is beautiful. As though carved by Michelangelo himself.

When he turns around with a mug in hand, my face grows all hot as I think of him taking me up on the counter. He places it before me and settles across from me, opening the bag of food I brought and unwrapping his bagel.

I quickly grab the steaming cup and drink it, hoping not to show how much he affects me. "How's your head and your arm?"

He glances down at his wound for a moment. "I'll be fine. Doc said to change the bandages every few days. I should be cleared to work soon too. So I hope you're not missing me too much." His teasing smirk just about evaporates all the air from my lungs.

"Nah." I flip a shoulder. "Rogue is doing just fine."

His smile immediately disappears.

"I'm only joking!" I let out a laugh.

"I don't find the thought of you and Rogue being that close to each other all that funny."

He's serious. If looks could kill…

I try not to laugh again.

I drag another long pull of my coffee before climbing out of my chair and walking around to him, cupping the stubble of his cheek. "If this is you being jealous, Devlin McHale, I like it. A lot."

He grabs my wrist and brings my fingertips to his mouth, kissing them as his intense gaze fastens to mine.

I inhale sharply from the way his mouth feels on my skin.

"Just because I said I can't be with you doesn't mean that the thought of any other man being near you doesn't make me want to rip out his bloody heart. No one is safe." His mouth tips up on one side.

In his words, I find warmth, like a blanket I'm wrapped up in. Yet at the same time, I'm cold. Because without him, I always will be.

"Then it's a good thing I plan to become a cat lady." I lift my chin with a tight, playful smile.

He bursts with a chuckle.

"What's so funny? Don't like cats? I'll have you know I plan to have a minimum of ten."

His laughter dies down as he shakes his head. "My God, don't think I've laughed like that in forever."

I run my hand through his thick hair and pull until he groans, shutting his eyes and tilting his head back. His mouth looks soft and firm all at once, and I want to lean down and kiss him.

Instead, I say, "Can I change your bandage before I go?"

I just want to take care of him the way he's always taken care of me.

His brows knit. "You'd want to do that?"

"Of course." My palm settles on the side of his neck, feeling his maddening pulse, the same way mine beats. "Just tell me where I can find the gauze and stuff."

"In the main bathroom, under the sink."

I start in that direction.

"Eriu?"

"Yeah?" My heart picks up speed when those eyes, those adoring eyes, stare back at me.

"Thank you."

Pain lodges in the back of my throat.

I love you.

"No problem."

Quickly, I scurry away, not wanting my tears to betray me. As soon as I'm in the bathroom, I kneel to grab the emergency kit. Taking a deep breath or five, I steady my precarious emotions before allowing myself to face him again.

When I'm ready, I walk back out, finding him facing away from the counter.

When his eyes connect with mine, that feeling of longing, that intense connection between us, returns. I fight it as I find my place by his thighs.

He drops his elbow on the counter, gazing down at me, and that just makes it hard to work.

Gently, I undo the medical tape and remove the gauze, full of blood. The cut looks deep, and I grimace.

"Does it hurt?"

He shakes his head. But I'm sure he's lying. There's no way it doesn't. He watches me as I unpack the new gauze and place it around his wound while he picks up the tape and cuts pieces for me. I avoid his gaze as I finish his arm and move on to his head, finding every atom in my body firing off.

Why does he have to watch me like that? Like he's dying to throw me on his lap and kiss me. My God, this is hell.

"All done." I take a step back, but his arm curls around the small of my back.

"Thanks, love. You really didn't have to do that." His warm breaths coast across my lips, and I don't even know if I'm capable of walking any longer. "Call me when you get back to your room or I'll worry."

"Mm-hmm."

His arm falls to his side, and he gets off the chair to walk me to the door, his body close behind, the heat of it radiating in waves.

He reaches around me for the door handle, but makes no attempt to open it. Every inch of me wants to fight to remain right here, but I know I have to go.

"I'll see you later," I tell him, and with a deep sigh, he lets me out.

Once he sees Rogue again, he growls right under his breath.

I stifle a laugh as he watches us all the way until we disappear out of sight.

And I swear I hear him mutter a curse as he shuts the door with a bang echoing through the hall.

Arriving back at my dorm, I head inside the building while Rogue stands in front of it.

I have nothing to do today except some homework that I'm behind on. Might as well do it now. I'm sure Karen will want to hang out later.

Entering my code, I strut inside.

And as soon as I do, all the air leaves my lungs. I back into the door, my heart beating right out of my chest.

"Wha-what are you…?"

"What am I doing here?" Mason rises from my bed, a menacing sneer on his face. "I came to see my fiancée, and she wasn't home, so I let myself in."

"How?" I whisper.

"I have ways."

In his hand is a large manila envelope. I'm afraid of asking what's inside.

"We need to talk."

"About wh-what?" I try to move past him, but he cages me in, and the terrifying look on his face has me trembling.

He catches my wrist harshly, pinching my skin as he drags me to the bed and throws me onto it. I remain seated, gasping and heaving as he towers over me, his glare cutting into me like glass. He rips open the envelope and throws photos at me.

"Look at them!"

With a jittery hand, I snatch one and gulp, sweat coating my brow. I pick up another photo and find more of the same.

Me with Karen and Adam. All of us in masks. Heading inside the club.

Another photo is of Karen and me in her car.

"You had me followed?"

He bends and grabs my jaw. "Of course I did. I knew I couldn't trust you to do your part. Instead, my man found these!" He glances at the photos in disgust. "Where were you going dressed like a whore?!" His hand whips out, and he slaps me across the face.

I wince, holding my cheek while it burns. Tears swim in my eyes.

"I—I was just going to a masquerade party. I—I didn't do anything." I sniffle, fearing the look on his face, wishing Devlin was here.

Oh, God. What is he going to do to me?

"Liar!" He yanks me by my hair and forces me to my feet. "I need this marriage, you bitch! Do you hear me?!" He locks my strands in his vengeful fist. "You're ruining everything!"

"Please," I cry. "You're…you're hurting me."

"Good." He laughs humorlessly. "I could do worse. I could show these pictures to your father. Let him decide where you were going. Because I don't believe you. This innocent virgin act isn't the real you, is it?"

He drops his face close to mine, and I taste the hint of beer mixed with his foul breath.

"I wasn't doing anything wrong. I was out with friends." Tears leak out of the corners of my eyes.

"If I catch you going there again, you will pay for this."

Once he releases me, I rub at my scalp, the pain shooting down my neck.

He gathers the photos from my bed and stuffs them back inside.

"Were…were you serious about me being a virgin before marriage?"

My pulse shoots out of my throat, like it's living outside of my body, but I need to know. I need to be sure before I do something I can't take back.

His palm snaps around my throat and squeezes so hard, I can't seem to breathe. "If you decide to fuck someone so I don't marry you, I'll make your life hell. I'll humiliate you. Make you a laughingstock. Let everyone know what a slut Eriu Quinn is. And no one will touch you. So go ahead. Do what you're thinking and see what happens to you."

My inhale catches in my throat, and I blink past the moisture continuing to build in my eyes.

With a final look of disdain, he marches out. As soon as he's gone, I rush for the door and let out a sob, pressing my back against the hard surface.

As I slide down against it, my face hits my knees while I silently cry. I can't go on this way. If no one is gonna help me, I have to help myself. And if he decides to spread rumors about me, let him. It'll just end up getting him killed.

I swipe under my eyes and get to my feet, knowing sitting here and crying isn't going to solve my problems. Getting my cellphone from my bed, I scroll through my emails to the one I'm looking for. Staring at the application the owner of the club sent me, I read over the questions before I get to the end, the fine print.

Carefully, I glance over the terms, chewing on the inside of my mouth.

Once I submit the application, it's non-reversable. I commit to this and can't change my mind.

What happens to the girls who do change their minds, though?

But with the kind of man who owns that club, I don't want to know.

Am I really doing this? Am I applying for the auction?

But I have to do something. I can't go on like this.

Before I change my mind, I fill it out, attach a photo of myself, and hit submit.

It's done. I did it. And I instantly regret it, my stomach knotting with tension, but this is the only way to get Mason out of my life for good.

I curl into a fetal position and wish this life away. But it's mine, and I have to do what I can to make it worth living.

There's a heavy knock on my door, and I instantly flinch awake, my pulse picking up speed as I realize I passed out on my bed.

I know it's probably Rogue checking in on me, but in my mind, it's Mason coming back to finish what he started. I still don't understand how he managed to get my code for the door.

I brush a hand down my face when another knock comes, harder this time.

"Eriu! Open up."

"Devlin?" Shock weaves into my voice as I jump out of bed and rush for the door.

As soon as I open it, a concerned Devlin looks me up and down. "Are you okay?"

"Um…"

My bottom lip quivers and my fingers rub at my neck. I can't seem to keep it together.

His nostrils widen, and he's forcing himself past the threshold and roughly shutting the door. "Eriu?"

His fingers find my chin, and he tilts it up to inspect my throat, anger flaming in his eyes.

"Feck…" His jaw twitches. "He left a mark on you?"

"What?" I choke out, my pulse quickening even more.

Is there a mark on my neck? Oh, no!

"It was Mason." He says it like he knows already. "He hurt you, right?"

My chin quivers, and a sob breaks free. Then I'm throwing myself into his arms and he's holding me, making me feel safer. I needed this more than anything.

"I'm so sorry. I'm gonna make this right. I promise. And no one will hurt you again. I swear it."

"Please…" I push back at his chest and stare up into his tranquil blue eyes. "Please don't do anything that could hurt you."

"Do you know what it does to me to know he laid hands on you and is still alive to talk about it?"

"Don't kill him. Not for me."

"I've gotta go." He cups my cheeks and his forehead meets mine, his mouth brushing against my lips until my heart skips a beat.

I want to feel his lips again and again.

He kisses me on my temple and breathes me in slow, like he's savoring me.

Before I can tell him not to leave, not to do whatever he's planning, he's out the door, and I'm afraid of what will happen when he's done.

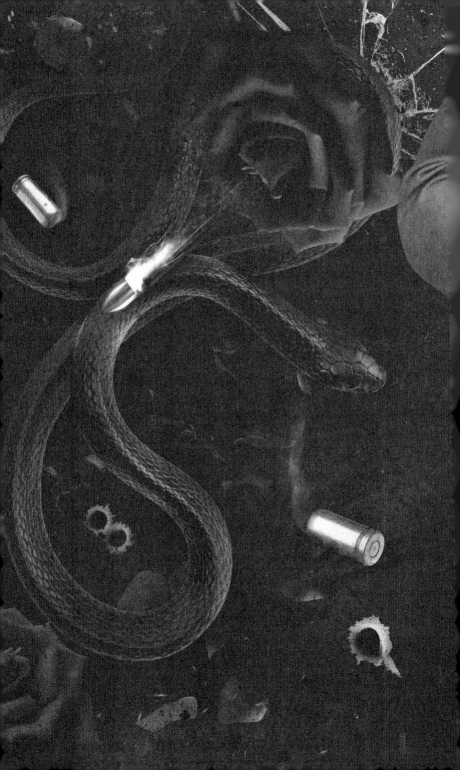

NINETEEN

DEVLIN

Mason lives alone in a house bigger than his balls, bought with his daddy's money. There are only three guards around the perimeter, and I already have a plan for how to take them out.

It only took me a couple of hours to get to his home with the traffic. I had to make sure the fecking prick was back before I did what I came to do. When I heard him hurting her, I rushed over, wanting to slice his goddamn throat. But I missed him.

I won't miss now.

I move toward one of the guards from behind, standing alone at the back at the house, and silently, I grab him around his throat and put a bullet in his temple. The shot is muffled by the silencer.

I slink toward the front of the house where the other two men are stationed, my nine at my side.

Something cracks beneath my foot. Maybe a branch.

Shite.

"Did you hear that?" one of the men asks.

"No idea. Go check it out. Let me know if you find anything."

"Yeah. Alright."

Here we go.

As soon as footfalls pummel closer, I get ready behind a shrub. When he comes around the corner, I manage to surprise him and step out, a bullet piercing his forehead.

He falls to the ground with a loud thud.

One remains between me and Mason feckin' Reynolds.

"Hey, you there?" The other one starts heading for my direction. "What the fuck you doing?"

I'm waiting there with a pistol pointing right at his head when he appears.

"What the…" Before his hand even reaches his waistband, a bullet rips between his eyes.

I brush past his dead body and head for the bastard who dared to hurt her.

Guess he thought I was bluffing when I warned him to keep his hands to himself. He's going to learn that I'm a man who keeps his word.

I know Mason is home. Only identified one body inside with my motion detection device.

Removing a keycard from one of the guards, I use it to scan the door and let myself in the back, careful to shut the door quietly. I already know where Mason is: past the long foyer, sitting in the den on his laptop.

He doesn't hear me as I start toward him from behind.

My gun is pointing at the back of his head. "Do you remember what I said to you at the diner?"

His body jolts as he turns his neck and stares right at me, laptop plummeting to the floor. He doesn't appear afraid. Not yet. He's used to making others afraid of him.

"What the hell are you doing here? My guards will have your head!"

I chuckle as I round the sofa, the pistol in my grasp. "Unfortunately for you, they're all dead."

"Wh-what? You killed them? Are you insane?! Do you know what I'll do to you?" He mashes his teeth.

"I asked you a bloody question, arsehole! Do you recall what I said to you when you touched her at the diner?"

"I don't care!" His fingers curl on his thigh. "Get the hell out of my house before I get the police. If you leave now, I'll tell the cops it was a robbery."

I continue to glare. "Seems you have a faulty memory. I told you that if you touched her again, you'd see what I'd do to your hand."

His fingers slowly slip under the sofa cushion, and I know immediately what he plans to do. But I let him, knowing he won't be able to take a shot before I do.

As soon as he removes a pistol, I pull the trigger, and a bullet rips right through his hand.

"Fuck!" he screams a deafening sound, his weapon falling to his feet.

I fling over my string bag from my back. The one carrying a cordless reciprocating saw.

"Please!" he begs, his eyes pleading as I remove it. "Wha-what are you gonna do with that?"

He gets up and runs.

"That was a big mistake." I release a groan, chasing him before I throw him onto the floor, settling over his body.

I grab the hand I shot and flip on the saw. The echoing sound makes the hairs on his arm stand up.

He cries real tears.

Now we're talking…

"Hold still." A smile flips up the corner of my mouth.

"Please, man. Please don't do this!" He fights me, shouting for help to no avail.

"You come after her, you come after me."

With no mercy, I pin his wrist to the floor and push the tip of the saw right into it.

There's blood everywhere. His screaming can be heard for miles. Flesh and bone ripped through, broken and shattered, until I have his hand in my grasp, completely dismembered.

"O-o-oh my God!" he hollers, trembling in agony, his chest pummeling with rapid breaths.

"That's what happens when you touch what belongs to me. And if you do it again—if you so much as look at her wrong—I'll take your other hand."

He sobs, grabbing his arm while I get off him and head for his fireplace. He bleeds across his porcelain floor, somehow watching me through it all. Which is a good thing. Wouldn't want him to miss this part.

I toss his hand into the fireplace, the skin blistering in the wild flames.

"NO!" he howls, but I ignore it.

"You will not marry her. Do you understand?" I stand over him now. "You will tell your father you changed your mind."

"No! Please. I—I have to!"

"You have to?" I kneel and grab his shirt, pulling him to a stand. "What are you talking about?"

When he continues to cry, my patience runs out.

"I'll make you bleed out if you don't tell me what that means."

"I—I can't disappoint my father. I have to do what he wants, or I don't get my inheritance! Oh, God, I need a doctor! Please!"

I let him go. This is about his money, huh?

I find his phone on the sofa and throw it at his chest. "If you tell anyone what happened here, I will kill you."

He shakes his head frantically. "I won't. I s-swear."

"I already took care of your cameras and wiped all the footage from today."

I take my shite and head back into my car, flipping my hoodie back over my head.

If this comes back to me, I'll serve my time with a bloody smile on my face because, for her, it's worth it.

I'm gonna be setting up a meeting with her father to tell him she isn't marrying Mason. After what he did to her, I won't allow it.

Too bad Patrick is away on business. But he should be back in a few days. Once he gives me the confirmation, I'll tell Eriu that she's finally free.

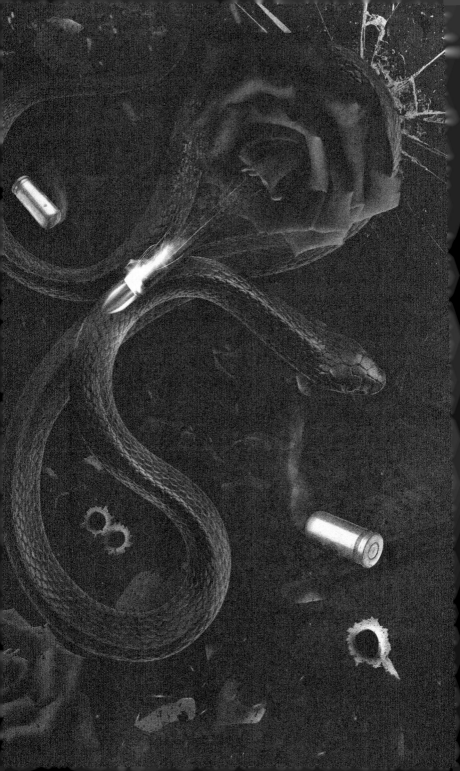

TWENTY

ERIU

Congratulations. You're in.

The words stare back at me on my cellphone screen. I can't believe it was this fast to get accepted to the auction.

There's no indication it's the club, except a logo on the bottom of the email, the same one they use with every text they send: a black circle with a red club.

I'm in. I'm actually doing this!

Oh my God! What have I done?

I pinch the bridge of my nose and go to my text messages, finding Devlin's name.

He hasn't called or texted me back after he saw what Mason did to me. I've asked Rogue if he's heard from him, but he hasn't. It's not like Devlin to make me worry this way. What if something happened to him? I've barely slept these past couple of nights anxious and afraid.

Heading to my morning class, I call Iseult, hoping she at least knows something. I'm afraid of telling her how Mason has been treating me. She'll go apeshit and definitely kill him.

My sister can handle herself—I've seen it firsthand—but I don't want her getting hurt because of me. I know how powerful the Reynoldses are. I've already lost a mother; I can't lose anyone else.

She answers on the second ring. "Hey, you're calling early. Something wrong?"

"Have you heard from Devlin in the last few days?"

"No. Should I have?"

"No, I was just curious. I haven't heard from him since I saw him a couple of days ago. He was upset about stuff with Mason, so I'm afraid he confronted him and something happened."

"What stuff? Did Mason do something?" Her tone is urgent and clipped.

I don't have to tell her everything, but I can tell her enough to help me find Devlin. If he doesn't call me today, I'm gonna go to his place and be the crazy non-girlfriend that I am.

"No, Mason is just…you know, Mason."

"You mean a self-entitled, pompous piece of horseshit?"

"Now that you put it that way…"

She laughs. "I'll find Devlin. But, Eriu? If Mason does anything to you, I want you to tell me, okay? Promise me."

I close my eyes and lie. "Of course. I promise."

"We'll figure a way out of this. You'll see."

I already did.

The email from the club appears in my mind.

Tomorrow is when I auction off my virginity, and I don't even know how I'm going to get through it.

I stop by Professor Montgomery's office the next day after one of my classes to return the books she gave me the last time.

Knocking softly, I wait for her to let me in.

"Come in." As soon as she sees me, her face lights up. "Hey, how are you doing?"

"I'm good." I force a smile and her brows furrow.

"What's wrong?"

Is it really that easy to see that something is going on with me?

"Nothing." My grin widens. "I'm totally fine."

She arches a single brow. "Sit."

With a shaky inhale, I settle across from her desk, resting against the black leather chair.

"What's really going on? I can tell you're upset. Is it the engagement?"

I nod. "I can't stand him."

"I'm sorry, Eriu." Her gaze grows sympathetic. "If there was something I could do, I would."

"I know. I think I may have figured a way out. It's just not the best option. But it feels like the only one I have."

My body sags. I'm so tired. I just want this to be over.

She nods thoughtfully. "Sometimes we have to make difficult choices, and sometimes those are the only ones that will create change." She leans forward. "You're strong. I've always told you that."

"Thank you." I reach into my backpack and retrieve the books she lent me, placing them in front of her. "I appreciate these. They were helpful."

"I'm glad. I'll have more for you next week. But listen, take my number down. If you ever need anything, call me anytime. I sleep late." Her mouth tips up, and I feel a little better talking to her.

She's right. I have to make a difficult choice, and it may cost me more than I realize. But marrying Mason is a fate worse than death.

She tells me her number, and I save it into my phone before heading for the door. "Thanks, Professor Montgomery."

"Always. Have a nice day."

When I head out of the building, I look around for Rogue, but don't see him standing in front of the humanities building anymore.

"What the…"

"Eriu," someone calls, and I freeze in place.

That rugged, masculine timbre sends a shiver down my body. I'd recognize that voice anywhere.

"Devlin?" I utter in absolute relief, spinning on my heels to find him standing there in one piece.

A short-sleeved black t-shirt accentuates every single hard square of muscle on his arms. My throat goes dry as he nears with a half-smile.

"Heard you were looking for me."

My face twists with aggravation. "Where have you been?"

I shove him hard on his chest, but the man doesn't even move an inch, simply stares at me with amusement meeting the tendrils of his blue eyes.

I go on, completely annoyed that he hasn't so much as apologized. "I called you yesterday and left you a text to find out what happened with Mason, but you never got back to me. I thought you were dead!"

The gash on his forehead still remains covered, but he looks fine overall.

Inhaling deeply, he slices away at the distance between us, his eyes tenderly boring into mine. "I'm sorry I worried you, love."

And just like that, my annoyance disappears.

His knuckles brush down my cheek, and I close my eyes, feeling it everywhere. It's been forever since he touched me last.

His lips jerk, and his eyes deepen with mine. "My phone broke yesterday, and I had to get a new one. Your message never came through."

"Oh." I swallow nervously from the hooded way he stares at me, eyes raking over my face, dropping to my lips before they climb back up. "What are you doing here? Where's Rogue?"

"You won't be needing him anymore."

"What? Why? Are you back?"

"Aye. Nothing can keep me away from you any longer."

What is he doing to me, saying things like that? It's already hard enough to know he has feelings for me and that we can't be together.

"But the doctor said you need rest."

My reminder only makes him chuckle dryly. "I've had enough of that. Saw him yesterday and he said I could return back to work." He gives me a crooked smile that drops right into my belly. "Doc called me a stubborn mule, but said as long as I don't get myself blown up again, I'll be fine."

I shake my head. "You forced the doctor to clear you, didn't you?"

"Aye." Tenderly, he cups my cheek, and his brows knit. "You know me so well, Eriu Quinn."

"I've aways known who you really are." I grasp his wrist, his gaze softening.

And my heart does what it always does with him: it beats to a tempo meant just for him.

With a long drag of air, he curls an arm around me and drops his forehead to mine. And every time he does, it feels like I'm home. Like this is what forever feels like.

But tonight, I'm going to have to give a part of myself to someone else just to avoid marrying a monster.

And I already hate myself for it because it won't be him.

TWENTY-ONE

ERIU

"**A**re you sure about this?" Karen asks as we finish getting ready for the club in her room.

No. I'm not sure.

Fear clenches its teeth around my chest. How will I ever get through tonight?

What if I get hurt? What if I can't go through with it? Will they force me?

Oh my God. I need a drink. Need something to numb my thoughts.

"Weren't you the one telling me I had to do this?" My foot bounces, shifting to the edge of her bed.

"I was. But now that it's happening, I'm nervous for you."

She runs her fingers through her long pinup curls, walking over to me. Her black gown cuts low in the front, beading sequins running up the sides.

Mine is bloodred, thin straps, and a sweetheart neckline. It's tight around my curves and sweeps out, hitting the floor. The curled ends of my hair annoy me, tickling across my bare back. I fling them over my shoulder and huff a breath.

She lowers beside me and throws an arm around my back. "I hate that you have to do this."

"Yeah, well, like you said, I don't have a choice."

"It's too bad we couldn't throw Mason over a bridge."

I grumble. "I may need some shots before I do this tonight."

"We'll get some drinks once we get there. I'll have you buzzed enough not to run off the stage."

I slap a hand over my face, not even caring that I'll ruin the makeup Karen spent an hour doing.

She gently tugs my wrist back and peers at me through concerned eyes. "It'll be okay. It's just sex. Means nothing, unless you want it to."

"That's right. Just sex." I straighten my spine and prepare for the hell waiting for me.

She slips her fingers through mine and gives me a reassuring squeeze.

As we pick up our handbags and head out the door, I try not to think about the man I'm in love with and how this will break his heart.

And mine.

We arrive at the club with Adam in tow. I can't believe he's going to witness what I'll be doing. The whole thing is mortifying enough without adding that to the mix.

I told Karen not to tell him before we get there. I don't want him looking at me and judging me. It makes me feel dirty.

My family would be ashamed of me. My face heats up at the thought. But none of them understand how it feels to be forced into a marriage you don't want, especially with a man like Mason.

My father has controlled every aspect of my life. It's time I take that control back.

When I received the acceptance to the auction, I was sent a list of instructions, like where to report and what time. They provide the clothing, so I didn't need to worry about that.

We head to the bar, and Adam buys us a couple of shots each, which don't temper my thoughts whatsoever. An ill feeling settled in my gut as soon as we left the dorm, and nothing will erase it. And if I drink any more, I'm going to end up facedown on the floor.

Adam finishes his old fashioned before Karen starts dragging me in front of a room with an orgy going on. Six people, too many body parts to keep track of.

I can't even focus on anything besides what I'll be doing in twenty minutes. That's when I was told to report to a red door by the stage.

Karen glances at me, her face sympathetic. "It'll be okay. You'll see."

I nod with a flicker of a smile, knowing that's a lie.

None of this is okay.

I'm about to lose my virginity, and it scares the hell out of me.

DEVLIN

She's back at the club, and I swear this is gonna be the final time. After today, her days of being in this filthy place are over. Gonna tell her I'm the man behind the mask and that she's not allowed to step foot inside here again.

Standing by the bar, I watch Eriu and her friends drinking not too far from me. My God, this girl is asking for trouble.

From my periphery, I find Konstantin strolling by.

"You're here. Was hoping you would be."

"Why's that? Got another brother who wants to shoot me?"

He chuckles. "You and that sense of humor. I'm sure they've missed you as much as you've missed them. Now, how about a toast?"

"No drinking for me. I'm driving."

He grabs a bottle and two shot glasses from the bar, pouring one for me. "Get a cab. This is my finest vodka."

"I'm sure it's feckin' fabulous, but I can't be piss-drunk. Gotta watch Eriu."

"Ah, yes, your young lover. She's quite pretty. I can see the appeal."

I grind my teeth, my glare tight as I stare into his eyes with growing ire. "Don't call her pretty. In fact, don't even say her bloody name. You understand me, Marinov?"

He chuckles, and then his smile disappears. "Devlin, Devlin…" He tsks. "You are in *my* place of business and you dare insult me?"

I don't relent, continuing to cut him with a glare. "Not an insult, but a promise. Don't mess with her."

"If I wanted the young Quinn, she would've been mine by now." His lips spread. "Unlike you, I take what I want. I don't hesitate. Lucky for you, though, I don't want her." He slaps me across my back. "She's all yours, McHale, but you still won't do a thing about it." He pours himself another shot and tips the glass to his mouth.

"Don't worry about what I do. Just keep away from her."

"I have no intentions of hurting her." He starts to walk away, but as he does, he turns to me. "Oh, I did forget to mention one thing. I have a special surprise for you. I think you're gonna find it quite entertaining."

His amusement makes me wanna rip out his throat. "Don't feck with me, Marinov."

"Fucking you isn't on my agenda for this evening. You're not even my type." His head tips to the side, taunting with a grin. "But I know who is."

When I glance back at Eriu, she's not there anymore.

Something cold washes over me.

His sinister smile never wavers.

"Where did she go?" I snap.

"That would ruin the surprise, and what fun would that be?"

I growl deep in my chest. He's up to something, and I know I'm gonna hate it. I have to find her.

"Better have that drink, my friend. You're gonna need it."

"What the hell does that mean?!"

But he's already stalking away, leaving me with too many questions that I'm afraid of getting answers to.

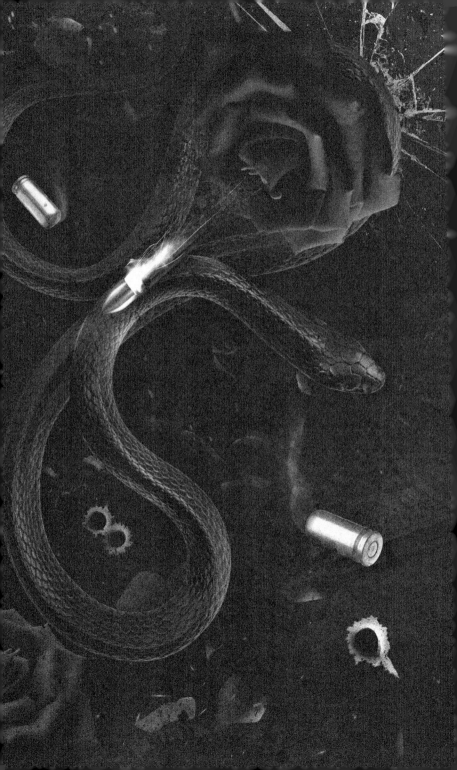

TWENTY-TWO

ERIU

"Come on now, honey. Take off your clothes, and I will help you slip into this gown." A blonde, blue-eyed woman waits for me to strip while in a dressing room.

She's assigned to help me. All the girls have someone, I was told. I guess the owner of the club wants to make sure none of us change our minds and run off. Which, I'll be honest, sounds tempting right about now.

The hairs on my nape prickle. I'm shivering, yet the room is warm. My arms curl around my body, and I can't seem to do this. I can't take off my clothes in front of her. This is humiliating!

"Sweetie, if you don't do what you're told, the boss is going to be very disappointed, and I don't want to be around when that happens."

She grimaces, crossing a long, tanned leg over the other. A tight black corset is the only thing she's wearing as she watches me from the red leather sofa.

When I don't listen, she shakes her head and rises, strutting right up to me. "Give me your hand."

Trembling, I remove one from my body, barely able to make it move. She pulls it into hers and looks right at me, running the fingers of her other hand over the top of mine.

"I know you're scared. Of course you are. Many of the girls are, but it's my job to make you feel as comfortable as possible. There's no shame in this. Not here. In fact, all the girls are treated well. So be a good girl and take off your dress, or I can do it for you. It's up to you."

Though she smiles, there's something cold in her demeanor, and it only makes me quiver even more.

I have to do this. I have to fight my nerves and get it over with. When I close my eyes, I see Mason and how angry he was with me.

That's all it takes for me to force my arms down and start undoing the side zipper.

"That's it. Keep going." Her lips twist.

I unzip the rest, and when the straps start to fall down my shoulders, she's there pulling them down, exposing my breasts.

Her eyes narrow as she takes in my beaded tips, her hands dragging down the dress until I'm in nothing but a pair of cotton panties.

"Those too." She eyes my underwear, and my face turns beet red.

But with a quick inhale, I pull them until they're on the floor.

"Beautiful." She smiles salaciously. "Now, I'll put these on your nipples." She picks up a pair of teardrop-jeweled pasties, removing the strip of paper from one before she presses the cover up to my breast, then does the same thing to the other.

"Let's put on your gown now, shall we?"

I nod, my stomach in knots. I feel beyond embarrassed from the way she's looking at me. I can't wait until this entire thing is over.

I know Karen is out there, sitting in the audience with Adam, and I'm completely mortified already. They're gonna see me naked on that stage.

Oh my God, what am I doing? What am I doing?!

The woman slips the see-through white dress off the hanger and approaches. It's exactly the same as the ones I saw the girls wearing when I watched the auction. My entire body there for everyone to see.

"Arms up, sweetie."

She holds it out, and when I raise them, she drops it over me.

"You're quite stunning." She gives me a slow once-over. "The winner will be a very lucky man. Or woman."

A single seductive brow hikes up, and I want to crawl into a corner and die.

"Now for your mask." She moves to the closet and removes a white one made with lace and feathers around the eyes.

She helps me put it on, then runs her fingers through my hair and fluffs the strands over my shoulders. "Now you're ready. You will be the third one up, so it will give you some time to prepare. Once the act is done, you will come back here to collect your money. Understand?"

"Yes," I whisper, nausea battling in my throat.

"Smile," she says. "Today you become a woman."

Yeah. Sure. That's definitely how that works…

I roll my eyes in my head.

"Now come." She starts for the door. "We must wait backstage."

"Okay."

Nervously swallowing down my fear, I follow her down a long corridor lined by a few men with weapons in their holsters. They don't stare at me or make me feel uncomfortable, which is a relief. They seem to have their minds trained on their task, which includes just standing around and looking scary. They're doing a pretty good job.

We arrive at a large backstage area, and I count about fifteen girls here, all nervous-looking, all seated in the chairs. One blonde woman is playing with her hair, her foot bouncing. Another is drinking something red through a straw. Probably liquor.

"Would you like a drink? I'm Esther, by the way." She glances at me behind her shoulder. "I can get you whatever you want. There's a bar over there."

She points to the left, and I see it, with a guy serving a woman who's dressed like Esther.

"No. I think I'm fine. I can't handle too much alcohol."

She laughs. "Of course. Well, go have a seat, and they will let us know when it's your turn."

I scurry to an empty chair, and a young woman beside me glances at me.

All our masks and dresses are the same, and I can see her brown eyes.

"Hi," she says. "I'm Susanna. What's your name?"

Can't tell her that. Especially with how different my name is, but they allowed us to pick our own stage names on the application.

"I'm Ellen."

"Nice to meet you." She brings her chair closer and whispers, "Are you nervous too? I'm second-guessing this entire thing. All I wanted was money to pay for college. But this was stupid and now it's too late."

"I'm sorry."

I feel bad for her. I've lived a privileged life. I've never had to worry about money, but so many people do.

"It's fine." She sits up straighter, as though that'll make it all okay. "It will be over soon. For both of us."

"Yes. That's right." The sooner, the better.

The first girl is called and brought out by a woman in a gold mask and black corset. The second follows not long after.

And I know what's coming.

"Ellen. You're up," Esther calls.

My whole body spreads with a wave of ice-cold fear. The kind that stops you dead in your tracks.

"Oh, God…" I whisper, my knees bucking as I force my legs to work.

Just stand up and go before she calls the boss.

"You can do this," Susanna attempts to reassure me, but nothing will help.

Curling a fist, I make myself get to my feet, my flesh riding with goose bumps.

Esther saunters over and slips her arm through mine. "Take a breath, honey. You'll be okay."

What a lie.

She leads me out another door, and bright lights assault me.

When I blink a few times, I realize…I'm on a stage, so many masked faces in the audience. Hundreds of them.

Oh my God…

Esther remains by my side while the emcee's mouth curls, his attention zeroing in on me.

"Welcome Ellen, contestant number three. A beautiful young virgin who loves to write and enjoys taking care of her animals. She's a straight-A student and takes her studies very seriously."

He gathers my hand and lifts it in the air, spinning me once on my heels. "She's looking to uncover her sexuality, and maybe tonight, the lucky winner will help her do that."

He gives me a smirking look, while I'm shaking all over.

My eyes bounce around the audience but I don't see anyone I know. Not Karen. Not Adam. Not even the man in the mask. There are just too many people here.

"The bidding will start at one hundred thousand."

Shit.

DEVLIN

Where the feck is she?!

I can't find her anywhere. I'm stalking through rooms, wondering if she's hanging from some contraption from the ceiling. Or worse, if she has another man's hands on her, and this time it isn't me.

But after the ominous warning from Konstantin, I have to expect just about anything. As I head down the corridor, passing rooms on both sides, I find a larger open area with seating, like at a show.

Unsure what the hell this is, I walk in and see a girl on stage and...

No...

My pulse throbs in my ears. "Eriu?"

But no one can hear me while she's being displayed on stage like cattle, wearing a fecking see-through dress, her damn nipples covered in rhinestones.

"Three hundred thousand." A man with a red devil's mask raises his auction number.

"What the feck?" My heart races, and my feet are moving of

their own accord, my hand on the weapon at my holster.

What are they bidding on?

"Five hundred," someone else calls.

And the numbers keep rising until they reach a million.

I grab the arm of one of the men standing beside a woman. "What is this?"

His mouth twitches and so does hers. "Auction. You can buy their virginity."

FECK!

She can't be doing this! I won't bloody allow it.

A vein throbs in my neck, my fist curling at my side as I walk toward the center of the room between the two sections of seats. And that's when she sees me.

But she has no idea who I am, does she? I'm a stranger yet again.

I won't be for long. I will not let her sell herself to anyone. Never. I'll maim and kill any bastard who thinks himself worthy of her.

My hand tightens around my weapon, heartbeats galloping in my throat. I know what would happen if I killed someone here. Konstantin would kill me.

But right now, I don't care if I live or die because I vowed to protect her, and this is what I must do.

"Three million dollars," a man with a deep Russian accent calls, and her audible gasp echoes.

He's not touching her. He won't even get the chance.

I prowl closer as he stands up, getting ready to claim her.

"Going once…"

I'm rushing toward the stage, hoping to cause a distraction and to reason with Konstantin somehow before I do something I can't take back.

My eyes land on hers, and I swear I want to rip my bloody mask off and tell her who I am. But I can't even think about that now. All I can do is concentrate on how to end this.

"Stop this shite!" I call, but besides a few passing glances, everyone ignores me.

She jerks back a step, body visibly trembling, and from my periphery, I find a few of the guards storming toward me.

"Going twice."

"Konstantin! You'd better put a stop to this!"

More people turn toward me, curious now that I've mentioned him.

But he never comes.

"Sold! To number 3762."

The rest happens in the blink of an eye.

The gun is out in seconds, and just as the winner starts toward the stage, my body roils with rage.

"Don't feckin' touch her!" A roar climbs out of my throat just as one of my bullets rips into the winner's head.

Screams erupt from the audience, and in the chaos, she stares at me, quivering.

"Devlin?"

Yeah, love. It's me.

TWENTY-THREE

ERIU

People start running toward the exits, in fear for their life as the man—no, not just any man, but Devlin—stands there with a gun in his hand.

Security locks the doors, not allowing anyone out, while my eyes never leave his.

It can't be him...

How could he not tell me? How could he pretend this whole time! The things he did to me...here!

I can't think straight.

"What have you done?" I whisper to him as his eyes connect with mine.

I know he can read lips. But he doesn't say anything in return, his body rocking with heavy breaths as men surround him, their guns pointed at his head.

At any moment, one of them could pull the trigger!

A door slams in the distance, heavy footsteps thundering, and the room starts to go quiet until a man I've already met, the owner of the club, stands on top of the stage.

Too close to me.

Esther grips my arm while my pulse thuds with harrowing speed. Whatever is about to happen won't be good for either of us.

The owner slips off his mask, not a care in the world that everyone can now see him. The hollows beneath his cheekbones deepen from the tension on his face.

"Oh, what a pity…" he tsks, staring down blankly at the dead, bleeding body. "I didn't expect so much excitement tonight, but here we are." He throws a hand in the air, his icy grin sending wafting terror down my spine. "You've created such a mess, my old friend."

The guards move on Devlin while he stares back at the boss who clutches a weapon at his side.

"Do you realize who you've killed?" The owner climbs down the steps of the stage and starts toward Devlin as the guests panic in his wake, moving as far away as possible, like they're parting the sea.

Not a pin drop can be heard except for the music coming from the rest of the club.

"Don't worry. We will clean this up for you. But you see…" He grabs the collar of Devlin's shirt, his chuckle a deadly sound. "Now you owe me three million dollars. And congratulations. You're now the proud owner of Eriu's virginity."

"Don't bloody do this," Devlin grits, pushing his hand off.

Do what?

My heart leaps into my throat. I just want to go home with Devlin!

"You're the one who came to *my* club and shot one of the

most powerful men in my circle." He releases his grip on Devlin, straightening the lapels of his suit jacket. "So, you see, now you're at my mercy, and you will do *exactly* what I say."

He reaches into his waistband and removes a gun before he points it right at me.

"Or you and the Irish princess die right here in front of all these people."

Women gasp. Some cry.

"You feckin' savage," Devlin growls, raising his weapon at the man.

"I'd be very careful where I was pointing that thing. Wouldn't want to give my men the wrong idea. Wouldn't be good for anyone, do you think?"

The boss lowers his hand, and I breathe a sigh when the gun is no longer ready to kill me. But we're screwed. Devlin must know that.

The owner glances around the room, at all the people in fear for their lives, and he grins. "Ladies and gentlemen, you must excuse this awful interruption. I promise to make it up to you, and we shall start right now. I think that will put us all in a good mood."

His tone is sinister, and my fear only grows.

"Our friend here has feelings for that woman on stage, the one who was about to sell her most prized possession. Now it's his." His laugh rakes at my skin. "And neither of them will be going anywhere until he claims it."

"What?" I peer at Esther, who shushes me.

What does he mean, claims it?

"I have decided to change the rules of the game, though. This one time, due to my friend's lack of manners…" He narrows his glare at Devlin. "You'll all get to watch as this beautiful girl's virginity is taken. Right here on stage."

"No!" I gasp, my body shaking, my feet backing off.

But Esther is there, snapping her fingers around my forearm, keeping me where I am.

"You're not going anywhere," she whisper-shouts. "You do as the boss says or you die."

"I—I can't do this," I cry.

"You don't have a choice." There's no compassion in her tone. She doesn't care.

No one here does. No one but Devlin.

"I'm not doing it." Devlin's eyes fill with rage. "You're gonna have to kill me, Konstantin."

Konstantin. Even his name sounds terrifying. I don't miss the fact that they know each other.

"If you insist," Konstantin muses. "But I will start with her, and I will make it brutal. So choose."

Then he's pointing the gun at me again, and tears well in my eyes, my breaths heaving.

"No!" I shake my head. "Please don't kill me!"

"Daragaya…" He gives me what one would describe as a tender look, but he's all devil. "I'm not the one killing you. He is." His attention snaps to Devlin. "You're in my fucking world now. So choose. Do what I said, or I kill you both."

"You're a feckin' sick bastard!" Devlin grits.

"I do enjoy the occasional compliment. But now is not the time." He inclines his chin, and his men grab Devlin. "My employees are bringing a sofa for your comfort. I cannot wait for the show."

A few seconds later, the curtains at the far end of the stage part as two men drag a blue velvet sofa out and place it in the center of the stage. One of them tosses a small box on top of it, and I can tell it's condoms.

My blood curdles. How will I do this? How can I?

My first time in front of all these people, and with Devlin? Oh my God. Everything is a mess.

"Let's go!" Konstantin howls, a vein popping in his temple.

The men shove Devlin forward, and even through the mask, I look at him, silently praying that we both make it out of here alive.

"Feck!" Devlin snaps, because he knows we don't have a choice.

Only a few feet remain between us, then he's climbing up the steps.

Konstantin jerks his head at Esther, and she disappears behind the stage.

"Eriu…" He takes my hands in his. "I'm so bloody sorry."

"It's okay," I whisper, slipping off my mask and dropping it at my feet. "I was going to do this anyway. It's better that it's with you."

My limbs tremble, and I fight to keep a brave face.

"I'm gonna do everything I can to shield you from the crowd. I promise." His knuckles dust over my cheek so tenderly, tears ache behind my eyes.

The room remains silent, and when I glance at the audience behind him, I find Konstantin sitting front and center. His arms are crossed over his well-built chest, his expression cunning as his eyes land on us.

Devlin drags me to the sofa, and I lower onto it, moving the box of condoms to the corner.

With a strain of his breath, his hands go to the mask, and he finally rips it off. And once I'm able to look into his eyes, tears fill mine.

I've waited for this moment for years, and now it's ruined.

"Don't cry, love. Your tears are enough to kill me." He tosses the mask onto the floor, his thumbs gently swiping under my eyes.

I nod as his lips fall to my forehead, remaining there, causing me to cry silently even more.

"You don't know how sorry I am." He holds my face between his palms. "But we don't have another option. He will kill us both."

"I know that. It's okay, Devlin."

He closes his eyes for a moment, kissing me on the forehead one last time before he pushes my body down and settles his large one over it. My legs instinctively circle his hips.

"This is not how your first time should be, mo stoirín."

My heart skips a beat.

He drags his knuckles across my jaw, dropping his mouth so close to mine, I can almost feel it. "But I promise to make it special for you. And I swear I won't let any of those bastards see an inch of you."

I nod, unable to fight my emotions, fight the tears, the humiliation of it all. Yet in my despair, there's some semblance of joy because I'm with Devlin, the man I've loved since forever.

He rips open the box of condoms and removes one, handing it to me while he reaches between our bodies and undoes his belt, his eyes never leaving mine.

"I don't deserve this," he whispers, groaning before he kisses me, like he can't stand the thought of not doing it.

Sharp palpitations grow in my chest. This is happening. This is finally happening.

"I don't deserve *you*." Raw emotions embed into the depths of his gaze. "I never have and I never will. And I'll always be sorry I'm taking this away from you. That you're not willingly giving it to me."

I shake my head, the back of my nose stinging as I place a hand over the stubble riding across his cheek.

"Don't you get it, Devlin?" My words are hushed, hoping that this conversation is solely between us. "You're the one I've always wanted to give myself to. I've hoped for this moment for so long, and now that it's here, I don't care how we got here. I just see you."

I push my mouth up to his, and I'm the one kissing him. And he lets me, staying still as I do, like he wants to feel it.

"You were always the one for me, Devlin McHale."

A low and approving growl vibrates against my mouth as he kisses me so hungrily, so full of passion and want, that I forget where we are. I forget what I did to get us there. All I know and want and feel is this man, the sensation of his touch, the embers that burn when we shine brightly together.

And in the end, isn't that what matters? Isn't that what people dream their whole lives to feel just once? And here I am, feeling it all.

He pitches back, heaving and breathless, his gaze a liquid pool of desire, of need, of unspoken longing. He's wanted this as much as I have.

"I'm scared," I confess on a throaty whisper.

"I know you are." He drops his lips to my forehead and drags a deep breath. "Don't be. You're always safe with me."

"I know that," I breathe. "I've always known that."

Slowly, I tug his pants and boxers down while he takes the condom from me, ripping off the wrapper with his teeth.

Those eyes, they steal every breath from my lungs, and I'd give up everything just to have him look at me this way all the time— like I'm his world.

His hardness presses into me there, and my core throbs for more, needing to feel full.

I force myself to forget where we are, focusing on his blue eyes instead, jutting my hips, wanting to feel his hard-on deeper.

He groans, dropping his forehead to mine. "You keep moving

like that and I'm gonna feck you so hard that we'll really put on a show."

My teeth sink around my lower lip as he discreetly slips into the condom.

He yanks my dress up between us, all the way to my hips, a finger stroking between my thighs.

I gasp from the zap of sensations, remembering the way he touched me not once, not twice, but *three* times before. I want to ask how he could lie to me, how he could pretend to be someone else, but that would be impossible at the moment. Not when all I need is to come.

His lips drop to the shell of my ear. "I think we need to discuss the importance of wearing panties, love."

He pushes his finger all the way inside me, my mouth widening from how good it feels. I let out a gasp as he adds another finger, and his teeth sink around my lobe.

"Gonna stretch you out a little first so you can take me better."

"Mm-hmm…" I pinch my eyes closed, not wanting all those people to hear me.

My God, they're still watching.

He takes one of my legs and pushes my foot down onto the floor, opening me up. The other remains pressed to his back, my heel digging into his behind.

His eyes bore into mine just as the crown of his cock dips into my entrance. I inhale sharply at the burning sensation, and he's not even inside.

"Don't worry, baby girl. I've got you." His hand lowers between our bodies, and I can feel him grab his erection. "Just look into my eyes and don't let go."

I nod, doing what he said.

"That's it. That's my good girl."

He works himself an inch inside and the throbbing pain rips through me. I grimace and hiss uncomfortably.

"Feck, I'm sorry." His anguish swallows his emotions, as though it's killing him to know I'm hurting.

"It's okay. Keep going." My lips flicker even as the stinging grows.

He's so thick, or maybe I'm too tight. Yet there's also this pleasure that's beginning to bloom.

His hand reaches between us, and his finger is there on my clit, slowly drawing circles.

I let out a moan, and my eyes round as I remember we aren't alone. I want to care, I really do, but it's impossible when he makes me feel so good.

"Will it hurt a lot more than this?"

"It could," he says, our eyes locked while he continues to touch me there, making this more palpable. He drops a kiss to the tip of my nose. "If you need to scream, bite into my shoulder, okay?"

I nod, unable to calm my racing pulse.

"Just do it," I pant. "Please. I can't take another second of waiting."

I'm scared, yet I want this so badly. I don't even care about the pain anymore.

He works himself in another inch as he continues to touch me there, and pain begins to morph into pleasure, like I'm floating.

Before I can think about whether he'll even fit, he thrusts inside me in one hard move. I let out a scream, biting into his shoulder, my body shaking from the feeling of pain and pleasure twining into one.

"You okay?" Concern lines his face, and I cup his cheek and nod.

"Keep going and don't stop."

"Are you sure?"

He sinks in deeper, and I feel myself stretch to accommodate his width.

"So good…" I stifle a moan. "Please…"

My fingernails rake his back; I need this man everywhere. He circles his hips, staring hungrily at my mouth before he slips out of me and slams back in.

Hard.

It still hurts, but it's less now, the feeling of pleasure overtaking me.

"More," I whimper.

He refuses to take his eyes off me, something carnal and possessive within them.

"I'm goin' straight to hell for this," he mutters, arousal coating his tone.

"Then take me with you."

With a deep-chested growl, he captures my mouth with his, kissing me with maddening passion, his body and mine as one as he pistons into me until every nerve ending I possess fires off.

I didn't think it was possible to ever feel this full, this wanted.

"So bloody tight," he rumbles, fingers fisting my hair as he pumps into me even faster, and I no longer much care about the pain.

His palm wraps around the side of my neck, thumb tipping up the underside of my jaw to kiss me deeper. His warm tongue sinks inside me, dancing with mine. I don't know if I'm even doing this right, but I don't seem to care, lost in the moment.

Lost in us.

His promise of being gentle is long gone as his hips pound into me, the sound of skin against skin echoing, his grunting desperate and masculine.

"You feel like bloody heaven," he rasps against my throat, kissing me there, my own cries of pleasure escaping past my lips.

This pulsating feeling grows inside my body, my limbs tingling, my core filling with a sensation I can't name. I've never felt anything like this. And I already can't wait to have more of it. More of him.

I moan against his mouth, no longer caring that a crowd of people is watching, that the man who made us do this is seeing me this way. That Karen is. That Adam is. It no longer matters at all.

He rams inside me, biting my lower lip, lips scorching down my chin before he takes my mouth again.

His thrusting increases and my moans are electrified, and he devours each one.

He wrenches back an inch, his lips drifting over my jaw. "I can feel you about to come, love. I can't wait to watch you give me what I've been dying for."

"Oh, God," I cry out, my back bowing, this feeling of something within me about to burst becoming stronger.

It's the same feeling I felt when he fingered me.

"Pleasepleaseplease…" I plead, not recognizing my own voice.

"You sound good beggin' for it. And I could listen to you beggin' for my cock all bloody night. But now I need you to come. Think you can do that for me, sweetheart?"

His finger returns to my clit, and he plays me so well, like he knows every inch of me. My body, my heart, my soul…all his, forever.

"Devlin!" I cry, as he coaxes me into the most powerful release.

I quiver and moan, and instead of kissing the sounds away, he gazes down with a fierce possessiveness. Like he wants the world to hear me.

"Beautiful," he whispers, his tempo unrelenting. "So beautiful and all mine. And the only thing I regret is this condom."

"Wha— Oh, God!"

He grabs a fistful of my hair and fucks me roughly. That sensation overtakes me again, growing until I'm whimpering his name.

"Devlin! Wha-what's happening?"

He chuckles under his breath. "Making you come one more time, mo stoirín."

"What does that mean? Mo stoirín? You…you always call me that."

He works my clit, using two fingers, rubbing me faster. And this time I'm more sensitive, needing the release badly.

"Yes, keep going!" I cry, forgetting my question already.

He groans, our eyes aligned, my heartbeats pounding right before I let go, screaming his name as he throws me over the edge.

Moments later, he's joining me.

Then reality sets in.

Crap.

TWENTY-FOUR

DEVLIN

O nce we're done, I can't stop staring at her. Can't believe I did that. Here of all places. But it was either that or Konstantin would kill us. There was no choice.

I slip out of her, hating that I can't stay inside her warmth. I reach over and toss the condom into the trash can they left us, then zip up before lowering her see-through dress.

Her arms are curled around her body as she sits there while I pull off my jacket.

"Put your arms through it. We don't have time to get your dress now."

She nods, her face tight like it's all just hit her. She nervously slides in one arm after another and tugs the lapels around herself. This jacket should be long enough to cover her entire body.

"Well, that was quite the show," Konstantin says, and she recoils instantly.

Of course Konstantin's voice ruins everything.

"May I say, that performance was even worth the death of my good friend."

He looks bloody pleased with himself. Now I have to pay this arsehole three million. Sure, I have the money, but I don't wanna give it to him. Don't have a choice, though, unless I want to wage war with the Marinovs.

I give Konstantin a hard stare.

His smile widens as he rises, glancing around to the audience before he begins to clap, and the people all hesitantly follow suit.

"Can we go now?" I grab Eriu's hand, and it trembles.

I hate that she's scared. That I couldn't protect her from this. Failed her again.

"Sure. You're more than welcome to go, but I expect the payment in full tomorrow." Konstantin says that so calmly, you'd almost think he doesn't care. "And you will get your portion, Ms. Quinn." He inclines his head toward her.

"Uh, yeah, okay," she whispers.

"Well, thank you for a fine evening," he tells us, then addresses the audience, glancing around the wide space. "The auction will continue. Everyone is welcome to stay and enjoy. I promise, my friend will not be shooting anyone else."

He chuckles, and some of the guests start nervously doing the same. Probably for the best. I think I once heard he stabbed a man in the eye when he didn't laugh at his joke.

He starts for the exit, and I pull Eriu to a stand.

"Come on, let's get the hell out of here. And you're *never* to come back. Do you understand me?"

She nods, her eyes glassy, face still flushed. My God, I wanna feck her all over again. Instead, I pull her down the steps and through the doors, leading us out of here. After pushing through closely sandwiched people, dancing and feckin', we're finally outside.

Welcome relief.

Hurrying off to my car, parked in the garage, I let her in first, strapping her seat belt.

A finger accidentally brushes over her breast, and her eyes snap to mine.

As soon as they do, she bites that bottom lip.

I groan. "Do you know how crazy you make me when you do that?"

Running my fingertips over her mouth, I release it with my thumb.

She doesn't stop staring, all innocent and beautiful. My maddening temptation. This is how sinners fall. And I've taken the highest leap down.

My heart thuds faster as I recall in vivid detail the way her body felt beneath mine, the way she sounded and cried my name as she came.

I drag in a long, shallow breath and close her door before rushing to my side and gunning the engine. I need to get her as far away from here as possible.

Minutes pass, and she still hasn't said a word except for the stolen glances and her trembling lips. I can tell she wants to talk. There is a lot to discuss.

"What is it, Eriu? What do you want to say?"

She presses two fingers into her temple, exhaling with frustration. "How could you not tell me you were the man in the mask?!"

Her brows tug and her eyes shimmer. I think the events of tonight are finally hitting her.

My palm clasps her upper thigh and I squeeze, just wanting my hands on her any way I can get it.

"How could you not tell me you let another man touch you, hmm?" My fingers climb up, and she bites on the corner of her mouth.

Lord have mercy on me.

"It was you anyway! You can't be mad."

"You overestimate my ability to be rational, baby girl."

She groans when my fingers slide up under her dress, pushing between her thighs, where she's still wet and warm.

"You had no idea it was me. So you did, in fact, let someone else touch you that way." I push my thumb in deeper, and she whimpers. "Bad girl."

"I…" She growls in frustration. "I just wanted to feel something for once in my life, and you were too damn stubborn to give it to me."

I flick her clit, and she cries out, dropping her head back.

"Feel that?" I smirk. "Don't appear to be stubborn right now, do I?"

"Keep doing that," she whispers, her fingers digging into the leather of her seat.

But instead, I drag my hand away, inhaling her scent on my fingertips.

"I think I'm good now." I curl that hand around the steering wheel.

"Not fair." She pouts, squeezing her thighs together.

I let out a chuckle. "You're lucky that's your only punishment."

"You're back to punishing me, huh?"

"Aye." I give her a hooded once-over, eyes back on the road. "You never seem to learn, though. Maybe I need to be harder on ya."

Her face flushes, and my grin widens. She's so damn adorable.

"You shoulda told me what you were planning. At the club."

If she'd confided in me, all of this could've been avoided. But now it's too late. I took her virginity. I have to make it right with her father.

"Like you should've told me you were the man in the mask!"

"You mean the man you let grope you like that!"

"We already established that was you!"

"Hell, woman, you didn't know that!"

She huffs and looks out the window.

"My God, Eriu, don't you fecking realize what you are to me?" My hand is back on her thigh, shoving the dress away so I can feel her soft skin. "You've always been mine, in my heart and in my mind, so you letting some stranger touch you like that...it makes me insane!" I tighten my grasp on her leg. "If you told me what you were planning, I would've—"

"You would've what?" She snickers. "Fucked me? Please, Devlin." Her laugh is cold. "You know you wouldn't have. You would've tried to convince me there was another way. You'd never want my dad to know what you did. Fucked his precious little daughter."

"Well, he's gonna know now, won't he?"

Her gaze narrows. "He doesn't have to know."

She's right. He doesn't, but it wouldn't be honorable to keep it from him.

"When your father comes back from his business trip..." I tell her. "I'm gonna talk to him about Mason, make him understand."

"He won't just take your word for it, and you know it. You'll need something more."

"I'm trying. Got one of Gio's friends looking into Mason for me."

She's back to staring out the window, like she's losing hope. I don't blame her. I can't imagine what she's going through.

"I promise…" I grab her jaw and force her to look at me, her eyes welling with bits of her broken soul. "You will not marry him."

Her lips thin into a barely there smile. "And how will that work? Will you marry me instead? Or should I wait for the next Mason?"

My exhale is heavy, the weight of it all crushing my damn heart.

"Don't you think I want to?!" I snap, pulling the car to a stop on the side of the road, the tires screeching in the darkness.

I grab the side of her throat, shifting myself closer. "Don't you think I've imagined being your husband? Imagined the way it'd feel to hear you tell me you love me?"

Her lips quiver, those broken eyes staring back at me.

"Since the moment I started to have feelings for you, everything changed for me…"

I release her seatbelt and grab her hips, throwing her on top of me. Both hands cup her face, our gazes boring, and I need her to feel it. Feel what she is to me and how hard it is to let her go.

A hand slides up her spine and sinks into her luscious hair, a hiss stemming from between my teeth when she moves her hips on top of me, trying to fix her position. But it only causes my cock to rub into her bare center.

Her mouth parts, and I pull her face closer, our lips stroking, heat rising from our breaths.

"I've wanted you more than I've ever wanted anything in my life. I don't know how to stop wanting you. But being with me is dangerous. I can't let anything happen to you."

"Don't think about that…" she whispers. "Just think about this."

Then she's kissing the corner of my mouth, unscrewing my head from all logic.

"Feck," I growl, arching my hips, needing inside her again, needing to make it all right somehow.

She shouldn't have lost her virginity that way. Her first time should've been special. She deserves special.

I pin her forehead to mine and let my lips kiss her slow, needing this woman again and again…

"Let's get you home."

She wrenches back. "Please stay with me. Don't leave me tonight."

My heart beats faster. "I won't leave you. I swear it. I'm taking you back to my place."

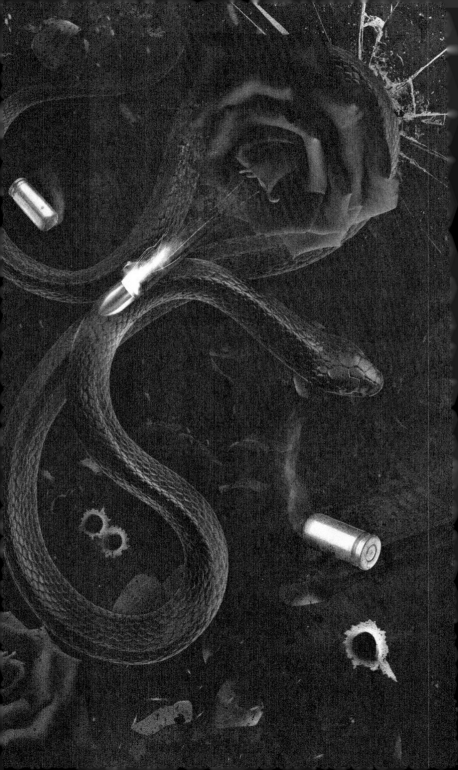

TWENTY-FIVE

ERIU

He closes the door of his apartment, and I follow him inside and to the kitchen, tugging his jacket to a close around me. Can't believe he brought me here. I can't stop grinning.

He opens the fridge and pours me a glass of water, bringing it to me. "Drink."

I take it from him, letting the ice-cold liquid douse the heat in my body, but I can't stop the flames he ignites, not when he's currently undoing his cuffs, pushing the sleeves up.

The thick veins from the top of his hand, running up his forearms, are enough to send me into a tailspin.

He's a beautiful man, and he admitted he wants me. Finally.

I never saw myself as anything special. Still don't. But somehow, the fact that someone who looks like him wants me... I don't know, it makes me feel beautiful.

"What are you thinkin' about over there?" He takes his glass of water to his mouth, and his thick throat bobs.

Even the way he drinks is attractive.

My eyes drop to his abdomen, and I try not to stare at the thick outline of his cock.

Oh my God, I can't believe that was inside me. It hurt. I can't deny that. I'm still in pain, but I loved every moment of it, knowing that it was Devlin and no one else.

I try not to focus on where it happened and who was watching. It'll only send me into straight panic.

I've already gotten ten worried texts from Karen. I told her I was safe and with Devlin, and that I don't want to talk about what happened. It's better to pretend it didn't happen the way it did.

"I was thinking…" I finally answer. "That I hope I'm done with this engagement now. If you can't convince my dad, then I'll tell Mason I'm no longer a virgin. I don't have to tell him it was with you."

A devilish smirk appears on his face. "Please do." He lowers the glass down on the counter and takes mine from my hands. "I'm not afraid to tell anyone what happened between us. We don't have to tell them where." He brushes my cheek with the back of his hand, his eyes locked with mine, causing my heart to tumble in my chest. "I wouldn't do that to you."

I nod, my mouth unable to form words when he's this close, his hands causing my skin to shiver.

His eyes turn heated, jaw clamping as his gaze sweeps down from my face to my thighs. "I don't know if I have anything for you to wear to bed besides one of my t-shirts."

"I can live with that," I breathe, my heartbeats echoing in my ears.

"Me too." He drags a long pull of air. "I like the thought of you in my clothes. My home."

He grunts under his breath, and if I wasn't already about to combust, this would do it. He's looking at me like he wants to repeat what happened at the club.

"Feck…" he mutters, grabbing the back of his neck.

"What is it?"

"If I tell you, you'll think me an animal."

"No I won't." I grab his wrist, my fingers barely able to close.

"You still sore, love? Because my God, I wanna punish every inch of you for driving me crazy, for being reckless, for letting someone you thought wasn't me touch you."

My eyes pop.

With a deep, throaty chuckle, he grabs a fistful of my hair and brings my face right up to his, stroking my lips with his mouth. "I wanna rip this flimsy dress to shreds, throw you on my lap and spank the holy hell out of this gorgeous arse you've been hiding from me."

I gasp.

"Mm-hmm, that's right." He grasps my jaw and runs a thumb over my lips. "Then I'd feck you and use your body all night. And I wouldn't hold back. 'Cause I already know how well you can take me."

My chest heaves, my core throbbing, begging for everything he just described.

With a quick jerk, he snaps my head back, his mouth sinking over the pulse beating frantically beneath my neck.

"Now that I've had a taste, I can't share you."

I don't know what that means. Has he changed his mind about marrying me? Or does he just mean sex? I'm afraid to seek clarification, fearing that whatever is happening will end.

From beneath the jacket, he clutches a handful of my behind, tugging me against his hard body. I yelp, then moan as he massages me there.

"This is mine." He slaps my ass cheek hard, and I whimper from the aching pleasure.

His heated gaze roves down to my lips, and my pulse skyrockets.

"How about I run you a bath?" Knuckles drag down my cheeks, making my skin prickle.

"That sounds nice."

Especially if you joined me.

But I don't tell him that last part.

"I'll go and start it for you."

I nod as he presses a kiss to my forehead, clutching my face in both hands, and I feel safe every time he does this.

With a sigh, he hurries off upstairs and I hear the running water within seconds.

A knot grows in my stomach and tightens until it's hard to breathe. I want to do something, but I'm so nervous and I don't have much time to decide if I will. What if he thinks it's silly? I'd die if he laughed.

But I told myself that I wanted to be braver, more like Karen, so I have to do this. It won't be like the last time. Things are different now.

My pulse hikes as I register his heavy footsteps coming back, starting for the stairs.

Before I can change my mind, I slip out of his jacket, then slide the dress from over my head until I'm in nothing but my jeweled pasties.

"Okay, the bath is—" The words instantly die in his throat.

He's definitely not laughing. The hooded perusal of his gaze has my entire body convulsing.

I don't even use my hands to hide myself, wanting exactly this:

his tongue raking over his lips, his eyes hungry for me.

"Jesus Christ, baby…" His low, gravelly voice greets me. "You're beautiful."

He stalks closer, and everything in me grows tight and needy.

"What are you saying to me right now?" His fingers trace down my sternum, and my nipples pebble in their wake.

"That I'm yours. You can do whatever you want with me."

He stares up at the heavens and mutters, "A Thiarna dean tròcaire orm."

I don't know what he said, but it sounded like he was pleading.

And this time, when he gazes at me, something shifts in his eyes, unspoken intensity within them. "Anything I want?"

I nod, swallowing the lump in my throat.

A delicious smirk crawls up to his mouth.

He reaches for my breasts, ripping off each covering, pinching my nipple and pulling it enough to send a zap into my core.

"Oh, God…" I throw my head back.

"You like that."

"Yes… I can feel it there."

"Where, love?"

He does the same thing to my other nipple, and I moan and pinch my thighs together, shameless throbbing there, needing him to take it away.

"Come on, don't be shy…" He kneads my breast, tugging my chin up to meet his height. "Tell me where you feel it when I do this…"

He pulls harder, and I swear I'll collapse.

"I wanna hear you say it. I wanna hear my innocent girl tell me all the dirty things she likes. Say it, Eriu."

Before I can utter a single word, his lips wrap around my beaded flesh, sucking and biting lightly as my hands sink into his hair, whimpering with need.

He pops a nipple out of his mouth and heatedly gazes up, and I know he's waiting for me to say it.

"My…my pussy. I feel it there every time you do that."

"Good girl," he growls, sucking on my other breast before he lifts me in the air, my legs wrapping around his hips.

He carries me to the island and places me on top of it, staring intently as he grabs behind my knees and spreads me open,

Placing the backs of my calves over his shoulders, he husks, "I can't wait to get a taste of this."

A finger lazily slides between my wetness, brushing over my clit.

My body bucks, hips arching. "Yes!"

His deep rumbling laughter makes it harder to breathe.

"This is such a beautiful pussy. Pink and wet and all feckin' mine."

Then his mouth is on it, and my brazen moans grow louder as he sucks and nibbles and makes my body climb. His own erotic sounds vibrate around me, making everything intense. It feels so good, all I can think about is my release. His gaze meets mine, and slowly, he slips a finger inside me, thrusting all the way in.

I couldn't tear my eyes from his if I tried.

His tongue swirls around me, torturing me, stars erupting before my eyes like a myriad of tiny embers burning brightly.

"Oh God, yes, please!" My hand reaches for his hair, and I grip and pull, making the masculine sounds from his throat turn raspier.

I can sense it happening, that feeling of needing to explode, and it's like he knows it too, ramming deeper until the need slams higher.

And I fall.

"Yes, Devlin! Oh God, yes!"

My body bows, my fingernails raking his back, his scalp, whatever I can touch.

"Mm-hmm," he hums, sucking me into his mouth and only slowing a fraction when my body ebbs and flows.

Those lips fall to the inside of my thigh and he kisses me there, squeezing my hips with both hands.

I wither on the counter, breathing heavy, slapping my arm over my forehead. "Wow."

He laughs. "That's right, wow."

I don't even have the energy to look at him, but he's there, lifting my naked and satiated body into his arms.

His smug grin causes me to smile. I run the back of my hand over his jaw, my heart full and happy. When have I ever been this happy before?

He leans in and kisses me, his tongue lazily rolling with mine. I follow his lead, tasting myself on him, and it's equal parts dirty and hot.

"Gonna carry you to the bath now and take my time washing you."

"What?"

Heat floods my cheeks, which makes no sense, because the man just saw me naked and did *that* to me in his kitchen. What's the difference if he washes me?

But something about this is different. It's more personal.

"You heard me." That smirk widens. "Got you all messy, and it's my job to clean you up."

"Okay." I nuzzle my face into his cheek, his heartbeats rapping wildly in his ribs.

He carries me up the stairs while my arms cling around his neck.

One look into his eyes, and I know he's happy too. I don't think

I've ever seen Devlin this happy, and my body warms knowing it's because of me.

He opens the bathroom door and walks us in, placing me on my feet. The steam is thick in the air, the water still running.

"Get in." He gestures with a jerk of his head while he starts unbuttoning his shirt, staring heatedly at me.

Swallowing nervously, I step in with one foot, the water warm and intoxicating, smelling a little like roses. I follow the rest of the way and slowly sink into it.

"I didn't have any bubbles." The corner of his mouth lifts in a lopsided grin that makes the butterflies surge in my stomach.

"It smells nice." My lashes grow heavy, arousal building in every inch of my body as I continue to watch this beautiful man strip.

He meets my gaze with equal fervor, doesn't even blink as he tugs the sleeves off, his abs contracting, the sneak of that deep V so insanely sexy, my mind goes blank.

"I got the shampoo you use."

He points behind me, and I see it then. On the corner of the tub is the same exact brand that I keep at school.

My eyes widen and I hike a brow. "Care to explain?"

"That my obsession with you is reaching a point of no return?"

"You're obsessed with me?" All the air stills in my lungs.

"To the point I'd smell this damn thing just to feel you close."

I swallow thickly, my teeth sinking around the corner of my bottom lip.

"You like that, don't you? You like that I've wanted you? Thought about fecking you all the damn time? Jerked myself off to thoughts of your sinful body?"

"Oh, God…"

Just breathe.

"Touch yourself." He grunts low in his chest.

"What?" I jerk, splashes of water escaping out of the tub. "I've never…"

"I know." He starts on the button of his slacks. "I want all your firsts to be with me. So come on now, slip those fingers inside you while I watch."

His possessive stare cruises down my body, and from beneath the water, he can see every inch of me.

The way he's looking, it's making me wanton and crazed, and even a little bit brave.

And I do it.

My fingers play between my breasts, gliding down my belly button, lower until I'm right where he wants me to be.

With a tip of a finger, I fondle myself, leaning my head back against the tub from the sensitivity still present in my clit.

"Eyes on me. Only me," he demands.

And I obey. 'Cause I want to. I want to give him everything.

"That's it, baby, keep going," he murmurs as he slides down the zipper of his trousers, pushing the pants down his thighs, along with his boxers, until his thick and hard cock juts out.

He takes it in his hand and strokes lazily as he watches me.

Desire unfurls within me, growing tumultuous as I watch him in return.

I push a fingertip inside me, bucking around it, dragging it out to roll it around my clit once more.

There's a tightening in my gut, a needy sensation I've come to know.

My eyelids flutter, the need climbing, my legs growing weaker. It's then he steps into the bath with me, and I gasp, freezing in place.

"Don't stop," his voice howls as he easily moves me enough to fit himself behind me.

With a rough hand, he grabs my hair, and his other slips between my fingers, coaxing me to finish what I started.

"Devlin…" I cry as he forces my finger back inside me. "Oh, God!"

"Now, don't go saying my name like that, love. I'm bound to feck you if you do, sore or not."

"Please, please touch me…" I whimper, needing him badly.

"You begging like that…feck."

He fists my hair tighter, dragging my head back until it's against his chest, those sapphire irises locking with mine.

Two fingers stroke my clit from both sides, and I lose all ability to speak. The sensations make my head spin, my body buck.

"Yes, yes, oh God!"

His fingers hasten, my moans escaping in gasping successions.

"Devlin…pleaseplease…I need to come so badly!"

He growls low against my ear. "Told you not to say my name like that."

And in an instant, fingers ram inside me so deep, I think he's reached the very depth of me.

"Oh, God!" I scream, my body spasming like it's trying to escape this feeling, yet wanting it all at the same time.

"You're gonna take it," he groans. "And you're gonna come. Then I'm gonna slam you on my cock until you come again. Until I tell you to stop."

He's saying words, but my mind isn't fully grasping that he's talking to me like that. It's all surreal, and before I know it, I'm screaming his name.

"Devlin! Yesyesyes!"

Every nerve ending in my body is crying out in mind-bending pleasure.

With a quick move, he flips me on top of him, throwing my legs on either side of him and smashing his lips to mine.

He kisses me like he's been possessed by the devil himself, and I've never wanted to go to hell as much as I do right now. I'd welcome the fire and burn at the stake just to have this man kiss me and fuck me the way he just did.

He clasps my nape, deepening our connection, gripping my hair beneath his fingers.

This passion, it's unbending, untethered by reality and rules and family alliances.

Right here, right now, we're just Eriu and Devlin, wanting and breathing in one another, as though our souls have forever been one.

The head of his erection nudges into my entrance, and he grunts, snapping my head back. "I'm not capable of being gentle right now. So this is your only chance to say no."

"Not in your dreams, McHale." I rock myself against his thick erection, wanting the pain and pleasure, wanting it all.

"I should've gotten a condom, mo stoirín."

"I'm on the pill. And those words, tell me what it means. Please."

A smile plays on his lips, his knuckles softly brushing down my face. "It means my little darling. 'Cause that's what you are."

Tears prickle my eyes, my heart aching not from sadness, but from pure joy.

He drags my face closer, pinning my forehead to his, and with his other hand, he guides himself to my entrance. "This is gonna hurt."

"Then make it hurt."

Without waiting another moment, he thrusts inside me with one quick move and swallows my scream with a brutal kiss.

Raw pain ignites, and I whimper, needing the pleasure to return.

"Shite." He pushes himself back, concern stitching up his eyes. "I'm sorry, love. I got carried away."

I shake my head. "It's okay. I want this." I bring his hand to my mouth and kiss the center of his palm. "I want you, Devlin. So please move and make me feel good. Make me come."

He nuzzles his mouth with mine and groans. "Keep talkin' like that and you're gonna have me blow a load before I've had my fill of you."

He circles his hips, and my spine curves.

"This is our first time," he says, placing a palm at the center of my chest, his eyes drowning with affection. "Right here. Together. This is our first time."

"Yes…" I cry out. "Our first time."

His chest rumbles with satisfaction.

I lower my mouth to his and kiss him slow, and that overwhelming feeling inside me returns—the desire, the need.

"I'll go slow and increase the pace once you get more used to my size."

I nod as he thrusts deeper, gaze leveled to mine as he bounces my body, sliding out all the way, then ramming me back down.

"Oh my God!"

He pumps me faster when he sees how much I like it. "This tight little cunt has been mine all this time, hasn't it?"

"Yes, all yours." My breathing hitches. "Always been yours."

His groans are ragged and gravelly against my lips.

My hands slide into his long, wet hair and I hold on with every fiber even while my body climbs, while he reaches between our slick flesh and plays with my clit.

He pummels deeper, the water making a mess of the floor. He's unable to peel his eyes from me, like he wants to watch my every move, my every reaction.

"Devlin, yes! Don't stop!" My orgasm starts to crest, and it's all I can think about.

"Come on now, let me feel this perfect greedy pussy come."

I wrap my arms around his neck while rough hands clutch my hips, fingers biting into my slick skin as he fucks me roughly, the pain now a distant memory.

My legs tremble, and within seconds, I fall, screaming his name, pulling on his hair, fingernails scoring his back.

"Yes! Yes! Oh God, Devlin!" I moan over and over.

"That's it, take every inch. Wish you could see how beautiful you look taking all of me."

His dirty words egg me on, the release never ending.

He grabs my hair and captures my mouth, pumping into me until with a deafening grunt, he releases inside me.

Draped in each other's arms, we hold on to something we may never have.

Because when has life ever been fair for a girl like me?

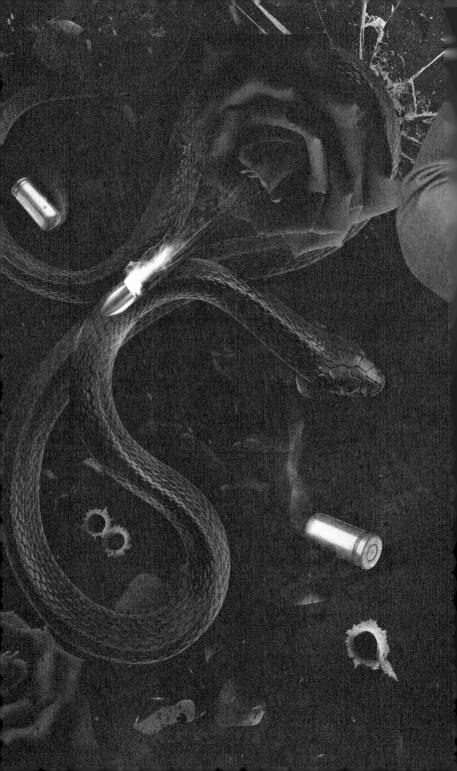

TWENTY-SIX

DEVLIN

I swear I didn't intend to feck her when I brought her to my place, but it was bound to happen. I can't fight her anymore. Not after the club. Not after everything.

Eriu will be mine. It's a matter of time. I just have to play things right. Talk to Patrick, then figure out the threat against her.

But she'll always be in danger from one person or another for the rest of her life. I can't let that stop me from being with her anymore. I won't do it. I won't give her up.

Patrick will have to understand what she means to me. I'll make him understand.

She draws circles on my bare chest, peering up at me beneath a fan of thick dark lashes. And all I can do is smile down at her, my arm around her back, palm on that perfect arse. She's in my shirt, but completely bare under it, just the way I want her.

"How did you know I was at the club?" she asks. "Did you

follow me each time?"

"Aye. I'm always watching."

She props herself on her elbow. "Oh my God, are you tracking Karen's car?"

She's smart. Of course she is.

I nod. "Been tracking her car since you started being friends with her. Think I was gonna let you drug me again and disappear?"

My palm wraps around her nape and I bring her lips to mine and kiss her once slowly, dragging my tongue around the seam of her mouth.

"I promise not to drug you again," she husks with feminine laughter.

"That really doesn't make me feel any better." My chuckling feels foreign as I flip her beneath me and stare down at this beautiful creature who wants me.

It's strange, you know, to have someone want you. Need you. I've never had that before.

I slide an arm under her and tug her to me, holding her tight, hoping she doesn't vanish right before my eyes.

I inhale her scent, and it always brings me a sense of peace. It smells like home, a future I was never good enough to have.

"You okay?" she asks sweetly, stealing my heart all over again.

She gently lays her palm over my cheek, and I burrow into it, needing it like a lifeline.

"I am now."

"Want to talk about it?"

I release a heavy sigh and flip onto my back, taking her against my chest. My attention lands on the ceiling as my fingers slip under the shirt and brush up and down her spine.

"I wasn't a good person, Eriu, even before I joined Palmer's crew. I'm still not. But back then, I had a family. A brother, my parents." I take a momentary pause. "They loved me, you know? Until they didn't. Until I was more of a burden than a son."

Her arms clutch around my torso reassuringly, as though saying she doesn't see me that way. I don't know if that's good or bad, because she's either in denial or she really can accept me the way I am.

I force myself to continue. "I was hurting people back in Ireland. Killing them for unpaid debts, for other things they were doing that went against the people I worked for."

I pinch the bridge of my nose, hating that I'm telling her this shite. But she has to know everything about me before she decides that I'm going to be her husband and the father of her children.

"I killed my first man when I was fifteen. It was scary, but the more I did it, the easier it became, until killing people was just a job I did. It didn't matter if they had families, kids. If I was told they needed to go, I did it, and I was good at it. Still am." I glance at her saddened expression, and my heart sinks. "It's why your father recruited me after I left the gang I was with in California."

"How long were you there?"

"About two years before your father came calling. I knew who he was, who his dad was back in Ireland. They were powerful, and I needed something new."

Her fingers drag over my chest as she listens intently.

"Before I came to California with my brother at twenty-one, my mum kicked me out of the house when I turned eighteen. She wasn't a bad person. Neither was Da. But they had become tired of me. They knew I'd never change. They weren't wrong. My ma told me I'd never find a proper woman to love me, but I was okay with that. I didn't need love."

"Oh, Devlin." Her eyes shine with tears as she tucks her chin in her palm. "You deserve love. You *are* loved. I love you! I always have."

An ache I've never felt slams into the center of my chest.

"Again," I breathe. "Say it again."

"I love you, Devlin McHale. And I'm never gonna stop."

I fight my emotions, my throat growing thick. "I don't deserve it. People like me, they don't deserve it."

"That's not true. Everyone deserves love. Everyone is worthy of it."

"When you say it like that, I somehow want to believe it's true."

With the back of my hand, I stroke the span of her jaw, wanting to say those words I know she's desperately wanting me to say in return.

But I want to save them. The first time I tell her I love her, I want her to be my wife. A McHale. Not a moment before.

Then I kiss her, her body melting into mine, and I grasp on to the hope that maybe she's right. That maybe, beneath the sinner, there's someone worthy of loving.

My phone vibrates while she's fast asleep, and I slip out of the bed so as not to wake her, gently removing my arm from underneath her hips.

When I find Grant's name on the screen, my pulse surges. Hopefully he's got dirt on Mason. The more I have on that bastard, the better my conversation with Patrick will go. He comes home tonight, and I intend to drive to Boston tomorrow and have that chat that we should've had a while ago.

When I make it to the kitchen, I answer. "What do you have for me?"

"Hey, so I dived into a few of his offshore accounts. The ones your people probably didn't find because he did a hell of a job hiding them under multiple shell corporations."

"And?"

"Someone is paying him weekly, fifty large."

"When did it start?"

"A little less than a month ago."

"You sure? Nothing before?"

"No."

"What else?"

"I tried finding out who's paying him, but it's untraceable. And you know I've tried everything. Whoever it is really doesn't want to be found."

"Shite."

"The account is coming from the Bahamas. But when I trace it, it jumps to another account, then another, all in different locations, then jumps back to the Bahamas. I'll send you all the info I have so far, but I'll continue looking." There's a tapping sound, like he's pressing some keys on a laptop. "There's one last thing. One of the accounts has a name."

"What is it?"

"Camora. Does that mean anything?"

All the blood rushes from my body. "You sure that's the name?"

"Yeah. It means something, doesn't it?"

"Yeah, bloody does. Keep looking and send me that info."

"Already in your email. Talk soon."

"Aye."

It's like they wanted me to find it. Like they knew if I did, I'd know it was them. Francis Palmer is alive. There's no doubt in my mind, and now I know he's been paying Mason. And it all began when he met Eriu...

Now, I know for certain Francis was the one who blew up the car and sent her that note. He will pay for it all.

My rage surges, my blood pumping loudly in my ears. "Son of a bitch!"

Mason is in with them. But how? Why? It doesn't make sense. Why would he need money? Is it for gambling? Greed?

I need to find out everything. He's going to squeal like a pig when I'm through. I just need someone watching Eriu while I do what must be done.

I think back on that name. Camora.

She was only one, maybe younger, when I killed her parents and left her wailing in the crib. She became orphaned, thrown into the system 'cause of me. They were the last two people I murdered for the Palmers before they killed my brother.

I'll destroy every one of them for trying to hurt Eriu.

The time has come for me to end this once and for all.

ERIU

I stretch my limbs, yawning with the biggest grin on my face, remembering every sordid detail of last night.

There's a throbbing between my thighs, but I enjoy every second of it, knowing why.

Rolling over, I no longer see Devlin lying beside me. His space is cold and empty. My eyes pop open, and I sit up immediately.

The clock on the wall reads seven in the morning. Where could he be this early?

As I swing my feet over, my eyes flick toward the nightstand, noticing a note there.

Picking it up, I find that it's from Devlin.

Hey, love. I had to go to a meeting. But I've got

Rogue watching you. Don't go anywhere. He's been instructed to keep watch and not to let you leave. Don't ask me why. I'll explain once I figure everything out. I miss you.

Devlin

He's drawn a trinity knot after his name, like the ones I drew when I wrote him letters in prison. I clasp the note against my chest, grinning like a fool, my heart flipping in my chest. That means more to me than he realizes. *And* he just admitted he misses me! Never in my wildest dreams did I think this was possible.

Of course, I'm gonna ignore the fact that I'm a prisoner in his beautiful apartment. But Devlin wouldn't keep me here unless it was for my own safety.

Needing a shower, I slip out of his shirt and head for the master bath, turning on the water and getting inside, the steam coating the prickles on my arms from the chill in the air. I grab my shampoo, pour some onto my palm, and lather my strands before washing my body and rinsing off completely.

Drying off, I roll a towel around my head before throwing on one of his shirts, then using his blow-dryer to dry my hair.

Not knowing what else to do, I return to the bedroom and open some of his drawers, finding everything neatly folded. I didn't expect Devlin to be messy. He's one of those kinds of guys, like military types, except as far as I know he's never been in one.

When I open another drawer, there's a piece of paper sticking out of the corner. Being nosy, I reach inside and grab it, finding a stack of papers.

As I unfold them, I realize they're the letters I wrote to him while he was in prison.

He kept them all. A sting creeps behind my eyes. That means so much to me.

I place them back where I found them, but when I do, I realize I missed two photos that lay hidden underneath.

I stare at a smiling Devlin, maybe twelve, with a younger version of himself. That must be his brother.

Emotions plague my vision at the thought of what he must've felt when he lost him.

The other photo is of a family, Devlin and his brother, and an older couple, who I presume to be his parents. They all look so happy. Devlin has his father's face, but his mother's eyes.

How could she give up on him? How could she throw him out the way she did? He was just a child. My heart breaks for all of them.

With a mournful sigh, I return the photos back inside and decide that's enough snooping for today.

My phone vibrates on the nightstand, and I rush back, hoping it's Devlin. But it's only Karen. Ugh, crap. She's gonna wanna talk.

KAREN

Are you okay?! CALL ME!

I plop down onto the bed. Might as well just get it over with. With a press of a button, the phone rings.

"Oh my God!" she exclaims. "I've been up all night thinking of you. Are you okay? That was insane!"

"I'm fine. I guess. I mean, as fine as can be, but I won't have to marry Mason anymore, so there's that."

She laughs. "Yes, that *is* the best news ever. Are you still with Devlin?"

"Yeah…"

"Ooh, did anything more happen? Did he confess his undying love for you yet?"

"Kinda." My mouth spreads. "But we have a lot to figure out first."

"I bet you do. But I saw the way he fucked you last night. I mean, I know it was in front of a shitload of people, but holy hell, I wanna be fucked like that. But I am sorry it happened that way for you."

"It's okay. It was my decision. I just hope my father never finds out."

"Why would he?"

"Mason threatened me the other day." I blow a breath. "He had us followed. He saw where we were going, but he didn't know what the place was."

She gasps. "Fuck! I hate that asshole!"

"Hopefully he's out of my life forever now."

"He'd better be."

"I'll see you tomorrow?"

"I have nowhere else to be. Maybe I'll get lunch with Kayla, since you're clearly busy fucking your new man." She giggles.

"Oh my God, shut up!" I snort. "Don't tell Kayla anything. I'll tell her on my own."

"I can't keep this to myself! You have to call her before I see her. I'm bound to slip."

I grumble. "Figured as much."

"You know me too well."

"You're a pain in my behind! But I love you. Talk to you later."

"Love you, bitch!"

As soon as the conversation ends, I call Kayla. Hopefully, she isn't too disappointed I went through with it.

"Hey!" Her cheery voice shines through.

"You're too happy for someone up this early." I pull the comforter over my shoulders, smelling Devlin, and my entire body tingles.

"I've been up since five, actually. Had a great session with my boxing coach, and now I'm heading to Helping Hand to assist Jade with the center."

Helping Hand is a center her friend Jade started for trafficked women and children, and it has grown to multiple locations. She's a hero. The things she's provided for these people are beautiful.

"Wow, you're too productive on a Sunday."

She laughs. "What's up? You never call this early."

I hesitate, nerves settling in my gut. "I have to tell you something."

"Okay... Do I need to kill anyone?"

I let out a laugh. Kayla, kill someone? I'd pay to see that! She's the sweetest, kindest person I know. She couldn't hurt a fly, let alone take a life.

"No, not necessary. But remember the auction I mentioned?"

"Oh my God, you did it!" Her voice shrieks.

"Well, yes and no..."

Then I tell her what happened last night, how Devlin saved me and killed someone in the process, and what he had to do to save us both.

"Holy shit," she whispers. "I'm happy for you?" A nervous laugh bubbles out of her. "I mean, I'm glad it was Devlin of all people, but wow."

"I know. I'm so scared my dad will find out. He'll be furious and he'll probably wanna kill Devlin for doing what he did. But he really didn't have a choice."

"Your father loves Devlin. He won't kill him. I mean, yes, he'll be angry, but he'll get over it."

"Spoken like someone who's only met my dad in small doses."

"It'll be okay, Eriu. You'll see."

"I'm gonna have to confront Mason and tell him what I did."

"Not by yourself, you're not!"

"No, of course not. I'll be with Devlin."

"Good." She releases a heavy exhale. "I love you, Eriu. You're a good person, and that's rare to find."

"You too, Kayla. I'm so glad you decided to come to college here."

"Me too. I'm at the center now, but call me if you need anything. Anything at all."

"I will. Have a good day."

"You too." I hang up and try to take a nap, my eyes heavy.

With a smile plastered on my face, I scoot to Devlin's side. Gripping his pillow, I close my eyes and let sleep call me.

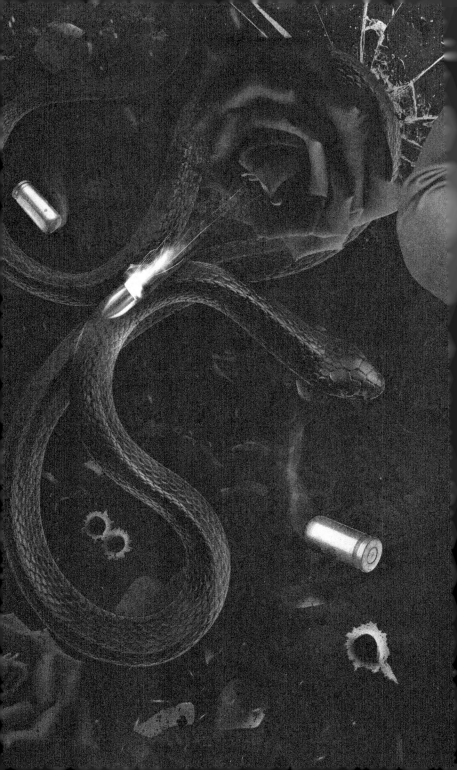

TWENTY-SEVEN

DEVLIN

I hated leaving her with Rogue. But if push comes to shove, I know he would put her life before his, and that's what matters.

Tynan told me Patrick was back, and I wanted to speak to him in person. This is a face-to-face type of conversation.

Parking in one of the garages at Patrick's estate, I grab my cell and check on a recent bank transaction. Three million dollars has been successfully sent from one of my offshore accounts into Konstantin's. I already paid him the five K I owed him for the membership. At least that shite is over with.

Getting out of my car, I head up the cobble steps, and the doors immediately open, two guards stationed on both sides greeting me with a tilt of their heads.

The smell of garlic and tomatoes permeates my nostrils. It's either Patrick cooking or one of his staff. The man is a damn good cook.

As soon as I head toward the stairs, up to his study, Tynan walks down and greets me.

He slaps a palm against my back. "He's waiting for you."

"Does he know what I'm here to say?"

"That you wanna marry my sister? Nah." Tynan smirks a fragment. "I thought the news would be best coming from you."

"Do you think he'll take it well?"

"I don't know. My father is…well, you know how he is." He shrugs. "You're on your own."

"Mm-hmm."

I don't know how Patrick will take the news. But I can't pretend that I can live without her anymore.

Heading up the stairs, I knock on the door, ready to get this over with.

"Come in," he says, reading through some papers on his desk.

The Quinns own a lot of property and businesses, most of them involving gambling. Patrick is constantly busy. But he's tired lately, and I think that's why he's pushing Tynan to marry. He wants his sons and daughters to pass his legacy on to the future generations.

"So, tell me…" He swivels back in the chair, eyes centered on me. "What did you have to discuss that was so urgent?"

Gripping the back of my neck, I figure out a place to start. "I can't let Eriu marry Mason."

"Oh? Why not?" He leans back in his swivel chair, rolling back and forth, brows set in a tense stare.

"Because…"

Just bloody say it, already.

He waits for me to continue, but my mouth won't move. No matter how many times I've rehearsed this shite in my head, it's not enough.

"I've never seen you look this terrified." Patrick laughs. "Just spit it out, son, or we'll be sitting here all damn day."

"Aye." I choke on an inhale and just blurt it out. "I can't let her marry him because I want to be the one to marry her. Sir."

Feckin' hell, I did it.

When his eyes widen and he freezes in the chair, I'm no longer sure if I should shut the hell up and leave or continue.

But I've gotta tell him how I feel. It's the only way.

"I know our age difference is big, and I know I've disappointed you in the past, failed her in the past. Feck, I've failed more people than I can count. But I love her, sir. I love her with all my heart and soul, and I need that to be enough. I need you to tell me that's enough. Because she's enough for me, and I wanna take care of her for the rest of my life."

At first, his mouth thins and thick brows tug, but then he breaks into a grin.

"Bloody finally!" He bangs a fist on the desk and shakes his head on a chuckle. "I've been waiting for you to man up and admit your feelings for my daughter since you got your arse out of prison."

"What? You knew? How?"

"You all must think I'm some idiot, not realizing when a man has feelings for my daughters. I mean, okay, fine…." He throws a hand in the air. "I was blind for a bit with Iseult and Gio, but they hid it well. You, on the other hand?" He snickers. "Son, I saw it the moment you stormed into my home, looking all bent out of shape after she was saved from the kidnapping. I saw it the moment you laid eyes on her. The relief. The love. I see it all. But I would never let my daughter marry a man who couldn't admit his own feelings. Because if you can't do that, how can you love her? So I was waiting patiently. Wanting to see what you'd do if she were to marry the likes of Mason feckin' Reynolds."

I almost collapse. But instead, I take a seat across from him, my elbows on my knees, unable to speak.

"You played us into believing she was gonna marry him?"

"Well, at first, I was considering it. For a second. The opportunity for our families was decent. But he was too much of a slimebag. Instead of telling his father the engagement was off, I let it continue. I needed you to finally man up and marry my daughter because there's no one in this world who can love and care for her the way you do. I know that in my gut. I just needed you to know that too."

Emotions punch in my throat, and I blink faster to hide it all, too consumed with it. He actually believes I'm right for her. That I, Devlin McHale, am right for his daughter.

"I have to admit, son, I was losing faith in you, but then I heard about poor Mason's accident." He smirks and shakes his head. "You know, the one where he lost his hand?"

"I have no idea what you're talking about, sir." The corner of my mouth jerks.

"Of course not." He feigns a serious expression.

"Mason, of course, told his father there was a burglary. The cameras were all conveniently disconnected too. No witnesses except good old Mason."

"How's he doing?" Mirth sets in my tone. "Must be terrible not to be able to use his right hand."

"Poor lad. Must've done something to deserve it."

"Aye." I glare. "He won't be touching my wife again."

"Again?" Patrick presses a fist to the edge of the desk, a glare tight on his face. "Bet your arse he won't. I shoulda killed him just for being a shite."

"It's over now." I nod. "But speaking of Mason, there's

something else you need to know."

I rehash the stuff with the Palmers, the name Camora found on the bank account, and its connection to Mason.

"How the hell did we miss this snake in the grass? What could he be up to with them?"

"I have no clue. Not yet. It might have something to do with Eriu. But Grant's still looking."

"What are we gonna do with him in the meantime?"

"Let's wait before we get rid of him. We tell him the marriage is off and see what he does and who he talks to, then we see if the money continues. I wanna catch Palmer. I want to kill him and his sons. And anyone who works for him. Until they stop coming."

Patrick angles in close. "I'm on board with that. I will make the call to Mason's father."

"No." I incline my chin. "How about I do the honors? I'll even bring him a *get well soon* card."

Patrick chuckles, shaking his head. "You crazy son of a bitch. Alright. Do it. Then tell me all about it."

"Aye." I start to rise, heading for the door.

"And, Devlin?" he calls, and I turn back to him.

"Yeah?"

"I always saw you as one of my sons. Now it's gonna be official."

Feckin' hell. I can't bloody cry in front of this man.

"Thank you."

"Does she know yet?"

"No, but I intend to go home after talking to that prick and tell her. But I was thinking, and maybe this is stupid, but can we have the wedding here? And maybe it can be a surprise?"

His eyes soften. "Well, I assumed you'd have it here. Of course. And the surprise? I like it! I'll speak to Fernanda. She's gonna have this place turned into a fancy wedding in a week. Think you can handle that?"

A week. Hell, what's a week when I'll get to spend the rest of my life with her?

"Yeah, I think I can."

"How are we gonna get her here and all dressed up?" he asks.

"I have no idea. But I'm thinkin' maybe Iseult can somehow help with that."

"Aye. My daughter has a creative imagination." He chuckles. "Man, I love weddings. Don't you?"

I shrug. "Never had a reason to. Not until now."

"Yeah, these women, they just have a way of doing that, don't they?"

"Thank you, sir."

"You don't have to thank me. I know you will do right by my daughter. You always have."

And I always will.

As soon as I get past Mason's security—again—and knock on his door, his eyes bug out. I almost feel sorry for him, standing there behind a flimsy glass door, trembling and backing away, holding out that one good hand, the other wrapped in thick gauze.

Nah, don't feel bad at all. He had it coming.

I fire a bullet into the doorknob, destroying the lock and stepping over one of his guards as I walk in.

"Hey, how's the hand?"

"P-please. I—I haven't called her! I haven't seen her. So get out!"

I shut the door behind me with my foot and lean against it. "How did you hurt your hand there?"

His brows snap, and he swallows thickly. "Burglary. That's what I said to everyone. I won't talk. I swear!"

"That's good. Wouldn't want whoever did that to come back and take more. It'd be a real shame to lose another fine hand. Don't you think?"

He starts crying, really crying. Ask me if I care.

"I came to tell you that Patrick is calling off the engagement. It's over. You're not to come near *my* wife, you understand me?"

"Your *what*?"

"You heard me. I'm marrying her."

He has the balls to laugh. "Oh man, I knew it! You wanted to fuck her the whole time, didn't you? I told her I had a feeling about you."

It's like he's asking for a bullet in his head.

"Did you fuck her already? Was she as tight as I imagined?"

That's it.

Feck it.

My tight fist lands square into his nose, and I swear I hear a crack.

"Shit!" he yells, holding on to it with his left hand, blood dripping in between his fingers.

With a dry chuckle, I open the door and start to head out.

"You seem to attract a lot of burglaries," I tell him over my shoulder. "I'd maybe switch up my security." I glance down at the dead guard. "Doesn't look like they do a good job."

I leave him behind, but I know I'll see him again soon, and he *will* tell me everything he knows about the Palmers.

Back in my car, I can't wait until I'm with her and she's in my arms. Just the thought of her lying in my bed, with my shirt on, does a whole lot of things to me. I never thought I'd have this: a woman like her, a life together. But it's right there, waiting for us.

When I put my phone on speaker, it rings as I head on the highway.

"What do you want?" Iseult answers in her usual polite tone.

"Hello to you too. I need a favor."

"What is it?"

"Promise not to ask too many questions?"

"I promise no such thing. Now tell me what you need."

"I'm gonna marry your sister in a week at your father's place, and we need to come up with a plan to get her all dressed up for it."

"Wait, WHAT?!"

I laugh at the shock in her voice.

"I don't understand what's happening exactly, but I approve. Good job, McHale. You finally got that stick out of your ass enough to see my sister has been crazy in love with you probably her whole life."

"Okay. Yeah, thanks. Now will you help me?"

"For Eriu? Of course I will. Leave it to me. I'm gonna have her looking like she's about to walk into her own wedding."

"Well…that's exactly what's happening."

"Whatever. Shut up." She snorts. "When a woman says she can help you, don't go pushing her buttons. But I have to know, how the hell did you convince my father?"

"Apparently he wasn't all that sold on Mason either. He's been waiting for me to tell him how I felt about her."

"Wow. Go Dad. I didn't think the old man had it in him to be this level of deceiving, but he is my father, after all. Oh, does Mason know yet? Please tell me he does and he's miserable."

"He's plenty miserable already. Did you not hear he lost a hand?"

"Keep going. This is getting exciting."

She's crazy, and it's why I like her. Iseult is one of the most skilled enforcers I have ever met. Sure, she's a little unhinged and has some anger issues here or there, but who doesn't? Her heart's always in the right place, and her love for her family and her sister is something to witness.

"Bastard had it coming."

"What did he do?"

"He put his hands on your sister."

"Excuse me? And he's still alive?! Are you fucking kidding me?"

"He won't be for long. Don't worry. But we need him alive for now. I found out he's being paid by the same people I was once connected to, so we're gonna have him followed to see what we can find."

"Fine." She huffs. "But you'd better make it quick, because he needs to go."

"Aye."

"Keep me informed. And promise me that when you do kill him, I get a front-row seat."

"Yes, ma'am."

"Ugh. Don't ever call me that."

"Fine, the devil it is."

"Now you're speaking my language. And, McHale?"

"Yeah?"

"You know what happens if you break my baby sister's heart, right?"

"Let me guess. You're gonna break mine."

"Yeah, but your heart is the last thing I'll break. Now that we've gotten that out of the way, congrats!"

"Yeah, thanks. A man has got to be crazy to have you as his

sister-in-law."

She laughs while my pulse beats faster, unsure if I can even pull this wedding off.

"Do you think my plan of surprising her is stupid?" I ask. "Because you can tell me, you know. You won't hurt my feelings. I mean, it's shite, right? Women don't like that? Ugh, I should just propose like a normal guy and let her plan a wedding and do all that girly crap."

She bursts with thick laughter. "Aww, nervous Devlin is adorable. I can see why she's in love with you."

"Shut up. I'm not adorable."

But she doesn't. She keeps laughing while I mutter a Gaelic curse under my breath.

When she finally stops laughing, she says, "No, the surprise isn't stupid. Eriu doesn't care about fancy weddings and all that stuff. She just wants you, and I think surprising her is gonna give her the biggest shock of her life. So, this is what we're gonna do…"

TWENTY-EIGHT

ERIU

Devlin called hours ago and said he's got news to talk to me about. Said he went to see my father. He didn't want to tell me more over the phone, but he should be back any minute now.

I switch between channels, trying to let the time go by faster. Did he finally convince my dad that Mason is a tool and I shouldn't be forced to marry him? That would be something. Would save me from confronting Mason. If I never see him again, that would be great.

As I put on a random TV show, the front door creaks, and in a flash, I'm off the bed and running toward him.

"Hey, baby…" His thick accent, that erotic look in his eyes when I jump into his arms, makes me feel like the luckiest woman on earth.

My legs tighten around his hips, my heels pressing into his ass.

"I've missed you." His voice drops into a seductive timbre, and arousal grows within me.

I lean down and kiss him once, and a growl rips out of him.

He fists my hair, his tongue invading my mouth as he backs me to the wall so he can kiss me deeper. My bare core rubs around his belt and I moan, needing more.

Breathlessly, he pitches back, hooded eyes raking every inch of my face, his palm cupping my cheek. My body warms, and I smile at him like he's the summer sun in the middle of winter, keeping me warm.

"Can you say that again?" I ask, pressing my cheek to his chest.

"I missed you, lass."

"Mm…" My flesh prickles. "I like how that sounds."

A moan slips out, and he pushes himself in between my thighs, a devilish grin fastening to his features. He holds me like I weigh nothing, working my hips on him as his gaze bores deeper.

"You're mine now. You're gonna hear it a lot."

The promise in his voice feels like he means it, that we can be together. His mouth latches on to my throat, and he kisses up to my jaw until his lips capture mine.

His groaning, the way he sucks my tongue into his… My God, I never knew how good it could be.

He pulls back and searches my eyes for seconds or minutes, I don't know, but I want it to last forever.

"I love you," he says, and my breath hitches.

"Wh-what?"

He laughs huskily. "You heard me. I love you with my whole heart, Eriu Quinn. I was waiting to say it after we were married, but I can't wait anymore."

"Oh my God… What?" My emotions slam into the back of my throat, and I kiss him with every passion in my being, my lips roughly moving with his. "Did you just say married?"

"Aye. It's exactly what I said, and I mean it. Once we figure things out and I get your father's permission, I plan to ask you if you'll be my wife."

The back of my nose stings, and tears fill the rims of my lower lashes. "Of course I'll say yes."

"You promise?" A hand sinks into the back of my head, his fingers slicing into my hair.

"With my whole heart."

With a grunt, he slams my lips to his and kisses me with fiery passion, my body blazing like the sun. He pushes our bodies deeper, moving us past the door. Every cell in my body needs this man.

Wrenching back breathlessly, his mouth glistens as he says, "I need you to hold on for me, love."

Before I can wonder why, he flips me upside down, and I yelp, my fingers grasping his thighs. He positions my legs over his shoulders and my pussy against his warm, enticing mouth.

"Mmm…" He grunts. "Been dreaming about you like this, taking your pink pussy into my mouth while your body trembles, unable to hold on."

"Oh my God, Devlin…" The heat of his mouth and the slow way it feathers over my clit has me jolting and begging. "Please! Please! Don't stop!"

I never knew I would beg for such things, but now it's all I wanna do.

"What do you need?" The tip of his tongue lazily swipes into my middle.

"I need to come… It hurts so bad…" I whimper, needing his tongue again.

His husky laughter vibrates into my center, making me throb

even more. "Greedy little thing, aren't you?"

The outline of his cock is thick and heavy. And I want to taste him too.

"Devlin, please, I can't take any more!"

"You won't have to."

Then his mouth latches on to my clit and he sucks, his tongue rolling there, flicking slow, then fast, bringing me to the edge and then back down.

"Oh God, yes!" My nails dig into his muscled thighs, my body trembling as the release makes its way closer.

The rush of heat permeates my veins, but he doesn't stop driving me wild. There's a tight coiling in my gut, the release so close I can taste it.

"Faster, please!"

I hold on tight, afraid I'll fall, but his hold on my calves is strong. He won't let me fall.

He groans, lapping and sucking until I'm there, screaming his name.

"Yes! Devlin, oh God!"

His own moans are deep and raspy, his expert tongue flicking faster. I jolt as he swipes me again and again before he slows, kissing up the insides of my thighs.

He flips me back, and my legs wrap around his hips as he takes my mouth, kissing me with a passion so intense, I don't know where I end and he begins.

Fingertips run up my spine, sinking into my hair like it's his favorite spot.

Roughly, he yanks me back. "We're supposed to be talking."

"We *are* talking." My teeth sink around my lower lip.

"Oh, hell. Don't bite your lip like that."

"Why not?" I hike a sassy brow.

"Because I'm gonna end up feckin' you before we have a chance to do more talking, and believe me, you're gonna like what I have to say."

"I bet I will…" I kiss along his jaw, his erection rubbing up against my center deliciously.

And a thought hits me…

Maybe I can give him what he gave me. Maybe he can teach me.

Hesitantly, I reach down, my pulse slamming in my ears as I curl a hand around his cock.

"Jesus Christ, baby…" He throws his head back and shuts his eyes. "What are you doing?"

My cheeks warm. "I want to learn how to do what you did to me."

His eyes bug out. I swear I have never seen them this way.

"Are you serious?" The disbelief in his tone is comical, and I stifle a laugh.

"Yes." Of course I'm nervous that I'm gonna somehow do it all wrong, but I wanna try. "Unless you think I'll be terrible at it. Which, in that case, maybe I shouldn't because, I mean, I wouldn't wanna embarrass myself and I—"

His jaw grits as he peers at me, his voice raspy as he says, "It'd be my honor to feck your pretty mouth, Ms. Quinn."

I'm not quite sure what just happened, but I think my heart may have stopped beating.

Nope, definitely did.

"Go on, then." He tucks my chin between two fingers. "Get on your knees and undo my belt."

I pant, my stomach tightening as he lowers me to the floor, and there's a fifty percent chance I may collapse.

Before I can change my mind, I drop to my knees and look up

at him, my nerve endings pulsating with desire and uncertainty.

His intense gaze meets my uneasy one, and I look straight instead, my jittery hands tugging his belt as I start to undo it. His breathing is heavy while the clasping sound of metal echoes through the room, inflating my already frazzled nerves.

"Look at me when you do that," he commands, capturing my hair and jerking my head back to meet his fiery stare—equal parts affection, desire, and dominance.

My God, I'll do anything he wants right now.

"That's it. Good girl. Keep going," he praises as the belt comes undone, the zipper sliding down.

With both hands, I grab his pants and boxers, dragging them down slowly, our eyes locked until his cock juts out, thick, hard, the veins practically ripping from within.

I can't believe that thing was actually inside me.

He must notice the feral attention I give it, because he chuckles. "Shall I remind you how well your pussy took me? Now let's see what your mouth can do."

Oh God, dirty-talking Devlin is even hotter than the broody one.

"What do I do first?" I breathe, my heart beating beyond control.

His smile treks up one side. "Wrap your hand around the bottom, like this…" He takes my wrist and curls my fingers around the base of his erection. "Now stroke up like this." He moves our hands up and down his shaft, from root to tip. "Jesus feckin' Christ. Just like that, but tighter." He cinches my grasp.

"I won't hurt you?"

"No, love. Do it just like I showed you. Then put your lips around the top and do as your hand just did. Suck it into your mouth and take as much of it as you can while keeping your hand wrapped tight."

I swallow the lump in my throat and nod.

He removes his hand from mine and clasps the back of my head instead.

"You may not be able to take all of me, not at first, but that's okay." He strokes my cheek with his knuckles. "Take your time and remember to breathe out of your nose. Don't want this to hurt you."

I drag in a silent breath, my insides quivering while I stare at his erection, not sure where I want to start.

"You don't have to if you don't want to." He tilts my chin to meet his eyes.

"I do want to. I'm just scared I'll do it wrong." My face heats up.

"Nothing you do would ever be wrong."

My heart skips a beat, and I drop my lips to the tip of his erection and plant a kiss there.

"Feck." He releases a groan, and his cock jerks.

I look up to make sure that was okay. Do girls do that? Or is this childish? I hate feeling like I don't know what I'm doing!

His brows furrow like he's in pain.

"Did I do something wrong?" My pulse speeds up.

I must've.

His mouth clenches into a tight line, and his fingers rough into my hair.

"Do that again." His voice is low and almost shaky.

"What?" I whisper.

"Kiss my cock like that again."

Oh...

My heartbeats soar to a hurried crescendo, and I do. I kiss him there once, twice, my tongue sneaking out to taste him. And the growl that emanates from his lungs is so masculine and deep, I squeeze my legs from the need unfurling there.

"I've never had anyone kiss me like that before," he husks.

A smile curls on my face as I peer up. "And no one ever will."

I don't know where that came from, but the thought of some other woman doing what I am to him… It would kill me.

"Mm." He rolls all my hair around his wrist and drops his face an inch from mine. "That's right, baby. Claim me," he says, stealing all my breaths away, kissing me hard and fast, before he pushes me into his erection.

"Suck. Now."

Without separating my eyes from him, I sink my mouth around the head of his cock and take it whole.

"Oh, shite, yes…keep doing whatever the hell you're doing."

I realize I like it when he praises me, so I continue to take more of him, his hard-on pulsating down into my throat until I gag so hard I can't breathe.

"Yes, feck, that's good."

His palm keeps me prisoner around him, like he doesn't want me to move a fraction. And neither do I.

I learn that I enjoy bringing him pleasure, and I want to do that. I want to gag on him. I bob my head up and down, trying not to use my teeth, but my God, this is hard. My cheeks burn, but I continue with fervor, peering up at him, his face twisted up in absolute want.

"That's it," he moans. "Keep sucking me with that virgin mouth. You're doing so good."

My own need becomes untamable, and all I want is to feel him inside me again, his eyes on me as he thrusts.

I keep working him, and his palm forces me all the way down until I gag again.

"You sound perfect taking me so deep. Never felt anything

better in my life except when I feel your pussy ripple around me."

Everything he says, the way he sounds, it's all making me more aroused, an achy throbbing between my thighs.

"Feck, I'm close. Keep suckin' me, baby." His fingers spread in my hair as I slide my mouth up, then all the way down. "Yes, that's it. Good girl. Don't stop. Gonna coat your throat with my cum."

My hand strokes him while I continue to pull him deeper into my throat, tasting his precum. His erection grows tight, jerking against my tongue.

Before I know what's happening, a loud groaning thunders in his chest. His hand keeps my mouth locked against the base of his cock as warmth shoots down my throat.

"Feck…yes…" His hips thrust into me over and over, as though he can't stop.

My body heats at the thought that I was able to do that. Give him this much pleasure.

When he's through, he yanks my head back and blows a whoosh of an exhale. "You sure you've never done that before?"

Gripping my lower lip with my teeth, I smile and shake my head.

"Good. Because that's all mine now too." He raises his pants back up, but leaves the zipper undone before he's lifting me in the air.

My legs wind around him as he kisses me softly this time. It's like he wants me to know that this thing between us is beyond just sex, beyond the physical. But I already knew that.

He carries me to the bedroom, lowering me onto his bed.

His hands grab his t-shirt, and he tugs it over his head before he's stepping out of his pants, and somehow he's hard again.

Lazily, he strokes himself, watching me, his erection getting thicker.

I follow his lead and slip out of my shirt too, and his jaw tenses, his fist tightening around the crown of his cock.

Hungrily, his gaze caresses a path down my body, every hill and valley his to climb. I feel not an ounce of shame. I'm every bit his, and he's every bit mine.

He stalks forward, settling on top of me, and I welcome his weight, spreading my thighs open for him.

"I'm not wearing a condom." He grabs his cock and the tip nudges my entrance. "If I'm lucky, I'll get you pregnant by the end of tonight."

"I'm on the pill, remember?" My grin widens.

But he only smirks and thrusts deep enough for the familiar stars to spread before my eyes.

"Don't worry, love…" His lips feather against my throat. "I'll find a way around that."

After the multiple orgasms, we finally started talking. I can't believe my father had this whole thing with Mason planned! He could've told me! But I understand why he didn't. Devlin had to see how scared I was, and in the end, it worked out anyway. I have no energy to be mad at my father.

"This is probably the best news ever." I grin.

Things are finally working out for us. We can be happy.

"Why didn't you just ask for my father's blessing when you spoke?"

He clears his throat. "I wanted to give him time to sit on the news. But he approves of us, so I'm sure he won't have a problem with it when I do. If he does, then I'll fight for you, Eriu. Because I'm not letting you go for anything or anyone."

My smile spreads so wide, my cheeks ache. I place a hand

across his stubbly cheek. "I love you, Devlin."

"That's a good thing." He winks. "It'd be a lot harder to marry you if you didn't."

With a sigh, I lower my face across his chest and burrow into him as he holds me close to his beating heart. I could really get used to this.

"So, about what you said? Getting me pregnant. Uh…"

"What is it?" He wrenches my chin up with a tilt of his hand.

"I don't think I'm ready for that yet. I want to finish school and get a job first. Is that okay?"

"Of course it's okay. We've got all the time in the world. I just got carried away." He places a palm against my abdomen, his eyes swelling with drowning affection. "Thinking about you growing our child…I don't know, it does things to me. But I'm willing to wait as long as you want because I love you."

"I love you too, Devlin. Always."

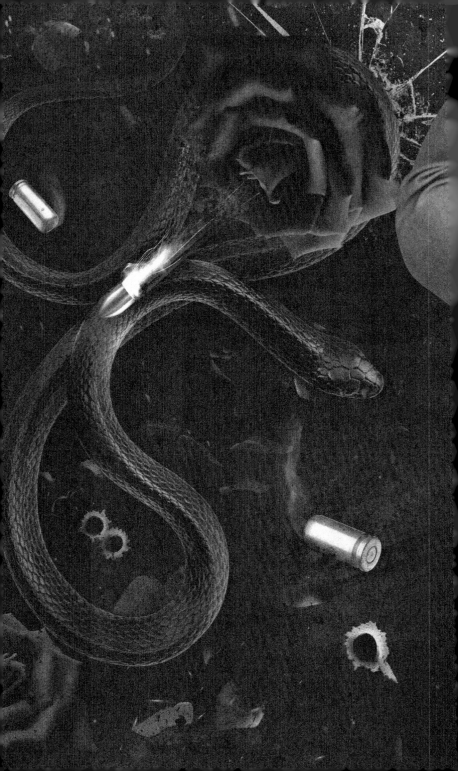

TWENTY-NINE

DEVLIN

The following day, we're in the shower together, having just made love, while I lather up her hair, her back pressed to my front as she sighs.

"I wanna take you out tonight," I tell her, and her eyes pop open.

"Like a date?"

"I guess, yeah." I scratch my forehead. "Never been on one, actually, but I think that's what you call them." My mouth jerks.

Her laugh is like the sunshine, an eternal heaven of peace and all the things I'd never dream to experience.

"You've really never been on a date?" She pivots around and wraps her arms around my torso.

"Aye. Never. I worked for your father and didn't have the time or interest. Before that, it was more of the same. My mother's words, they kind of always stayed with me, ya know? Never thought I was good enough for anyone."

"I'm so sorry. But…" Her voice trails and her cheeks turn a slight shade of pink.

"Ask." I cup her chin in my palm and raise her eyes to mine. "I'll tell you anything you want to know."

"But you're not a virgin like me…"

Ah, I see what she's asking.

"No." I brush her lips with my thumb. "Believe me, right now I wish you were the only woman I've fecked, because you're the only one that matters."

"Oh." Her face falls.

"Hey, don't do that." I tug her chin toward me and brush my nose with hers. "I love you. I've never loved anyone in my life."

A smile returns to her face.

With my eyes closed, I lay a kiss on her forehead, keeping my mouth there, breathing her in and wondering if it could really be this perfect.

My heart grows heavy, memories of my brother and what happened to him cutting through my thoughts.

But I won't allow history to repeat itself. I will protect her like I couldn't protect him, even if I pay the ultimate price to do it.

ERIU

We arrive at a steakhouse on the Upper West Side, a sparkling chandelier hanging brightly above. A beautiful place for a first official date.

He said he wanted me to stay with him for a while, so earlier, he brought me to my dorm so I could gather some clothes and toiletries. I grabbed my things as quickly as possible, taking some extra clothes to sleep in, not knowing how long I will be there.

I hope it continues. I've loved waking up beside him, seeing those blue eyes play with a smirk when he sees me first thing in the morning.

He even gave me space in his closet for my things, like it's already *our* place.

His hand is tight around mine as we're led by the maître d' to a private corner table. As we pass, a man gawks at me, looking down my body, cloaked in a tight ruby-red knee-length dress. Devlin just about rips his head off, casting him a terrifying glare, and the man's eyes shoot up before he turns back to the woman he's with.

What a pig!

"A waiter will arrive shortly to take your orders," the maître d' announces, his thick black mustache jerking.

"Thank you," I say as Devlin pulls out a chair and waits for me to sit before he takes his spot across from me.

"This is nice." My eyes glance around the lavish restaurant.

I never in a million years would've thought we'd be here, together. I've dreamed of it for so long, it's hard to believe it's reality.

"I'm glad you approve." Above the candlelight, his eyes shine brightly and I wonder if people like us truly can have it all.

Once the waiter arrives and takes our orders, I excuse myself to the restroom. But, of course, he follows me.

"You know, this isn't necessary." I hook my arm through his. "I'll be fine."

"Not leaving you alone for a moment. I'd follow you inside if I could."

I roll my eyes. "Come on now. That's ridiculous, don't you think?"

He grabs my nape and presses his forehead to mine. "You don't understand how much you mean to me. If anything happens to you…"

"Nothing will."

He exhales. "Go before I change my mind and take our food to go. This was already a risk."

He finally lets me go, and with a shake of my head, I strut in through the double doors, the floor gleaming beneath my feet as I find an empty stall and head inside.

But before I can even shut the door, someone pushes it open.

A man in a ski mask.

Fear claws at my throat, my chest heavy.

His hand clasps around my mouth to keep me from screaming.

"Shh." He places a finger across his mouth. "Don't scream, or I'll kill you before he knows I'm even here."

My pulse rips through my neck, terror like I've never known simmering in my gut.

I nod frantically, tears rolling down my cheeks.

"I need you to send Devlin a message. Or should I call him Scott?"

I recoil, needing this man to go.

Please go.

"Tell him we know where he's been hiding and we're coming."

Something burns through my arm, and I realize I've been slashed. I whimper, my whole body quivering.

"Don't worry, it's just a cut. It won't kill you, but it sure as hell will kill him."

He digs the knife in deeper, and I wince, unable to stop my quiet sobs.

"Now, you'll wait five minutes for me to leave before you go and get him. Nod if you understand."

I nod, nausea churning, my head spinning.

"Good."

He backs up, and my shaky fingers feel for the cut, right below my shoulder. Crimson crawls down my hand, my blood everywhere.

Walking out, he leaves me there, unable to move or breathe, or do anything.

I don't know how long I remain there, staying in the same spot as though frozen. But after some time, the main door to the restroom makes a creaking sound, or so I think, and voices of women flow through.

"Excuse me?" one calls, snapping me from my trance, a soft knock on the door to my stall. "Are you okay? You're…uh… bleeding?"

She knocks again, and the door falls open. One look at me, and she screams for help.

"Oh my God! She's bleeding. Someone call an ambulance."

"Eriu?"

Footsteps. Heavy footsteps. Then he's there in front of me, rage and terror filling every line on his face.

"Feck! Who did this to you?" He ties something around my arm and scoops me against his chest as the women holler at him.

"Hey! Where are you taking her?"

"To safety."

Moments later, I feel the cool breeze against my skin.

"My God, I'm sorry." Emotions swim in his tone.

But I still don't look at him. All I see is that man in the mask.

He cups my face. "Baby, please, tell me if you saw who did it."

"I—" The words are caught in my throat.

"It's okay. You're safe now. I won't ever let you go again."

He makes a call on his phone, but I'm barely paying attention.

"Tell him…" I whisper. "Tell him we know where he's been

hiding and we're coming."

"What?"

"That's…that's what he said. He called you Scott."

"Feckin' hell!" A rumbling threat swims out of him. "I'm so damn sorry. It's all my fault."

My head falls against his shoulder.

I should've known this was all too good to be true.

DEVLIN

"It was the Palmers," I tell the Quinns and Messinas.

All of us are gathered in the waiting room of the hospital owned by the Messinas.

"And they're who again?" Gio scratches his temple.

"The gang I was with before I joined the Quinns. I left, so they want payback."

"They're the ones that killed your brother?" Michael asks, the scar on his cheek jerking.

I don't know how he got the damn thing and I have no desire to ask, but it's a part of him, like he was born with it. Like it belongs there, brutal as much as he is.

I nod. "Killed him in front of me. Had me bury him on their property."

"So you want our help finding them?" Gio asks this time.

"Aye. I think if we unite forces, we stand a better chance of getting rid of them."

"They came after my daughter." Patrick grinds his teeth, his nostrils widening. "They will not survive the week. I swear on my life."

The Quinn boys all look just as pissed, but it's Iseult whose rage is written all over her face.

"How the *hell* did he get to her in the women's bathroom?!" She rakes me with coals.

"The window," I tell her. "I sent Rogue back there and had him check it out. He told me the assailant climbed through the window in the stall next to hers."

"And none of the cameras caught his face?" Tynan asks.

"No. He wore his mask the entire time he drove off, then we lost him."

"We need to get Mason. Now." Iseult curls and uncurls her fingers.

Gio grabs her hand and brings it to his mouth. She glances at him, her brows knitted, emotions swimming in her eyes. She was really worried about Eriu when I called in to Gio, asking to use their hospital.

I know the girls are close, and I'm glad Eriu has someone who looks out for her with such force the way Iseult does. It's important to have a family that gives a feck. It's one thing I had with my brother.

"I agree. We need to move on Mason." Tynan cracks his neck. "He will talk. And he will tell us everything."

"I won't leave Eriu," I tell them.

"I'll do it." Iseult volunteers. "He doesn't know me, and I'm sure a man like that doesn't think a woman can hurt him."

Her lips curve, and I pity any man who gets in her way.

"We'll all go together." Tynan removes his phone and starts to dial, speaking to someone. "Gather the men. We leave in an hour. Will send you details." He returns the phone to his pocket and says to me, "We'll keep him alive for you."

"I'll get there as soon as I can. I just hate leaving her alone."

"She won't be alone, son," Patrick adds. "I'll be here, and so will my army. No one will touch her. I'll be outside that room twenty-four seven."

Maybe I should go with them. I want to hear what that rat Mason has to say firsthand, but I need to see her before I go.

The doctor is still working on her, and I don't know how long that'll take, but I won't leave without seeing her first. She lost so much blood. I can't get it out of my head.

Over twenty minutes pass, and finally, one of the doctors steps out from behind the doors, removing his blue scrub cap.

"How is she, Doc?" I rush forward, my pulse blasting in my ears.

"She's fine. No serious damage." His attention flicks to everyone. "We gave her some blood, stitched her up, and she's resting now in room seven. But she was asking for you," he tells me. "So if you wanna go—"

I don't even wait for a response, running through those doors and down a hallway until I find room seven.

Through the glass window in the center of the door, our eyes connect. And with a trembling bottom lip, she starts to cry. Immediately, I rush inside and reach for her, my arms tighten around her while that soft crying rips at my heart.

I scoop her up and place her on my lap. "Don't ever scare me like that again, mo stoirín."

Her sobs grow heavier. "It all just hit me." She sniffles. "It could've been so much worse."

"I know, love. I know." My own emotions pound through me. "The thought of losing you, the one person in this world I love more than anything… I did this to you, and I need to end it."

She slants back. "End it how? Are you leaving?"

Her whispered worry makes my chest tight.

"I have to find out how Mason knows the people from my

past, the ones who came after you. I'm going with your sister and brothers to get answers. But I swear..." I grasp her jaw and kiss her slow. "I swear I'm coming back to you and making you my wife."

Tears gather in her eyes. "Please don't let anything happen to you. I won't survive it."

"I promise to do everything I can to come home to you, lass. You've given me purpose. Made me believe that I'm a man worthy of something. Worthy of a love from a woman like you."

She lifts her good arm and clasps a palm around my cheek. "You have always been worthy of love, Devlin. I'm sorry your parents made you believe otherwise."

She lays her head against my chest, my fingers stroking her back as we stay there, minutes bleeding into one another, until it's time for me to go.

Before I do, I vow to come back to her one last time. I just hope it's a promise I'm able to keep.

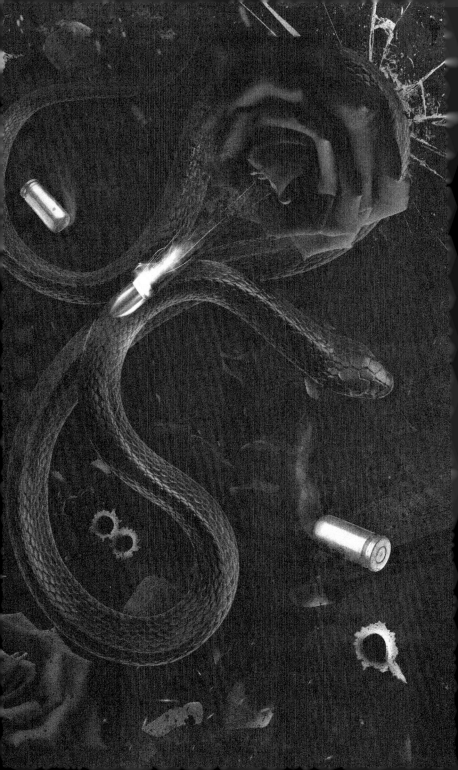

THIRTY

ERIU

O nce he's gone, it's like a piece of me is missing. I can't
stop the scary thoughts in my head. What if something
happens to him? To my sister? My brothers? What if I
lose someone else like I lost Mom? I don't want anyone else to die.

My eyes sting. I swipe at them just as the door opens, and in
walks my father. We haven't had a moment to talk. After Devlin
left, Iseult and my brothers came to check on me before they too
left.

"Hi, darling. How are you feeling?" He strides toward the bed
and takes the chair beside it.

"Could be better." I shrug.

"I'm sorry this all is happening to you." He sighs. "I've spent
my entire life trying to shield you from the dangers of what we do,
but it seems like there's no escaping it."

I glance down at my lap, unsure how to respond. Of course

there's no escaping it. We are Quinns. We are the Mob. I still don't see us that way. It's all just strange.

"Dad." I reach my hand for his, and he scoots to the edge of the chair so he can grab it. "I'm not a little kid anymore. I know how dangerous our world is. I saw it with my own eyes when I was kidnapped by that Russian guy."

"Yes, Konstantin's father. How could I forget?" His features twist with indignation. "If he wasn't dead already, I'd have killed him."

"Can I ask you something?" My stomach tenses. "And please tell me the truth."

He sits up straighter. "What is it?"

My stomach twists and turns, pulse unsteady. "Did Mom really die in an accident?"

He draws in a breath that he doesn't let go of. When his eyes shut for a moment, I know I was fed a lie.

"I'm sorry, Eriu." His face turns with sympathy and regret. "You were so young when it happened. I just…"

"What happened to Mom?"

I need to know the truth. It's killing me not to know.

"Sergey, he took her after we had a dispute over property and…" He fists a hand, and in his silence, there's despair. "He burned her alive. He sent me the video to prove it."

"Oh my God!" My vision blurs and I slap a hand over my mouth, my tears falling silently for a woman I barely remember. For the one who loved me, but whose love I can't seem to hold on to.

But it's there, like the wind kissing your skin, like the sun sprinkling you with its heat. Yet you can't touch or keep it. You have to be content to simply feel it and let go.

My father's arms are there, clasping around me. "Your mother was a great woman, and she loved you with all her heart, my darling."

I nod, sobbing against him, mourning her in my own way.

I don't know how long I cry, but it somehow feels good to. It's cathartic, like I'm shedding a part of myself I no longer want to keep.

My father kisses me on the top of my head and goes to the mini fridge to get me a water bottle. I take a few sips and place it on the nightstand beside me.

"So, you and Devlin, huh?"

He quickly changes the subject and I'm instantly relieved. Because as soon as I hear his name, I can't help but smile. "Yeah."

He grins, settling back on the chair. "You think I didn't know you had a crush on him?"

My mouth pops.

"That's right. Your father isn't always blind as a bat. Sometimes I wear my glasses."

I roll my eyes. "You never wear your glasses."

"I'm being figurative here, alright?" He chuckles. "He's a good man."

"I know. Now Mason…" I grimace. "Really, Dad? You couldn't even give me a little heads-up about your plan?"

"I'm sorry, sweetheart. I just knew I had to do something a bit drastic for Devlin to admit his feelings for ya. I think everyone knew but him."

"He was just scared of disappointing you and feeling like he wasn't good enough for your daughter. His parents never accepted him, and he carried that."

"Yeah, well, he's got a family now."

"That's right." *I can't wait until he returns.* "I hope nothing happens to them."

"It won't. They have each other's backs. And now we have the Messinas on our side, thanks to your sister marrying Gio."

"Well, I'm just glad I wasn't the one to marry him. Two failed arranged marriages for me. I'm on a roll."

He laughs. "Never thought your sister would marry before you. That's something I didn't see coming."

"There was *no* way Gio was ever gonna let her go."

His laughter grows. "You're not kidding. I thought he was gonna have my head when he barged into my office that one day and told me he was marrying her and I had no choice in the matter."

My heart warms at the way Gio loves my sister. He'd do anything for her. Burn the world down just to see her smile.

"I'm happy for her. She deserves it."

"Aye. She does. And so do you."

"Speaking of my happiness, I need to talk to you about something else."

"Of course, darling. Anything."

"I know when I've brought up writing as a career, you've dismissed it. But I really want to do this, Dad. I wanna try. And it doesn't mean I won't help you on the farm. I just want more, you know?"

He shrinks back against the chair and searches my eyes, then says something I never thought I'd hear him say.

"Then do it. I won't stop you. Not anymore."

"Really?!"

"Aye."

"What happened to…" I mock his tone of voice. "'Writing isn't a career. You need a job worthy of your name.'"

"I just want you all to be happy, and if this makes you happy, then that's all that matters to me."

"Well, that was much easier than I thought."

"See?" He throws his hands in the air. "I'm easy to talk to."

"Mm-hmm." I pop a brow.

His eyes crinkle with a hard chuckle. "I love you, Eriu. I want you to know that."

"I do know that."

"Good. Now, why don't you rest? I'll be here the whole time."

But even though I try to sleep, it never comes. I won't be able to. Not until I know Devlin and my family are safe.

DEVLIN

Mason's guards are lying on the ground. Again. Seems like he didn't learn his lesson after all.

While Gio and the Quinns surround the property, Iseult walks right up to the front door, with me wedged between two shrubs not too far from the entrance.

She rings the bell and waits for Mason to answer.

A creak echoes.

"Who the hell are you, and how did you…" Mason's voice trails, and I'm thinking he just caught the bodies on his lawn.

"Aww," Iseult tsks. "Now is that a way to treat your almost future sister-in-law?"

He gasps right before she kicks him hard, and he grunts as she rushes inside. And that's when I join them. The other guys all follow us in.

Iseult grabs Mason by the hair, and he winces.

"What the hell is this?!" His eyes bounce between her, me, and the rest of the room. "I didn't do shit! I left her alone like you told me to." His frantic attention flies to me.

"Cut your bullshit." I step up, removing my nine from my

waistband and angling it into his throat.

"Wh-what are y-you talking about?" He practically shakes in her grasp. "I didn't do anything! You're making a big mistake!"

Tynan brings a chair over from the kitchen, and Iseult pushes Mason into it.

Her palms drop to his knees, and she bends forward. "Now, if you're a good little boy, I won't cut off your tiny penis." She kneels and retrieves a knife from her ankle, swinging it in the air. "I may have a little fun, though." She grins, staring at the glistening blade. "How much depends on you."

When his face goes white, she grabs his throat and places the blade against his carotid.

"We know someone has been paying you fifty K every week," I tell him. "We know it was the Palmers."

"Who?" His hands shake, his body growing rigid as she slowly turns to look at me, the knife still at his throat.

He's either stupid or really doesn't know who that is.

"Who's been paying you?" Iseult asks, digging the knife just enough to draw a little blood.

"Oh, f-f-fuck… I—I don't know his name. H-he just—oh my God, I'm bleeding!"

She yanks his head backward. "Tell us everything about this man. I'll know if you're lying."

"Okay, okay! I…I'm in deep in gambling debts. Owe a lot of money to scary people," he pants. "More than I can get from my father. I couldn't let him know what a big disappointment I am. So when some guy named Ethan approached me, saying his people would pay off my debts if I volunteered to marry Eriu, I said yes. My father knew her father, so when I mentioned it to him, he thought it was a great idea, and so did her father."

I grind my jaw. "And?"

"Ethan sent in money every week as promised, splitting up what I owed, as long as I don't back out of the engagement. All I had to do was tell her I wanted her to be a virgin, scare her a little. They told me if I needed to go through with the wedding, I should do it. Once I did all that, they'd pay me what I owe in full."

My pulse turns demonic in my head. I dig the barrel of my gun into his temple.

"Did you see this Ethan's face? How old was he?"

"Please, please don't kill me!"

"TALK!"

"I—I—I saw his face. I—I can identify him for you. I swear! Just don't kill me!" he wails. "I fucked up!"

"Did you ever see or hear about a Francis Palmer?"

He shakes his head. "Ethan didn't tell me anything. I knew enough not to ask questions."

When I reach into my pocket, he shrinks back.

Removing my phone, I shove it into his face. "Need you to tell me if one of the guys on here is Ethan."

He starts nodding frantically. "That one. He's older now, but I recognize him."

He points to one of the Palmer boys. His name isn't Ethan, of course. That's Roy Palmer. The oldest one.

I nod at Iseult, and without hesitation, her knife slashes Mason across his throat. The shock on his face comes swiftly.

He thought he would survive such a betrayal. But no one fecks with the Quinns and lives to tell about it.

And soon enough, the Palmers will learn the same lesson.

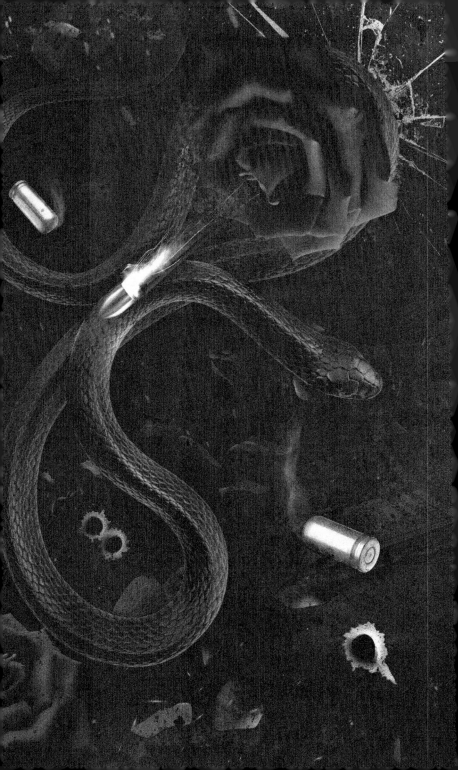

THIRTY-ONE

ERIU
ONE WEEK LATER

My arm has been healing nicely, and it only throbs a little. I've had people ask what happened—including Karen, of course—and all I said was some lunatic attacked me in the bathroom. I mean, that *is* accurate.

Devlin no longer wants me at the dorm, so I have been living with him. He drives me to school and brings me back, and I'm limited to where I can go. Not that I'm at all surprised. With everything that has happened, I don't want to wander far either.

I step into Professor Montgomery's office, needing to tell her that I want to sign up for another advanced class she's offering next semester. Since I no longer have to hide what I want to do from my dad, I decided to switch my major from business to creative writing.

"Hey, Eriu. How's that assignment going?" Her brown eyes

gleam. "I know it was a tough one, but I have no doubt you're going to come up with an amazing short story, like you always do."

"Thank you. It's getting there. I did want to discuss next semester with you."

"Please tell me you're not dropping out of writing." She shuts her laptop. "Because I swear if your father is giving you a hard time again, I will speak to him. Tell him how talented you are. It's a shame to let all that talent go to waste. I'm sure he's not that stubborn."

I scrunch my nose. "You've never met my father. But actually, he approves of me switching majors to writing."

"Wow. Great news! And the engagement? Has he changed his mind about that too?"

My lips spread. "He has."

"Well, look at you making moves. I'm proud of you."

"It wasn't all me. I have good people in my corner."

She nods contemplatively. "Having the right people makes all the difference. As far as my class next semester, I will always have a spot for you."

"Thank you. I don't know what I would do without your support."

We spend the next few minutes discussing my assignment and where I plan to go with it. She listens like she always does and offers fresh perspectives.

When my phone vibrates with a text, I find that it's my sister, wanting me to meet her at a store in the city. My father and Fernanda are having a party tomorrow for Dad's birthday, and it's black tie. But I have no desire to go. A party is the last thing on my mind, especially with those people still after Devlin and me. But I know my sister is not gonna let this go.

So I say goodbye to the professor and head outside toward Devlin, who's standing right at the door of the building.

He stares at me, a twitch of a smirk appearing.

"What?" I ask him, my cheeks heating up from his deep perusal.

"Nothing. Just admiring my future wife."

My body spreads with tingles. Every time he refers to marriage or me being his wife, I can't help getting all giddy at the thought. He hasn't asked me or anything, but it sounds like it's on his mind.

"My sister texted. She wants me to meet her at the Dior store." I roll my eyes. "For Dad's party tomorrow. I'm being forced to buy a new dress."

He laughs and tugs my chin into his face, giving me a quick kiss. "I don't know, love. I like the idea of you in a new dress. Something else I can rip off of you."

My face heats up.

His chuckling rises as he slips his hand into mine and leads me to his SUV. He helps me in, and when he's setting the car to drive, his palm clasps around my upper thigh.

Now, suddenly, buying a new dress doesn't sound all that bad.

We arrive at my father's estate by the next evening. Acres of property have been transformed into a lavish affair. Twinkling lights hang over trees, like a myriad of tiny stars outbound in the endless sky.

A band plays a rock song I don't know, people already dancing with glasses of alcohol in their hands.

There's more food here than anyone ever needs, but it's how I grew up: always having more of everything. I never took any of it for granted, though. I don't know what it was, but even from a young age, I knew not everyone was as lucky as we were—

with money, anyway. We're definitely not lucky about many other things.

I run my palms down my ivory mermaid lace dress. I have no idea why I agreed to it, but once Iseult saw me in it, I swear she cried. Or maybe something was in her eye. In either case, she wouldn't let me leave the store without it.

Who needs a dress this fancy for my dad's birthday, and why in the world are we even having his party a month before? But Dad said he won't be here for it then, so Fernanda planned this crazy event.

"Having fun?" Iseult shimmies beside me.

"It looks nice, but since when is Dad into fancy crap for his birthday?"

Iseult throws an arm over my shoulders. "You know Fernanda loves to throw a party. I'm sure she convinced Dad."

"Yeah, probably." I glance around, wondering where Devlin went to.

He was just talking to Tynan and Gio, and now they're all gone.

"Is Devlin still with the guys?"

"Yeah, I think they went inside the house. I'm sure they'll be out soon." She tugs me to her. "Let's go get a drink."

She pulls me toward one of the bars and orders us both watermelon margaritas.

"What are you so worried about? They're here. Nothing's happening to Devlin, I promise." Iseult hands me my drink.

I nod and force myself to take a sip so I can calm down. She's right. Nothing will happen to them at my father's house.

"If you're concerned about Mason, don't be. He'll never bother you again. I promise."

It hits me then, the meaning of her words.

"Oh my God." My hand falls across my mouth. "Is he…"

"I won't lie to you. You know that."

A pulse throbs in my temple. They killed him.

"Don't feel sorry for him." Her face twists. "He hurt you. He betrayed us. Worked with the people coming after you and Devlin. If he wasn't dead, I'd kill him again."

My eyes pop wider. It's all too much.

"This is why Devlin didn't want to tell you," she says, taking my hand in hers. "He wants to protect you. He loves you, Eriu."

"I know he does. I just don't understand how easy murdering someone can be for you."

"I never want you to understand." Her lips thin as she blows a breath. "Come on, let's go dance."

She drags me toward the dance floor, and after a few minutes, I start to move, closing my eyes and trying to forget everything. Song after song, I'm there with my sister until we both find ourselves laughing and having a great time.

"Let's go powder our noses." She takes our drinks, leaving them at the bar, before we head into the guest bathroom, right through the first set of glass doors.

Waiters bustle around with more food, bringing out trays for the one hundred-plus guests in attendance.

I don't see Devlin anywhere as we enter the restroom. I can't help but worry, even when it's kind of irrational.

He's fine here. He can take care of himself. I give myself a quick pep talk.

"I think you need some more lipstick." Iseult removes the deep red tube she had me use when she did my makeup earlier. She inspects me inquisitively, then proceeds to add blush to my cheeks.

She takes a few steps back and narrows her gaze as she looks me up and down, and I'm surprised her five-inch stilettos aren't getting caught in her long emerald-green gown.

"I think we're good now." I snicker. "It's not like this is my wedding."

Her eyes go round.

"What's that face…" My voice trails. "Iseult?"

But she doesn't say anything. Then it hits me…

She did my hair and makeup. She pressured me to buy this dress as opposed to the colorful ones I was trying on.

"Oh my God. No!" My head spins. "Iseult! Tell me this isn't my wedding?"

She shrinks back and winces. "Ugh, damn it! I'm so bad at keeping surprises!"

"Oh my God! How could you not tell me?"

"Don't be mad." She scratches her nose. "I promised him I wouldn't."

"Who? Please tell me Dad didn't back out of his word and set up a secret wedding for me to someone else. Please, Iseult!"

"No! Of course not! You think I would let that happen?"

I release a relieved exhale. "Then what is this?"

"Devlin." She grins. "He wanted to surprise you."

I gasp. "He planned this?"

"Yes." Her eyes glint. "He did. So please, can you pretend to be surprised?"

I grab her purse and retrieve her mascara, nervously adding some to my eyes. I chew on my bottom lip, yet I can't stop smiling.

"Oh my God! I'm getting married!"

Her expression softens, her palms gripping my shoulders from behind as our eyes connect through the mirror. "Yes, you are. I wish Mom was here to see it."

"Me too," I say, tucking her hand in mine. "But I know she's always with us."

Out of nowhere, a gentle breeze sways across my face. And I

smile as though she's standing right before us.

DEVLIN

"Jesus Christ, would you stop pacing?" Tynan shakes his head as we wait for Eriu to appear, a priest standing to our right.

While Iseult took her to the bathroom, the staff got to setting up the canopy with a whole lot of lilies on the top.

Iseult is supposed to keep Eriu occupied until she gets a text from Fernanda. And I hope she can manage it.

I keep second-guessing this whole thing. Not the wedding, but the way I did it.

What if she hates it? What if she decides not to marry me?

That's not gonna happen, though. This is for life.

I need to put this ring on her finger so I know that she's mine.

The music starts to play.

Feck. It's happening.

I ignore Tynan's snicker.

"You are gonna give yourself an aneurism." He continues to poke fun at me.

"Shut up, will ya? Maybe some of us actually wanna get married."

"Better you than me."

"Gonna remind you of this when you meet someone who makes you forget you hate weddings."

"Never gonna happen, McHale. Never gonna fall in love. I'll bet you a million dollars."

I grin, extending a hand for his. "I'll take that bet."

He confidently shakes hands with me. "Hope you like losing money."

"I like making it."

Everyone starts to rise, and both of us immediately stop talking.

Before I can respond, she's there, her father beside her, tears in her eyes as she catches my stare.

The room disappears, and all I know is this breathtaking woman—a true piece of my heart, the only way it beats right.

She marches closer, and my feet are already moving, needing to be near her. Through the thick emotions veiled in her gaze, her smile grows, and my heartbeats echo in my ears, never having known a feeling like this. It's big enough to consume me. My love for her. My devotion. There's no end to what I feel for her.

I make it to her before she even reaches the end, and I take her hand in mine. "Hi."

My face splits, and she bites that lip.

My Lord, this woman.

"Hi," she whispers, her eyes glimmering. "We're getting married."

"It looks like it, lass."

Beside us, her father chuckles. "Can you let me give my daughter away properly, son?"

A few of the guests laugh as he takes both of her hands and kisses each one before he kisses her cheek.

"I love you both very much."

He looks at me for a moment, and I incline my chin in gratitude. Because I've finally found people I belong with.

"You take good care of each other, will ya?" He slaps me across my back before he heads to sit in the front row next to Fernanda.

"Let's get married, mo stoirín."

Hand in hand, we stand before the priest, who's reciting his part while I grow insanely impatient, needing this to be over.

"Can we get the CliffsNotes version?" I say. "Wanna get to the part where I kiss my wife."

Eriu elbows me, fighting a smile, while a few cheers from the crowd have the priest smiling too. He finishes his part, and it's her turn to say her vows, then it's mine.

Taking both her hands, I lock eyes with her as I recite them.

"I, Donny Devlin McHale, take you, Eriu Charlotte Quinn, to be my wife, to have and to hold from this day forward, for better or for worse, for richer or for poorer, in sickness and in health. I promise to love and cherish you for all the days of my life."

Tears well in her eyes, and she fights not to let them free. I can't believe we are finally here. I can't believe she's mine.

We exchange rings, and the priest recites some other shite I'm barely listening to, unable to peel my gaze off of her. It's like I won the damn lottery. Wish my brother was alive to meet her. He would've loved her.

"I now pronounce you husband and wife. You may kiss your bride."

"Feckin' finally."

Grabbing her face with both hands, I kiss her with every drenching ounce of love I possess, knowing for her, I'd do anything, kill anyone, die a thousand deaths just to keep her safe.

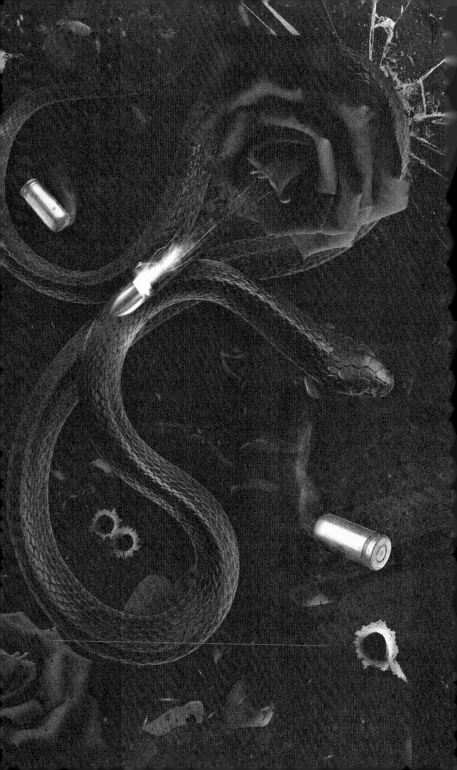

THIRTY-TWO

ERIU

With the wedding over, a limo my father hired takes us to Devlin's penthouse. His arm holds me tight against his side, like he never wants to let go.

"I can't believe you planned a secret wedding!" My eyes take in the large solitaire ring sparkling on my finger. I can't get over it.

Not long ago, I only knew his rejection. The idea of us felt like it'd never happen. But now we're married. Husband and wife. No one can break that.

"I didn't exactly plan anything." He chuckles. "I just had the idea. Fernanda is the mastermind."

"Well, if you hadn't had the idea, there would have been no wedding." I glance up at him, unable to stop smiling. "So thank you. This has been the best day."

His gaze deepens, and his hard knuckles brush over my cheek. "I'm glad I was able to make you happy. There's nothing in this world rarer and more precious than you."

My stomach tugs, and I lay my palm over the top of his hand, my heart beating in double time.

"I have a surprise for you at home." He says that like it's ours already, and I guess it is.

"Oh, yeah?" My grin spreads. "What could that be?"

My mind roams with illicit thoughts, and he must realize that, because he chuckles knowingly.

"My God, my wife is a dirty girl," he teases, rubbing his rough thumb over my lips. "But no, that's not what I meant." His eyes turn hooded. "But if you're wondering if I'm gonna feck you tonight, then yeah, baby. I am. Gonna make you sore enough to stay in bed for days. Then I'll feck you again until you can't take any more of me."

"Devlin…" I whisper on a groan.

His eyes deepen with mine, possessive fierceness within them.

He clenches his jaw and fists my hair, his mouth dropping against my ear. "I can't wait to be inside my wife."

"Oh God, that sounded so hot," I pant, glancing at the driver, hoping he doesn't hear us. "I don't think I can wait until we get home."

I was only half joking, but he's already closing the partition that separates us from the driver.

My long gown from the ceremony has been replaced with a short cocktail dress thanks to my sister, and right now, I want to send her a thank-you card. Because I think my new husband is gonna take me in the limo.

His fingers crawl up my inner thigh.

"Lie back," he commands as he pushes me down by my chest. He sits at my feet, spreading my thighs easily, fingers tracing my slit through my panties. "Need to come, don't ya, lass?"

"Yes," I moan. "Please."

He grunts, fingering my panties and flipping them to the side, exposing me.

"You're already wet." He sinks a single digit inside me. "And so damn tight."

His thumb rolls around my clit as he grunts. "Mine. This is all mine."

"Yes…" I cry as he tortures me, making my eyes roll back.

He adds another finger, and it burns a little, but not as bad as when he's inside me.

Will it hurt again? Or will it feel better this time since we've done it a few times?

My need grows as he rocks his fingers deeper.

"So beautiful," he rasps before he drops to his knees.

"What are you—oh, God!" I cry as his tongue answers my question, sweeping around my clit, then inside me.

I let out a scream, forgetting that we're not alone. That this man who works for my father can hear us. But I stopped caring the moment Devlin touched me.

He sucks me into his hot mouth, fingers pistoning inside me, his deep groans vibrating over my pussy until my body trembles, my walls clenching as he thrusts faster. And I fall into the wild rush of desire, this unbending need that never yields when we're together.

"Yes, Devlin! Oh, God!" I cry, my hand in his hair, tugging hard.

But he doesn't slow. He thrusts faster, flicks to a hurried pace, as though he wants everything I have to give.

My body feels like Jell-O once he stops, a smirk donning his face as he fixes my dress and sits back beside me. He scoops me onto his lap and kisses me slow.

"Mm," I murmur. "That was nice."

"Nice? That's all you've got for me?" There's humor in his voice.

A smile twitches on my lips as I close my eyes and burrow deeper into his chest.

"I'd feck you so hard right now, but I want our wedding night to be special."

My God, he's the sweetest man alive. Also the dirtiest. Which is quite the combination.

Wait until I tell Karen about what he just did to me in the limo. She'd be proud. That's for sure.

Speaking of Karen, I need to call her tomorrow and check on her. Devlin said they invited her to the wedding, but she couldn't come because her grandma died yesterday.

I didn't get to talk to her yesterday after classes ended, and now that I'm not at the dorm, I don't see as much of her as I used to. I talk to her every day, but yesterday, she never texted back. I just thought she was caught up with studying for one of our midterms. Now I feel bad I didn't know her grandma died.

The limo arrives at Devlin's building, and he gets out first, coming around to open the door for me. He extends a hand for mine and helps me out, and together, we head inside, taking the elevator up to the top floor.

He removes his keys from his pocket, and something catches in his eyes when he looks at me. Something warm and beautiful.

My heart thuds as he opens the door. And as soon as I see what he's done, I gasp, emotions clouding my vision. Candles are everywhere, the room bathed in a soft light, rose petals leading from the door and into the house.

"How?" I whisper.

"I asked Rogue to do it." He chuckles.

"What? Rogue?" I jerk back.

He shrugs. "We made peace. He didn't mind."

"I can't imagine either of you guys doing something like this." I giggle.

He wraps his arms around me from behind as I stare at how beautiful everything looks.

I quickly turn to him and grin. "Who knew you were so romantic?"

"There are a lot of things I didn't know about myself. Not until I went and fell in love with you."

His smile sets my world on fire.

"I love it when you look this happy," I tell him.

"That's easy when I have you."

In an instant, he's pushing the door to a close with his foot and lifting me up in the air. My legs close around his hips, his hands in my hair while he groans as he drags my lips to meet him.

"I love you," I breathe, rocking my core against him.

He pulls my head back, kissing up my throat, my jaw. "My God, I'll never tire of hearing you say that."

My legs tighten around him.

"Do you know what that accent does to me?" I admit something I've been dying to for a long time.

He laughs all low and seductive. "No, so how about you tell me all about it?" He pushes me down onto the kitchen counter and spreads my thighs wide open. "After I've had my fill of you."

"Oh my God," I cry out as he lowers his mouth to my core and sucks my clit into it through my panties.

My fingers slide into his thick, long hair, pulling hard as he trails love bites down my inner thigh. My body is ready to combust from the sheer effect this man has on me. I've never felt so alive, so needy. I rise on my elbows so I can watch him, the visual making me even more turned on.

With his thumbs, he lowers my panties, locking his eyes with mine as he tugs them to my lower thighs, then flattens his tongue around my pussy.

"Devlin!" I gasp, my eyes rolling into the back of my head.

I'm still sensitive from what he did to me in the car, but it seems like that wasn't enough.

"Please, please," I beg, and that causes him to groan around me like a madman.

My body jerks, my legs closing around his head. But his palms snap around the insides of my thighs, and he forces them apart, slapping them on the counter.

He adds two fingers into me, and I can feel them curl inside while his mouth does sinful things.

This is too good. I can't believe I've been missing out all this time. But Devlin has been the one for me, and this has been worth waiting for.

He pistons faster, his tongue rolling against my clit. My body falls back, unable to keep myself up anymore. And with his next thrust, I shatter, his name on my lips as I do.

"Devlin! Oh, God!"

He sucks me into his mouth, coaxing every drop from me, before he slows and looks up at me with the cockiest smirk on his face. "Was that just nice too?"

My lips tremble, but no words come out.

He chuckles, scooping me up into his arms bridal-style.

Every inch of me is satiated, and being in his arms... I could die happy.

He kisses my forehead as I stare at him with hurried breaths.

"I'm not through with you yet," he husks as he carries me to our bedroom where more candles flicker from every corner.

He places me gently on the bed, then starts removing his tuxedo jacket, eyes boring into mine.

Devlin stripping in front of me is quickly becoming one of my favorite things.

He starts on the buttons of his cuffs, and that familiar build of desire dances across my flesh.

"You like what you see, wife?" His fingers go to the buttons of his dress shirt as he starts to undo them.

"Yes…very much."

My heart thuds faster in my chest as he drags the shirt off before tossing it on the floor, his large hands reaching for his belt, undoing it slowly.

He drags the zipper down, the sound echoing before he completely pulls his pants and boxers off. My hand runs down my abdomen as I grow intoxicated, unable to stop these shivers coasting down my body from the sight of him.

"Take off that dress." He grabs his erection and strokes. "And strip for me."

My face grows warm but I slowly rise to my knees, my hand tugging at the side zipper as I start to pull it down, going slow as he continues to touch himself.

"Slip off the straps," he rasps, and the pulsing in my core swells.

I swallow down my nerves, grabbing one strap and pulling it lower, then the other, slipping my arms out of them, holding the dress against my breasts.

His tongue traces his bottom lip before he bites it.

My God. I've never seen Devlin look at me this way.

"Drop your arms and show me."

I don't hesitate, doing what he's commanding. Loving the way he does.

When he sees my breasts, he hisses. "Feck."

Then he's on me, pushing my body flat on the bed, mouth hungrily capturing mine with a growl. His palm finds my hair, fisting tight as he kisses me hard, his fingers lowering between us as he thrusts them inside me.

"Come for me, lass," he grunts against my ear.

My walls squeeze and my body jolts before his mouth is on me again, wringing every bit of pleasure from my willing body.

He captures my moans as I come, wet and willing to be his anything. His lips sink around my jaw, kissing and biting his way down my throat before he takes a beaded tip into his mouth and sucks. His free hand drags my dress down until it's lost to the floor, our bodies bare, our skin and flesh molded as one.

He takes my other nipple and does the same.

Before I realize what he's doing, he's on his feet, grabbing a candle from the dresser.

He looms above me, the light bathing his body in a warm glow. "Do you trust me?"

I nod.

"Good girl."

He flips the candle over a little, spilling the hot wax over my tight nipple, then the other, as I cry out from the instant burn. But something in it feels good too. He drags the candle in the air, stopping above my core. When I arch up, he spills the liquid onto me there.

"Oh, God!" My body bows off the bed while the wax cools against my clit. "This is so good."

He chuckles, removing the wax from me, then blowing the candle out and placing it on the nightstand. His heavy body lowers onto mine and he cups my face, his eyes tender.

"I love you," he vows as he positions his cock against my opening. "I promise to never stop."

He slowly pierces my entrance, robbing me of all breaths. His erection surges inch by inch, his thrusting deeper, and I groan, needing more of him.

I can't take this torture. "Please, fuck me."

His eyes narrow and his teeth snap, and with a quick jerk, he pummels inside me until I'm full of every thick inch of him.

"Yes, that's it…" He peppers kisses down my throat. "You take me so good, mo stoirín."

He throws one leg over his shoulder, ramming harder, slanting back to look at me.

The new position is intense, and I gasp on a string of moans, staring at my husband, feeling all these different emotions at once.

But most of all, I feel grateful to have him. Because I know how fleeting moments like these are, especially for people like us.

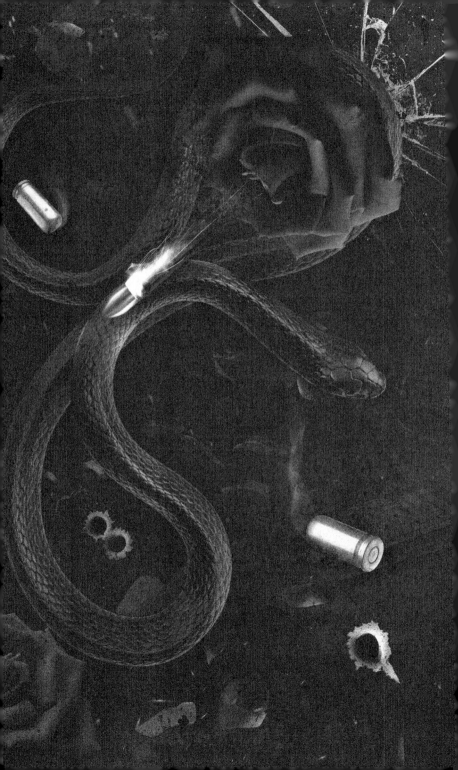

THIRTY-THREE

ERIU

T he next morning, I stretch away, feeling a little different, even though I'm still the same woman I was before. But I'm married now, and that somehow changes everything.

The space beside me is empty, but the aroma of eggs and coffee fills the room. I quickly sit up and head for the dresser, grabbing one of his t-shirts to slip into.

Picking up my cell from the nightstand, I stare out the window, admiring the view of Central Park. Trees lining the street. Benches with people on them. Two runners pass a large German shepherd, his owner petting its head.

Unlocking my phone, I send Karen a quick text.

ERIU

> I'm so sorry about your grandma! I feel like such a bad friend that I didn't know.

Call me when you can. I love you!

It's not like her to be so quiet. Even when she's upset, she always calls me or at least texts.

There's a small banging noise coming from somewhere in the apartment, and with a sigh, I head toward it, wondering what Devlin could be doing so early.

When I head out of the room and turn toward the foyer, I find him shirtless, gray sweats hanging low as he stands on a small ladder, changing a lightbulb.

He doesn't notice me at first while I wonder if this man can get any hotter. Even something as simple as him changing a lightbulb is attractive. But I've never seen Devlin look so domesticated before. I'm gonna enjoy this marriage.

The muscles in his abdomen stretch and flex, the V lowering into the place I've become quite friendly with.

He clears his throat as his gaze flicks to mine. "Been wonderin' how long you're gonna stand there and check me out." A wicked smirk lines his mouth. "Not that I mind my wife looking at me like that."

His wife...

That sounds so good.

"It smells amazing in here. You cooked?"

He climbs down, swooping an arm around me. His lips brush against mine and my eyes fall to a close, the sensations warming me from the inside.

"Aye. I like cooking for my woman."

A dreamy sigh escapes me. "I don't think this will ever get old."

"It better not."

He grabs the back of my neck and kisses me, his soft lips molding with mine, my tongue sweeping along his as I feel this kiss in my marrow. My fingers sink into his solid back as he lifts me up and carries me to the kitchen. Breathless, he pulls back and searches my eyes deeply with unreserved passion.

"Being with you, having all this. I never thought…" He drops his forehead to mine, his breaths as warm and vulnerable as his words, aching through his soul.

"You'll never have to wonder how much I love you," I whisper. "Because my love for you is unconditional."

His exhale is sharp. "You don't know that. You don't know if I'll do something that'll make you stop loving me."

I place a palm across his nape. "Nothing you do will ever make me stop loving you, Devlin."

He shuts his eyes, his face tense.

"Look at me." I stroke his jaw with my thumb. "Devlin, please…"

With his brows furrowed, he stares up at me, and it breaks my heart to see his pain so clearly.

"I'm not them. I'm not your parents. I won't ever give up on you."

His eyes pinch closed, and he buries his face into my chest.

"Thank you," he whispers. "If anything ever happens to you, I won't survive it."

"Nothing will happen to me." My arms squeeze around him.

But promises are strange like that. We don't actually know if we can keep them.

After breakfast, we returned back to bed and he made love to me, slow this time. It was powerful the way we connected, the way our bodies and our souls moved together.

He sleeps soundly beside me, his arm heavy over my hip, my

back molded into his front.

I hate to wake him, but I have a surprise of my own. I know he won't like me leaving the apartment without him, but the grocery store is only a few blocks away.

Since he cooked me breakfast, I figure I'll make us dinner. Maybe buy some fresh flowers and a nice tablecloth, make it romantic. Show him how much I appreciate him.

A smile curls on my face. I was thinking of making chicken marsala with some homemade Caesar dressing and freshly baked bread.

My father is a great cook, and he taught me a lot when I was young. One day, when Devlin and I have kids, I want to teach them too.

Gently, I lift Devlin's arm and slip out, tiptoeing to the walk-in closet to grab some clothes.

I should be gone no more than half an hour.

Slipping into a pair of sneakers he bought me, I grab my bag and phone. But before I go, I open the nightstand and take out a pen and Post-it note so I can let him know where I went. If I text him, his phone will go off.

He dismissed Rogue for today, or I know he would call Devlin and tell him I left. I can't wait until everything with those Palmer people is finished so he can stop worrying about my every move.

Heading quietly for the door, I give him one final look before I start toward the foyer and out of the apartment.

Once in the elevator, I breathe a relieved sigh. It feels like I'm escaping a prison. The doorman greets me as I head out of the building and into the chill of a spring day.

The clouds above are dark, but a little sunshine seeps out. Geez, I hope it doesn't rain. I didn't bring an umbrella.

Deciding not to go back for it in case Devlin wakes up, I rush for the store, running through the ingredients in my head. Maybe I should make him cupcakes too for dessert. He once told me he loves strawberry cupcakes.

A little girl, maybe around seven, passes by with her mom. The girl smiles at me, a big pink bow in her dark ponytail.

Thoughts of my mom suddenly jump into my head. Did she take me to stores with her? Did she put bows on my head?

I still have all my pictures of her in my room in Boston. If I'm going to live in his apartment, I want to bring all my stuff there. This wedding happened so fast, we haven't had time to talk about the future or where we plan to live. I do like the city and wouldn't mind making it my official home.

Finally at the store, I start grabbing all the things I need as fast as I can because Lord knows if that man wakes up and knows I disappeared without him, he's going to raid the city.

"Need any help?" a young man who works here asks as he stocks the shelves with pasta boxes.

"Nope." I grab two boxes of spaghetti. "Just need these. Have a great day."

With a sleazy gaze, he scans my body, and I roll my eyes as I head to pay for all my items. The line goes quick, and I throw everything into two bags, which are quite heavy. Didn't exactly think this through.

Thanking the cashier, I head out, and as I walk past the first block, thunder rolls across the sky and it starts to pour.

"Are you kidding me?! Ugh!" I groan, shaking my head as I try to run home, but with these damn bags, it's more like a jog.

"Hey!" someone calls. "Eriu? Do you need a ride?"

I blink through the drops of rain on my lashes, seeing Professor Montgomery pulling up on the corner.

"Oh my God! Please! I'm just a few blocks that way." I point north.

"Hop in. I was just getting breakfast. Do you live here now?"

I open the passenger side and place my wet bags on the floor before hopping inside.

"I guess I do." I give her Devlin's address.

"You're soaked. Take this." She reaches to the back and hands me a sweater.

"Thank you." I do my best to wipe my face and hair. "I can't believe the rain came so hard and fast."

"I know. They said it might hold off until tonight, but I guess Mother Nature had other thoughts. So, what brings you all the way up here?"

"Oh, well, I kind of have some news." I grin, extending my ring finger to show her the round diamond and matching band.

Her eyes grow as she glances at it before staring back at the road. "Wait, you're married? Please tell me it's not to that awful man."

"No." I shake my head and grin. "The one I've always liked. Loved, actually."

I breathe in and smile, unable to wait until I surprise him with dinner tonight.

"That's great." Her eyes shine as they look at me. "You deserve it."

She groans when we happen upon some traffic cones in the middle of the street, blocking our access to the next block.

A construction worker points left, indicating where we can go. Of course they're doing this in the middle of the day, in a crowded street in the city. Makes sense.

"We can head up this way," she says. "Then I can take you around to your new apartment."

"Do you live around here?"

"Oh, yeah. Only a few blocks away. It's a lovely area to live."

I nod. "I like the city, especially Central Park."

She rounds the corner to a one-way street, the rain pummeling against the hood of the car.

A vehicle behind us honks, getting closer.

"What the hell?" she snaps. "Doesn't he realize there's nowhere to go?"

She honks back, but instead of slowing down, the driver goes faster.

My skin prickles.

Professor Montgomery shakes her head, and when she reaches the corner of the street, she turns onto a two-way road. Instead of driving straight past us, the car follows right behind.

"Oh my God!" she screams as another vehicle speeds the wrong way and right toward us. "He's gonna hit us! Get out!"

But it's too late.

One moment, she's telling me to go, and the next second, there's a loud boom before my body jolts, the car flipping to its side.

Groaning, I blink past the blurriness.

"Professor?" I mutter. "Professor?"

My eyes fill with terror as I find her on the bottom, her eyes closed, a gash on her forehead, blood running down her face.

"Professor Montgomery!" I scream. "Wake up!"

Someone pries my door open, and I'm relieved that we have help. She has to be okay!

I should've listened to Devlin. I should've stayed home.

"P-please help—" But the words seize in my chest as I stare at a man whose eyes I immediately recognize, even through the ski mask. "No!"

I try to get the seat belt off. To run. To do anything I can to escape. But there's nowhere to go.

He reaches for me, something in his hand. A cloth of some kind. And as soon as he places it around my mouth and nose, my screams die.

The fight in me disappears.

And everything goes black.

THIRTY-FOUR

DEVLIN

Jolting awake, I find the space beside me empty. Instant alarm wakes me up completely when I don't see or hear her in the shower.

"Eriu?" I rush out of the room, thinking she's probably in the kitchen getting something to eat.

But the place is empty, and she's nowhere to be found.

The rain falls from the sky, pummeling the ground below, and I start to wonder if she's out there. But what reason would she have to go out?

I grab my phone, intending to text her, when I find a note she wrote lying beside it.

Just went to the store on 65th to get some stuff for us. And I can already see you worrying. Don't. I love you. I'll be back in thirty.

With a growl, I text her.

DEVLIN

> I'm coming to pick you up. Stay at the store.

Luckily, Patrick had my car sent over after the wedding. He just didn't want me driving on our wedding day.

I slip into my shoes and rush out and into the elevator. When I make it down, I ask the doorman if he's seen her. He confirms she left an hour ago.

Something stirs in my gut. That's too long. She should've been back by now.

Getting in my car, I press a few keys on my cell and try locating her phone. But nothing comes up. Breaths burst in and out from my constricted chest.

Something happened to her.

Something bad.

"Feck!" I start the car and speed down toward the store I know she went to, calling Iseult as I do.

"Hey, what's up? Everything okay?"

"Listen. I'm afraid something happened to Eriu."

"What?" Alarm lines her voice. "What do you mean?"

"She left me a note an hour ago saying she was heading for the grocery store, but the GPS on her cell has been tampered with."

"God damn it! We're on our way to you." She takes a long, ominous pause. "Do you think… Do you think they got to her?"

My hand clamps around the steering wheel. I don't want to

admit it to myself, but what else would it be?

"Aye."

"I won't lose my sister. You hear me, Devlin?! I won't lose her."

"Can't lose her either." My adrenaline spikes.

"Then we figure out how to find her. Call the Russians. I don't care! Find her!"

She drops the call, and with a growl, I pound the wheel with a fist. How do I constantly keep failing her?!

"Feck!" I can't lose her too.

I knew I shouldn't have married her. I put her at risk even more.

Taking Iseult's advice, I call Konstantin.

He immediately answers. "Hello, friend. I received the money you owed me. Much appreciated. What can I do for you?"

"Look, I need your help. Someone took Eriu. Someone from my past. This gang run by Francis Palmer from California."

"And why would they want to hurt you or the lovely Ms. Quinn?"

"Actually, it's Mrs. McHale now."

He chuckles with a twinge of shock. "Well, well. Pozdravleyu. You finally wised up. I guess you have me to thank for my part in it."

"Maybe not. Now that she's my wife, they're going to kill her just to hurt me."

"Did you betray them?"

I can't exactly tell Konstantin everything, so I give him a little bit of the truth.

"I left, and they didn't approve. Killed my brother for it, and now they're gonna kill her."

"Nu da. You have a problem. Let me get some people on it, and I'll call you if I have something."

"Thanks."

He ends the call, and I drop the cell into the cup holder, turning left on a street with some construction going on.

Muttering a curse, I turn onto another block, but this time, something else stops me.

Ambulance lights flash, a fire truck in front of it.

My heart stills as I parallel park and jump out, running toward the scene, needing to make sure she isn't hurt…or dead.

The cops have the area taped off, a car flipped onto the passenger side. I recognize one of the officers who works for Patrick and get his attention.

"Devlin, hey," he whispers. "You shouldn't be here."

"What happened here?" I glance at the car, the front windows smashed like someone broke it.

"Car accident and possible abduction. Witness said someone went straight into it."

Feck.

"Who was inside?"

"No one that we saw when we got here." He glances at the other cops as he continues, like he doesn't want them to overhear. "Witness said he saw a man in a ski mask heading for the car, and he dragged two women out, then brought them into a black SUV."

"Bloody hell!" I grab the back of my neck and squeeze. "What did they look like? Did he say?"

"One was in jeans and had darker hair, maybe black. The other had long brown hair and light pink sneakers. That's all I know for now. We're waiting on cameras."

His voice trails. There's a ringing in my ear, so loud I can barely hear him.

Light pink sneakers…

It's her. It's the shoes I got her.

They have her. The Palmers have her. But whose car was she in and why? They wouldn't hesitate to kill an innocent bystander if they had to.

"Which way?"

"What?"

"Which way did they go?!" I snap, and the other officers all turn to me.

He gives them a quick nod and waves off their concern like I'm some nosy citizen. "Shut up before you make a scene."

"Just tell me what I need to know."

"They headed down that way." He points to his left. "That's all we have so far. We have people looking at nearby cameras for the SUV."

They won't find it. I'm sure they've had the car destroyed by now.

"You know my number if you find out anything else."

Running back to my car, I intend to call Patrick. He must be going insane right now.

As soon as I start to dial, it rings. And it's a number I don't recognize.

"Yeah?"

"You'll get an address," says a man. "Come alone."

"Is she alive?"

"Devlin!" she screams, and relief and rage take hold of me simultaneously.

"Don't you feckin' touch my wife!"

"You're not the one making demands here. Now shut up and hurry. Or the boss will get trigger-happy."

"Tell Palmer I'm coming."

The line goes dead, and a text immediately comes through with an address.

I don't know that area. Somewhere in Queens, outside the city, probably commercial with not much foot traffic.

Ignoring his threat, I give Iseult the info. I know she's gonna be smart about it. The Messinas and the Quinns will have the place, and the arseholes inside won't even know it.

I just hope they keep her alive long enough for me to save her the way I couldn't save my brother.

THIRTY-FIVE

ERIU

I blink through the darkness clouding my vision. Voices, too many, ring in my ears.

"What do you wanna do to the girl before he gets here?" a man asks, but it's like he's far away, or like I'm underwater.

"We wait. Nothing happens without my say-so. Got it, Roy?"

I instantly shrink back.

That voice…it causes a gasp to escape.

I know that voice. Heard it countless times.

This can't be happening.

This isn't real.

I can't breathe.

Can't run.

My body, it feels like lead.

Anger and fear tangle furiously inside me as I pant, reeling from the realization of it all.

I've been betrayed.

"I want to see the look on his face when I slit her throat."

Every hair on my body wakes, and I'm instantly doused in absolute mind-crunching panic. The kind that seeps into your marrow and wakes up every nightmare you've ever had.

Why? That's the question that plays in my head. Why would she do this?

"Oh, look, she's awake." Someone yanks the blindfold off me and I blink faster, registering her face.

The woman I trusted, the one who was like a mentor to me, was nothing but an enemy.

Professor Montgomery snaps my chin, turning my head both ways, a gun in her other hand.

"You're not hurt, right?" She feigns concern while quiet sobs rip from my throbbing chest.

Her forehead is bandaged, but she's clearly fine.

"I thought the accident was a bit too much." She rolls her eyes, glancing back at the man behind her. "But the boys can be a little dramatic."

Her laughter makes my sobs grow louder.

"Now, now," she tsks. "I know this is all scary, and I'm sure you have a lot of questions."

"W-why?" I wrangle out the word, sticky in my throat. "Why would you do this to me?"

My wrists pinch, tied behind me on the cold floor in a building of some sort.

"I'm not doing it to you, sweetheart. I'm doing it to Scott. Or Devlin." The scrape of her laugh is like a knife puncture to my throat. "If he hadn't betrayed us, we wouldn't be in this mess."

"Us?" I whisper. "You're…"

My head spins. She can't be. How? Nothing is making sense.

"Yes, sorry." She hikes up a well-manicured brow. "Getting ahead of myself. Let's start at the beginning. My name is Lordes Palmer. I'm the youngest daughter of Francis Palmer. Nice to officially meet you, Eriu Quinn." Her eyes narrow, a seedy look within them.

She's a Palmer. She's one of them. How the hell did she manage this?! Is she really a professor? Did she start working at the school because of me?

"See, Devlin betrayed us to the feds. And after we killed his brother, they came for my dad and my brothers. My father killed himself to avoid prison, and my brothers finally got out recently."

Her heels clack as she ponders the rest, gripping her gun tightly in her grasp. I just need to keep her talking long enough to survive. I have to believe Devlin will save me.

"Is Roy your brother?" I ask her.

She freezes, snapping those cold eyes at me. "One of them. The other two are with our men downstairs, waiting to kill your husband."

All the blood leaves my body.

"Please don't. I beg you! Don't you want to move on from all this?" My chest shakes with each word. Maybe there's some hope to convince her to let this go. "I know you're hurting, but killing his brother should've been enough."

"Enough?" She laughs, then her face goes hard. "No. It'll never be enough. I made my father a promise that when he was gone, I would continue his legacy and I, *me*..." She slaps a palm over her chest. "...would bring our family justice." She grabs a fistful of my shirt and nears her face to mine. "And that will only happen when I hurt Devlin by hurting you, right before I kill him."

I pant with silent whimpers. She won't let this go. I've never seen her this way. Never knew she hated me this whole time.

She releases a dramatic exhale and drops her hand off of me.

"I've always wanted to prove myself to my father. You see, he never saw me like one of my brothers. I was a girl. Weak. Pathetic." She rolls her eyes. "But I wish Dad was still alive to see what I've managed to accomplish." Her chin inclines with indignation. "Sometimes it takes a woman's touch, don't you think? For these men to see us? It's what you fight for, isn't it? To be seen by your own father?" That gaze takes me in coldly. "It's a shame I have to kill you. I saw a lot of myself in you."

"Please," I cry. "I don't want to die. Please don't do this!"

"Hush now. Save your tears. There's nothing you can say to change my mind."

My body sags, and I continue to sob. "D-d-did you really work with Mason? For what?"

Her grin spreads. "We've been following Devlin and your family for years. I knew Devlin, and I knew he'd never wanna get married after his brother, even if he did like you." She runs a finger through the hair lining her face. "But see, I also suspected that if I paid off some asshole to marry you, Devlin would wanna take his place, especially if you decided to sell your virginity."

"W-what?" I can barely speak, not sure what she's trying to tell me.

She laughs. "I mean, I didn't know if you were brave enough to go through with it, but bravo. You fell right into my trap."

The room spins as my mind races, taking short, shallow breaths.

I don't understand what's happening.

"How would you even know about the club?"

"Knew about it?" She scoffs. "I made sure you went." With every footfall, she comes closer until she's kneeling in front of me, the back of her hand gliding down my cheek until I recoil. "Wanna know how?"

But I don't. I can't take any more. My chest snaps so tight I can barely breathe.

She continues to look pleased with herself, straightening before glancing behind her shoulder at her brother. She tilts her head to the side in a quick snap, and I have no idea what that meant, but I'm sure it's not good.

My entire body tremors, gasping for air, the pulse in my ears louder.

Her brother disappears for a moment, and in the next, another guy returns with him, dragging someone.

Not just someone.

"Karen? Oh my God! Don't touch her! She has nothing to do with this!"

But the professor simply laughs like I've said something ridiculous. "Nothing to do with this? Oh, she has everything to do with this. Don't you, sweetheart?"

"What?" I whisper, my eyes growing large.

"Please, Mom! Don't do this!"

"Mom?" I gasp.

And in that split second is when the realization finally hits and everything changes.

Everything I believed, everything I've clung to, simply vanishes. And in its place is darkness, so black I can't see through it.

Fresh tears blanket my vision, nausea swirling, my head spinning until I feel as though I may pass out.

"Nonono!" I whimper, my chest heaving while fat tears roll down my face.

But no matter how many times I close my eyes, I see the same thing: Karen stands in front of me, her eyes glassy, face blotchy, calling this woman *Mom*.

"Karen? What's going on here?! Please tell me she's not your mother! That you weren't… Oh my God." I crumble, sinking deeper into the cold floor, weeping and shaking my head.

My best friend stands there calling this woman her mother. She lied to me? Was our friendship all a lie too? Were all the people I trusted just out to hurt me?

"Oh my God." I can't breathe.

Karen doesn't meet my gaze, and every ounce of blood rushes out of my body.

"Karen?" I sob. "Look at me."

But she still refuses, peering at her mother through red-stained eyes. She looks nothing like the well-put-together, confident woman I've always known her to be. In her place is someone broken.

"You stupid girl!" The professor slaps her hard across her cheek. "You got too close, and now look at you!" Her upper lip curls in disgust.

Karen weeps, holding her face.

"Don't you remember what Scott did to your grandpa? Your uncles? We lost *everything* because of him, and now he gets to feel what I did all those years!"

"But, Mom," she whimpers. "It's not her fault. Please, please, if you love me, you'll let her go!"

Professor Montgomery blows a disappointed breath. "This is why you'll never be in charge of this organization when I'm gone. Your twin brother will have it all. He has our interests at heart. You, on the other hand, are a constant disappointment. You couldn't even attend the wedding so we could take her then. Because of you, we had to do something drastic."

She was going to take me at my own wedding… She's insane!

"I'm sorry," Karen whispers, finally looking at me, and for a moment, it feels as though I have my best friend back.

But she was nothing but a lie.

"Shut up!" her mother hollers. "She isn't your friend. I know I had to constantly remind you of that."

The professor's bemused smirk lands on me.

"Karen being my daughter must come as a huge shock. I mean, she did do her job. I have to give her that." She gives her daughter a passing look. "When I found out you'd be transferring to the same university as her, it was like fate. I easily got a job there thanks to a fellow colleague and told Karen to befriend you. And my plan of getting back at Devlin seemed easier than ever."

Karen quietly sobs, shame lining her gaze.

"The club, that was an added bonus. I knew Adam's father. So I asked him for a favor, and that is how you got the invite. All Karen had to do was make sure you went and joined the auction. I must say, I had very little faith she'd actually do it. Isn't that right, darling?"

Her eyes narrow at her daughter, and I almost feel bad for Karen, if that's even her real name.

"I'm so sorry, Eriu!" She cries, shaking her head. "I had no choice!"

"Shut your damn mouth!" The professor glares, and Karen shrinks into herself.

A sudden loud smashing sound causes me to jerk, my heart racing until it feels as though it'll jump out of my throat.

Please, let it be Devlin and my family! Please!

"Go check with them downstairs," she tells Roy, who immediately does, leaving us alone with her and the henchman who's holding Karen.

The professor kneels, lowering her hand to her ankle, and pulls out a flip knife. She eyes me with a brutal stare, strutting up toward me.

"I hope that's him." She grabs my hair from the back and lines the knife against my carotid.

"Mom!" Karen sobs. "Please don't hurt her!"

But she ignores her, staring ahead, waiting for Devlin.

She doesn't wait long. The door flies open, and he rushes in, holding a young man in his grip, a gun pointed at the guy's temple.

"Get your hands off my wife!" His eyes go to mine, and in them, I find pain, so much of it.

"Ah, there you are. Took you long enough."

My scalp burns as she yanks harder, making me wince.

"Been listening to every word you said, Lordes. It's a shame it took us this long to meet, wouldn't ya say?"

"Believe me, I've been waiting a long time for this. Now, drop the boy and come fight me like a man."

The guy holding Karen points his weapon at Devlin, and my nerves can't take it anymore.

"I don't think I'll do that," Devlin says. "See, you've got a knife to her throat and I have a gun to your nephew's head. And I have a feeling you'd rather me kill your daughter than him, isn't that right?"

At that, Karen wails, and I wish I could hold her. I know she betrayed me, and I'm so angry, but I can't help but want to comfort her too. Clearly, she didn't have a good family life.

"Fuck you, you traitor!" The blade deepens against my skin. "Let my brother's boy go! Or I kill her right now."

The boy isn't that young, a few years older than me.

"You're gonna kill her anyway, so why would I let him live?" He tightens his arm around the guy's neck. "See, you thought you were smarter than me. That your people would easily overpower me and I'd let history repeat itself. But not this time. So, what will it be? Blood for blood, or do we let them go?"

"I will kill you!" she snaps.

"You could, but I have the place surrounded. Got the Irish, the Italians, and even the Russians ready to light your arse up. So, you may kill my wife and me, but you'll all be dead too."

"You bastard! My father trusted you. He treated you like a son!" she hollers. "And you gave us up like we meant nothing. And for what? For some junkie brother who would've ended up dead on the street with a needle in his arm anyway?" She snickers. "I'll never stop hunting you. No matter where you go, I'll be there, taking everything from you. It's why I needed you to marry her. Being together wasn't enough. I wanted to take her from you in the worst way. To make it hurt as much as I could."

"Well, you've done that. Now let her go and take me."

"That'll never be enough, and you know it. Not after the way you destroyed my family!"

I pinch my eyes closed, my body trembling, gasping for breaths that never come. Fear for Devlin and for myself hits me hard.

This could be it. Our future could vanish right here and now.

"My father never paid much attention to me," she goes on. "You never even met me because I was never a part of the business. But little did my father know, I watched him and learned everything." She sounds proud of herself. "You may have not known me, but I knew everything about you. I knew how you'd react if someone like Mason married her. I mean, he was already an asshole. Didn't take much to make him threaten Eriu about her virginity."

Devlin's face contorts with rage, even while he tries to remain calm.

"I figured that would make little Eriu desperate enough to join the auction to avoid marrying him. I love being right." Her voice mocks. "The only hiccup was if you'd actually marry her. I wanted her to be your wife when I took her from you. When I made you watch as another person you love got taken from you. If you'd been loyal, none of this would've happened. It's all your fault."

Devlin grunts low in his chest, glancing at me, jaw flexing. "I did what I had to do to keep the feds from taking my brother to prison."

She claps, slapping one palm on her other forearm. "Bravo. Except he ended up dead anyway. Prison would've been better."

"It's over, Lordes," he warns. "Give up now."

"I'll never go down like a coward. She's gonna—"

Pop.

I gasp, screaming as a bullet flies through the window and enters her temple.

And in a flash, another enters the man holding Karen.

He falls with a thud.

"No!" Karen runs toward her mother's dead body lying on the ground. "Mom! No!" she shrieks. "Mom!"

There's a sudden pang in my chest from her heavy wails. No matter how terrible she was, that's still her mom.

The whole thing hasn't really hit me. Karen and my professor were mother and daughter. How did I not see any of it? But Karen never mentioned much about her family. Now I see why.

"Devlin!" I call to him while he throws the nephew on the ground.

The man holds out his hands in front of his face, breaths hitched. But nothing will stop a bullet.

Devlin shoots him once in the head, and my chin trembles. He just killed someone. Right in front of me.

I pinch my eyes shut, muttering and whimpering to myself as I cry.

"I've got you, lass. It's okay. I've got you."

Devlin.

He cuts the zip ties from my wrists, and my arms jump around him. And when he holds me, when I feel his intense breaths, that's when everything in me cracks like a dam. Feeling his heartbeats next to mine, his hold around me tightening, my body sags.

I'm safe. He's safe.

We're okay.

"I thought I'd lost you." His own emotions wreck through him. "Don't ever scare me like that again."

My hands grip his shirt in tight fists.

"Let's get you out of here." He lifts me in the air and gathers me in his arms, cradling me.

When I look around, I see familiar faces: Gio, my sister, some of the Messinas. They're all here. They all came for me.

But someone else is here too. Someone I didn't expect to see. My stomach churns.

The last time I saw him, I was on stage losing my virginity.

"Hello, daragaya. I see you're in one piece, and what a relief that is." His mouth tips up.

Konstantin.

They all must've killed the men downstairs, the ones working for the professor. I look for Karen, not seeing her at first, until I find Rogue holding her by the arm.

"What do you wanna do with her?" he asks Devlin.

"Kill her."

"What?!" Spasms wrack my muscles until it seems like my bones will snap, and I force him to put me down. "No! You can't!"

"Please," Karen cries. "Please, I swear I won't say anything. I'll disappear. I—I'll get out of the country. Just don't kill me!"

"Devlin." I grab his arm and give him a stern look. "Don't do it! You can't!"

"Mo stoirín, she hurt you. I can't let her live." His finger brushes across my lips.

"You have to," I plead. "You have to do this for me, or we have no future. I won't forgive you for this."

His eyes slowly close, and he inhales a long breath.

"Fine. But if we catch wind of you here again…" he tells her. "You're dead."

She sags with relief, and Rogue lets her go.

"Eriu." Tears roll down her face. "I'm sorry I hurt you. I swear I didn't know how far she'd go. I never wanted you to find out because I love you. I wasn't lying when I said you were the best person I knew."

I swipe under my lashes. "Is Karen even your real name?"

I don't know why that's important in the grand scheme of things, but somehow it is.

She nods. "Yes. She made me become your friend, but I need you to know my feelings became genuine." She wilts like a flower, slowly dying right in front of me. "I had no choice. Not with her."

I nod with some form of understanding.

"You'll never see me again. I promise. Bye, Eriu. Please be happy."

Her lips quiver into a broken smile, and with a final look she turns and heads toward the exit.

Pop.

A bullet pierces the back of her head and she falls instantly.

"No!" My agonizing scream pierces through the echo of the gunshot as I run for Konstantin, his weapon still pointing in her direction. "No! Why?" I bang my fists on his chest. "Why did you kill her?! Why?!"

He just stares at me and lets me hit him, completely unaffected. "You never leave loose ends, daragaya. That's how you get killed."

With my hands quivering, I stare up at him with grief-stricken eyes, and I run for my friend's dead body and drop to the ground beside her. Laying my cheek on her stomach, I hold her as blood seeps from the hole in her head.

She didn't deserve this. She deserved more, a mother who loved and protected her, but instead she ended up a casualty in her mother's war for vengeance.

"Why did you do this? Why couldn't you talk to me? I could've helped you!"

But she doesn't answer. She can't say anything else ever again. She's gone. Just like that.

I don't know how long I stay there, holding her that way. But I can't seem to let go.

DEVLIN

The place is no longer filled with people. It's just Eriu, Karen, and me. She sobs over her dead friend while I want to choke the life out of Konstantin.

He did the right thing. I can't tell her that, though.

Karen could've come after her. Give someone enough rage, enough years to feel it, and they can do anything.

We managed to kill everyone who was at the abandoned sawmill where they kept Eriu. All the Palmer siblings are dead. And anyone left will be wiped out too. This needs to end once and for all.

"Baby, we have to go now." I lower beside her, and she doesn't even glance at me, her face hidden against her friend.

"We have to bury her," she whimpers. "We can't leave her here."

"Of course we will. I promise. The guys will take care of her properly once we're gone, and you can choose the spot, okay?"

She sniffles and nods, finally lifting her head upward. "I can't believe it. I really can't believe it. I trusted Professor Montgomery. I thought she cared about me. That Karen cared about me."

"I know. I'm sorry. I missed it too."

I slip my hand into hers and lift her to a standing position. She stares down at her friend and starts to sob again. But this time, she buries her face in my chest, and I hold her against my own broken heart, hating that she had to endure this much hurt, wishing I could do something about it.

THIRTY-SIX

ERIU
FIVE DAYS LATER

"We're gathered here today to remember Professor Montgomery and Karen Stuart, both of whom we lost on the same day in a tragic car accident," the dean says to a packed outdoor vigil. "We mourn together and remember all the memories we shared with them. They will never be forgotten because they live in our hearts."

Devlin stands behind me, his arms clasped tightly around me like I'm fragile and broken.

But I'm not broken. I'm angry.

Swiping at my eyes, I blink away the tears, hating that they're there. Hating that I still cry into my pillow at night.

They lied to me. Used my good nature against me. And for what? It got them nothing in the end.

"You're going to be an amazing writer one day. You'll prove

your father wrong."

I can just see her face. Professor Montgomery—or Lordes, whoever she was. I remember her when she said that to me. It was the first time I really believed in myself. Believed that I could be a writer.

But maybe she was lying. Maybe she just wanted to trick me into believing that I was good so I could fail at something. Were my grades even real? Or were they inflated so I thought I was better than I really am?

I can't even ask her now, 'cause she's dead. In the dirt rotting where she belongs.

I quietly sob, my body breaking along with my heart. She was more than a professor to me. I wanted to be just like her, but she was a monster. A liar. A murderer! The whole time she was being nice to me, she was planning to kill me! Everything was her doing! I was nothing but a puppet!

"Come on, let me paint your toes!"

Karen's smiling face appears before me now, and no matter how hard I fight the pull, the memories carry me back in time. Us in her room, her painting my toes yellow because it was pretty. I hated it, but I didn't tell her that because I loved her and wanted to make her happy.

"I'm so happy I met you."

Was she, though? Or was that another lie? If I just close my eyes, I can feel it…her arms as she hugged me.

Remembering Karen is even more painful than what the professor did. Karen and I were inseparable. I thought we would be friends many years from now.

How wrong I was…

I remembered something recently. There was one day she got a call from her mom. She left the room, and when she came back, I could tell she had been crying. She didn't want to talk about it and immediately acted like she was fine, grabbing the remote to turn on a comedy until we were both laughing. Now I wonder what that call was about. What her mother—the professor—was making her do.

My friend was never a friend. She was a spy.

I pinch my eyes closed, my pain seeping from every corner. I can't be friends with anyone anymore. No one can be trusted. I have Kayla, Devlin, and my family. That'll be enough.

I thought I could live a normal life. I was wrong. Normalcy doesn't exist for people like us.

"It'll be okay." Devlin's whisper comes through, but I just ignore him.

It won't be okay. Nothing will ever be okay.

He's urged me to visit Karen's grave. To talk to her. What a joke. She can't hear me. She's dead! Gone.

The back of my nose throbs, and I fight it. I don't want to feel anything for her. She doesn't deserve it. Yet she does…

"I never wanted you to find out because I love you. I wasn't lying when I said you were the best person I knew."

Her words echo in my mind from right before she was shot. I can't come to terms with these two opposite emotions—the betrayal and the friendship.

I can't even go back to school. This was the first day I returned, and that was only because Devlin said I needed to attend the memorial. Everything reminds me of Karen or Professor Montgomery.

Is this who I am now? An angry shell of a woman? Is that what happens when people are betrayed?

I thought I could handle going back to school the day after it happened. Thought I was strong even when everyone told me to take time off.

But as soon as I passed the professor's office, I had a panic attack. I had to leave school. Haven't been to Karen's dorm room either. I hear there's a whole memorial on her door—photos, ribbons, notes taped on the wall. I can't look at any of that. Easier to pretend it doesn't exist.

"If anyone needs to speak to someone..." the dean goes on. "We have resources available for you."

I look around at the stricken faces, students crying as they hold each other. I just shake my head because they have no idea who they're crying over. The professor had everyone fooled.

But my family didn't want her true identity coming out, so they kept it under wraps. Paid off the cops so they could forge the reports to say that Karen was in the car with the professor. That they both died inside on impact. And that was it. Not like anyone will dispute it.

Karen's father apparently died a couple of years ago. Devlin says there's talk that her mom did it when she found out he was cheating.

I turn to Devlin. "Can we go now?"

He sighs. "Yeah, sure."

I start walking away, shoving a few people as I try to maneuver myself out of here. Devlin follows me, walking right up beside me.

"Can we talk?" He grabs my hand, but I shove it off.

"There's nothing left for me here. I'll finish the semester online if they let me, or transfer out."

"Eriu. We need to talk about this." He stops mid-stride and curls an arm around my back to keep me close. Tentatively, he cups my cheek. "I don't want you stuffing this down and dealing with it on your own. Nothing good comes from that. I'm telling you from experience."

"Please, I don't wanna hear this right now." Ignoring him, I head for his car.

"I love you, lass. I don't want to see you hurting this way. Just talk to someone."

I snicker, rolling my eyes.

"Talking won't make it better," I snap. "Every place reminds me of Karen. I hear her laughter in my sleep. The things she'd say to me. The fun we had." Bitter laughter escapes me. "And it was all a lie. Do you know how stupid I feel?"

I stop in the middle of the street and grab my head, squeezing my temples.

He tugs my jaw up between two fingers. "Maybe it wasn't all a lie. Maybe what she said was true. She did a bad thing, but she regretted it. She loved you. I saw it. You saw it too, and that's why it kills you, isn't it? Because you love her too."

My chin trembles, tears blanketing my vision, and with a sob, I throw myself into his arms and cry against his chest.

I cry for our friendship. I cry for the way she hurt me. But most of all, I cry because I can't tell her that I forgive her.

I want just one more day to tell her that I love her too.

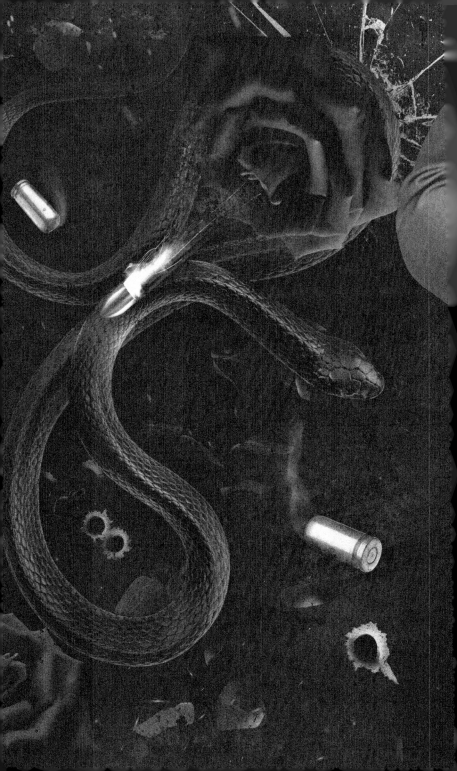

THIRTY-SEVEN

DEVLIN
TWO WEEKS LATER

E riu refuses to talk to me. She'd rather pretend it never happened. She puts on a happy smile, but I hear her crying in the shower. I know she has a lot of emotions she's not dealing with.

After my brother was killed, I didn't deal with shite. I kept it all in, and I don't want her to suffer like I did.

But I can't force her to talk either. Iseult has tried too, but she shuts everyone down, saying we're not helping by bringing up what happened.

It's easier to hide from pain. The hard part comes from embracing it and learning to let it go. I hope she realizes that sooner than I did.

I have eyes on Eriu at all times. But it's Rogue and another Quinn enforcer who are keeping tabs when I'm doing work for the

Quinns. I still hate having someone else watch her, but I can't be everywhere at once.

She doesn't know I've got two people on her. But I've learned my lesson when it comes to this woman. It's for her own safety. And for my peace of mind.

I can't lose my wife. I'd die without her.

The Palmers are no longer a threat. Anyone who was loyal to them was taken out too, including Karen's twin brother. With them gone, there's no one left. We're free of them.

My cell rings, and I glance down to find Iseult calling.

"Yeah?" I answer.

"Is she doing any better?" Concern weaves in her tone.

"No. She needs help, and I don't know how to give it to her."

She sighs. "She keeps dodging me too. Dad still wants to have her birthday party in two weeks. Think she'll wanna come?"

"I'll try to get her there. I'll tell her it'll mean a lot to your father."

"Not sure if that'll do anything. She's been rejecting his calls too."

I rub a palm over my face. "We've just gotta give her some time. This is hard for her."

"I know that. I just wish I could do more."

The water in the bathroom shuts off, and I know I have a few more minutes while she's drying her hair.

"Look, I've gotta go. She's done with her shower, and I don't want her thinking we're talking about her behind her back."

"That's literally what we're doing."

"Yeah, genius, I know that. Going now."

The door starts to open, and I immediately end the call and drop the phone on the bed beside me.

Eriu comes out with a towel wrapped around her body, her

brows pinched tight. "Were you just talking to someone?"

"Aye." I scratch my temple. "Just work stuff for your dad."

"Oh, okay…"

She starts for the dresser, and I breathe with relief. I hate lying to her.

My eyes linger on the backs of her bare legs and my cock swells, missing her, craving and needing her. I haven't attempted to touch her, merely content with holding her as she drifts off to sleep. When she's ready, I'll know.

She slips off the towel, still facing the dresser and starts getting dressed.

"Do you want to go out for dinner tonight?" I ask, my fist curling, everything in me snapping.

I've never felt this helpless.

"Sure." She gives me a wide grin over her shoulder.

But I know better. She's hurting, and I can't fix it.

"What do you wanna go for?"

She shrugs, avoiding my eyes now. "Whatever."

"Eriu…"

"Yes?" She clears her throat and starts refolding some of her shirts in the drawer.

"Talk to me. Talk to someone."

Her hands still, and her body rolls up and down with deep breaths. "If you plan on doing this all day, then maybe we shouldn't go to dinner."

"I'm sorry." I rise, placing my palms on her shoulders from behind, gliding them up and down her arms.

With a huff, she sags against me. "It's okay. I know you mean well."

"We all love you."

"I know that too."

"Your birthday is coming up, and your father would like to throw you a party, but before you say no—"

"I wasn't going to say that." She pivots around, and a small smile makes it on her lips. "A party may be just what I need."

"You sure, love?"

"Yeah." She throws her arms around my neck, and I see it then: a glimpse of the woman I married.

And I want her back.

"Lord, every time I remember that you're turning nineteen, I feel ancient."

"Oh, shut up!" She gives me a playful swat on my chest. "You're my sexy older husband and I like it that way."

"Do you now?" My voice drops deeper, and her eyes instantly turn hooded, her tongue darting out to lick over that bottom lip I want to suck into my mouth.

"I do…" Her tone turns huskier, and it doesn't help my raging hard-on.

I can't think about feckin' her right now. It wouldn't be right.

Yet my lips drop closer, needing to taste her, to let her know she's not alone. She rises on her feet, her mouth brushing over mine.

"Feck," I groan, my fingers slipping in her soft strands, gripping them tight in my grasp. "I've missed you."

"Missed you too…"

She kisses me slow, her soft lips sliding around mine. I don't dare kiss her back, needing to simply feel her.

Her fingers sink into my shoulders, and she pushes our bodies closer, forcing me backward until my legs hit the edge of the bed.

She looms over me, cheeks a little flushed as she starts to pull her t-shirt up until it's falling to the floor, her nipples hard, and I ache to take them into my mouth.

"Are you sure?" I ask, not wanting to push this, no matter how badly I may want her.

She nods, drawing her leggings down and stepping out of them.

My cock throbs, and I pull it out, fisting it tight, dragging my hand up and down as I stare down her body. My God, it's been too long.

She gazes at me hotly, running her fingers past her abdomen, right above where she's warm and wet and mine.

"Come on now, lass. Stop teasing me and put this cock inside you and feck it."

She tugs on her bottom lip as she struts closer, settling over me, her knees dropping on each side of my hips. She flips her hair and leans her chest flat against me, her enticing breaths mingling with mine. Her core rocks against me like she needs this.

And so do I. The feeling of her wet cunt against my hard-on is making me lose all my control.

My hand reaches for her hair, wrapping it tight around my wrist, and I slam her mouth to mine. Growling, I take the lead this time, kissing her with raw, aching passion, flipping her around as my mouth feasts on her neck. The pulse beneath pounds as fast as my heart does.

My tongue rolls over her beaded flesh, teeth wrapped around it as I pull and flick.

She bucks and moans, her back arching as I lower down her stomach, pulling her thighs apart, needing to taste her.

"You smell so fecking good, baby, and you taste even better." My tongue sweeps up from her opening to her clit. "All feckin' mine."

"Oh, God!" she whimpers, thrashing beneath me, the desire tethered to every inch of her flesh.

I live to make her happy.

"You're mine. You hear me? Mine to love. Mine to take care of. And I will do that for the rest of my life."

She's beyond the ability to speak, her body lost to the things I make her feel. When I roll the tip of my tongue around her clit, she cries out, gripping my hair hard.

I grunt, enjoying her brand of pain, sucking her into my mouth, needing her to come undone, to let me have it all just so I can do it all over again.

There's no way I can stop, not until I have her screaming my name. Not until she forgets what happened, forgets the ugliness, even for a moment. Because later, she'll remember it all over again, and I won't be able to do a thing about it.

When her release comes, shattering with my name branded on her lips, I flip her over and force her knees up, thrusting all the way inside, until we're both lost to it. Lost to the feeling when the world disappears and it's just the two of us to hold on to.

THIRTY-EIGHT

ERIU
TWO WEEKS LATER

W e're almost at my father's estate, minutes remaining until I have no choice but to face my entire family. Their looks of pity. Or worse, walking around me on eggshells, like one wrong step and I'll crack.

Maybe they're used to death, the betrayal of others from being who we are. But I'm not. I'd like to say the time has helped somehow, but that's a lie.

I don't know if anything will erase the pain I feel every moment I think about Karen. I try to pretend I'm okay, but I know Devlin sees right through me.

Unfortunately, I had to return to school. They wouldn't allow me to take courses online mid-semester, and switching to a new school would've been even more of an issue for my credits, so I decided I had to go back. I can't allow my grades to plummet.

Those first few days I was back, students would come up to me and tell me how sorry they were about Karen. They'd cry and hug me while I had to stand there and console them. It was awful. Luckily, over time, they forgot about me. Karen didn't really mean anything to them. Not like she did to me. I was her actual friend.

Sure you were, you idiot.

Feeling like a fool, I bite down so hard, my jaw aches.

She was never my friend.

My knee bounces, and Devlin's palm is there, squeezing my thigh as we pull up to my father's estate, the guards letting us through the gate.

"It'll be okay," he reassures me.

But I don't know if I believe him.

He parks in the driveway beside one of my father's old-fashioned cars, and when I open the door, my stomach knots. I've never dreaded seeing my family, not until now.

Devlin comes around to take my hand, bringing my knuckles to his lips. "Your father assured me no one will talk about what happened."

I purse my mouth. "Okay."

He pulls me to my feet, and together, we make it up the cobblestones, where two more guards are nodding to us in greeting before letting us inside.

Noise carries into the foyer, laughter and the clinking of glass reverberating.

He clutches my hand as he leads me toward my family, and when we enter the twenty-seat dining room, every pair of eyes lands on me. Even the Messinas are here, and why wouldn't they be? We're all one big, happy family now.

I instantly want to run, to escape this awkwardness, but Devlin simply squeezes my hand reassuringly, and I feel a fragment better.

He clears his throat, and my father and Fernanda immediately stand from their chairs.

"There she is! The birthday girl!" He rushes to me and hugs me tight, kissing the top of my hand, his eyes searching my face for signs of my broken heart.

He sighs and gives me one last kiss before Fernanda comes to embrace me affectionately.

"Happy birthday, sweetheart." Her brows tug, and she pats me dolefully on the shoulder before walking away.

I hate this. I truly hate it.

Fionn comes up to us next, with my other two brothers trailing behind.

Iseult, though? She remains seated beside Gio, her eyes holding mine.

"Before you know it, you'll be as old as me," Fionn teases.

He's only thirty-one. Not old at all.

"Or better yet, like this one." He slaps a palm across Tynan's back, who's seven years older.

Tynan's not amused, giving him a stern look, but when he looks at me, his eyes grow softer.

That was always the thing with Tynan. He was the one most people feared, but I knew my brother. He was hard on the outside, too hard, but he had to be, growing up the way he did: the oldest, the one who would one day take over for my father. But he was a good big brother. He looked out for me growing up. Read to me when I'd wake up in the middle of the night with a nightmare.

"Want a drink?" He leads me to the bar, and I pass Gio and Iseult, both looking up at me.

I can tell from her face she wants to say something, probably something I don't wanna hear.

But instead, she says, "Happy birthday, sis."

"Thanks."

Tynan reaches for a glass and pours me some white wine.

"I'm not supposed to drink." My grin grows.

"I won't tell if you don't." His lips play as he hands me the liquor.

I take it to my mouth, the murmur of a burn gliding down my throat.

"So, how's married life?" he asks, tossing back a whiskey neat.

"Good. I guess." My eyes wander around the room, catching sight of eight-year-old Brody.

He sits beside Sophia as she chats him up, showing him something on her tablet. But the boy with the golden-brown hair and green eyes remains silent. Because silence is all he knows now. After all the trauma of losing his father, then his mom to suicide not even a week later, he stopped speaking, and no one can get him to talk again.

Tears bathe my eyes just imagining what he went through. I wouldn't want to talk to anyone either.

But our fear is that this is now permanent. The doctors tell Tynan that he needs time and more counseling, but that hasn't helped.

"How's he doing?" I ask Tynan, glancing between him and Brody.

He blows an exhausted breath, running a hand down his face. "Not well. He still wakes up from nightmares and jumps into my bed, shaking and crying until I can get him back to sleep."

I blink past my emotions. "I'm so sorry."

"It's him I'm sorry for. Everything he went through…it's not right. And for what? Fuck, Eriu. Maybe I'm not cut out to be a father."

"Hey." My face falls, and I place a hand on his shoulder,

looking squarely at him. "You're amazing with him. You give him stability, love, acceptance. You don't push him. You let him be. That's what he needs."

"Maybe that's the problem. Maybe I should do more. He misses his parents, his mom especially. They were close. And she just—" He pinches his temple and shuts his eyes, shaking his head.

"She was hurting, Tynan. She loved Aiden. They were high school sweethearts, remember? And she couldn't see a way past her grief. She loved Brody, but she was in pain, and sometimes when we're hurting, *that* seems like the only way to escape it."

He exhales sharply. "Yeah. I know. I don't hate her. I just wish I could do more for him. But I'll never be enough."

I fear he's right. That Brody will always feel this emptiness where his parents' love once was.

Suddenly, my father clanks his glass, getting everyone's attention, and the room falls quiet.

"Thank you, everyone, for coming to celebrate my baby girl turning nineteen." My dad's eyes crinkle at the sides as he looks at me with a smile. "You have grown into a beautiful, smart young woman, and every day, I'm even more proud of you." He clears his throat. "I can't wait until you become a bigshot author so I can read your books and tell everyone my daughter wrote them."

"Thanks, Dad." I swipe under my eyes, feeling his words in my heart.

His acceptance is what I've always wanted, and now I have it.

I rush over and give him a hug.

He holds me tight, whispering, "I love you, darling girl. Your mother would be very proud of you too."

Kissing the side of my head, he pats my back, bringing me to his side as he looks around the room. "Before the cook brings our appetizers, I wanted to make an announcement."

Devlin comes over to Tynan and gives him a knowing look.
What was that about?

"So, as some of you know, I plan on retiring." He reaches for Fernanda's hand. "My beautiful wife and I want to do some traveling, and I want to give her everything she wants. Therefore…" He locks eyes with Tynan. "It's gonna be on you now, son. I need you to take over for me, but you know the condition I have. You have to get married."

Tynan grumbles a response.

"Don't give me that look," he tells my brother. "I want our bloodline secured. You hear me? You've been postponing it long enough, and you're gonna be forty soon. It's time."

Fionn chuckles under his breath and Cillian looks equally amused. Everyone knows my brother's feelings on marriage: he wants no part.

I don't know why. He would make a good husband. After a while…

"Why the hell do I need a wife? I have an heir right here." He gestures toward Brody with a tilt of his chin. "And you've got other kids who will give you plenty."

"Never enough, son. Not with the life we live. And you know it. You have two months, tops. Find a respectable young woman and make her your wife. Maybe smile a little, would ya? Give her some incentive to say yes." My dad's features light up from Tynan's annoyed expression.

"Yeah, whatever. Fine," he grunts.

"Great! Hear that, Fernanda? Greece, here we come."

She rolls her eyes. "You take your time, Tynan. Getting married is a big responsibility, and you want to ensure you choose the right one to raise your children. I'll deal with your dad." She pats Dad on the back.

Tynan pours himself another drink, shaking his head while continuing to mutter to himself.

Iseult finally strolls up to me and throws an arm around me. "Hey, sis. Happy birthday."

"Thanks."

I can feel it coming. When my sister wants to say something, nothing can stop her.

"Let's go take a walk."

And there it is.

When I give her an irate look, her arm tightens around me.

"Please?" She glances at me, leading me out of the room and past the foyer. "Just ten minutes, then you can tell me to fuck off, okay?"

"Fine." A woosh of a breath leaves my lungs.

We make it out to the back of the estate, the perfectly manicured lawn smelling as though just freshly cut.

Lights illuminate the vast property as we start away from the towering mansion.

"I hate beating around the bush, Eriu. I hate not being able to speak my mind with you like I always have. And you have always listened to me, so please…" She turns to me and takes my hand. "Listen to me now. Okay?"

I nod, glancing down at my feet, my heart beating faster. Part of me doesn't want to hear it, but another part wonders if my big sister can maybe help me somehow. I hold on to that hope as we settle on a bench, both staring out into the darkness.

"I know how much this hurts. How badly it feels to be betrayed by someone you opened up to. Someone you considered your best friend. You were there when my own friend betrayed me. You know what I did. What I had to do. So when I say I know what you are going through, I mean that."

She's right. She does. I haven't even thought about how similar our situations are.

"At least Karen felt remorse," she continues. "She was forced into this, and of course that's horrible too. But she did love you." She faces me now. "It's okay to love her and hate her at the same time."

An ache stings behind my eyes.

"And I know you must wrestle with all these emotions, seeing her everywhere, in everything you do, because that's what happened to me. But if you can't talk to us, then you have to talk to someone." She reaches into her jeans pocket and retrieves a card, handing it to me. "She's a therapist. I vetted her before I saw her myself."

"You went to a therapist?" My eyes grow.

My sister was always against shrinks. Our mom's death hit her hard, still does, but she never wanted to talk about it.

"It was Elsie's idea, actually, and she was right. I feel lighter somehow, like I'm not holding on to this baggage that was weighing me down, you know?"

I start to consider it...

"Can I tell this therapist the truth?"

"That's the best part. You can. She works at Helping Hand, and she's discreet."

Maybe I should give it a try. What could it hurt? If it doesn't help, then I don't go back.

"How long did it take for you to feel better?"

"Everyone's different. You have to give it time, and you have to be honest."

I straighten my spine. "I'll go."

She breathes a sigh. "Proud of you." Her hand squeezes mine. "Now, how about we go and get at least a little buzzed, because this heavy shit isn't my forte."

"I think you're doing just fine," I say as we get to our feet. "Maybe Gio is rubbing off on you."

"He wishes."

DEVLIN

I watched as Eriu left with Iseult, and I knew she was going to talk to her like she said she would. I just hope it works. I want my wife back.

Tynan tosses back what may be his sixth drink already.

"Told ya this was coming," I tease, throwing a piece of bacon into my mouth.

"Don't gloat, asshole."

Fionn and Cillian walk over, Gio following them.

"Don't look so miserable." Gio throws a palm on Tynan's shoulder, but he shakes it off. "Marriage isn't so bad." He laughs. "Except for the unlucky woman who ends up with you."

"Yeah, yeah, fucking comedian," Tynan barks back.

Fionn reaches into his pocket and removes his phone. "By the way, got the 411 on the lady friend you're stalking."

"Wait, who are we stalking?" I ask, glancing between the brothers.

"Oh, he didn't tell you?" Fionn laughs. "Elara Hill, Brody's new teacher. She recently replaced the last teacher the kid had, so Tynan had me digging for dirt on her."

Tynan grunts. "Just being careful."

"Right." Cillian snickers. "It has nothing to do with her great ass or her crystal-blue eyes."

"I'm not interested," he mutters under his breath. "Never even met her in person."

"I guess you also wouldn't like to know that she was once engaged." Fionn glances at his phone.

"What?" Tynan's eyes snap to his brother. "Let me see that." He grabs the phone from his grasp and scrolls the screen.

"Now I have his attention." Fionn grins.

"Why'd she end the engagement?"

"Don't know. Maybe you should ask her over a glass of wine."

"I saw her photos too." Cillian smirks. "She's pretty. Maybe you should make her your wife."

Tynan scoffs. "Never gonna happen. Not getting married."

"Well, if you don't want her, I'll give my Irish luck a chance."

I know exactly what Fionn's doing. And if the glare on Tynan's face is any indication, he's succeeding quite well.

"Keep your fucking hands off of her. I don't care that you're my brother. I'll kill you."

Fionn chuckles. "Yeah, you're right. You don't like her at all."

"I don't want you ruining this for Brody. He likes her. She's the only one that has him smiling lately, and I don't want anything to get in the way of that." He grabs a fistful of his brother's shirt. "If you fuck her and break her heart and she leaves, I'm gonna break your legs. You got it?"

"Damn." Gio smacks him on the back. "You've got it bad."

"Enough!" He lets his brother go. "All I care about is the boy and making sure that his new life is stable, and that includes his school life. I want to make sure she stays."

I glance at Brody at the far end of the room, playing with Sophia. It's a shame what happened to him. We all want to do more for that boy, but our hands are tied.

He'll talk again once he's ready. But Tynan isn't wrong. The right teacher could make all the difference.

And this Elara may be the one to do it.

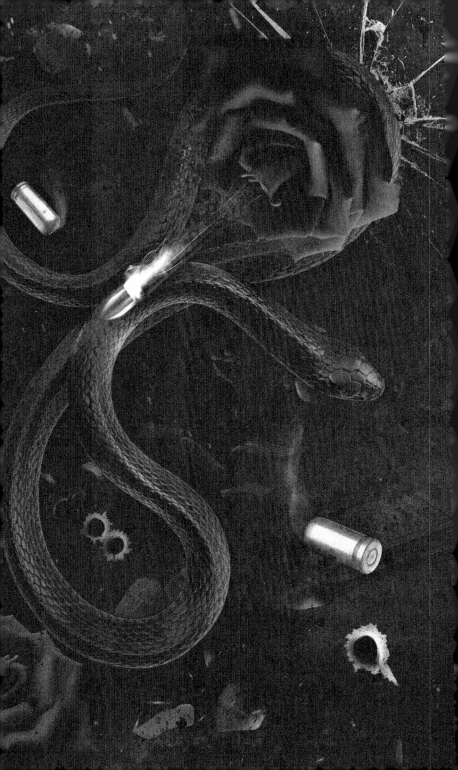

THIRTY-NINE

ERIU
THREE WEEKS LATER

My heart thuds, growing louder with every step I take. My breathing turns shallower, the ache in my chest throbbing.

But I have to do this. I have to go to Karen's dorm room. I have to stop avoiding it. It's what the therapist recommended.

My legs are as heavy as bricks, shivers running up my spine as I grow nearer. One more step and...

A sob breaks free, and I cup my mouth when I'm in front of her door.

The photos and ribbons are still here. So many, I'm overwhelmed by it all. But through the tears, I somehow smile, tracing a photo of her, me, and someone else making silly faces.

"I miss you," I whisper as my fingers reach for another photo, my vision murky from the overwhelming emotions pounding within me.

I went past Professor Montgomery's old office too, now with someone new working there. I didn't take the class, though. I couldn't. Maybe next semester, I'll be ready for that again.

My hand reaches for another photo, and as it does, I push the door open on accident.

"Hi there," a woman in black pants and a red blouse says, collecting Karen's things in a simple brown box. "Are you the next of kin?"

"Ugh, what?" I stride in, and a swell of painful emotions wage war inside my heart.

Memories flood my mind like a stampede of wild horses, endlessly galloping while I lie there on the ground.

It's her I see. Her smile. Us getting ready for the club. Her doing my makeup. Studying together. It's all there, weighing me down.

I swallow down the lump in my throat and face this woman, whoever she is.

"Did you hear me?" She smiles kindly, narrowing her brows. "I'm Stella from admissions. We've been trying to reach Karen's family to collect her belongings, but no one has gotten back to us. I'm hoping you're related and that's why you're here?"

"Uh, yes." I nod. "I'm her cousin. Her mom died, and her dad... He, uh, passed away a while ago."

"Oh, wow. How tragic." She blows a breath. "I'm truly sorry for your loss. I'm so glad we didn't have to throw her things away. Now that you're here, you can go through it all and see what you want to keep. I'll give you some time alone, okay? I'll be back in twenty. Does that work?"

She places a pink journal in the box and starts toward me.

"That's good. Thanks."

She purses her lips and brushes past me, closing the door behind her.

I stay rooted in place, afraid to advance forward, like something in that box will hurt me more. But I can't fear the memories any longer. I have to cling to the good ones, or what happened, her betrayal, will eat away at me until I rot.

Taking a long, deep breath, I gather the strength to reach the box and peek inside. Picture frames, books, notebooks lie there abandoned.

I glance at the closet, wondering if her clothes are still inside it. They must be. I should take them, or the school will just throw them out.

Grabbing the box, I settle on the bare mattress, picking up the journal, wanting to see the photos of us.

But as I place the journal on my lap, it opens, and my heart almost stops when I see the first two words.

Dear Erin,

I slam the journal shut, my inhales and exhales battling for space. There's no way I can read whatever she wrote. No way I can make it through without crying. Without my heart completely breaking.

Why would she write something to me in a journal I've never seen before? Why wouldn't she just show it to me when she was alive?

It makes no sense.

Curiosity gets the better of me, and I find myself opening it back up, and when I read her words, I wish I hadn't. Because it hurts more than I even imagined.

Dear Eriu,

If you found this, it means I'm probably gone. Hopefully not dead, because that would be a complete bummer. I'm hoping I'm on a beach somewhere, sipping a margarita, missing you, wishing I was able to tell you everything.

I don't even know why I'm writing this. The chances of you even reading this letter, in my private journal that I hide behind my bed, are very slim. I'm clever, I know. But on the off chance that you are reading it, I just need you to know that I'm sorry.

I haven't been honest with you since we met. I've been lying. Carrying too many secrets I've been forced to keep by my mother. Every time you talk about her, I want to scream. Or slam a fist into the wall and imagine it's her face. Because she's the reason I'm hurting you without you even knowing.

But see, I consider you my friend, no matter what she thinks. I'd do anything for you, even when she tells me what a weak, pathetic girl I am for letting you into my heart. But how can I not? You're an amazing person, Eriu. Even she has to see that.

I'm sure you're confused. Or maybe not. Maybe you somehow discovered my deception and are sitting there crying while reading this letter thinking what a terrible person I am.

And I won't dispute that. I am a terrible person. If I was a good person, I'd have told you the truth a long time ago. But I'm a coward. Yep, me. A coward.

If I was brave, I'd have told you what my mother makes me do. How much she hates Devlin and is using you to hurt him. I'd never let her do anything to you, though. I swear. But she has so many people behind her, and my word has always meant very little. You know her as Professor Montgomery, but I call her Mom. Or Satan. She responds to either.

Before I met you, I had no friends. I mean, the people at school don't know me. Not really, not the way you do.

I know you're probably thinking, "I don't know you either." But you do, Erin. With you, I am myself, more than I have ever been, and I need you to know that. I need you to know that I love you and I'm sorry. I wish I could've done things differently. But I was afraid. And now I've lost the one person who mattered to me most.

Please forgive me. I know it's a lot to ask, but it's the one thing that would mean the world to me.

Maybe not today or tomorrow. But someday I hope you can look back on our friendship and realize everything I've said here is true.

Love,

Karen

As I clutch the letter against my chest, a sob wrenches out of me, cracking through my bones, sinking into my marrow.

I'll never get to see her again. Tell her that I understand. This is all I'll have of her: a ghost of what was. And no amount of wishing will ever bring her back again.

ONE WEEK LATER

Thorny vines pierce my skin. Deep red roses were her favorite. Devlin spared no expense to ensure Karen got the kind of burial she deserved. I place the flowers by her headstone and sit across the grass to face it.

KAREN LUCIA PALMER

The school didn't have her real last name. Her mother made sure it was forged on the paperwork, so it's why Devlin never caught on.

This is the first time I've come to visit her. The first time I've truly felt ready to say goodbye. To say I'm sorry. That I forgive her.

And I do forgive her now.

With time and therapy, I've come to accept that she was two different people, yet still somehow the Karen I loved.

She begged her mother not to kill me. She didn't want me to die. That means something.

I no longer hold any hate toward her. And that in itself is freeing.

I keep her journal with me, and the photo of us that she had in her room is now in the foyer of the apartment I share with Devlin.

I decided to donate her clothes to Helping Hand so that they could be passed on to those who might need them. Karen would've loved that.

"School isn't the same without you," I tell her, playing with the sleeve of my sweater. "I miss you so much. Every time I go to lunch, I see you sitting across from me, checking out the boys from the swim team." I choke up a teary laugh. "I wish you were here. I wish I could just hug you one more time." Tears lie trapped in my lower lashes. "I'm sorry for everything you had to live with. I know it wasn't easy to deal with your mom. Please know I forgive you. And I will never forget you."

I stay there telling her about my classes, about the editing internship I recently got with a publishing house in the city. I know she'd be proud of me. I can feel it.

Life is just unfair sometimes.

Wiping under my eyes, I start toward Devlin, who waits patiently a few feet away.

"You ready to go?" he asks.

"Yeah." I look up at my husband and smile, grabbing his hand and bringing his knuckles to my mouth. "I think I am."

SIX MONTHS LATER

Devlin and I remained in the city. We love it here and have no plans to leave. We've talked about the future and what happens when I'm done with school, and we've considered eventually moving to Long Island so I can be closer to Iseult. But that's years away, so for now, we're enjoying ourselves here.

Therapy has done wonders, and I no longer need it. I'm glad I listened to Iseult, and she sure likes to remind me of that.

I stare up at my husband, his eyes scanning my body as I lie there on our bed in nothing but his t-shirt while he starts undoing the buttons of his cuffs, his knuckles bloody.

I don't have to ask why they are. I know what he does for my family.

"You stay right there until I'm done with the shower." There's a warning glint in his eyes, his arousal thick in the air.

He frees his shirt from his body and lets it fall on the floor, undoing his belt next, then his slacks, his rough, manly hands doing things to me.

My knees press into one another, my eyes drowning over him, body tight with desire.

"Better hurry, then, or I might decide to do something about it." I run my hand between my thighs.

"Bloody hell, woman. You keep those fingers away from that pussy until I return."

"Or what?" I spread my thighs and flick my clit.

He grunts deep in his chest, fisting his cock as he strokes it. "Or I'll punish you, and I promise you won't like it."

"I've always loved your punishments." My mouth curls.

"Bloody hell, if I wasn't this dirty, I'd be inside you right now."

My face flushes, nipples pebbling beneath the thin cotton. With a curse, he rushes for the master bath and shuts the door, the water pounding.

A laugh escapes me, and I give him a few minutes alone before I'm off the bed, heading into the steamy bathroom.

Through the glass door, his eyes snap to mine, holding me still in the bright embers of his gaze. Slowly, he opens it, his long strands dripping down his face. He doesn't say anything, but his expression hardens when my hands grip the edge of my shirt, his eyes following my movements.

I pull the t-shirt off and toss it at my feet, his gaze feasting on my every curve.

As I strut forward, his fist wraps around his cock, and he strokes it slow, groaning as I make it closer.

"Come here, love. Let me get you all dirty."

The possessiveness, the desire slinking in the dark timbre of his tone, has my body wanting his. He grabs my hand and tugs me into the shower, shutting the door behind us.

And in an instant, he slams his lips to mine and kisses me ruthlessly, backing me up against the cold tiles, lifting up one of my legs as his mouth rolls down my jaw, my neck.

The sounds we make, the way our bodies move together… It's erotic and blissful and freeing to love him the way I do.

His other hand falls across my throat, fingers winding around it as his kisses grow more insistent. Full lips tug and bite on mine, madness rivaling violent urgency. He sets me aflame, like he has from the moment I wanted to be his forever.

Now it feels like we have it all. A life I once only dreamed of.

He backs off enough to look at me, and I see it there in his eyes, the same feelings filling up my heart.

He lowers a hand between us, stroking between my thighs, sinking two fingers inside me, watching me as I groan. Removing them, he grabs his cock and positions it at my entrance, the crown sinking deeper as he stretches me.

"I look at you…" he says. "And I don't know what I ever did to deserve you."

"I've always been yours, Devlin McHale." I stroke the stubble of his jaw with the back of my hand. "It just took you some time to see it."

He growls, thrusting all the way inside me, capturing my lips and my heart at the same time.

And together we fall, because together, we can do anything.

BONUS EPILOGUE

ERIU
FIVE YEARS LATER

"This is great work, Mrs. McHale." My editor, Kate, at Main Books glances up from reading an excerpt from my new romance novel, which they will be publishing next year.

I can't believe I get to not only work here as an editor myself, but have my dream of becoming an author come true.

Much to my father's dismay, writing romance novels felt right to me. It was the most natural thing, and I'm quite good at it. I've had three published already, with the latest hitting a bestseller list. My father and my entire family are proud of me, of course. I sought out to do something and I accomplished it.

But my biggest cheerleader is my husband. He's the one who has read every book, tells everyone about his "famous author wife."

I grin at the thought. Marrying him was the best thing I've ever done.

"Thank you," I tell her, my face flushing.

I'm still not used to getting compliments about my work. In all honesty, I don't even feel like a real author most days. It's all crazy to me. The book signings, the readers coming just to see me. I guess they call it imposter syndrome, and I'm a full member.

"This is probably your best book yet, Eriu. I see it hitting a list." She closes her laptop, while I start to rise.

"I hope so," I tell her. "That's the dream."

"I'd say you've already accomplished a lot of your dreams." Her tight-rimmed mouth flicks at the corner. "I still remember when you first joined us, and look at you now."

I shrug. "It feels like forever ago, yet also like no time has passed."

"You're not kidding." She shakes her head. "Well, I will see you tomorrow morning. Have a great rest of your day."

"Thanks." I head out, saying goodbye to the secretary up front before I start toward my car, with my new bodyguard, Tony, right behind me as I enter my sedan and slide onto the road.

A lot might have changed, but some things remain the same. My family is still who they are. And the danger? Well, I've come to accept it as part of my life.

As for Karen, I still miss her, and the hurt from what she did is just an echo now. I wish she was here. I wish I could talk to her and tell her about my life. She would've had one of her own. Would she be married too? Would she work in fashion like she once wanted to? Would she and I still be friends, or would we have lost each other to the years and the time slipping by?

I don't have any of those answers. I never will.

Almost two hours later, and I'm finally home at a sprawling

mansion on Long Island, not far from where my sister lives. We moved last year, and it felt right.

Especially now.

Parking in the driveway, I head inside, opening the door, hearing my husband whistling somewhere in the kitchen. It's his off day today, and I knew he'd make sure I had a meal to come home to.

"Love, is that you?" he calls from the distance as I strut into the kitchen.

He's cutting up some tomatoes, and of course he's not wearing a shirt. Definitely just got hotter in here.

"Well, if it wasn't, we'd have a real problem, wouldn't we?" I pop a hand on my hip.

He lowers the knife and runs a hand through his hair, brushing it away from his face, a grin spreading. "Get your pretty arse over here and give me a kiss."

My teeth sink around the corner of my bottom lip, gaze slinking down his body. The muscle in his chest jerks and his jaw clenches deliciously, those eyes heated as he watches me ogling him.

"Got your fill yet there, lass?"

I blow a breath. "Not even close."

He groans, stalking over to me until his body is pressed up to mine.

"My God, I've missed you," he husks, his mouth brushing over my lips.

"Me too," I pant as his mouth slinks down my throat, kissing and sucking down to my collarbone.

My hands spread across his hard back, the ripples of his muscles straining against my fingertips. He lifts up one of my legs, hooking it around his hip as he circles his groin into me, his cock pressing exactly where I want him.

"There's something I have to show you," I gasp as he arches

deeper into me, my pussy throbbing for him.

He's bound to make me forget what I have to tell him, so I need him to stop before we lose ourselves.

He wrenches back, breathing heavy through his nose, gripping my jaw in his masculine grasp. "What is it, love? Been dying to feck you up against this wall all bloody day, and I don't like to be interrupted."

"Jesus. You're trying to kill me."

A deep, raspy chuckle makes it out of his chest. "Definitely not trying to do that. Maybe stop your heart once or twice."

"Maybe that can wait a few minutes?" I grimace. "I wrote a new scene for that book you've been reading, and I really need your opinion. You know how I get in my head and can't write more until you tell me how amazing I am."

"And we have to do this right now?" His hand grazes down my stomach, ending up between my thighs, pressing his fingers into me through my black dress pants.

"Oh, God," I gasp, nodding. "Yes, it's important."

"Alright." He backs off of me and grins. "I'll read it just so I can tell you to stop doubting yourself because you…" He cups my cheek. "…are amazing."

My face heats up, and I throw my arms over his shoulders and stare up at him. "I love you."

He grits his teeth and shuts his eyes, lowering his forehead to mine. "Thank you for loving me."

My heart swells and tears prickle my eyes. I still have to constantly remind him how worthy he is of this life we've created, because behind this strong, powerful man is a boy who never felt worthy of much of anything.

"You never have to thank me for that. Being your wife has been better than what I've ever imagined. And trust me…" I hike up a brow. "Young me imagined our entire life together."

"Really, now?" He grabs my hand and pulls me to the den. "I must hear all about what you imagined."

I reach into my handbag, getting my cell out before pushing him down onto the sofa. "I will. After you read this."

I open up the scene I wrote last night and shove it into his outstretched hand. "Promise to be honest?"

"Always." He glances down at the screen before grabbing my attention. "But you always blow me away, mo stoirín."

He starts to read, and I start to pace, my heart hammering in my chest. Hands curl and uncurl as he continues while I grasp the strap of my handbag, my nerves eating away at me.

His brows knit as he glances up at me.

"It's one of *those* scenes, huh?" He smirks.

I nod. "Read it out loud."

His tongue darts out, and his arousal oozes from his heated gaze before he starts to read, and I hope it's at the part I want to get to.

"She straddles his hips, lowering on top of him," he starts, and I do exactly what the character in my book does.

The shocked expression on his face when I lower myself on top of his lap has me smiling.

"Keep going," I tell him.

"Jesus Christ, a man needs strength for this." He blows a breath, but continues to read. "Her lips softly land on his neck, her hands in his hair as she kisses him slowly…oh, feck."

He grunts when I do the same, clutching his long hair between my fingers. His quickened pulse scatters against my mouth, fast and hard.

"Don't know how much more I can read before I lose my patience and feck your pretty little pussy."

"Just keep going," I breathe, needing him to finish.

"Alright, but you're the one killing me now."

I hope what I'm about to do doesn't actually kill him.

I stare down at him. "Promise to go easy on you, baby."

My mouth lands on his, and I kiss him slow. And the way he growls and fists my hair has me wishing I'd just tell him what I need to tell him. But I wanted to do things differently. Our way.

"Keep reading," I say, running a hand through his hair, and with a muttered curse, he does.

"He doesn't notice when she sneaks a hand into her bag, retrieving something she's been dying to show him all day, wanting to see how he'll react to the news. Butterflies spread in her gut at the thought of what she's been keeping from him."

My own hand slides into my bag, rummaging quickly to find what I'm looking for. He still isn't catching on, but he will soon. He stares at the screen while I'm staring at him. Why am I so nervous?

"He doesn't know that his life is about to change." He continues to read my words, and I swear my heart beats right out of my throat. "He has no idea that the woman he loves is about to give him someone else he's going to love more than he ever imagined."

I tuck my hand under my thigh as he looks up at me.

"Is she pregnant?" he asks.

Tears well in my eyes as I nod. "She is."

"What? That's great! He's gonna be happy, I know it."

I laugh, blinking back tears. "Yes, he will."

He's still not getting it, and he continues to read, like he can't wait to see the hero's reaction.

"She places her palm against the side of his throat, and he stares at her with longing and love and a piece of his heart beating outside of his body."

My palm lands at the same spot on his neck.

"When she lifts her hand in the air and he sees what's in it, he can't believe his eyes. He—"

The words die when he sees what's in mine.

"Eriu?" Emotions cloud his vision. "What are you telling me? Are you?"

I nod frantically as he finally understands, finally sees the pregnancy test in my hand.

"Oh my God." He inhales deeply, and in an instant, his arms come around me and he tugs me to him, his mouth landing hard on mine.

His kisses are urgent and demanding, tongue slipping around mine, before he pulls back breathlessly.

"But you're on the pill. I thought you wanted to wait."

"I did, but I was done waiting."

His knuckles brush across my jaw.

"I wanted to surprise you," I tell him. "After our wedding, I thought it was only fair, and I wanted to make this one even more memorable."

His gaze grows misty. "Are we really having a baby?"

"Yes, we're really having a baby."

He drags in a long breath and lowers his forehead to my chest. "I'm gonna love this child with all my heart. No matter what, he or she will have my love, my acceptance. Everything."

I brush my fingers up and down his back and hold him to me. "Our child will be the luckiest in the world, because they will have you."

"And you, lass." His eyes glimmer as they happen on mine. "I never thought my life would be so fulfilled. Thank you for giving me so much." His thumb strokes my lips. "I'll do everything I can to protect it."

"You just be you, Devlin. That's all I want."

He moans deep in his chest as he flips me beneath him and settles his body on top of mine. "I can do that."

And he does.

For years to come.

THE END

THANKS FOR READING!

Up next is Tynan Quinn and Elara Hill, Brody's teacher. *Brutal Savage* will be a forced marriage, hate to love you romance with all the secrets and spice!

Want to know what happened when Eriu was kidnapped? Find out in Gio and Iseult's story, *Twisted Promises*!

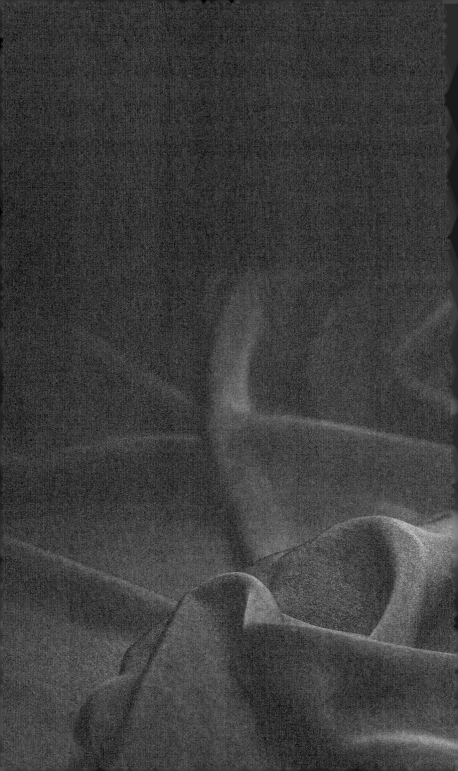

PLAYLIST

- "Ruthless" by Bookish Songs Collective feat. Kendra Dantes and Nino Tosco
- "Six Feet Under" by Billie Eilish
- "Blindside - Acoustic" by James Arthur
- "Work Song" by Hozier
- "Always Been You" by Jessie Murph
- "Insane" by Kendra Dantes
- "Sunday" by Dermot Kennedy
- "Moments Passed" by Dermot Kennedy
- "Always Remember Us This Way" by Noelle Johnson
- "Everybody Wants to Rule the World" by Lorde
- "Faithful - Stripped" by BOBI ANDONOV
- "Can't Catch Me Now" by Olivia Rodrigo
- "Constellations" by Jade LeMac
- "Making the Bed" by Olivia Rodrigo
- "Talk to My Skin" by Stalgia
- "Nothing Breaks Like a Heart" by Mark Ronson feat. Miley Cyrus
- "If I Don't Laugh, I'll Cry" by Frawley
- "Hurt Me" by Suriel Hess
- "Ruin in the Stars" by Kendra Dante feat. Sleeplore
- "Endgame" by Katie Garfield
- "The Pines" by Roses & Revolutions
- "Nightmare" by Kendra Dantes feat. Nino Tosco
- "Under the Spell" by Roses & Revolutions
- "One Day" by Tate McRae

- "That Part" by Lauren Spencer Smith
- "Grave" by Tate McRae
- "Moon Song" by Roses & Revolutions
- "Tattoo" by Loreen
- "No Love for a Sinner" by Shaya Zamora
- "Free Falling" by James Arthur
- "Curls in the Wind" by Mark Amber
- "Lucky" by Dermot Kennedy
- "Terrified" by Vincent Lima

ALSO BY LILIAN HARRIS

Fragile Hearts Series

1. *Fragile Scars* (Damian & Lilah)
2. *Fragile Lies* (Jax & Lexi Part 1)
3. *Fragile Truths* (Jax & Lexi Part 2)
4. *Fragile Pieces* (Gabe & Mia)

Cavaleri Brothers Series

1. *The Devil's Deal* (Dominic & Chiara)
2. *The Devil's Pawn* (Dante & Raquel)
3. *The Devil's Secret* (Enzo & Jade)
4. *The Devil's Den* (Matteo & Aida)
5. *The Devil's Demise* (Extended Epilogue)

Messina Crime Family Series

1. *Sinful Vows* (Michael & Elsie)
2. *Cruel Lies* (Raph & Nicolette)
3. *Twisted Promises* (Gio & Iseult)
4. *Savage Wounds* (Adriel & Kayla)

Savage Kings Series

1. *Ruthless Savage* (Devlin & Eriu)

2. *Brutal Savage* (Tynan & Elara - September 6th, 2024)
3. *Wicked Savage* (Fionn - January 6th, 2025)
4. *Filthy Savage* (Cillian - May 5th, 2025)

Standalone

1. *Shattered Secrets* (Husdon & Hadleigh)

WITHIN EVERY HEARTBEAT,
THERE'S A STORY.

For Lilian, a love of writing began with a love of books. From *Goosebumps* to romance novels with sexy men on the cover, she loved them all. It's no surprise that at the age of eight she started writing poetry and lyrics and hasn't stopped writing since.

She was born in Azerbaijan, and currently resides in Long Island, N.Y. with her husband, three kids, and a dog named Gatorade. Even though she has a law degree, she isn't currently practicing. When she isn't writing or reading, Lilian is baking or cooking up a storm. And once the kids are in bed, there's usually a glass of red in her hand. Can't just survive on coffee alone!

Lilian would love to connect with you!
Email: lilanharrisauthor@gmail.com
Website: www.lilanharris.com
Newsletter: https://bit.ly/LilianHarrisNewsletter
Signed Paperbacks: https://bit.ly/LHSignedPB
Facebook: www.facebook.com/LilianHarrisBooks
Reader Group: www.facebook.com/groups/lilianslovlies
Instagram: www.instagram.com/lilianharrisauthor
TikTok: www.tiktok.com/@lilianharrisauthor
Twitter: www.twitter.com/authorlilian
Goodreads: https://bit.ly/LilianHarrisGR
Amazon: www.amazon.com/author/lilianharris

Printed in Great Britain
by Amazon